THE TYPO

IN THE NAME OF GOD

WILLIAM LOWER

I&P

Ink & Pixel
PUBLISHERS

To Rosario.
And all those who worship Love

PRELUDE

Antonio Strozzi, a renowned Florentine manuscript illustrator, was putting the final touches on his artwork, carefully dabbing his precious ultramarine-blue ink. This regal color was possible only with lapis lazuli, an expensive pigment (as pigments went) reserved for important work for well-paying clients. The San Miniato al Monte Monastery was that well-paying client. Hopefully, this work would bring a smile to Abbot Fransisco's face. Those smiles were profitable. After all, while an art, manuscript illustration was also a business.

Overlooking Florence was the San Miniato al Monte Monastery, and Abbot Fransisco was penning the final schedule and invitations for the following day's viewing of the Monastery's new treasure. Florence's finest would be there, including Cosimo de' Medici. The Monastery's Gutenberg Bible had arrived and was to be unveiled.

The Monastery's Prior Lorenzo, knowing Cosimo de' Medici would attend the following day, ensured his wardrobe—modest white monks' attire of linen and undyed wool—was clean and in suitable condition for an audience with such an esteemed guest. His leather belt and sheathed knife were polished.

Gabriele, head of security for the San Miniato al Monte Monastery, was reviewing the following day's guest list with the Monastery's guards. Gabriele and the guards checked and rechecked every name.

Security's protocol at the monasteries reflected the times. If they expected uninvited and unwanted armed guests, security would be at the gates, ready with swords and shields. If it was a time of peace, love, and happiness, security was not to be seen—although they were always there, lurking.

Meanwhile, in a small walkway between two buildings on a Florentine side street, Guglielmo, a family-less, homeless, and unemployed man in his early twenties, curled up in a crevice between the buildings, thankful for the blanket left anonymously for him. Florence's February nights were bitter.

Miles north of Florence on a muddy but well-trodden trail, Heinrich, a man with no known last name and traveling on foot, encountered three men on horseback on the outskirts of Bologna. The three men, led by burly Alfonso, were highway bandits and, seeing Heinrich, thought they had found a new target. What they learned was that Heinrich was also a highway bandit but one whose horse had died. Hearing of Heinrich's profitable exploits, they thought he could be a valuable team member. He just needed a horse. For that, Alfonso knew a trader in Bologna who could help. His name was Jacopo.

Halfway across the Holy Roman Empire in Mainz, Germany, Johannes Gutenberg walked out of a Mainz courtroom, downtrodden, depressed, and destitute. His business partner and financier, Johann Fust, had successfully sued him for failure to repay funding used to create Gutenberg's press. With that courtroom victory, Fust was awarded possession of Gutenberg's press and the rights to all its revenue.

Half a continent away, in a fieldstone house hidden in a forest somewhere south of Bologna, Seraphina was organizing her plants, herbs, and tree-bark shavings into small clay pots and then covering each pot with a cloth to preserve its contents' freshness and potency.

In the days and weeks that followed, their fifteenth-century lives would collide, and those collisions would shape the world you live in today.

THE FINISHING TOUCHES

THE VIEWING

Florence, Italy

February 15, 1461

Wrapping his brush into a moist, clean cloth, Antonio leaned back to stare at the page on his art board.

This one was precious.

He looked up from his art table and glanced out the studio's window. Florence was flourishing, and soon the streets would bustle with artisans and tradespeople leaving work and stopping to collect staples for the evening's dinner.

The late afternoon sun cast deep golden rays, creating the long wavering, animated shadows trailing people as they made their way through Florence's winding streets and alleyways. Vespers and calls for religious observance from the church enforced obedience and order, but the sun determined the workday. As the sun set, tradespeople, artisans, and merchants put away their tools, closed their shops, and made their way through the block-stone streets and cobblestone alleyways to home and family for the day's evening meal. Under a canopy of red tile roofs, the Florence passageways became alive as people transitioned from the routine of work to the routine of worship and family living, which would culminate into rest, sleep, and journeys into the surreal cerebral universe of fifteenth-century dreams and nightmares.

Antonio took one last look at the page he had just finished. It took three days to create, but it was time well spent. Antonio's attention to minute details was one reason he was the Monastery's preferred master illustrator.

This page was truly wonderful. He would present it to Domine Fransisco, the Monastery's abbot, tomorrow for approval. With that, the manuscript production would progress and be completed in time for the Christmas services and celebrations.

Antonio slid off his stool, grabbed his overcoat, and said, "Good evening," to the apprentices and their masters, all still laboring over an assortment of art boards and assignments, trying to make the most of the day's dwindling light.

Antonio stepped onto the cobbled walkways that wound their way through the city's center.

Florence served as the center of the publishing industry, employing many tradespeople and artisans.

For now.

No matter what he planned for dinner, whether he decided to shop for dinner staples or to eat at Osteria della Storia or Ristorante della Fiera, Antonio always stopped at Mario's bakery. It wasn't the focaccia he was so interested in but more an excuse to chat with Andrea, even if just briefly.

At twenty-four, Antonio was an attractive man. He was slender, fit, and well-groomed, an established tradesman and, by most accounts, a suitable prospect for any young woman looking for a life mate. Moreover, he was still a virgin.

Andrea was Mario's seventeen-year-old daughter, who, most days, tended to end-of-day customers stopping on their way home to stock up for the day's dinner.

Andrea's slender beauty was striking. Her atypical emerald eyes sparkled, always with a hint of mischief. She knew her beauty and why her father's bakery became so busy when she was working. She was aware of her appeal and enjoyed it. Her smile was both inviting and knowing, a subtle promise of charm that never failed to tease.

Andrea was at the blossom stage of life: vibrant, seductive beauty that attracted the bees—both married and single—driven by the power of procreation. Andrea knew her allure, and Mario knew why his bakery was so busy at the end of the workday. Andrea toyed with customers, always just a little more than simply friendly and welcoming. There was nothing deceptive in Andrea's flirtatious interactions with male clientele; she was just living through the natural life cycle of the human condition. The flower in full, vibrant bloom attracting the bees to ensure the species' pollination. In ten years' time, she will likely have chosen a bee and polli-nated, bearing three children, her blossom aging and fading and the prod-ucts of her father's bakery adding pounds—unlike when she was young and in full bloom, when she could eat as many *schiacciata* and biscotti as her heart desired without adding an ounce to her lissome female flower.

Andrea was living life as life intended: drawing in the bees to play her role in ensuring the species' continuance. For now, it was sexual playfulness. And Andrea played it exceptionally well.

"Antonio! How wonderful to see you!" Her greetings always carried a subtle hint of longing, the key ingredient to the tease to attract the bees.

Equipped with a working knowledge of five languages—Latin, Florentine Italian, Greek, German, and French—as well as the works of Homer; Plato; Pico della Mirandola; Marsilio Ficino; Dante Alighieri; Petrarch; and, of course, the various authors and translators of the Bible, it was a challenge for Antonio to make small talk. To anyone.

Antonio had his mother to thank for his language prowess. While his father was a bookbinder, it was his mother who ensured Antonio had access to and could study the manuscripts that passed through his father's workshop. It was his mother who pressured his father to fund tutors and encouraged Antonio. Even as a young boy, his tutors would take him to conclaves of scholars discussing Greek texts.

While he was initially scorned, people soon saw him as a prodigy. His mother would encourage him to mingle on the streets with merchants, who daily traded with merchants from across the Holy Roman Empire, from France to Germany. With that came increased language understanding and critical thinking skills.

However, in the age of the Inquisition, critical thinking was best kept to oneself. While it was his father, the bookbinder, who encouraged Antonio in his pursuit of manuscript illustration training, it was his mother who nurtured his mind. As an intelligent woman in a patriarchal medieval society, she lived vicariously through Antonio's intellectual growth and taught him to guard the privacy of his thinking carefully. Even small talk could be dangerous, and Antonio did little of it. Even with Andrea. However, in his brief encounters with her, it was not his intellect that thirsted.

It was his heart.

Antonio had convinced himself he was in love with Andrea. But then, almost every other male customer was in love with Andrea. The fresh flower in the garden of procreation keeps our species going, whether continuing as a species makes any sense. Or not.

Most evenings, Antonio left Mario's with a fresh panini or focaccia, his mind filled with fantasies of Andrea and what-ifs.

Tonight, however, was an exception.

Less than half a decade earlier, a German entrepreneur and inventor had created a mechanical printing process and, hoping to ease his financial pressures, had printed Bibles. These became known as the Gutenberg Bibles. Although their price of thirty florins each was a year's salary for many individuals, the Gutenberg Bibles were a bargain for monasteries, universities, and wealthy nobles such as the Medici, who usually paid four hundred to five hundred florins for manuscript Bibles similar in quality to those from Antonio's workshop. Besides, it would have taken someone, even with Antonio's skill and efficiency, at least a year to produce the same product by hand.

The Monastery had ordered a copy of this Bible, and once it arrived, the abbot decreed a viewing for the Monastery's clergy and prominent Florentines. The Monastery's special event coincided with Antonio's scheduled progress presentation the following day. Respecting Antonio and knowing he planned to be at the Monastery, the abbot invited him to the presentation and ceremony. It was to be a prestigious social event, with the Bible displayed on the ambo as visitors lined up to take turns viewing.

Being of his lower social status, Antonio was at the rear of the viewing line.

As each visitor took their turn viewing the Bible, many gently felt the texture of the paper. Some even leaned into the book to smell the ink, and page turning was done with the utmost care.

When it was finally Antonio's turn, he studied the pages intensely, looking at the crisp type and the details of the engravings. After scanning one page, he gently turned to the next. With a trained eye for detail, Antonio was shocked by what he saw before him. There, in plain sight to a professional's eye, was a mistake. On page 149, the engravers had failed to capitalize the "d" in the word "*Deus*."

Antonio stared in disbelief.

Antonio Strozzi had discovered the world's first typo.

The Guarded Approach

Florence, Italy

February 16, 1461

Antonio had not slept well. Someday, someone would notice. Should he pretend he never saw the error that was, to his eye, a glaring flaw?

How long would it go unnoticed? Just imagine the wrath if he had made such a mistake on a page intended for the Holy Scripture. All hell would break loose. Not to mention the abbot's loss of faith.

He had to bring it to the abbot's attention.

Quickly.

He had no appointment scheduled, so he would have to go unannounced and explain to the guards that the matter was urgent and that he should speak to Domine Fransisco. Guards were not a mainstay at most monasteries. They were mercenaries hired if rumors of pending trouble from pesky neighboring city-states surfaced, but here at the San Miniato al Monte Monastery, guards were a mainstay at the suggestion of the Medici family. The Monastery housed too many valuable manuscripts to be left vulnerable to theft. And a suggestion from the Medicis had a way of being interpreted as an order. Guards were a permanent fixture at the San Miniato al Monte Monastery.

Antonio awoke before the rising sun, dressed appropriately for an audience with the abbot, and made his way to the Monastery, timing his arrival to be after morning prayers, rituals, and a meager monastery morning meal.

Two guards attended the Monastery's entrance. All the guards knew Antonio, and he knew them, even by name. Antonio was a regular visitor. However, there was an appointment for each visit, and the guards knew the day's schedule and what guests, dignitaries, and tradespeople were to be expected and when.

And when not.

Antonio had no such appointment that day and knew what to expect from the guards. The guards would not admit him without consulting the prior, the abbot's number two, even though they knew Antonio and his role with the Monastery.

Today, Gabriele and Rinaldo were on duty. Gabriele was head of security and, as such, was the senior of the two. So, Gabriele's subordinate, Rinaldo, first addressed (and questioned) Antonio.

As Antonio approached the door, Rinaldo took one step forward, standing between him and the entrance.

"Antonio. We don't expect you today. What brings you here?"

"Good day, Rinaldo. I have an urgent matter to discuss with Domine Fransisco, and he would be sorely disappointed if I were to delay bringing this to his attention immediately."

No one enjoyed their day if they played any role in disappointing the abbot. Antonio knew that. The words "disappointing" and "abbot" in the same sentence always got the listener's full attention.

"What may I tell the duty prior is the nature of this matter?"

"Rinaldo, while I trust both you and Gabriele, I think the abbot would also be sadly disappointed if he discovered I had given out this information. Even to you, his most trusted guards."

Antonio glanced over Rinaldo's shoulder to look Gabriele in the eye. Indeed, Gabriele paid close attention to the conversation and stared intently at Antonio. As a well-trained and experienced guard, Gabriele remained stone-faced, scrutinizing the interaction between Antonio and Rinaldo.

You could never tell what Gabriele was thinking. You could only tell when Gabriele was thinking.

And Gabriele was.

Antonio always thought it peculiar that the head of security was a man of such slight build. Those answering to him had much greater physiques. Perhaps it was Gabriele's piercing focus. Like the focus on Antonio right now. Nothing escaped Gabriele's attention because some of the greatest threats were the ones that were subtle and to most people, unpercieved. Until it was too late.

Rinaldo turned and walked over to whisper in Gabriele's ear. While listening, Gabriele's eyes remained locked on Antonio. When Rinaldo finished, Gabriele nodded to the door but never lost eye contact with Antonio.

With Gabriele's approval, Rinaldo entered the Monastery, closing the door behind him.

Antonio stood, slightly shuffling his feet, and offered Gabriele a nervous, feeble smile.

Expressionless, Gabriele said, "Always good to see you, Antonio."

Relieved at the respite from the tension, Antonio replied, "You as well, Gabriele."

Rinaldo returned and, holding the door open, said, "The prior will receive you."

Antonio passed the guards, politely nodding to both, and as soon as he was inside, the doors behind him closed with a thud that echoed off the winter-cold stone walls.

Although he knew his way through most of the Monastery, no one was in sight, and he was unsure what permissions he had. Or where to go. So, he stood at the entrance.

And waited.

There was not a sound.

It was so quiet Antonio swore he could hear the cobwebs.

Then, faintly, he heard footsteps approaching from an adjoining corridor. But whoever was approaching was in no hurry. They were shuffling toward him slowly.

After a brief eternity, Prior Lorenzo emerged from the corner of the hallway leading to the abbot's study and quarters.

At thirty-five, topped with dirty-brown hair and standing at five foot seven, Lorenzo had reached his peak on many levels. He would grow no taller. And he felt chained to a second-in-command stature at the Monastery. Advancement never advanced.

Prior Lorenzo was the senior clergy member and the one Antonio trusted the least. It was in his eyes. Antonio sensed Prior Lorenzo could read his mind, which was the one thing Antonio did not want read.

Certainly not here.

Prior Lorenzo's greeting smile emerged like a snake slithering from one ear to the other. His stubby, gaped teeth were yellowing with age. There was never warmth in Lorenzo's smiles.

"Antonio, it's so good to see you again and so soon! It was just yesterday. What do you need to tell Domine Fransisco today that you overlooked discussing during your appointment yesterday?"

The snake was parked, just waiting for prey. And a response.

"Prior Lorenzo, I am so grateful for your time and attention."

No response.

"I indeed need to speak with Domine Fransisco concerning yesterday's event. I said nothing yesterday, not wishing to cause any interruption or disturbance to the day's event."

"As I understand it, Domine Fransisco was most pleased with your work. As he always is, Antonio. Was there some misrepresentation in it?"

The snake seemed to wiggle.

"No, Prior Lorenzo, I would certainly bring nothing to him—or you, for that matter—if I felt something was less than perfect. It is not about my work, but it does concern sacred texts."

"You wish to change these texts?"

Check. And snake-mate. Lorenzo believed he had achieved a "gotcha" moment.

12

He had not.

"Heavens, no, Prior Lorenzo!" Antonio tried a self-demeaning chuckle. "Me?"

"What, then, do you wish to discuss?"

"The Bible."

"The Bible?" The snake retreated, morphing into a water-hunting witching stick.

"You wish to discuss the Bible, Antonio? And with no appointment? Antonio, you are a master artisan, and we certainly appreciate and … yes, respect your work, but Antonio," Prior Lorenzo lectured, as he often did to underlings, "each of us here has studied the Scriptures for years. What enlightenment about the Bible has created this urgency for an audience—with no appointment, mind you—between yesterday and today?"

The snake was back.

"A potential blasphemy."

Centuries later, a Norwegian artist would capture the look on Prior Lorenzo's face in a painting titled, *The Scream*.

In the age of the Inquisition, anything deemed a blasphemy had unpleasant consequences.

"Potential blasphemy? *Potential blasphemy*? Antonio, there is no such thing as potential blasphemy! It either is or it isn't!"

"Exactly, Prior Lorenzo. That is precisely why I need to speak with Domine Fransisco. What I have discovered is not for me to determine whether it is blasphemy. I certainly don't have those credentials."

The snake was gone. The gaping, *Scream*-like astonishment had vanished, and the witching-stick frown had evaporated.

Speechless, Prior Lorenzo was left with nothing but a blank stare and the recognition that he, too, lacked the credentials and authority to proclaim anything a blasphemy.

Antonio offered a slight smile. Or was it a smirk?

Prior Lorenzo stared into Antonio's eyes, now with yet another reason to distrust and dislike him.

What was it about Antonio?

"Wait here."

Prior Lorenzo spun around and scurried down the corridor from which he had skulked, but now with much greater urgency than when he had entered from it.

Within seconds, all Antonio could hear was a spider walking across its cobweb.

The Proof Is in the Reading

Florence, Italy

February 16, 1461

When Prior Lorenzo re-emerged, his snake smile had shed its skin. Instead, he bore the smile of a usurped authority, now a mere messenger and butler. He did not look Antonio in the eye but stared into Antonio's forehead: the pretense of contact while providing none.

"Abbot Domine Fransisco is pleased to receive you. Follow me."

Prior Lorenzo turned and, with a much-quickened pace, led Antonio down the corridor, which was lined with tapestries and frescoes. Despite Antonio's familiarity with the Monastery's main passageways, he'd never had the privilege of venturing into its inner sanctums. Windowless, the corridor was lit by flickering wall oil lanterns, creating an illusion of animation on the frescoes. The corridor had a sweet smell only produced when olive oil fueled the lamps, not the pungent smell associated with animal fats, which so many households used. While humble, the Monastery had subtle luxuries.

He was now being led to the abbot's primary study. Clearly, the mention of blasphemy had struck a chord.

Maybe this was not such a good idea after all. Every meeting Antonio had attended with the abbot previously was in the scriptorium, with several others in attendance. Those meetings always focused solely on the work at hand: creating and producing the Monastery's manuscripts. While detailed and focused, there was never much discussion of the manuscripts' substance. That was always preordained and not the responsibility of the manuscript illustrator.

When Prior Lorenzo reached the door at the end of a winding corridor, he opened it, and his unctuous smile re-emerged as he turned to Antonio.

"I hope your meeting with the abbot addresses your issue in a timely manner. The Reverend Father has a full schedule today. Consider yourself blessed. He has found time to see you."

Prior Lorenzo summarily ushered Antonio into the abbot's study, closing the door behind him as he left, leaving Antonio to stare at Domine Fransisco's back as the abbot leaned over his desk, putting papers in order and out of sight.

The chamber was lined on three walls with bookshelves stocked with manuscripts, some of which Antonio recognized as his work. The chamber's natural light source was a large arched window on the south wall overlooking the Monastery's inner cloistral courtyard.

When Abbot Fransisco turned to greet Antonio, his demeanor was warm and benevolent, as it always was in greetings. He carried his weight and stature with grace, disarming anyone, even the most polished of politicians. It was rumored he could have Piero di Cosimo de' Medici's ear at a moment's notice.

"Antonio," he purred while presenting his ring to be kissed, which Antonio did with grace, as was his practice.

"You wish to speak to me of blasphemy? That must surely be a weighty topic for even as storied and respected a manuscript illustrator as you. Please. How can I help you?"

There was no denying the abbot's seductive warmth, a well-sewn wardrobe to his power.

Antonio's first maneuver, learned from years of serving all within the clergy, was to bow and scrape.

"Reverend Father, it was such a privilege to be invited to yesterday's presentation and ceremony introducing the masterful machine creation of the Holy Bible."

Abbot Fransisco simply smiled, saying nothing and waiting for this impetuous tradesman to get to the point.

"The typography was masterful, and the illustrations a marvel to the eye."

Abbot Fransisco simply smiled, saying nothing and waiting for this impetuous tradesman to get to the point.

"In the brief moments I had to explore this incredible treasure, I did notice one thing I thought should be brought to your attention."

Abbot Fransisco simply smiled, saying nothing and waiting for this impetuous tradesman to get to the point.

"It would seem the work's creators were not as well versed in biblical verse as you would certainly demand."

Abbot Fransisco simply smiled, saying nothing and waiting for this impetuous tradesman to get to the point.

"There was a mistake."

Antonio had finally gotten to the point and had gotten the abbot's attention.

"A mistake? What manner of mistake?"

"Abbot, I believe it was on page 149, although I am uncertain of that; it was in the Book of Luke, Chapter 4, verse 18, when Luke is discussing God having instructed Jesus to announce that there is good news for the poor."

It's been over two thousand years, and while we are still waiting for this good news for the poor, when it comes to faith, we are a patient species.

"Yes. What about this?"

"*Deus*. The word '*Deus*.'"

By now, the abbot was getting impatient, and his veneer of benevolence was beginning to wear thin.

"What is it about the word '*Deus*,' Antonio?"

"It wasn't capitalized."

The abbot just stared blankly at Antonio, speechless.

Antonio waited for the weight of his message to register.

"Good God."

The abbot was registering the implications. Where could this lead them? This disrespect? This mockery of the Scripture? And yes, this blasphemy.

Again, "Good God."

"With no capital 'D,'" Antonio added.

"This cannot be."

"No, it was a small 'd,'" Antonio replied.

The abbot stared at Antonio, thinking, "He always strikes me as quite intelligent, but then he acts like an idiot. I wonder if he does that to make me think he is stupid when I know he is not?"

"Antonio, come with me. I would like you to show me this egregious oversight."

Antonio followed the abbot as he walked to a bookcase and pushed on one side to reveal a hidden, tight, winding corridor lit solely by wall-mounted torches that led to a narrow, twisting stone stairway. At the top of the stairway, the abbot pushed on the stone wall to reveal this wall was actually a door that opened to the rear of the altar in the congregation room.

There, still on the ambo, was the Gutenberg Bible, now closed.

"Where was this error?"

"I believe, Abbot Fransisco, it was Luke, Chapter 4, verse 18."

The abbot opened the once sacred, now blasphemous volume and mumbled to himself in search of the text in question. "Let's see … Luke, Chapter 4, verse 18 … that put it somewhere here …"

"I believe page 149, Your Worship."

The abbot turned and looked at Antonio as if studying him.

"You are indeed a gifted manuscript illustrator. Such a detailed memory from such a short viewing."

When the abbot had found the page, Antonio pointed to the flawed text.

"Good God."

"Yes, but without a capital 'D.'"

"Antonio, we cannot have the Holy Scriptures with such a glaring error. You are correct in your assumption that some might see it as blasphemy."

The abbot stared at the page, then turned to Antonio, saying, "You are such a gifted master artisan. Perhaps you could correct this oversight?"

"Thank you for your kind words and confidence, Reverend Father, but my correction—any correction—would be very noticeable. Despite my skills and those of others in my workshop, getting an exact match to the color of the text would be, to my knowledge, technically impossible. There is black. And then there is black. And the serif of the lowercase 'd' would extend beyond the edges of the uppercase 'D.' My concern is that it would look amateurish, drawing more attention to it than the uncorrected error itself."

"Hmmm. Amateurish. In the San Miniato al Monte Monastery? Amateurish? That cannot be."

The abbot slowly closed the Bible, deep in thought.

"Antonio, accompany me back to my study."

They retraced their steps through the secret passageway—now less of a secret—and once they were back in the abbot's study with the bookcase returned to its place against the wall, Domine Fransisco motioned for Antonio to sit in a chair facing the desk as the abbot slowly reclined in his chair.

The meeting was losing its formality as the abbot sat there, silent, clearly lost in thought.

Then he looked Antonio in the eye and said, "Antonio, you are one of, if not the best manuscript illustrators in Florence, and ours is a city renowned in the publishing industry."

From the dawn of time, flattery has often been the precursor to asking for the impossible.

"Given the circumstances and given your skill and knowledge in publishing, what would you do?"

"I'd ask for my money back."

"And do what with the Bible?"

"Return it?"

Talking out loud but clearly to himself, the abbot mumbled, "Return it, yes, return it … but now that we have made such a public announcement and presentation of Gutenberg's 'genius,' what do you say has happened to the book? Yes, return it … Yes! Return it! And get Gutenberg to fix it!"

"A wise decision, Reverend Father, if I may be so bold to say so."

"Yes. And I know *exactly* who to send on such an urgent mission."

"If it is not imprudent for me to ask, who might that be?"

"You."

"Me?"

"You."

"I am deeply flattered you would consider me for such an urgent mission, but I am merely a manuscript illustrator. Why me, if I may ask?"

"You are the one who discovered this wretched carelessness. Who knows what other oversights might lurk on those pages? I'm confident that with your sharp eye, you will ensure no other inaccuracies or flaws remain hidden. I know I can trust you to ensure that scoundrel Gutenberg fulfills his responsibilities. Rumor has it Gutenberg is in financial difficulty, and in my sense, he is in the Bible business purely for the money."

Antonio processed the words as quickly and efficiently as possible, knowing the abbot's time was valuable and wanting to avoid another unscheduled meeting, especially if Prior Lorenzo was the gatekeeper.

"Reverend Father, so I am clear, you wish for me to inspect the new Bible for any further errors and then proceed to Gutenberg's facilities and have any necessary typographical errors attended to, then return with the corrected Bible?"

"Precisely, Antonio."

Antonio thought for a moment, then asked, "Where shall I review Gutenberg's Bible? With my experience reviewing our manuscripts, I believe it would take several days. Where would I do this?"

"Here. I will arrange for you to be granted daily entry to the Monastery without the formalities you encountered today. Lunch is after midday prayers. A place for you will be arranged at the table with the resident monk manuscript illustrators."

That table would presumably exclude Prior Lorenzo. Exquisite.

"I do apologize for so many questions, Reverend Father, but is Gutenberg not in the German territories of our Holy Roman Empire? Praise be to God."

"Yes. In the town of Mainz."

"And how shall I travel this considerable distance?"

"Antonio, yours will be a mission requiring utmost discretion, drawing as little attention as possible. You will travel by horseback, accompanied by one of our guards, for your security and protection."

Antonio struggled, sensing his job description was entering uncharted territory.

"If I may ask, which guard did you have in mind?"

"Given the nature of your journey, I think Gabriele would be best suited for this delicate mission."

Antonio stared expressionlessly at Domine Fransisco, desperately trying to find an appropriate response without appearing to question the wise abbot's wisdom.

"I am fortunate to know the Monastery's guards and have great respect for Gabriele. But while highly attentive and focused, he is slight in build.

When confronting the inevitable highway bandits, would not a guard with a more substantial and intimidating physique provide better protection?"

The abbot smiled. "Have you not witnessed Gabriele's swordsmanship?"

"Reverend Father, I confess my work has so occupied me I have not attended the tournaments."

"Antonio, I am not speaking of the tournaments. Few people know this, but I would not be alive today if it were not for Gabriele's skill with the sword. Trust me."

"Most certainly."

"That's settled then. We shall expect you tomorrow morning to begin your review of this mechanical monstrosity we seem to have on our hands, this Gutenberg Bible calamity the Lord has delivered to us, God knows why."

"Reverend Father, what about my duties at the workshop and the work in progress for your manuscripts?"

"Worry not, Antonio. I shall see to it that you are excused while you continue to be compensated."

This was followed by the smile only a man with unquestionable control of finances could produce.

Just twenty-four hours after discovering the world's first typo, Antonio Strozzi would become the world's first proofreader.

Let It Be "D"

Florence, Italy

February 17, 1461

Unbeknownst to Antonio, Domine Fransisco gathered the Monastery's senior clergy and informed them of the travesty and the plan to remedy this careless oversight. As such, the corrected Bible should be back in the Monastery in two months' time, and no one was to talk of this matter to anyone, not even amongst themselves.

He had them swear an oath of silence on the matter, then dismissed them back to their duties, studies, and prayers.

Prior Lorenzo bowed, smiled, and scraped as he left, shuffling down the winding corridor to his privileged dormitory—privileged because besides a bed, Lorenzo also had a desk and chair he had convinced the abbot were needed so that his contemplations, the fruit of deep thought, could be documented for others' study and consideration.

Tonight's contemplation was how to prevent a flawed, mass-produced Bible from being corrected.

"Let the world discover this flaw. A mass-produced Bible? Has the abbot, or even His Holiness, the Pope, for that matter, thought this through? A Bible produced without the Church's blessings and approval? For hundreds of years, we have worked to establish, with no uncertainty, the Church's authority. Now the Scriptures are to be produced by some … some … layperson? A Germanic layperson at that!"

Lorenzo lit his desk's candle and turned his gaze out his window just in time to see a guiding star blaze across the sky. He knew, with no doubt, this was a sign.

As he stared out the window at the star-laden sky, an epiphany hit him: "Disparate times demand desperate measures."

But what?

Then it became as clear as the night, a problem-solving procedure as old, tried, and true as civilization itself: disappear the messengers, a procedure sometimes (and distastefully) referred to as "murder."

Disappear the messenger. And Gutenberg's blasphemy, of course, which *must* be seen for what it is. Untrustworthy.

But how? Who?

As soon as he thought of it, the answer was obvious: Subprior Paola at the Monastery of San Domenico in Bologna. Antonio and Gabriele would certainly stop there for lodging and food.

Subprior Paola and Lorenzo had met a year prior at a meeting hosted at Lorenzo's monastery. They had discussed this very topic at length: the printing press and the Church relinquishing control over the Scriptures. Lorenzo had framed it well and Paola agreed: "Lose authority and you lose control. Lose control and you lose authority," he quipped. Or was it pontificating?

He and Paola had much in common. Both were sons number two from wealthy families. Sons number one were the ones who would inherit their families' wealth and property. Lorenzo and Paola's best option, available through family connections, were lives within the monasteries and the Church.

Lorenzo and Paola differed in one significant way. While Paola admired and looked up to his older brother, Lorenzo resented his. The elder brother prevented Lorenzo from inheriting wealth and notoriety. For that, he would have to advance himself through the ranks of the Church. Unlike through inheritances, through the Church, there were no guarantees.

With the Medicis' growing influence at the Monastery of San Domenico, Subprior Paola would welcome the opportunity to be recognized and appreciated within the Medici circle. And he looked up to Lorenzo much like he looked up to his older brother. Lorenzo knew how to work within the Church's system.

Lorenzo and Paola shared beliefs and motives. They both wanted to advance. And were there not monks who had risen to Pope?

Lorenzo took a sheet of paper, dipped his quill pen in his desktop ink, and began.

"My dear friend, fellow messenger of God's word, Paola, I bring to you an urgent matter. My holy abbot has spent considerable sums acquiring a copy of the scandalous Gutenberg Bible, which you and I discussed in our meeting a year ago. As you and I recognize, the Scriptures should remain solely in the clergy's domain.

"Both bad and good fortune have come from Gutenberg's Bible. On viewing, a lowly manuscript illustrator, a tradesman named Antonio Strozzi, identified a flaw—a blasphemous flaw, at that. The careless creators of Gutenberg's Bible failed in their respect for God by failing to capitalize the Almighty's name.

"The abbot has tasked Strozzi to take Gutenberg's Bible back to Gutenberg himself in Mainz, Germany, for correction and has issued strict instructions that knowledge of this effrontery remains within our monastery's walls.

"Ours is but one copy of the many copies Gutenberg produced and sold. Should it become common knowledge Gutenberg and his printing apparatus are not to be trusted with the distribution of holy teachings, ours will be protected positions.

"This letter comes to you from a villager, Guglielmo, whom I will engage for discreet and speedy delivery. I will tell him he is to tell no one of his mission and that he can keep the horse I provide from our stable for his journey as payment.

"Strozzi will travel with letters from my abbot addressed to the monastery abbots on his journey. The letters will request safe passage, food, and accommodations for him, his guard, and their horses. He will travel with but one guard.

"My dear, cherished brother, first, I ask that you provide comfortable accommodations for my messenger, Guglielmo, and see that he enjoys a sound, deep sleep.

"Into eternity.

"And into God's arms.

"His horse should bear good market value to use at your discretion.

"As we both know, the power of gossip is far more powerful than the power of truth. Should villagers learn a traveler with gold and a priceless artifact will pass through, bandits whose livelihoods depend on robbery will surely hear this news. Antonio and his sole guard, Gabriele, should prove easy prey to seasoned highway bandits. Antonio is a manuscript illustrator, and I was surprised by the abbot's choice of Gabriele as his guard. Gabriele is slight, not the muscular type at all.

"I shall ensure that the Medici family knows your name and of my high regard for you.

"I remain your Florence colleague and companion, Prior Lorenzo."

Lorenzo returned his quill to its well and lifted the letter, gently blew to dry the ink, then carefully folded it. He warmed a sealing wax, poured it over the folded letter, and imprinted the Monastery's authoritative seal.

Lorenzo sat back, stared at the sealed, folded letter on his desktop, and thought, "This will seal more than a letter."

He got up, changed into his night clothes, and slipped between his bed's blankets; and as he laid his head on his pillow, he glanced out the window in time to catch sight of another shooting star.

Lorenzo smiled as he closed his eyes.

He knew God's signs when he saw them.

The Unwitting Messenger

Florence, Italy

February 18, 1461

Prior Lorenzo rose hours before the morning sun, dressed, and quietly slithered to the novices' dormitory and roused the newly arrived monk wannabe. Lorenzo held his finger to his lips, directing the slumbering novice to be silent, then whispered instructions for him to dress, hastily make his way to Florence's Piazza di Santa Croce, and find a young man named Guglielmo. "Instruct him that I, Prior Lorenzo, urgently requests he meet me immediately at the Monastery's stable. Speak to no one of this request!" Then, as an afterthought, he added, "You, too, must keep our conversation this morning secret, but rest assured: this discreet task will benefit you as you continue your studies toward ordination."

"Of course, Prior Lorenzo, I am privileged you have trusted me with your mission. But exactly how will I find this Guglielmo?"

"He will be the one sleeping on the street."

Guglielmo was the perfect choice. He was a nobody, and nobody would miss him—if they even realized he was no longer to be seen. Perhaps he had moved on to grovel and beg elsewhere. Who would know? Who would care? Occasionally, he would come to the Monastery when hunger gave him no choice, and he was always given a piece of bread, some cheese, and a preachment on the Scriptures.

Lorenzo then turned and snaked his way through the dormitory's doorway and through the back corridors to the stable's rear entrance, moving so silently that not even the horses sensed his presence. And the stable keeper, Pietro, had not yet risen and arrived.

The stable housed twelve horses, each named after a station in the Stations of the Cross du jour. The stations have been fluid throughout history. Once there were said to be seven. In Antonio's time, twelve; later fourteen; and at one point, thirty. Their locations were as elusive as their number.

Following the path of the Stations of the Cross through history is like trying to understand the flight plan of a fly.

Given the three times Christ fell under the burden of the Cross' weight, naming those three horses proved challenging, but logic prevailed with names "Once," "Twice," and "Thrice."

Each stall bore the name of its horse: "Pilate," "Mary," "Simon," "Veronica," "Cavalry," "Spirit," "Once," "Twice," "Thrice," "Between Thieves," "Burden," and "Given."

Prior Lorenzo slid onto a stool, sizing up the horses. Guglielmo would "steal" the swiftest, ensuring he reached the Monastery of San Domenico in Bologna before Antonio and his guard.

Burden was swift, but it was a given that Given was twice as fast—but not as fast as Thrice. However, Thrice was more than once outpaced by Twice, although Once was more reliable on long-distance journeys. Pilate worked best pulling a plow but only when led by Mary, but even then, only after Cavalry arrived. Simon was useless.

As Lorenzo sat studying his equestrian options, one stood out. He stared at him, and after careful consideration, his mind was made up. It was common knowledge that nothing moved faster than Between Thieves. It was Between Thieves that would carry Guglielmo and the urgent letter. This is how this story would unfold: Guglielmo had stolen a horse, apparently ridden it toward Bologna, then disappeared. It would be easy to make this story credible, just as convincing Guglielmo to carry out his mission would be easy. After all, there is no one easier to scam than someone in need.

Dawn light seeped over the horizon as a scrawny, slouching young man cautiously entered the stable doors. He was dressed in fraying clothing that had probably not left his back in weeks. His entrance did not go unnoticed by the horses.

"Prior Lorenzo?"

Lorenzo rose from his stool in the shadows.

"Guglielmo. So kind of you to come on such short notice. How are you, my son?"

Guglielmo had never been addressed with such warmth and kindness by anyone with any form of authority, and he searched for an appropriate and respectful reply.

"I am better for seeing you, Prior Lorenzo."

Lorenzo returned with a simple, ingratiating smile. "Guglielmo, I have a very urgent mission, and it is one that demands utmost secrecy. As I considered who I could trust with no worry, you were the first person who came to mind."

Guglielmo was stunned by the honor, thinking, "The prior not just thinking of me but turning to me?"

They stood in the rising morning light, and Lorenzo bore his trademark rattlesnake smile, waiting for a reply.

"How may I serve and honor you, Prior Lorenzo?"

Snake-mate. Victory. End game. "Serve and honor." Exactly what Lorenzo wanted. To be served and honored, but most importantly, not questioned.

Lorenzo reached into his jacket pocket and produced his urgent letter.

"This needs to reach Subprior Paola and *only* Subprior Paola at the Monastery of San Domenico in Bologna, as swiftly as possible."

Guglielmo struggled and failed to conceal his terror at being tasked with the impossible. Bologna was over sixty miles from where they were standing, and the day had already begun.

Lorenzo wanted the impossible to register with Guglielmo before he unleashed his ministerial powers, making the impossible possible. He walked over to Between Thieves' stall and, reaching for a saddle on the opposite wall, said, "Guglielmo, this is our fastest and finest steed."

Guglielmo glanced at the horse's name, painted over the doorway of the stall.

"Between Thieves?"

"Guglielmo, each of these twelve horses bears a name borne from the twelve Stations of the Cross of our Lord and Savior, Jesus Christ."

Guglielmo was quick to respond: "Amen."

Although he had very little education or even religious upbringing, Guglielmo knew to follow any mention of Jesus Christ with "amen."

"As you know, Guglielmo, they crucified our Lord and Savior, Jesus Christ, between two thieves. Rumor has it, though supporting texts are yet to be found, that the two thieves converted to Christianity before their deaths.

"Between Thieves will carry you to the Monastery of San Domenico faster than any other horse from our stable."

Then Lorenzo reached into his other pocket and produced a handful of coins, saying, "And you will certainly need food on your journey. We would not wish you to travel hungry."

Accepting the coins, Guglielmo recognized that the gift would feed him for over a week. He felt as though the hand of God had found him after living with no blessings for so long.

Lorenzo saddled Between Thieves and helped Guglielmo mount and settle. Guglielmo led Between Thieves out of the stable and galloped down the trail but then stopped, turned to Lorenzo, and said, "Which way to Bologna?"

Standing in the stable's doorway, Lorenzo pointed to the northeast and said, "That way."

Guglielmo then broke Between Thieves into a gallop and rode off into the sunrise.

The Word. By Word.

Florence, Italy

February 18, 1461

The day broke after another night of unsettled sleep. Antonio's nocturnal torment consisted of tossing and turning, contemplating the eternal question each human faces at least once in life:

"Should I have just kept my mouth shut?"

However, he had not. And here he was.

His flat overlooked southwest Florence. He had prepared his wardrobe the night before, no small task. His regular garb for his workshop duties or attire for a more respectful appearance expected for a monasterial engagement?

"Dress for the occasion," his inner voice suggested; however, that same inner voice had also led him to reveal Gutenberg's glaring error.

From his apartment on Via del Garbo, it was a ten-minute walk to his workshop on Via dei Calzaiuoli. He would have to requisition his workshop's only reference Bible, which was used when creating new works.

How else could he assure the abbot there were no other defects in Gutenberg's monstrosity if he had no known sanctified manuscript?

How would he explain to his workshop employer, Matteo, that he needed to remove this treasured reference for several days without explaining why? Domine Fransisco had made it clear he did not wish to suffer the humiliation and embarrassment of people knowing he made such a purchase as a Bible containing such a biblical blunder.

Did Domine Fransisco think Antonio knew the Bible so well that he could identify all mistakes and omissions?

The more Antonio thought about the task that lay ahead, the greater his sense of dread became.

Matteo's shop stood out with its dark wood paneling and inviting display of manuscripts in the window. As he approached the workshop door, Antonio let out a deep sigh; but when he opened it, Matteo stood in the entranceway with the illustrated Bible in hand and offered it to Antonio without saying a word.

Antonio was stunned.

"Domine Fransisco sent a messenger informing me you must borrow this for a few days. The messenger did not explain why, so I assume it would be best not to ask."

Matteo then reached into his jacket pocket and produced fifty florins, over two months' wages, and handed them to Antonio, saying, "He also provided a generous two-month salary advance to give to you."

Before Antonio could respond, Matteo added, "Plus 10 percent for my trouble," which was not really for his trouble but for his silence. So many things go unsaid with an exchange of money. Silence is indeed golden.

"Good luck with your assignment. Your position will be here for you when you return—whenever that shall be. I am truly impressed you seem to have earned Domine Fransisco's confidence and trust in your work. He is, as you know, our most beloved client."

Most beloved client, indeed. And coincidently, the highest paying.

Matteo closed the door, leaving Antonio standing alone on the early morning Via dei Calzaiuoli.

The rising sun's glow illuminated the colorful buildings and cobblestone streets of Via dei Calzaiuoli, casting a golden hue over everything in sight. The hustle and bustle of Florence was awakening. But at that moment, the street was still quiet and empty, giving Antonio a sense of seclusion despite being in the heart of the city.

The buildings were so close together they almost touched and cast shadows on the street below. Antonio's eyes lingered on the door that Matteo had just closed, wondering what rumors would stir inside.

Antonio had not planned such a brief stop at his workshop, so he found himself standing on the street with the city only beginning to wake. While the city and its tradespeople were rising, it would be another hour before the monks completed their morning prayers and breakfast.

His first thought was to stop at Mario's bakery for coffee and a *frittelle*. Andrea would most likely not be working. She was, by all accounts, a more nocturnal creature.

As he stood motionless, sanctioned reference manuscript in hand, the city's morning aromas wafted through the crisp Florence air: wood burning, bread baking, and fresh-ground coffee brewing.

Only five minutes later, Antonio sat at a table at Mario's with fresh coffee, fresh *frittelle*, and confirmation Andrea had not yet risen.

Chatting with Mario was not that different in substance than chatting with Andrea. The only difference was Antonio had no romantic interest in Mario.

With coffee and *frittelle* consumed to sustain his trek, Antonio gave a polite *"arrivederci"* to Mario and stepped back into the Florence street, now becoming overcast and gloomy, as he made his way to the Monastery.

When he arrived at its entrance, guards Rinaldo and Gabriele were again on duty; only now, as Antonio approached, Gabriele greeted him, saying, "Good to see you again, Antonio. The abbot is expecting you. Please. Allow me."

Gabriele stepped back and opened the door. Once Antonio crossed into the Monastery's hallway entrance, the door behind him closed with the familiar echoing thud he heard what seemed a lifetime ago but was only yesterday.

Silence.

A cat scurried by.

Today, the cobwebs were quiet. Perhaps they were drowned out by the shuffling footsteps, although today's steps were not as slow and menacing as yesterday's. From the corridor, it was Prior Lorenzo again who emerged.

Today's greeting smile was feeble.

"Antonio. I understand your matters with Abbot Fransisco are of the utmost importance. He has assigned a private space for you to conduct your work. If it is your pleasure, please follow me."

Slouching, shuffling, the monk turned and led Antonio along a torch-lit adjoining corridor to a small wooden door Lorenzo opened for Antonio. The snake smile had slithered back across Lorenzo's face, and after ushering Antonio into his assigned workspace, Lorenzo closed the door behind him.

The room was small, furnished with only a desk and chair. Light filtering through small arched windows highlighted the walls' frescoes, which depicted biblical scenes and saints themes he would recognize as he plodded his way through the two Bibles.

On the desk were flickering candles providing more light for the task ahead.

Antonio sat the illustrated Bible beside Gutenberg's, sighed, and settled in his chair.

Opening each cover, the only sound in the room was the crinkling of page turning.

It was going to be a long few days.

THE JOURNEY BEGINS

NOTHING TO WORRY ABOUT

Florence, Italy

February 23, 1461

It was another night of troubled sleep. Abbot Fransisco had said, "You have nothing to worry about," which almost always meant you have something to worry about.

Antonio's position at his workshop was guaranteed to be there for him upon his return; the same was also true of his flat. And the Monastery's guarantees were as good as guarantees could get.

It was common knowledge that guarantees backed by the Monastery were guarantees backed by the Medicis.

Required was clothing for all weather—including wearable shoes and cumbersome boots—and writing instruments, all now packed as per Gabriele's instructions.

At the stable the previous night, Twice and Thrice were identified as the best suited for Antonio and Gabriele, while the steed Pilate would carry the burden of supplies.

Pietro, the Monastery's stable keeper, arrived pre-sunrise with a carriage to carry Antonio and his travel belongings to the stable, where he would meet with Gabriele, load the horses, and start their journey.

A light snow was falling, leaving Antonio with a heavy heart. Big flakes, small snow. Small flakes, big snow. Would they make it to Bologna by nightfall? Unlikely. But by being light, this snow was not wet.

Gutenberg's Bible would be weatherproof, wrapped, and buried with Pilate's cargo containing Antonio's and Gabriele's provisions. Bandits and robbers would be more interested in what Antonio and Gabriele carried on their person than what might be buried in piles of their undergarments.

The predawn light seeped through Antonio's bedroom window, ending the nightmare of another sleepless night and beginning a daylight nightmare— one that would last for many days.

Antonio slid out of bed, thankful for the one thing he had: a pot to piss in. Done, he took the pot, opened the street-side window, and tossed its contents onto the street below, only barely missing Pietro, who looked up, saying, "Good morning, Master Antonio. Are you ready to go or do you require more time?"

"I am prepared, but a few more minutes would be appreciated. Perhaps wait up the street for a moment or two."

A more substantial return to the pot was in order. It was best for Pietro to wait up the street.

Several minutes later, when Antonio finally emerged, Pietro stepped from the shadows to help with Antonio's bags.

Bags loaded, Antonio and Pietro climbed into the Medici-supplied carriage, making their way through the dawn's falling snow, along the cobblestone streets, to the Monastery's stable.

Gabriele was already there, standing at the stable's entry. Twice and Thrice were saddled, and Pilate, loaded with their supplies, was tethered to Gabriele's horse, Thrice.

"Good morning, Antonio. Twice is saddled and waiting for you. Load your saddlebags and we can be on our way."

Pietro took Antonio's saddlebags and, calming Twice, he secured Antonio's gear to his steed.

Antonio turned to Gabriele and began to speak, but Gabriele cut him off. "And the—"

"It's packed. Securely."

Gabriele wore a hooded woolen coat with a sheathed sword strapped and ready. Mounting Thrice, Gabriele turned to Antonio and said, "Do you carry any weapon …? Beyond a paintbrush?"

Slightly miffed, Antonio replied, "I always carry a dagger."

Gabriele, lightly laughing as Antonio mounted Twice, thought, "A dagger versus a sword. If only he knew."

As they guided Twice and Thrice with Pilate in tow out the stable doors, Prior Lorenzo stepped from around the stable doors, smiling as he said, "Abbot Fransisco requested I come to tell you he bids you good wishes for safe travels and has provided these letters of introduction to the monasteries you will encounter in your journey."

He handed a pouch to Antonio, then produced a second, heavier pouch, adding, "And for other needs in your travels."

Money.

Then, turning to Antonio, still smiling, Lorenzo thought to himself, "There is something about this tradesman I don't like."

Antonio returned the spurious smile, thinking, "There is something about this 'man of God' I really don't trust."

The wind veered from the west, creating a thick haze of snow that soon enveloped Antonio and Gabriele as they rode into the distance.

Lorenzo watched as they faded out of sight, but certainly not out of mind.

The First Supper

Sasso Marconi, Italy

February 24, 1461

Twice and Thrice, with Pilate in tow, plodded their way north, saddled with Antonio, Gabriele, and their belongings.

Occasionally, Gabriele would produce charts from a few sources, one a hand-drawn version of the Tabula Peutingeriana, a Roman-era guide to roads and pathways. Some routes were still functioning, while others were long since reclaimed by nature. The other navigational aids were rudimentary manuscript charts produced by monks, merchants, and scholars with varying cartographic skills. Captured on the parchment were roads, rivers, towns, and landmarks (as many as they knew).

Gabriele motioned them to stop, studied the crumpled cartographic reference, and then motioned them forward in a northeasterly direction. Antonio glanced over his shoulder at the distant silhouette of Florence's cityscape, wondering what he had gotten himself into: the unknown, trouble, or (most probably) both.

The trail forward led them through winter's dormant vineyards, orchards, and root vegetable gardens.

For hours, they spoke little, and once beyond the sounds of Florence, the only sounds were the horses' breaths and the varying pitches of wind whistling around them.

Occasionally, Gabriele would issue directional comments, commands, or questions.

"I think this trail is best." Or "Am I traveling too quickly for you?" Sometimes a veiled command to keep up the pace, or occasionally, "How are you managing?"

It was cold. After hours of plodding, they reached a forest grove that would give them some shelter from the wind. Gabriele spotted a small clearing and said, "Let's give ourselves and the horses a brief rest."

Dismounting, Gabriele instructed, "Gather some twigs and branches, and we'll make a fire to warm up for a moment."

Antonio brushed off the powder snow on the forest's offerings of twigs and small fallen branches and brought them to Gabriele, who said nothing but piled the smallest twigs and grass into a fireboard, spun the spindle until a spark ignited the dried grass, then added the larger twigs. Within a few moments, they were standing, rubbing their hands over the flames of a small fire. Much of the conversation was clipped, some statements even lacking a verb. "A bit cold." "Hungry?"

With the winter ground providing little for the horses to feed on, Gabriele kept rest stops brief. After stomping out the fire, Gabriele merely said, "Okay," meaning, "Let's get going."

Even though the trek would be long, it appeared conversations would be short.

They had just turned onto a path leading through an olive tree grove.

From behind a tree, two men emerged: one in his mid-forties, an elderly man, and with him a muscular younger man, twenty-ish. As the elder spoke, the younger stepped forward.

"These are our lands. Who gave you passage? What business do you have here?"

The younger stepped closer and was about to grab Thrice's reins; but as his hand reached out, in the blink of his stupefied eye, Gabriele's sword greeted his wrist. The weapon did not break skin or draw blood, only drew his attention to the notion that any further aggressive action might not be in his best interest.

As this scene became a tableau, Antonio said as calmly as he could, "Kind sirs, Abbot Fransisco of the San Miniato al Monte Monastery has sent us on an urgent mission. Perhaps you have heard of our abbot Fransisco?"

Both the elder and the younger stood silent.

Antonio could smell the angle of attack to take.

"Which church do you attend?"

With but a split-second pause, Antonio added, "You do attend church, do you not?"

The elder quickly responded, "But yes, of course, we attend and are thankful for the blessings our tithes have granted our crops." He cast a pious look skyward and continued, "While we have heard of Abbot Fransisco, we are lowly farmers and have not had the good fortune and opportunity to meet the Reverend Father in person. But please, tell us: how can assist you on your mission?"

The younger farmer let go of Thrice's reins, and as he did, Gabriele re-sheathed the sword.

Antonio said, "Would you know the best direction to Bologna?"

The elder quickly pointed in a northerly direction as the younger pointed more easterly toward a distant forest. They simultaneously uttered, "That way."

Antonio and Gabriele cast a quick look at each other, then both looked in a somewhat northerly direction. Antonio replied, "Thank you, kind sirs, for your courtesy. We shall be off. Ours is a long journey. May the good Lord grant you bountiful crops."

Antonio and Gabriele then steered Twice and Thrice in a somewhat northerly direction and continued on, saying nothing.

With the olive grove in the distance, Antonio said, "I don't think I have ever seen anyone yield a sword with such speed and precision as you, Gabriele. Not that I have witnessed much in the way of sword fighting, neither in sport nor conflict. How did you come upon this skill, if I am not prying?"

"My father."

"Your father?"

"Yes."

And so ended the prying.

They rode in silence across the fields in a somewhat north or north-north-easterly direction. As they crested a hill, they saw a village lining a meandering stream below them.

"Twice and Thrice will be thirsty, as I am. Hungry as well. Pass me three of your coins. I will find us food."

Antonio was confused. "Why should I not just ask to purchase a meal?"

Gabriele turned and stared at the novice in the ways of man. With a sigh, Gabriele gave the first of what would be many lessons in being trail-wise.

"If people see you reach into a deep pouch laden with coins to pay for a meal, I can assure you we will be greeted again once we have left town and are alone on the trail. Under those conditions, the use of my sword will need to be less polite than it was in the olive grove."

Antonio stared into Gabriele's eyes, then replied, "That was polite?"

"Three coins, Antonio. If you please. I am hungry. But not for trouble."

Antonio turned in his saddle and reached into his saddlebag, digging in the buried pouch. From there, he pulled out three coins, handed them to Gabriele, and, wishing to demonstrate his acquiring trail wisdom, added, "Don't forget to ask for change."

Gabriele stared at Antonio as he passed the three coins, then turned skyward, thinking, "God, what did I do to deserve this?"

About forty houses and huts, mostly of fieldstone construction, lined the stream in the village they entered. At the east end of the village stood a church of finer stone construction. In the town's center, on the far side of the stream, a larger stone building stood with smoke billowing out its chimney.

"That is probably a tavern," Gabriele suggested. "And it is midday, so most likely lunch is being served. If so, let's hope they prepare generous portions to accommodate unexpected guests without their regular patrons noticing their portions are less while their bills are not."

Gabriele turned to Antonio and smirked. Antonio smiled and thought, "Am I sensing humor?"

They trod down the hillside to the stone bridge at the village's center and made their way to the tavern.

The tavern itself was but four buildings away from the carved stone church, both of which were on the stream's south side. As they dismounted and hitched their horses outside the tavern, Gabriele turned to Antonio and said, "We need to keep watch."

Peering through one of the tavern's windows, Gabriele spotted three people leaving a table close to both the burning fireplace and a window providing a clear view of their steeds.

"Antonio, please go in and ask for that table. It will be warm by the fire, and we can watch our horses. I'll also see that they are watered and fed while we eat."

Antonio made his way into the tavern, where the arched, thick wooden door served to help keep the cold air out and the noise in.

The ten tables were all occupied except the one the guests—who were now at the counter paying for their meals—had just abandoned. As Antonio walked in, a few heads turned, and the tavern owner smiled and said, "Welcome. If you're hungry, you'll find the best food in the village here."

A few men at one table laughed. One said, "Stranger, this is the only food you'll find in our village," which brought lots of laughter from the room.

From another table, a burly man (most likely a farmer, judging by his girth) added, "That's right. It's been over a year since someone has died after eating here."

Now everyone was laughing, and all focus was on Antonio.

The tavern owner took the joke at his expense in good stride, laughing and adding, "You'll find my food as hearty as the people who eat here, and almost all live to tell of it."

At that point, Gabriele walked in, and the one who appeared to be the village humorist looked at Gabriele and said, "Now, here's someone who could use some fattening up. Friend, are you fasting for atonement for past sins? We enjoy discussing our sins here. It's down the street where you have to be careful about that."

The room erupted again, and Gabriele replied, "I'm certain your sinful stories could keep us engaged for days, but we have a long journey ahead of us and, sadly, will only have time to eat."

Then, turning to the tavern owner, Gabriele said, "Are we welcome to the table by the fire? It's a pleasure to come into your warmth from the cold today."

The tavern owner gestured to the table, saying, "It is my pleasure to serve you."

Gabriele and Antonio settled into the table, and Gabriele, taking the seat facing the room, explained, "In my line of work, my back is always to the wall. I'm just fortunate that today, the wall has a roaring fire."

Antonio smiled. "I'm sure the perks in your line of work are few and far between. Enjoy the fire. I am thankful for your company on this journey."

They had just settled when the tavern owner arrived at their table with two goblets of red wine, saying, "It is my pleasure to serve you the best Tuscany wine as my guests. My compliments. I am always hopeful travelers will tell fellow travelers of my tavern and of a pleasurable experience."

Antonio and Gabriele both graciously nodded, thanked him, and asked what was on the menu.

"Today, we have the Medici Beef Medley, Traveler's Savory Stew, Tuscany farm-fresh potpourri, and the daily special."

Antonio, being a Florentine, could not resist asking, "What is the Medici Beef Medley?"

The tavern owner, with an Italian flare that over the centuries would become world-famous, replied, "It is capon stuffed with roasted chestnuts and served with tenderized turnips and carrots, smothered in olive oil infused with our secret house blend of rosemary, sage, thyme, and parsley, topped with a dash of carefully aged fresh saffron."

Antonio, often burdened with unwelcomed but instinctive critical thinking, asked, "How can something be 'carefully aged' and 'fresh'?"

The tavern owner smiled, leaned forward, and whispered, "That is a safely guarded house secret."

Gabriele nodded, then asked, "What is the Tuscany farm-fresh potpourri?"

The tavern owner, now with a more intimate and almost whispered delivery, replied, "It is capon stuffed with roasted chestnuts and served with tenderized turnips and carrots, smothered in olive oil infused with our secret house blend of rosemary, sage, thyme, and parsley, topped with a dash of carefully aged fresh saffron."

The tavern owner then added, "Our house tradition is to serve a cup of Pinot Noir with your meal. Our compliments."

Antonio, multilingual and, through his profession, somewhat culturally astute, asked, "Pinot Noir is from Burgundy, France. How do you get that in Tuscany?"

In a rare moment of honesty, the tavern owner confidentially replied, "We steal it."

Gabriele replied, "I confess—"

"No, you confess down the street," the tavern owner interjected.

Without losing composure, Gabriele continued to say, "I'm afraid to ask—"

"Fear not, for here you are among friends. It's not like down the street where it is best not to ask."

Gabriele leaned closer to him and whispered, "Dare I ask: what is the daily special?"

In what would also become universal Italian body language, the waiter shrugged and said, "I go in the kitchen, I look around, and I think, 'Anything goes.' Daily."

Antonio looked at Gabriele.

Gabriele looked at Antonio.

Both were speechless.

From across the room, the tavern humorist shouted, "I'd go with the Medici Beef Medley. Apparently, it's Michelangelo's favorite."

Antonio spun around, looked at him, and said, "But he's not even born yet!"

With the universal Italian shrug, the tavern humorist shot back, "Let the book editor worry about that."

Antonio looked at Gabriele.

Gabriele looked at Antonio.

Then Gabriele said, "I think I'll have the Medici Beef Medley."

The tavern humorist shouted to Antonio, pointing to Gabriele, "Friend, I'd have what he's having. It's to die for. And we have the bodies to prove it."

The tavern's laughter faded, and the waiter returned to the simmering stove to prepare Antonio's and Gabriele's meals.

Antonio raised his glass of Tuscany wine to Gabriele and said, "To think the journey has only just begun."

For the first time in their journey, Gabriele inquired about Antonio's life.

"How did you become a master manuscript illustrator?"

"I've been drawing since I can remember. My father was a bookbinder connected to many prominent artists and manuscript illustrators, including Fra Angelico."

"*The* Fra Angelico?" Gabriele asked.

"Yes. My father shared some of my childhood drawings with him, and Fra Angelico took me in as an apprentice on my eleventh birthday."

"A birthday gift indeed," Gabriele replied.

For the first notable time, Gabriele smiled, raised the glass of whatever

Tuscany or stolen wine they were about to sample, and toasted, "Life is a journey."

They clinked their goblets, eyes engaged, then sipped.

Lowering his glass, Antonio said, "From France."

Somewhat surprised, Gabriele replied, "How would you know?"

"I have some well-traveled friends who occasionally bring gifts, and wine is always the most appreciated. This is from France."

Gabriele cast a glance at the tavern owner and then turned back to Antonio, leaning forward and whispering, "Stolen?"

Antonio raised his glass, took another sip, and then responded, "I'm certain they would prefer it to be referred to as 'imported.'"

For the first time since their journey began, Antonio's guard smiled.

Holy Shit

Somewhere in the Middle of Somewhere En Route to Bologna

Daybreak

February 20, 1461

Guglielmo woke to the aroma of something cooking; he looked and saw Seraphina stirring whatever she was preparing in a cauldron hanging over the fireplace's low flame. Although he had made no sound as he woke, and even though Seraphina's back faced him, without turning she said, "You slept well. That's good, Guglielmo. You will need your strength and wits about you today." She then turned to face him, smiled, and said, "And I have prepared my favorite concoction for cold winter days, so you'll have a full stomach to give you strength for your journey."

Guglielmo swung out of bed and put on his worn leather shoes. They weren't boots, which would have been so much better for this weather, but they were what he had. Seraphina glanced down as he put them on, and it was as if she could read his mind. With her apparent skills in enchantments, perhaps she could.

"In the chest at the foot of the bed, you'll find a pair of woolen socks I think would fit you. By looking at the size of those shoes, I don't think the extra socks would prevent you from fitting in them. Where on earth did you get them?"

"They were given to me."

"By someone with larger feet, it would seem. Get the socks, and then let's get you fed."

Guglielmo went to the foot of the bed and opened the chest. Inside were blankets and a thick woolen sweater; and to the right was a thick dark-green pair of woolen socks, the same green as Seraphina's cape. He took them, sat back on the bed, and pulled over his thinner, worn socks these new ones that fit like a glove. Then he pulled his shoes back on. As

Seraphina had suggested, the shoes were a better fit with these socks, and his feet would be protected better from Tuscany's February weather.

"Thank you. I have never seen socks this color. It's like your cape. I have never seen it before."

"And you probably won't again anytime soon."

"How do you make clothes the color of the forest?"

"First dye with weld, then dye with woad, and green comes to life."

"Die with weld? Die with woad? And then come to life? How can that be? You *are* a witch!"

"Not 'die' as in 'dead.' 'Dye' as in creating color by soaking in extracts from plants. Weld and woad are plants."

Guglielmo stared at Seraphina, trying to accept the reality that someone from the Church was trying to kill him, while someone who seemed every bit a witch was trying to help him.

Or so it seemed.

Seraphina put her hand on his shoulder and said, "Those green socks seem to suit you. So now you have a bit of forest in you as well. Come. Let's eat."

Seraphina took two wooden bowls from the fireside shelf, one bowl larger than the other. She then dipped her ladle into the cauldron, stirring up the scents as she filled the bowls and set them on the table. Guglielmo took the chair from the fireside, and Seraphina sat on the wooden bench on the table's opposite side.

"This smells delicious. What is it?"

"A bit of this, a bit of that, some pork I traded for herbs, a dash of whatever strikes me while I'm cooking. So far, the recipe has never failed me."

Guglielmo took a sip and, with bulging eyes, looked at Seraphina and said, "I have never tasted anything like this! Never. It's unbelievable." Guglielmo ate as if he had not eaten in days, which was often the case for him.

Seraphina watched him eat and smiled to herself. There is a unique pleasure in providing pleasure, and Seraphina was savoring that pleasure.

With his bowl emptied, Guglielmo sat back in his chair, let out a sigh, and said, "How can you prepare a meal like this? Your home is not a farm. Where do you shop for your ingredients?"

Seraphina let out a laugh and said, "Shop? Shop? That's what they do in towns. I don't shop."

Clearly confused, Guglielmo asked, "Well, where do you get your meat for meals like this?"

"I trade."

"Trade? Trade what?"

"Recipes."

"Recipes? That's it? Recipes?"

"Yes, that's it."

"Recipes for what?"

Seraphina turned and looked out the window to the forest, then turned back to Guglielmo and said, "Things that ail or help people."

"Ail people? Help people with what?"

Seraphina remained silent for a moment, then, looking Guglielmo in the eye, answered: "Nausea and digestive issues; irritable bowel syndrome; indigestion and bloating; coughs and bronchitis; colds; respiratory congestion and infections; asthma; pain relief; headaches and muscle pain; joint pain; burns, cuts, and skin irritations; inflammation; insect bites; a variety of random infections; fever; low blood sugar levels; irritation in the ear canal; stress level changes; trouble sleeping; anxiety; heart health and circulation; allergy symptoms; healing of wounds and fractures; regulation of menstrual cycles; alleviation of menstrual cramps; improvement of kidney health; soothing of irritated eyes. As examples."

"Holy shit."

"We'll get to that."

"This, whatever it is, is delicious. Why don't you sell your recipes in a store?"

Seraphina stared silently at Guglielmo and then gestured for him to lean forward toward her until they were almost nose to nose. She then said, "People might think I'm a witch."

Guglielmo sprang back in his chair, alarmed and distressed, and blurted, "Are you a witch? I ... I ... I am staying with a witch? Holy shit!"

"We'll get to that."

"Get to that? Get to that? I could go to hell for being with a witch! Oh my God! Oh my God!"

"Yes, people often say that when they think they are in the clutches of what they think is a witch. But you're not going to hell. You're going to the Monastery of San Domenico."

"Holy shit."

"We'll get to that."

Guglielmo was hyperventilating.

Seraphina said, "Guglielmo, take deep breaths. Watch me and just do what I do."

Seraphina began slow, deep breaths through her nose, held them for several seconds, and then exhaled.

"Again. And again. And again."

After a few minutes, Guglielmo's fear of going to hell subsided, only to be replaced by his fear of going to the Monastery of San Domenico.

"Seraphina, I'm frightened."

"I understand. They have swords, daggers, halberds, maces, and the power of God. Right?"

"Yes."

"But do you know what you have that they don't have?"

Guglielmo stared at Seraphina, silent. He turned and looked out the window, then turned back to Seraphina and said, "An extra pair of socks?"

Seraphina stared back at Guglielmo, locking their eyes; she would not let him escape but remained silent.

After letting the silence sink in, she said, "Despite everything they have, you have something they don't."

Guglielmo said nothing.

Seraphina gave a smirk and a wink. "Guglielmo, what you have that they don't have is knowledge. You know Prior Lorenzo's motives, you know Subprior Paola's motives. *But*," Seraphina said, giving another smirk and wink, "they don't know that you know."

"Holy shit."

"Yes. And timing is everything."

"For what?"

Seraphina reached into her jacket pocket and produced a small tightly closed leather pouch, placed it on the table, and responded, "Holy shit."

Baffled, Guglielmo stared at Seraphina as her eyes twinkled. With a small mischievous, demure smile, she leaned and said, "Guglielmo, your journey will take you to the Monastery of San Domenico, and we both know their motives. You will be invited to join them for dinner. Following that, you will be escorted to your quarters and at some point during the night you will be disposed of. Correct?"

"Yes, so the letter seems to instruct."

Seraphina smiled and said, "Remedies from the forest have many powers. And the powder in this pouch has one particular function."

"What is that?"

"Holy shit."

"You mean …"

"Yes, you, Guglielmo, need to sprinkle but a little of the powder in this pouch into either their wine or something to be served on their plates."

Still confused, Guglielmo asked, "What does it do?"

Seraphina leaned again into the table's center, gesturing for Guglielmo to lean in so they were again nose to nose.

"It gives them the shits."

"Holy shit."

"Precisely."

"How quickly?"

Seraphina raised her right hand and snapped her fingers; her signature mischievous, demure smile followed.

Guglielmo then asked, "What do I do then?"

"Leave. And leave the horse. Its sale will leave a trail." She added, "That is but one reason I don't own a store. Make your way to the forest's edge from the Monastery. It's less than a hundred meters. I, or someone, will be there to meet you."

Guglielmo tried to peer behind Seraphina's twinkling eyes but was unsuccessful.

"Why are you doing this? Why are you helping me?"

Seraphina took Guglielmo's hand and replied, "It's not me, Guglielmo. It's the forest. It speaks. You just have to listen."

Guglielmo took Seraphina's hand, kissed her, turned, and left the cottage. Mounting Between Thieves, he began his journey to the Monastery of San Domenico; but before he could get far, Seraphina's door swung open, and she called to him.

Guglielmo pulled back on the reins and brought Between Thieves to a stop. He turned to Seraphina, who yelled out, "Guglielmo, after you administer the powder, be certain to wash your hands."

"Holy shit, thank you for that."

"Holy shit indeed."

A Toast to the Living

Bologna, Italy

February 21, 1461

The Monastery of San Domenico in Bologna sat atop a hill on the north side of the town, appearing almost as an architectural protector of the town below or, conversely, as a guard tower—and Bologna's inhabitants its prisoners.

Guglielmo cautiously guided Between Thieves through the town's narrow, winding streets, which were lined by an assortment of thin stone buildings, some reaching four floors high.

It was just past midday, so midday meals had ended and the Bolognese had gone back to their duties, their labor, or—for those chosen few who had the means and who answered to no one but themselves and God—the freedom to pursue cerebral, social, or carnal pleasures, depending on the day and their dispositions.

Guglielmo was not an educated young man. Though he did not know the word "irony," its meaning did not escape him as he made his way through the streets of Bologna. It felt like Between Thieves was indeed carrying him between thieves.

As he emerged from the town's northern edge, Between Thieves carried him up the winding road to the Monastery's entrance. There, he was greeted not by thieves but by two guards who, despite their attire, looked like thugs. As Guglielmo approached, one held out his hand and said, "Who are you? And what is your business here?"

Both guards wore helmets, held shields and sheathed swords, and looked combat-ready. Clearly, they were not hotel greeters. Why guards?

"My name is Guglielmo, and I come from Florence."

The other guard responded, "So do whores and football players. What business do you have here?"

"I have an urgent letter to deliver to Subprior Paola."

Both guards remained silent, then the first asked, "Who has sent this 'urgent letter'?"

"Prior Lorenzo of the San Miniato al Monte Monastery."

"Of Florence?" It was the lesser of the two guards speaking again.

"Yes. Where I am traveling from. Florence."

The second of the two guards—and what was becoming clear, the one with authority and some critical thinking skills—asked, "May I see this letter?"

Reaching into his saddlebag and producing the sacred letter, Guglielmo said, "Certainly, sir." The guard approached, and as he was examining the letter, Guglielmo said, "You'll see, sir, the San Miniato al Monte Monastery's seal is to be broken only by Subprior Paola. It is from the Monastary's Prior Lorenzo."

The critical-thinking guard cast a quick look into Guglielmo's eyes, by no means a friendly, welcoming look. Turning toward the Monastery entrance, he said, "Wait here."

"At your command, sir."

When in doubt, bow and scrape.

As Guglielmo and the first guard maintained their positions and waited for the critical-thinking guard's return, the guard, sizing up Between Thieves, said, "That is a fine-looking steed." Then, suspiciously, "Where did you get such a horse?"

No one of Guglielmo's status would have such a prized stallion.

Guglielmo motioned for the guard to come closer for a more intimate response. When he did, Guglielmo said, "Please do not share this, but I am to gift Between Thieves to Subprior Paola."

The guard stared at Guglielmo, glanced back at the horse, and said, "This horse's name is 'Between Thieves'? Who names a horse 'Between Thieves'?"

"The San Miniato al Monte Monastery. They named their horses after the twelve Stations of the Cross of our good Lord, Jesus Christ."

The guard quickly crossed himself, adding, "Amen."

Rumor's seed was planted. The most effective way to get someone to tell everyone is to ask them to tell no one.

The critical-thinking guard returned from the Monastery's entrance and, with a smile usually reserved for co-conspirators, looked at Guglielmo and said, "The subprior is eager to receive you."

As he dismounted, Guglielmo surveyed the Monastery's landscape. As Seraphina had said, a forest's edge was but a few steps from the Monastery's back wall.

The other guard took Between Thieves' reins and said with a most uncharacteristic kindness, "I will tend to your horse and see he is watered and fed." What the guard was trying to plan was a way to profit.

Guglielmo gathered his belongings and the letter. As he stepped away from Between Thieves, he turned to the guards and humbly asked, "Where might I find the necessarium? It is that time of day for me, and I would be relieved to have its use before meeting with the holy subprior."

Guglielmo had no such need. His need was to know where the monks would scurry after he applied Seraphina's magic and to know his way out once they were tending to their needs.

The critical-thinking guard sighed and said, "Follow me."

The guard led Guglielmo through the Monastery's entrance and, pointing to a fresco-lined corridor to the left, said, "Subprior Paola will greet you in the scriptorium at the end of this corridor." Then, pointing to a less ornate corridor to the right, he said, "You will find the necessarium at the end of this hallway. I encourage you to be quick about your business. The subprior has business to attend to as well."

The guard then turned and left. Guglielmo ventured down the hallway to the necessarium, noting adjacent corridors and where they might lead.

What Guglielmo was mapping out was an escape route; he did not want to have to leave through the front entrance with the attending guards. And he found it. Past the entrance to the necessarium was a small door leading to the outside world and all that the necessarium had to offer. It would be through this door that the laypeople would carry their buckets of water to cleanse—not their souls but the monks' offerings to the necessarium gods.

With the escape route in mind, Guglielmo hurried back to the fresco-lined corridor and the scriptorium, where Subprior Paola stood waiting. Arched windows let the heavenly southern light pour in. The northern and western walls were lined with bookshelves cramped with manuscripts and oil lamps to aid night reading when the winter sun set early, leaving the monks in darkness.

When Guglielmo first entered the room, he was not sure if Subprior Paola was standing or sitting. He was standing. Subprior Paola was not tall. His thin, cropped, oily hair clung to his head while his eyes bulged out. With a nervous smile he said, "Welcome! I understand Prior Lorenzo has a letter for me. I am eager to read it. What was your name again?"

Guglielmo handed the letter to Paola, saying, "My apologies for not introducing myself. My name is Guglielmo."

As he began to tear open the letter and break Seraphina's forged seal, the subprior said, "Please … what was it again?"

"Guglielmo."

As Paola eased himself into a chair, he replied, "Yes, Guglielmo, please be seated."

Guglielmo sat across the table and watched as Paola read the secret letter, which, unbeknownst to Paola, was no secret to Guglielmo.

Paola's face remained expressionless as he read. Once finished, he folded the letter and pocketed it. Then he looked up to Guglielmo, smiled, and said, "Guglielmo, you have no idea how important this letter is and how grateful I am for your services in bringing it to me so quickly."

Guglielmo smiled, nodded, and replied, "It is an honor to be of service."

Paola smiled.

Guglielmo smiled, wondering, "What will he say next?"

Paola turned and stared out the window at the setting afternoon sun, wondering, "How do I dispose of this man?" Noting that night was approaching, Paola thought to himself, "I wonder how much of life's dark deeds are done under the cover of night's darkness."

He turned back to Guglielmo, smiling, and said, "Yours has certainly been a tiresome journey. I will see to it you have a place to rest your head here tonight, and I would be pleased if you would join me and my fellow brothers to dine this evening."

A layperson invited to dine with the clergy's monks? To most laypeople, this would be an extraordinary honor. However, Guglielmo knew the trap was being set.

Smiling, feigning astonishment, Guglielmo replied, "I cannot believe such an honor. Of course, I humbly accept your gracious courtesy!"

Now the trap within the trap needed to be set.

"Wonderful. We dine at the conclusion of the Vespers in the refectory. The guards will show you to your sleeping quarters, and until we dine, I encourage you to take refuge in the central church area for prayer and contemplation. It is in the church that we find ourselves closest to our God and Savior."

Paola thought offering Guglielmo a sanctuary to commune with God before meeting Him was the greatest courtesy.

Guglielmo thought it would provide a time and private place to plan.

Paola rose, walked to the scriptorium door, and opened it. He called out for the guards, who were astonishingly close, Guglielmo thought.

The guards gave Guglielmo a tour that would prove more useful than they could imagine, and at the tour's end, Guglielmo asked for privacy in the cloister while he took the time for contemplation and prayer.

No one in a monastery could say no to anyone who sought time to pray, so the guards obliged and left Guglielmo alone in the cloister.

The guards gone, Guglielmo clasped his hands, bowed his head, and thought, "Seraphina, what the fuck do I do now?"

Guglielmo considered Seraphina's tightly closed pouch in his pocket. But how to administer this potion?

Dinner. Would his food be poisoned? Would wine be served? This was a monastery. Of course wine would be served.

Guglielmo rose from his "prayers," and with no one to prevent his wandering, he made his way through the snaking monastery corridors and found the kitchen, where the evening's meal was being prepared. Three monks were busy at the counter, chopping and stirring, all with their backs to Guglielmo.

A wine urn, on a counter to their right and out of sight, sat full with its wine breathing. Guglielmo silently slipped in and sprinkled Seraphina's potion into the urn, then, just as silently, slipped away.

Guglielmo returned to the cloister, sat, and this time bowed his head in genuine prayer, saying nothing more and nothing less than, "Please, God."

Wide, open-ended prayers have often proved to be the most fruitful.

After a short while, one guard arrived and directed him to the dining chamber.

Paola was there with four other monks and warmly greeted Guglielmo, then introduced him to Brother Marco, Brother Franco, Brother Vincenzo, and Brother Tommaso.

Once seated, Brother Marco reached for the wooden urn and poured wine for everyone at the table.

Everyone raised their glasses in a toast, including Guglielmo, but he was careful not to let the liquid even touch his lips. However, Guglielmo was pleased to see these Brothers drink heartily.

As they set their glasses back on the table, Guglielmo closely watched the looks on their faces for signs of internal trouble.

The first to exhibit them was Subprior Paola himself, whose bulging eyes seemed to bulge even more. An assortment of looks followed: astonishment, fear, and terror.

One by one, they quickly excused themselves from the table. Scurrying out of the room in the necessarium's direction, they took tiny tight steps, and it looked as though they were squeezing their buttocks.

Once they were out of the refectory, Guglielmo quickly slipped into the corridor leading to the back entrance, made haste to the exit, and slipped out the unguarded door. The forest's edge was less than a hundred feet away, and Guglielmo slipped into its cloak of invisibility in less than a minute.

But once inside the forest, Guglielmo had no idea which direction to walk and could see no trail to follow. Seraphina had said she or someone (whoever "someone" might be) would be there to meet him.

He saw no one.

He did not want to call out for fear he might be heard; once the Brothers finished with their duties in the necessarium and found him missing, they would search for his whereabouts. Between Thieves would still be there, so he couldn't have gone far. Had he fallen down the well? One would hope not because that would poison the water.

It was a moonlit night, which was both good and bad. He could see but also be seen. Then, from nowhere, he felt a hand take his hand, which frightened the devil out of him. It was Seraphina. She was wearing her heather-green hooded cloak, which made her appear as part of the forest itself.

"You frightened me!"

"Shhhh!"

In a whisper, Guglielmo asked, "Where do we go now?"

"Home."

"How do we get there? We have no horses."

"We walk."

"At night? Through the forest? Won't that be dangerous?"

"When you are with me, you have nothing to fear in the forest."

"Why not?"

"Because I am part of it. But we keep to the forest's shadows."

"Why are you helping me?"

"Retribution."

"Retribution? For what?"

Nodding her head at the Monastery, she said, "They burn people like me at the stake."

"So you *are* a witch!"

"No, I am a healer. It is the Church that calls people like me witches. Come. Let's go."

"How long will this take us?"

"All night."

Paola and his Brothers had spent longer at the necessarium than was their norm. Finally relieved on many levels, they each collected themselves, one commenting, "That was so sudden!"

Paola was the first of the five to step into the refectory to discover Guglielmo was absent. As the monks gathered at the table, they looked around and at each other, bewildered.

After they all quickly confirmed they had not seen him, Paola was quick to send them off in different directions to search for their missing guest. While all curiously scratched their heads, it was Paola who was most concerned.

"Brother Vincenzo, please look in the cloister; perhaps he needed fresh air. Brother Luigi, look in the kitchen and then the infirmary. Perhaps he, too, was stricken with whatever attacked us and went looking for assistance from the attending Brother in our infirmary."

Brother Tommaso offered, "Perhaps he sought a moment for prayer and is in the church proper."

Paola had not thought of that and replied, "Of course, Brother Tommaso, it could be that simple. Please have a look for him there. I will search the grounds myself."

The search party dispersed, Paola exiting through the same rear door Guglielmo used to make his escape only moments before.

Stepping into the frosty night air, Paola glanced from side to side, determining where to start his search. To his left was the cemetery with only tombstones reflecting the moonlight. Guglielmo wouldn't be there.

At least for now.

He strolled across the grounds, looking side to side, all to no avail. Then he thought, "Is it possible?" Anything is possible until it isn't, he reasoned, so he walked over to the Monastery's well, which sat in the shadows with less than a two-foot stone wall surrounding it. Paola leaned in and yelled, "Guglielmo? Guglielmo? Guglielmo!" his voice echoing off the well's stone walls and rebounding in the cold night air.

Seraphina and Guglielmo were weaving their way through the forest's shadows, staying out of the moonlight, when they heard Paola's call in the distance; it sounded like the howl of a lone, nocturnal wolf.

Seraphina said nothing, only turned to Guglielmo and smiled as they silently slipped away into the forest's protective shadows.

Mystery in the Monastery

Approaching Bologna, Italy

Falling Night

February 24, 1461

It had been a four-hour ride from the respite of stolen Pinot Noir, capon stuffed with roasted chestnuts and served with tenderized turnips and carrots, smothered in olive oil infused with our secret house blend of rosemary, sage, thyme, and parsley, topped with a dash of carefully aged fresh saffron. Both Antonio and Gabriele looked forward to the sight of the Monastery of San Domenico in Bologna.

Antonio bore letters of introduction and requests for his and his guard's welcome, meals, and overnight accommodations, letters signed and sealed by Abbot Fransisco. Only a request from the Pope would have commanded more attention.

The late afternoon sun was setting, and the little warmth an Italian February sun could provide was fading as quickly as the sun itself. The cold became conquering.

As they topped a hill on the outskirts of Bologna, the town's skyline rose just as the sun retired. The Monastery of San Domenico stood on a hilltop dominant over the town, commanding both authority and reverence.

"Twenty minutes," Gabriele announced.

"To what?" Antonio replied.

Gabriele said, "Hopefully, a meal, care for Twice and Thrice, and a bed to sleep in." After a moment, the guard added, "That is, so long as our letters bear authority."

Antonio turned to Gabriele, smiling, and replied, "And fruit."

They led Twice and Thrice through what they hoped would be the last leg of the day's journey.

In 1461, neither Antonio nor Gabriele would know that the town's name would become the namesake of mystery meat. At that time, all that was a mystery was what might lie ahead in the dominating monastery overlooking Bologna's twisting streets and fieldstone buildings.

Gabriele, ever the guard, said, "You can fetch the abbot's letter of introduction?"

Unsaid at the end of that question was the qualifier "I hope."

Proudly, Antonio replied, "Yes, of course."

"Antonio, I think it is wisest to have the letter in hand before we dismount."

Antonio wondered, "Why the caution?" This was a monastery, and they had the abbot's letter of introduction.

"Have you ever been to the Monastery of San Domenico before? Do you know anyone there?"

"No. Antonio, as your guard, your safety is my responsibility. Escaping an undesirable situation is better on horseback than on foot."

Antonio stared into Gabriele's steely-blue eyes and said nothing. They just stared at each other silently, and Antonio reached into his saddlebag. There were several letters, each bearing the abbot's powerful seal and each addressed to specific monastery abbots. He shuffled through the sealed letters until he found the one addressed to the abbot of the Monastery of San Domenico.

"Here."

"Then let's continue on."

As they departed the town's northern edge, winding up the road to the Monastery, the sun had set on the Bologna February landscape.

Two guards stood at the Monastery's entrance. Gabriele was well versed in the guards' body language. The junior of the two always approached arrivals first while the second stood guard over the guard. It was the same as when Antonio had arrived with no appointment at the San Miniato al Monte Monastery a few days before.

So while one guard approached Antonio to question his purpose in coming, it was the second guard Gabriele watched like a hawk, hand sliding subtly to the sword's handle.

"What is your business?"

Antonio proudly produced the letter for the Monastery of San Domenico abbot and said, "We are on a mission for Abbot Fransisco, and he sends this letter of introduction."

The guard took the letter and examined it. He looked as though he might break the seal to read its contents, so Gabriele said, "That is the abbot's seal. Do guards at the Monastery of San Domenico have the authority to break abbots' seals? At ours in Florence, they do not."

The two guards cast glances at each other, looked back at Gabriele, and then turned to Antonio and said, "Wait here."

The lesser of the two guards turned, opened the Monastery doors, and entered, closing the door behind him.

The senior of the two stared not at Antonio but at Gabriele, expressionless. Then Gabriele feigned flattery, saying, "Yours is a weighty responsibility: protector of this hallowed ground and sacred sanctuary of faith."

"Thank you. What might your role be, if I might ask?"

"Similar to yours. A protector."

The doors to the Monastery opened, and the junior guard, accompanied by Subprior Paola, stepped out to greet them. Subprior Paola, bearing a large overly welcoming smile complemented by his signature bulging eyes, said, "Welcome, pilgrims, to the Monastery of San Domenico! The abbot is eager to receive you and the message you bear from Abbot Fransisco. Please. Come. The guard will tend to your horses."

Gabriele took no time to respond. "I will help with attending to the horses."

Dismounting, Antonio shook hands with Subprior Paola as Gabriele took the reins of Twice, Thrice, and Pilate and followed the subordinate guard as he led the way to the stable.

As they entered the stalls, one horse stood out. Black with white patches above each hoof, Gabriele could recognize Between Thieves immediately. What was he doing here? Neither the guards nor Paola had mentioned any other visitors from the San Miniato al Monte Monastery.

With Twice, Thrice, and Pilate settled, Gabriele collected their belongings and, from the underbelly of Pilate, took Gutenberg's Bible.

Curious, the guard said, "What's that?"

Gabriele cast a stern and admonishing glare to the guard and replied, "The Holy Scriptures. We read them each night. Don't you?"

"Yes! Yes, of course! But ours are not of such size and substance as that."

"We bring one with larger type for times when we read with the elderly, whose vision cannot accommodate a smaller-type version."

"I see."

"Exactly. Some of them can't."

The guard led Gabriele to the dormitory, saying, "This is where you shall bed tonight. I believe you are in time for the evening's meal. I see your companion has found his bed. You may take the one beside his. Dinner will be served shortly. We are pleased to have you as our guests."

With formalities and responsibilities dispensed, the guard turned and left the dormitory, returning to his duties at the Monastery's gates, where he hoped to get a good night's sleep.

After settling the belongings, Gabriele sat on the bunk next to Antonio's, leaned forward, and said, "Antonio, something doesn't smell right."

"You went by the necessarium, too?"

"No, I went by the rectory."

"And it smelled like the necessarium?"

Leaning closer to Antonio, Gabriele whispered, "Antonio, there is something fishy going on."

"Is today Friday?"

Gabriele's eyes rolled to the heavens and then back to Antonio.

"One of our monastery's horses is in the stable."

"Besides ours?"

"Yes. Between Thieves. That's our fastest horse."

"What's he doing here?"

"I don't know, but something doesn't feel right."

For the first time, Antonio felt the weight of the Gutenberg Bible's mission. For a few moments, he just stared at Gabriele, realizing that having a guard was more than having a traveling companion. In an effort to dismiss any relevance to Between Thieves, he said, "Maybe someone else from the Monastery has business here that has nothing to do with us. Maybe it's just a coincidence."

"If there was other business here, I would know about it. Don't forget, I am the head of security at the Monastery. I know the its business."

"What do you suggest, Gabriele?"

Gabriele glanced around the dormitory. There were fourteen straw-mattress beds, and at the foot of each bed there was a neatly folded woolen blanket. These were the sleeping quarters for the privileged. And the informed.

Gabriele's gaze turned back to Antonio.

"Abbot Fransisco's letter of introduction obviously requested we be treated well. And we have been. Shortly, we will be invited to the rectory to dine. On what, might be the question."

Gabriele sat staring at Antonio, lost in thought. Then a mischievous smile found its way to Gabriele's face.

Antonio could see the wheels turning but could not hear the sound they were producing.

"What?"

"Confusion."

"I am already there."

"Prior to the subprior's presentation for dining, I will make my way to the kitchen with a great sense of urgency."

"And do what?"

"I will tell the kitchen chefs that everything you eat must be gluten-free."

Antonio stared at Gabriele. Gabriele stared at Antonio, the mischievous smile firmly in place.

"Isn't that what they feed horses?"

"Antonio, it doesn't matter. What matters is that they don't poison our food. And there's nothing like chaos to prevent that."

With Gabriele's eyes glimmering with a guard's dark humor, Gabriele added, "Imagine if they accidentally poisoned Subprior Paola."

"What about the wine they will serve?"

"Appear to sip and don't drink."

As they sat knee to knee at their adjoining straw-mattress cots and stared each other in the eye, Antonio, beginning to realize the complexity of his pending journey, said, "Gabriele, I am a manuscript illustrator. My life has been one buried in manuscripts, looking to bring new ones to life through skills and techniques taught to me by some of Florence's best."

Though their glares did not break, both sat silently until Gabriele replied, "Antonio, I don't know your world of manuscripts. I only know you are one of Florence's most respected talents. Your skills come from an inkwell-dipped quill. Mine come from a sword's sheath."

Their eyes remained locked for a moment more.

"Let me tend to the kitchen," Gabriele then said, standing and giving Antonio a wink, and a mischievous grin.

Antonio watched as his guard walked away, wondering, "What is it with this Gabriele?"

Who's on First

Monastery of San Domenico

February 24, 1461

Subprior Paola stepped into the refectory, flashed an oversized smile, and said, "Antonio!" Then, seeing Gabriele was not with him, he added, "And where is your companion, Gabriele?"

"Gabriele had a couple of matters to attend to but will be back momentarily. Your hospitality, Subprior, is appreciated. Journeys can be tiring."

Then Gabriele appeared in the doorway and flashed an undersized smile to Subprior Paola, saying, "Subprior, your attention to Antonio and me is appreciated, and I will be certain to tell our Abbot Fransisco of the attention you have bestowed on us."

Subprior Paola's smile diminished slightly as he replied, "Please. Make no mention at all. It is nothing. Now, if you will, dinner is being served in the refectory, and we look forward to your company."

Paola turned and vanished down the biblically storied corridor, passing pastel depictions of the confusing Sermon on the Mount. Was it a sermon or a lawyer's argument? God only knows.

Paola whisked by the fresco of Christ miraculously feeding a multitude with five loaves and two fish. Then he passed, as he did every day, the frescoes of Christ healing the sick, the lost sheep, The Woman at the Well, Christ showing compassion for the outcast, His rising, His blessing of children, the prodigal son, and the Last Judgement.

Gabriele quietly said, "I think our meal service will be safe."

Antonio asked, "How so?"

"They don't know what to serve first."

"You mean, who to serve first."

"No, I mean what."

"What to who?"

"That depends on what's second."

"Second? But what's first?"

"That depends on who's first."

"Who's first for what?"

"I just told you. That depends on what's second."

"Don't you think meals are served in hierarchy?"

"No, I made sure the meal today will be served in anarchy."

"How?"

"Because of your diet."

"Diet? I'm not on a diet."

"I know. But I told them that's why you're so thin."

Gabriele turned to head toward the refectory, with Antonio close behind.

Antonio sighed, "I hope they serve wine."

"One of the kitchen staff said to be cautious with the wine. Apparently, it recently caused some intestinal issues with the monks."

"Shit."

"You heard, too?"

As they entered the refectory, all heads turned to them, all smiling, and Subprior Paola stood from his table. "Please join me here. I have saved two spots for you," he said.

There were two long tables, and the monks were seated in prayer while waiting for the food and wine to be served.

Paola said, "Brother Franco, please read for us Psalm 51 as we eat."

When he got to the line, "Behold, I was shapen in iniquity; and in sin did my mother conceive me," Gabriele looked up at him, and Antonio sensed disdain.

They ate in silence, and both left the wine served untouched.

At the conclusion of the meal, as the servitors cleared the plates and cups from the table, Paola turned to Gabriele and asked, "So what route will you take tomorrow? Where do you hope to reach tomorrow?"

"So many questions," Gabriele thought.

"We shall follow the Po Valley and hope to reach Ferrara."

"That is such a journey! But thankfully, at this time of the year, the ground should be solid, and you will not have mud to bog you down. I hope your sleep tonight provides rest and comfort to prepare for your day's journey tomorrow. I have seen to it that you are provided with extra woolen blankets. Our nights here in February are cold; and while humility and bare creature comforts are our way of life, they may not be yours."

Paola served up a fawning smile, followed by, "Brother Vincenzo will ensure you have a hearty breakfast to start your day. A prominent family in Bologna has requested I attend and deliver the last rites to the family's patriarch, a kind and God-fearing man who has been generous to our humble monastery and will soon be delivered into the hands of our Lord. It is a privilege to be asked to deliver his last rites."

Antonio thought, "Oh, the pious, how ingratiating their journey through life."

Standing to make his grand exit, Paola said, "I wish you a good night's rest and a safe journey tomorrow."

With an obsequious smile and lightless eyes, Paola turned and left the refectory.

The tables were cleared, and the monks were making their way to evening prayers, their last task before retiring to their austere dormitory cots.

With the refectory empty, Antonio and Gabriele silently stared at the frescoes, the duo deep in their thoughts as they pondered where they were, what lay ahead, and how they had gotten here in the first place.

Without breaking his stare at a fresco depicting the Parable of the Lost Sheep, Antonio said, "Gabriele, what do you think?"

Gabriele, staring out the window at the starlit sky, responded, "Antonio, I was about to ask you the same question."

"You are the head of security at San Miniato al Monte Monastery and know the ways of monasteries."

"You are a respected manuscript illustrator and a man of words and know the way of the monasteries' senior clergies' minds."

"Gabriele, I don't believe that is humanly possible."

For the second time since their journey together began, Gabriele smiled.

They turned and looked at each other.

Antonio said, "I'm not sure how well I will sleep in the dormitory tonight. I have never slept in a roomful of monks before."

"Neither have I. We guards usually sleep where we stand."

"Sword in hand, I hope."

"Always."

Antonio and Gabriele stood and made their way to the dormitory. Monks were settling, extinguishing the wall torches. They murmured to each other, or maybe themself, before slipping into the silence of a night's sleep. However, it was not that silent. Three snored, one loudly. And as the night's nocturnal symphony played its tuneless melody—accompanied by random voices of sleep talking—Antonio and Gabriele, unbeknownst to each other, both stared wide-eyed at the ceiling, wondering when the morning's sun would end their torture of a sleepless night.

Antonio was the first to whisper. "Are you awake?"

"Yes."

"Have you managed to get any sleep?"

"No."

"The snoring is a challenge. And a couple have been talking in their sleep."

"I know. And I don't want to know what they're saying."

"Imagine what they might be dreaming."

"No, thank you."

Antonio sat up and turned to sit on the edge of his cot. Facing Gabriele, he asked, "Gabriele, how did you become the head of security at the Monastery? And why you to protect me?"

Gabriele lay motionless and silent, still staring at the ceiling.

Sensing discomfort, Antonio apologized. "I'm sorry. Your role and the affairs of the San Miniato al Monte Monastery are none of my business. I am simply a manuscript illustrator. But reading what I illustrate often curses me with a nagging question—'Why?'—about almost everything."

Suddenly, Gabriele swung out of the cot and sat facing Antonio, knee to knee with him.

"My father."

"Your father? What about your father?"

"My father taught me how to be a man. A man skilled with the sword."

"What about your mother? What did your mother teach you?"

"My mother died during childbirth."

For a moment, there was a silence between them. Even the monks' snoring paused.

Gabriele then said, "Did you listen to the dinner's reading?"

"Not really. I have read and written these Scriptures many times. In fact, in several languages. Listening to someone read them means little to me. What did I miss?"

Gabriele quoted, "'Behold, I was shapen in iniquity; and in sin did my mother conceive me.'"

Gabriele stared at Antonio, then added, "So my mother died for her sin, and here I am, right? Did your mother die for her sin, or did you have a mother?"

Antonio stared Gabriele in the eyes for long, intense moments while neither spoke. Then Antonio said, "Gabriele, it was my mother who encouraged me to read and study the languages in manuscripts I was illustrating. Latin. German. French. Italian, of course. Greek. But thankfully, she never tasked me with learning Hungarian."

"What was it like to have a mother?"

"I don't know. Just life. What was it like to be raised by a father who had to be both father and mother?"

Gabriele smirked, looked down and then back at Antonio, answering, "Unique. From a very early age, he trained me to be who I am."

"Swordsmanship?"

"Absolutely."

"When did he start training you?"

"When I was three."

Antonio cast a glance at the sword that never seemed to leave Gabriele's side and said, "How does a three-year-old pick up a sword such as that?"

"That was my father's profession. He was a sword maker, considered the best. So when I was three, he made my first sword, created for my size. This amused his clientele, and they would engage in little sword battles with me, basically teaching me the art of swordsmanship as an entertaining game.

"As I grew, so did the size of the sword my father made for me. And the games with his clients continued. As did their intensity.

"For my seventeenth birthday, my father gifted me the sword you see with me now. He invited a group of his clients for a birthday celebration and playful bouts. Each one left commenting, 'I could not beat Gabriele.' Those are the roots of my career as a monastery guard."

Antonio and Gabriele studied each other turned away and said, "Let's try to get some sleep. It will be a long day tomorrow."

They both swung back into their beds, wishing each other a good night's sleep.

Both lay silent, staring at the ceiling above them.

When Gabriele should really have been asleep, Antonio said, "Gabriele?"

There was a pause. Was Gabriele asleep?

"Yes?"

"I am sorry about your mother."

"Thank you."

Head over Heels

Monastery of San Domenico

February 25, 1461

A tuneless chorus of Latin chanting woke Antonio from his sleep; centuries later, with the aid of synthesized music, a quicker tempo, and local languages replacing Latin, it would become known as "rap."

Moaning, Antonio muttered, "For the love of God."

From the adjacent cot, Gabriele responded, "Apparently."

Antonio whispered, "Did you get any sleep?"

"I have better sleep standing on guard at San Miniato al Monte Monastery."

"Well, no doubt breakfast will soon be served and then we can be on our way."

"Have you ever had breakfast in a monastery?"

"No."

"Expect bread, butter, if we are lucky some form of pastry and fruit, as well as herbal tea."

"No coffee?"

"No coffee. Antonio, this is not Florence."

Antonio's thoughts drifted to Mario's bakery, this time fantasizing not about Andrea but about the aroma of fresh-brewed coffee, the warmth holding the cup on a Florentine winter morning, that first sip and the spark it brought to the day's beginning.

Herbal tea?

Then Antonio thought of the many letters of introduction he had to the en route monasteries and began budgeting what money they had for the cost of inns and taverns that would provide snore-less overnight stays and mornings that served coffee.

The roommate monks stopped their chants, and it seemed it was finally time for breakfast.

And herbal tea.

Gabriele and Antonio gathered their belongings, including the clandestine-wrapped, errant Gutenberg Bible, and made their way with the flow of monks to the refectory.

Subprior Paola was absent, as he said he would be, now possibly delivering last rites to one of Bologna's finest.

Antonio and Gabriele took the same spots on the bench where they sat for dinner the night before. The monks on either side nodded to them and smiled but said nothing.

The monks on duty then served breakfast, which, as Gabriele forecast, consisted of still warm, freshly baked bread, a humble serving of butter, and a pastry-like thing Antonio had never seen served at Mario's bakery.

And herbal tea.

Breakfast was not a long dining experience, and there were no long, lingering, cordial goodbyes, only one Brother who said, "Allow me to escort you to the stable. Your horses have been well fed and watered."

Antonio leaned into Gabriele's ear and whispered, "We should have been so lucky."

From that emerged Gabriele's third smile. But when they entered the stable, Gabriele's demeanor changed instantly.

"Between Thieves is no longer here."

As they saddled Twice, Thrice, and Pilate and Brother Franco excused himself, Gabriele turned to Antonio and said, "Perhaps Between Thieves is delivering last rites in Bologna."

Antonio and Gabriele stared at each other, neither saying a word. Then

Antonio said, "Gabriele, I am a manuscript illustrator. The intrigues of monasteries are not my world."

Smiling and trying to comfort him with a hand to his shoulder, Gabriele said, "They are now."

Saddled and packed with Gutenberg's Bible discreetly tucked under Pilate's belly, they left the stable and turned north toward Ferrara. Getting there would mean another long day of travel if things went well. Two days if not.

The Italian February sun was a tease. While bright, sunny, and cheerful, it was cold.

Their trip began through a small forest of coppiced trees, primarily oak and chestnut, serving as a source of wood for heating and construction. The forest was under the care (and ownership) of the Monastery. With the trees leafless in the winter months, sunlight poured into the grove and made following the trail easier than it was in summer.

Raised with no mother, Gabriele was captivated learning how Antonio's mother inspired him to learn languages.

"Women typically don't play a role in their children's learning. They cook. They clean. They bear children. Unless you are of nobility. Were you?"

Antonio laughed. "Our interaction with the nobility was limited. What I remember most of the nobility from when I was a child, when we did have such an interaction, was their shoes."

"Their shoes?"

"Yes. When you are bowing and scraping, you see more shoes than faces."

Gabriele chuckled. It seemed the stone face of the attentive guard when Antonio groveled for an impromptu meeting with Abbot Fransisco would crack. The guard was becoming less guard-like, even laughing occasionally—if a chuckle constitutes a laugh.

"Are there any particular shoes you recall?"

"Oh yes. Cosimo de' Medici's shoes."

"You met Cosimo the Elder?"

"Yes. Well, more of his shoes than him, actually. I was about thirteen or fourteen, and Fra Angelico had taken me on as an apprentice. One day, while I was working, he came to me and said, 'Put your paints away and come with me.' Of course, an apprentice does exactly what he is told. A few minutes later we are walking toward the river, and I ask, 'Where are we going?'

"Gabriele, I'm sure you're familiar with the Medici residence."

"'Of course.'

"Well, Fra Angelico raised his hand, pointed to it, and said, 'There.'

"I didn't know what to do or think. And I don't know why he had me accompany him. Perhaps it was to impress upon me his stature in Florence's art and social world, although he really didn't need to."

"So when you met him, Cosimo de' Medici, what did you do?"

"I bowed and scraped and stared at his shoes."

"And you still remember them?"

"They were a light-green leather with pointed toes, and the rim was lined with tastefully placed little studs that I am certain were made of gold. I only think that from working with gold leaf in manuscript illustration. You can't fake gold."

The forest grove cleared into open agricultural land, and the trail they had been following became more ambiguous. The myriad of creeks and streams draining into the Po river were also the water source for the multiple crops encircling villages dotting the landscape ahead of them. A trail to this village, a trail to that village, but which trail would lead them directly to Ferrara?

As they stood there studying the landscape, Gabriele heard the pounding of galloping horses coming from the left, at the other end of the forest grove they had just left.

"Look."

Antonio turned and saw four men on horseback making their way toward them, making good speed.

Watching as they approached, Gabriele said, "Jesus Christ."

"What?"

"That horse in the middle? That's Between Thieves."

"Apparently."

As the four horsemen of the pending apocalypse approached Antonio and Gabriele, they slowed and encircled them. Although all four horsemen were armed, they carried only swords. No crossbows or serious battlefield weaponry. Simply the basic hardware of thieves. The one riding Between Thieves—big, burly, bearded, and the clear leader—laughed and said, "Well, what might we have here? Give us your saddlebags and you may be on your way."

Gabriele replied, "Certainly," and dismounted, unhitched the saddlebag, and tossed it to the ground. Then, standing in front of it, Gabriele said, "Come and get it."

The four horsemen of the robbery simultaneously burst out laughing, looking at each other. After a few moments, one of the thieves—who most likely wished to impress—looked at the clear leader, responded, "Allow me," and dismounted. Like the leader of the team of bandits, he was brawny and bullnecked, and each step was plodding. As he got to within striking distance he drew his sword and swung it high over his head. Gabriele had remained motionless.

Until that moment.

Two things happened simultaneously: Gabriele flicked a dagger from under the left sleeve while unsheathing the sword with blinding speed. For a split second, the appearance of the dagger distracted the bandit, and that split second was all Gabriele needed. Before the thief could even put his sword in action, in a lightning-swift blow, Gabriele severed his head.

In the few seconds after a head departs the body, there is still blood in the brain, and the eyes can, for life's last moment, register to the brain what they see. The last thing the thief saw in this life was his headless body collapsing to the ground.

With dagger in one hand and bloodied sword in the other, Gabriele said, "Next?"

None of the thieves moved or spoke.

Gabriele then walked over to the leader of this woeful gaggle of thieves and asked, "Where did you get this horse?"

"It was a gift from a monk."

"Monks don't give gifts. They take them. Where did you get this horse?" Gabriele raised the dagger to the horse's jugular. From the guard's right hand, the sword that severed the thief's companion's head was upright, ready to strike.

Calmly, Gabriele asked, "And what is your name?"

The thief sat mounted in his saddle, wishing to ignore the question; but with Gabriele's blade positioned at his horse's throat, the sword held ready for combat, and one of his comrades lying on the ground with his head several feet from his body, the bandit reluctantly answered, "Alfonso."

"A Ferrara name. Is that where you're from?"

"No. That is where my mother was from. She was sentimental. I am from wherever things take me."

Gabriele smiled and replied, "Like here? Like now?"

The guard glanced around to the remaining two thieves still mounted and, glancing first at the head of their companion and then his body, said to them, "Unless you would like to join him, I suggest you remain mounted." The thieves sat on their horses, neither speaking but both wondering how such a scrawny person could have undone their hefty, now-headless companion.

Turning back to Alfonso and Between Thieves, Gabriele repeated, "Where did you get this horse?"

"It was a trade."

"A trade for what?"

"A little bit of money and the secret of a treasure to steal."

"Treasure? What treasure?"

"The treasure you're carrying."

"Treasure? What treasure are we supposed to be carrying?"

"A book."

"A book? Do you know how to read?"

"Tavern signs, yes."

"So, what is this book?"

"Apparently, it's an important Bible."

"Bible? Have you ever read the Bible?"

"No, it's in Latin."

"So how do you know what the Bible says?"

"The monks tell us."

"How did you know we would have this treasure you don't know how to read?"

"The horse trader told us."

"How would a horse trader know we would have a Bible to steal?"

"A monk told him. The monk gave him the horse to sell and told him about the book to steal."

"So we're back to a monk trading a horse and telling tales about a book to steal that you don't know how to read? What did this monk look like?"

"I don't know. I never met him."

"So you got the story that a monk gave a horse to sell and told a secret of a treasure to steal all from a horse trader?"

"Perhaps we should be on our way."

"Not so fast. That's our horse."

"You know this horse?"

"Yes."

"What's his name?"

"Between Thieves."

"It is!"

"But not for long. Take your friend's horse. He won't be needing it."

Alfonso glanced first at his dead colleague's body, then his colleague's head a few feet away, wondering how such a gangly man could have so easily overpowered such a proven bandit as Heinrich.

"How do you know this horse? Who are you?"

"I am a guard from the monastery that owns this horse and I suggest you get off him and get on your way."

Dismounting and taking the reins of the headless horseman's steed, he looked woefully at his comrade's two parts, saying, "What about Heinrich?"

"Was that his name?"

"I think so."

Gabriele smiled and replied, "Fly food and fertilizer. I'm a naturalist."

As the would-be robbers rode off, Gabriele took the sword and sheath from Heinrich's headless body and turned to Antonio, who was still mounted. The guard handed them to him, saying, "Have you ever used one of these before?"

"No."

Sighing, Gabriele then mounted Thrice and, as they returned to their journey, said, "Training begins in the morning. Wherever that might be."

As the meager band of thieves rode away, Alfonso turned and yelled, "This time, you were lucky. Next time, you won't be. Trust me."

By then, the flies had already found their day's dinner and were settling on Heinrich's head and body.

Gabriele turned to Antonio and asked, "What is it about this Bible?"

"A simple mistake."

"Apparently not as simple as you might think."

Gabriele took the reins of Between Thieves and tied them to Twice, Antonio's horse, saying, "And now we will drag the fastest horse from the Monastery's stable like a packhorse. Don't you wonder, 'Why?'"

"Why? How? I am a manuscript illustrator. How did I get into this?"

Gabriele smiled, looked at Antonio, and replied, "Lucky, I guess."

The Forest Comes to Life

Bologna, Italy

February 22, 1461

Seraphina and Guglielmo padded through the shadows of the moonlit forest night. Whenever Guglielmo stepped on a twig or branch, breaking the silence of the night, Seraphina would, scolding, whisper, "Watch where you step! Best to be silent in the forest at night. There are things you don't want to wake."

Seraphina walked as though she were following a trail on a map, although she had neither. Guglielmo followed behind, hoping not to step on anything that would break the silence of the nocturnal, moonlit forest.

Suddenly, Seraphina stopped and raised her hand, signaling Guglielmo to stop as well. Guglielmo stood in Seraphina's shadow and whispered, "What?"

Seraphina whispered back, as softly as the wind, "Pig."

Guglielmo nervously looked side to side, thinking she meant boar. Wild boars were dangerous, he had been told, although he had never seen one.

"Can't you smell it?"

"No."

Pointing to the southwest, Seraphina whispered, "That way."

Guglielmo's eyes, ears, and nostrils strained toward Seraphina's outstretched index finger, but he could sense nothing.

Moonlight and shadows were all Guglielmo could sense.

Turning in the scent's direction, Seraphina blew a whisper. "Follow me. And please. Try to be mindful of where you step."

Seraphina wove her way through the shadows and, following her in every footstep, Guglielmo soon picked up the scent. Pleased with himself, he whispered, "I can smell it!"

"Quiet, Guglielmo! They might hear you!"

Hear him? Guglielmo was surprised Seraphina could hear him. And exactly who were "they"?

As they thread their way through the forest's groves, they saw a golden fire's glow straight ahead. As they got closer, they could hear voices and laughter, but the horses at the encampment began to stir and neigh when they smelled the newcomers.

The laughter and banter suddenly stopped. Whoever they were knew something was stirring in the surrounding forest, and if it made the horses nervous, it made them nervous, too.

Seraphina could sense this in an instant.

From the invisible shadows of the forest, she called out, "Travelers! My name is Seraphina, and my companion, Guglielmo, and I are unarmed and mean no harm. May we approach and join you for a brief respite?"

Seraphina could hear a murmur from the group, and then one voice called out, "Make yourselves apparent so we may see you."

Seraphina gestured for Guglielmo to follow her, and they stepped out of the forest's cloak and into a clearing encampment.

Six men and women sat around a fire pit, where a small pig was roasting. Behind them were three wagons and four horses tied to the low-hanging branches of trees lining the clearing.

One member of the group, a man most likely not long past his thirtieth birthday, stood. Seeing that Seraphina and Guglielmo were, in fact, apparently unarmed, he said, "Welcome. We are the Florentine Players theatre troupe. Who might you be, and why would you be traveling alone and unarmed through the forest at night?"

Seraphina was not just adept at herbal remedies; Guglielmo witnessed she was also an artful strategist. Before answering the question, she said, "You are not *the* Florentine Players theatre troupe? I have heard of you from so many villagers, but I am embarrassed to say I have not been fortunate enough to see one of your performances. What play are you touring with now?"

Before the man could respond, a woman sitting on a log by the fire's edge proudly said, "*Everyman.*"

"*Everyman?*"

"Yes, *Everyman*," the woman replied.

"*Everyman* except we are missing a man," an older man who appeared to be the leader of the group said.

"Death died," the woman explained.

Guglielmo was both confused and startled, saying, "Death died? How can death die?"

Seraphina turned to him, explaining, "Death is a character in the play *Everyman.*"

"That sounds like a frightening play," Guglielmo replied. "Especially in the middle of the night."

The leader said, "My name is Franco, and you still haven't explained who you are and what you are doing walking through the forest in the darkness of night."

Seraphina laughed, answering, "It isn't dark at all under this moonlight. As I said, my name is Seraphina, and this is Guglielmo. I am an herbal tea maker, and Guglielmo helps gather herbs. We delivered a batch of my teas in Bologna, and I wanted to be back to my home by daybreak. With this moonlight, we thought it would be a simple journey."

Then the others introduced themselves. Properzia, Andrea, Serena, Alessandro, and Giulio. Three men and three women.

"Alfonzo was Death, but alas, he is no longer of this world," Franco lamented.

Guglielmo was still struggling with the idea of someone playing a character named Death. "What would a character named 'Death' say? Sounds scary."

Serena, the youngest of the theatre troupe, replied, "That's the basis of the play *Everyman*; Death comes to visit every man."

"And woman," Andrea added.

"People pay to see this play?" Guglielmo asked.

The troupe burst into laughter.

"Everyone pays the Reaper," Properzia added, which only brought the laughter to new heights.

Guglielmo's confusion only grew with the laughter.

"It's a comedy?" he asked.

By now, even Seraphina was laughing.

Guglielmo asked, "What other characters are in this play?"

Franco, clearly the troupe's director, answered, "Well, besides Death, there is Everyman, who represents all of us; we are all Everyman. Then there is Good Deeds, who accompanies Everyman on his journey to the ever after; there is the character Knowledge, who guides Everyman on what he must do; then there is Fellowship, Goods, and Strength, who are Everyman's worldly things that will matter not where Everyman is going."

Andrea added, "Don't forget the voice of God, heaven forbid!" which was followed by a chorus of amen.

Franco stared at Guglielmo, sizing him up, then asked, "So that's what you do? You collect herbs for tea?"

Seraphina was quick to answer for him. "He helps from time to time."

"So, what other work do you do?" Franco was grilling, and Guglielmo shuffled, uncomfortable with the truth.

"I do work when people need help with something." That was neither a lie nor the truth. He did work when he could find it, but it wasn't that often.

"Do you live with your parents?" Franco's grilling continued, and as it did, Guglielmo's humiliation became more pronounced.

"No, my parents are no longer alive."

"Where do you live?"

"Florence."

"Where in Florence?"

Seraphina put her hand on Guglielmo's shoulder, giving him what he felt was little in life: comfort.

"Wherever I can."

Franco just stared at him without saying a word.

The campsite was still and quiet, and Guglielmo just stared at the ground.

Then Franco said, "Guglielmo, how would you like to join us and play the role of Death?"

"*Me*?" Guglielmo looked up from the ground, looked Franco in the eye, and said, "But I don't know how to act. I am not an actor."

For the first time, Franco smiled and said, "Guglielmo, I can teach you."

"How are you going to teach me how to be an actor?"

"Guglielmo, acting is basically quite simple. All you have to do is pretend to be somebody you're not. People do it all the time."

Guglielmo turned to see Seraphina staring at him, smiling, almost gleaming.

Death had brought life to Guglielmo.

WITCH WAYS

SAY WHAT?

Florence, Italy

February 20, 1461

In the known history of the known world, no one had ever been responsible for proving that two different items were not different.

Later, it would become known as proofreading.

At the time, Antonio looked at it as a task for career preservation.

For the third day in a row, Antonio sat at the desk, the illustrated Bible open to one side and Gutenberg's to the other.

He tried not to think about what could be proven from anything he was proofing.

Genesis 38:8-10: So, the man took his concubine and sent her outside to them, and they raped her and abused her throughout the night.

Briefly, Antonio wondered what form of abuse would take after rape. And who were "they" and how many of "them" were there? Perhaps the translators misconstrued something. But that was not for him to question.

As the day wore on, the light moved to highlight the wall's frescoes one by one.

Kings 2:23-24: "He turned around, looked at them and called down a curse on them in the name of the Lord. Then two bears came out of the woods and mauled forty-two of the boys."

One of Antonio's many inconveniences was his instinct to question. "Forty-two of the boys"? Were there more? Who was keeping count?

Midafternoon, the study's door opened, and the abbot himself stepped in.

"How goes it, Antonio? Have you found other grievances?"

"None so far, Reverend Father. Everything seems as written."

"Good, my son."

The abbot then walked over to Antonio, holding a piece of paper in his hand. "As I understand it, Antonio, you are a lover of manuscripts, and I believe you read and are fluent in several languages."

"Five if you include Latin, Reverend Father."

"All the more perfect. Please. Read this."

The abbot then handed Antonio the paper in his hand. It was a letter written in Latin and addressed from Domine Fransisco to … Could this be true? Pope Pius II himself. As Antonio read, his eyes widened, his mouth went agape, and he looked up at the abbot, stunned.

"For me?"

"Yes, Antonio, for you in gratitude for your service to not just our humble monastery but the Church itself. Now that you have read the letter, it will await your return in my study. Then I shall seal it for you, requesting your admission to the Vatican library. Now, let me leave you to your work."

The abbot retreated as gracefully and silently as he entered, leaving Antonio in disbelief at what he had just read: a request to grant Antonio, a lover of manuscripts, access to the Vatican library, the mother lode of manuscripts.

But first, back to his work.

Numbers 31:18: "But all the women children, that have not known a man by lying with him, keep alive for yourselves.."

Always questioning, Antonio thought, "And how would 'yourselves' know? And how old would a woman child be?"

As Antonio's left-hand index finger followed, word by word, the accredited and blessed text of the illustrated Scriptures, his right-hand index finger followed the text trail of this, so far, blasphemous Bible imposter. Each word was a potential trap. If he overlooked even one discrepancy later to be discovered, Antonio's reputation, as well as his career, could be in shatters.

The more he read, the more he believed the Church benefited from these sacred texts being written in Latin, a language only the educated could understand.

Matthew 5:28: "But I say unto you, that whosoever looketh on a woman to lust after her hath committed adultery with her already in his heart."

Antonio's thoughts wandered to Andrea from Mario's bakery and how it must be getting close to dinnertime.

Ezekiel 4:12-15: "And thou shalt eat it as barley cakes, and thou shalt bake it with dung that cometh out of man, in their sight."

At that moment, just as the day's light began to fade, a monk ambled through the corridors, ringing a bell to announce dinner.

Antonio closed the sacred texts for the day. Then, anticipating the honor of joining the Monastery's clergy for the end-of-day feast, he hoped he wouldn't be seated near Prior Lorenzo and served a plate of steaming, warm barley cake.

Saddling Up

Florence, Italy

February 22, 1461

The Monastery assigned Piero, a novice, to ensure Antonio and Gabriele had everything they needed for their journey even though he was unaware of its destination or purpose. They met in the calefactory after all the monks had retired to their quarters for meditation, contemplation, and prayer.

And privacy.

When asked about their destination, Gabriele responded, "North."

One of the first lessons of wisdom applicants to the Monastery learned was the art and insight of knowing when to ask questions and when to be obeisant and serving.

"North in February. I will collect blankets for you and your horses. I suggest you bring one horse to carry provisions. Does that meet with your approval?"

"Yes."

Gabriele had long mastered the husbandry of language. And those answering to Gabriele had long mastered the art of servitude. A manuscript illustrator traveling with the Monastery's most trusted guard was something that could bring the rumor mill to life if you lacked the insight to avoid bringing it to anyone's attention.

"Might I ask how long you plan to be traveling?"

"Six weeks," Antonio replied, reflecting an artist's timeless predisposition to optimism.

"Eight weeks," Gabriele corrected. The guard didn't verbalize the completion of the thought: "… if we're lucky."

"I see," replied Piero, who did not. He had never in his eighteen years traveled more than five miles in any direction from the center of Florence.

"If you will allow, I shall collect your provisions, bring them to the stable, and meet you there in an hour's time. Is that suitable?"

Gabriele replied, "My travel needs are packed and ready in my quarters. I will bring them when we meet. Antonio, have you prepared for travel?"

Even as an educated, well-read, multilingual artist, Antonio was at a loss for words. The best he could come up with, although he could have said it in Latin, Florentine Italian, Greek, French, and German, was, "No."

Gabriele stared at him, expressionless, then advised, "Perhaps we should go to the stable, select our horses, and arrange saddles and packs. Piero can also load packsaddles in the morning, giving you time, Antonio, to return to your quarters, collect your things, and meet us back at the stable at dawn." Then, after a brief pause, Gabriele added, "Are you able to do this, Antonio, or do you require help? I can send Rinaldo to assist you if need be."

Gabriele had wasted no time establishing who was in command of the pending journey.

"No, thank you, Gabriele, I do not need Rinaldo. I am quite capable."

Gabriele locked gazes with Antonio, ensuring he understood the command of authority. Then, turning to Novice Piero, Gabriele issued the next command: "With that settled, let's get the stable business in order. I would like to get sleep tonight before tomorrow's journey."

Gabriele stood, followed by the two attentive sheep.

Piero took a lit torch from the wall, and they wound their way through the back corridors to the stable.

Their arrival, unlike Prior Lorenzo's, stirred the horses. There were a couple of minutes of snorting, hoof stomping, and neighing before the horses settled. Gabriele, familiar with all of them and their idiosyncrasies, was the first to notice the empty stall.

"We're missing Between Thieves."

Antonio's anxiety about the pending journey took a sudden jolt. They had not even left. How could they be missing between thieves?

Nervously, he responded, "What thieves?"

Gabriele's eyes rolled before turning to Piero. The guard asked, "Where is Between Thieves?"

At that moment, the stable keeper, Pietro, entered the stable and the chaos.

Although Piero was not responsible for stable management, Gabriele's intensity in questioning made him feel that somehow he was. He reminded Gabriele that his knowledge of the stable was merely its location, then, seeing Pietro, asked, "Pietro, where is Between Thieves?"

Although one should never answer a question with a question, that is precisely what Pietro did.

"He's not here?"

As though thinking out loud, Gabriele mumbled, "Fastest horse we had. Curious."

Piero, eager to oblige and help, jumped in, "We have a horse named Curious? Where shall I find it? Shall I bring Curious to you?"

Gabriele eased onto the same stool where Lorenzo had sat just three days before, then said as one might talk to an aspiring monk simpleton, "No, thank you. Please help Pietro collect saddles and saddle packs. Antonio and I will review our options here and then tell you which horses we will take. You can read, can't you?"

"Yes, Gabriele, but not Latin."

Gabriele glanced at Antonio, then at the stable signs, clearly not written in Latin, and then looked back at Antonio. It was a flicker of wordless communication, leaving Antonio wondering, "What am I getting myself into?"

Gabriele rose from the stool and sauntered down between the stalls, considering their options. Then a thought struck, and quickly turning to Antonio, Gabriele asked, "You do know how to ride a horse, don't you?"

The insult of assuming he could not pack for himself was one thing, but this was another. Antonio paused, returning Gabriele's stare, and then replied, "And paint, too."

Gabriele smirked, adding, "At the same time?"

Centuries later, this line of thinking and questioning would morph into one's ability to walk, talk, and chew gum at the same time, which, in turn, would condense into an efficiency known as "multitasking."

After considering the options, Gabriele thought the wisest choice would be for them to ride Twice and Thrice, with Pilate bearing the travel burdens.

Settled, Gabriele instructed Piero to ensure all was in place for a dawn departure and dismissed him. With the sun long gone, Gabriele solicitously suggested a guard accompany Antonio home for added safety.

"Thank you, Gabriele, but I should be fine to find my way home."

"Antonio, given the nature of our assignment, I think I would be more comfortable if someone escorted you. Allow me a moment to collect my gear."

As Gabriele left the stable, Antonio realized this was the first time he had seen Gabriele without a sword and felt it odd that he had not noticed.

Piero had left with the torch, so Antonio found himself alone in the darkened stable, listening to the horses' breathing and a northerly wind. A few moments later, Gabriele returned armed, saying, "I do not know where you call home. You'll have to lead the way."

"Via del Garbo but a ten-minute walk."

As they walked in silence, Gabriele thought, "Via del Garbo. Such a colorful neighborhood. How appropriate."

Antonio and Gabriele had never conducted any casual conversation whatsoever. On duty, Gabriele did not engage in idle chitchat under any circumstance.

While they walked, they each considered the unknowns. Gabriele knew nothing of Antonio's private life. Was he married? Did he have children?

If so, how would he explain to his family the need for a two-month journey?

Antonio's mind became rutted in one question: "What does a monastery guard do when they are not guarding?"

After several blocks, Gabriele was the first to speak.

"Have you traveled beyond Florence before?"

"Once to Venice."

"Venice? That is a long journey. What took you there?"

"My studies. What about you? Have you traveled beyond Florence?"

"I am not from Florence. I grew up in the countryside."

There was a finality to how Gabriele answered the question, and the conversation ended.

As they reached Antonio's doorway, Gabriele reminded him to pack keeping in mind they were traveling north and it was February, adding that in the morning Piero would arrive to help carry his belongings. Then Gabriele turned and walked away.

Antonio watched for a moment, wondering what it would be like traveling week after week with an enigma.

Strangers in the Fight

Somewhere in the Middle of Nowhere, En route to Bologna

Falling Night

February 19, 1461

Guglielmo, driving Between Thieves as best as could be expected, was still at least a day's ride from Bologna, and the wind had picked up, carrying light snow. He entered a forest with a narrow trail that was disappearing under a light blanket of fresh falling snowflakes.

The only navigational aid Prior Lorenzo offered was assurance that the trail to Bologna was clear and well traveled. He guaranteed Guglielmo would fail to find his destination by uttering the age-old curse, "You can't miss it."

Although Guglielmo had found the trail into the forest, it soon blended into a uniform white veneer. And more than snow was falling. So was daylight. And his confidence.

Guglielmo pushed forward, guiding Between Thieves between trees, and was now looking for a sheltered grove, one protected from the westerly blowing snow and suitable for a night's rest—as much rest as one could expect from a night exposed in a forest with nothing but Between Thieves for comfort and solace.

With his senses keen and alert, Guglielmo caught a faint whiff of something burning. He did not know what because it was not a scent he recognized; he only knew something was burning. And if something was burning, there was heat. And maybe even hope.

His navigational aid was now his nose rather than his eyes. Between Thieves kept him between trees as they weaved their way to the scent's source, but with blowing snow and growing darkness, they were quickly traveling blind. But the smell was growing stronger.

As they negotiated around a cedar grove, there sat a small fieldstone house complete with a smoking chimney, the source of their olfactory navigation.

Thirty feet from the house, Guglielmo brought Between Thieves to a halt and called out, "Hello?"

Nothing changed. The snow continued to blow, smoke wafted skyward, and all was still except for the beating hearts of Guglielmo and Between Thieves.

Guglielmo called out again. "Hello? I mean no harm!"

The snow continued to blow, and smoke wafted skyward, but no sound stirred inside the tiny impenetrable stone house.

Being left outside the walls of home comforts and refuge was not new to Guglielmo, but being exposed to a forest's wilderness, blowing snow, and dangers was.

"Hello? I need help, and I am frightened."

Something from inside stirred. Maybe it was a chair shuffling across a floor.

Seconds later, the arched wooden door opened. In its doorway stood a contradiction: a young-looking female apparition with the snow-white hair of the aged and wise, which glowed from under the hood of her dark-green cape. He had never seen a woman like this nor clothing of a dark-green color.

"Exactly what help do you need? And who are you?"

"My name is Guglielmo, and I am from Florence."

He started to dismount Between Thieves as he spoke, but she quickly interjected, "You do not need to get off your horse yet."

Guglielmo resettled in his saddle and his known station in life, saying, "My apologies. I do not wish to impose or assume."

She stood there, staring at Guglielmo and then Between Thieves, and asked, "Why are you here?"

Proudly, Guglielmo said he was on a mission from the San Miniato al Monte Monastery to deliver an urgent message to Subprior Paola at the Monastery of San Domenico.

The woman, stern now with squinting eyes, asked, "Are you with the San Miniato al Monte Monastery?"

Guglielmo was quick to dispel any impression he may have made of his role. "No, no! I am just a Florentine. I have no position in the Monastery but am sometimes blessed by its good graces."

She stood there, still glancing between Guglielmo and Between Thieves, and said, "You have a fine horse, even for a Florentine."

Quickly, Guglielmo injected, "This is not my horse. I was assigned him, as he would get me to Bologna the fastest. Or so I was told."

"Who assigned this horse to you?"

"Prior Lorenzo. He wrote the letter for me to deliver to Subprior Paola in Bologna."

"Paola? And you have this letter with you?"

"Yes. With the Monastery's seal."

She stood for a moment and stared at Guglielmo. Seraphina understood both nature and the nature of man. What she sensed in Guglielmo was naïve innocence with a whiff of pending victim. But why? Seldom were Seraphina's senses wrong.

"My name is Seraphina. Please come in. You may tie your horse where you wish. I will fetch him feed and water."

Inside, a cauldron hung over a fireplace glowing with embers. Guglielmo had no idea what was simmering in the cauldron. It was like nothing he had ever smelled before.

A small table sat against the wall adjacent to the fireplace with two chairs tucked into the sides. On a second table under a small window at the end of the room was a cup of quill pens, glass jars of inks, and other writing paraphernalia, and centered on the table was a closed book. On the other side of the door's entrance was a cot with two pillows and several woolen blankets folded at its foot.

Seraphina blew in, closing the door behind her, and said, "Perhaps you're hungry. When did you eat last?"

"This morning before I left. Prior Lorenzo was gracious to bring me food from the refectory for my journey. I felt blessed."

"And fed." For the first time since they had met, Seraphina smiled. Then she said, "So by now, you must be hungry again."

Guglielmo glanced at the fireplace cauldron and replied, "Yes, I am. What are you preparing? I don't recognize the broth or stew. What is it?"

"Food."

"Food?"

"Yes. Forest food. Sometimes foul, sometimes rabbit, but always with things I grow in the shade or in the sun from my surrounding forest garden."

Seraphina got up, took a wooden spoon from the table, scooped up a sample from the simmering cauldron, brought it to Guglielmo, and said, "Taste."

Cautiously, Guglielmo took a sip and then looked up to Seraphina, who was smirking as she watched him say, "Delicious! Like nothing I have ever tasted before!"

"Or will again. Such is the variety of the forest garden. Let's eat."

Seraphina prepared two bowls, scooping the contents from the cauldron. They sat at the window-side table, eating and savoring in silence.

After eating and tidying the table, Seraphina said, "Now, let's see that letter you are bringing to Paola."

Shocked and suddenly alarmed, Guglielmo said, "But it's sealed!"

Seraphina smiled and said, "Bring it to my worktable." There, she lit a candle and warmed wax. Then, taking the sealed letter, she created a wax forgery of the Monastery's wax seal, carefully removing the seal and opening the letter.

"Latin," she remarked.

"So you can't read it, I am guessing."

Seraphina reached and opened the book on the table. It, too, was in Latin.

"I write in Latin. So yes, I can read Latin."

Then, translating from Latin, she read the letter out loud.

As he listened, tears began to trickle down his cheeks, and he felt shame for believing the prior. Where had believing in things gotten him before? Nowhere. Only now, it seemed worse. After Seraphina finished, he said, "I live on the streets. And from serving the Monastery, I thought I was being shown kindness. And worth." He laughed as the tears flowed. "That doesn't even exist."

Seraphina took his hand and said, "I found it in the forest."

Guglielmo looked at her, saying, "What should I do?"

"Deliver the letter. But don't eat the food they offer or drink the wine they serve. Just make them think you have."

"Then what?"

"Slip out under the cover of night into the forest."

"Then what?"

"The forest looks after its own, Guglielmo."

"Is that where I should stay tonight? In the forest? I could stay with the horse."

Seraphina's was a small house hidden in a forest sanctuary and had but one cot for a bed.

"No, Guglielmo. You take the cot. I will take blankets and sleep outside. The forest knows me. And I know the forest. I can also ensure your horse remains calm. I'm sure he's frightened, too."

Seraphina took a pillow from the cot and blankets from a chest at the foot of the bed. As she went to open the cottage door, Guglielmo asked, "Why are you being so kind to me?"

Seraphina looked at him, smiled, and replied, "Is there a reason I shouldn't be, Guglielmo? Please blow out the candle. I will see you in the morning."

As Seraphina closed the door behind her, Guglielmo went over to her worktable to blow out the candle; there on the table was the letter he was to deliver, its wax seal perfectly forged, a letter meant to seal Guglielmo's fate. And it would. But not the way the letter's author intended.

ON THE ROAD AGAIN

MONEY-BACK GUARANTEES NOT GUARANTEED

Bologna, Italy

February 25, 1461

The three thieves strode back into Bologna at dusk, missing two things: the horse Between Thieves, for which they had paid handsomely (they especially liked its name), and Heinrich, who was the one to actually pay for Between Thieves. In the heat of the moment, Heinrich had lost his head, and as a result, they had lost the horse.

Thieves, too, demand justice.

Alfonso, stocky, heavily built, and good with his fists, was the leader of the three. Niccolò and Alessandro were the underlings, underlings in both brains and brawn. Still, they aided Alfonso by joining his attacks and ensuring the victims' pockets were fully emptied of any belongings.

Today, they were looking for the man who had sold them a stolen horse: Jacopo, the sleazy horse trader from Venice. Alfonso thought, "He probably had to flee Venice after swindling someone who had the means and money to achieve revenge."

By this time in the afternoon, Jacopo could usually be found in the tavern, where he often lay in wait for travelers—or as he jokingly called them: "moving targets."

As expected, Jacopo was there when the trio walked into the tavern. Seeing them, he stood up, smiled, and said, "Hello, my friends. So good to see you again and so soon!" Alfonso said nothing, walked up to him, and decked him with his right fist. Jacopo fell backward, knocking over a table. Reaching up to his bloodied mouth, he cried out, "What was that for?"

"You sold us a stolen horse."

"What do you mean? I never sold you a stolen horse. Alfonso, I know what you and your men are capable of. Do you think I would be stupid enough to cross you?"

"If you thought you could get away with it, yes."

"It saddens me you would think I would cross you, Alfonso."

"Where'd you get the horse?"

"A monk gave it to me."

For a split second, the three thieves stared expressionlessly at Jacopo; and then, simultaneously, they burst into laughter.

Alfonso, still laughing, replied, "Jacopo, do you honestly think—" Turning to his underlings, he interrupted himself, saying, "Honestly think … now there's a good one." Turning back to Jacopo, he continued, "Do you honestly think we dumb thieves are so dumb that we would believe a monk gave you a horse? We just tried that joke, and it didn't work out so well."

Desperately Jacopo insisted, "It's true, Alfonso! A monk from the Monastery of San Domenico gave it to me to sell and said I could keep half the proceeds and give the other half to him."

"Why would a monk be so generous? Monks aren't generous. So. Have you given half the proceeds to this monk?"

"We are to meet early tomorrow morning."

"So you still have the money?"

"Most of it." Then he quietly added, "I did have some tavern expenses here to settle."

"Jacopo, did you notice there are only three of us now?"

"Well, yes. I just assumed your colleague was in the latrine."

"No, our colleague lost his head."

Shocked, Jacopo responded, "He went out of his mind?"

"No, it was more like his mind went out of him. He was beheaded."

Up to this point, all the tavern guests who had gone back to their meals after Alfonso had landed his hefty opening blow to Jacopo had been merely eavesdropping. But at the mention of beheading, all returned their attention to the scene unfolding in front of them.

Beheadings were always an attention-grabbing topic, with many, in the back of their minds, thinking, "There but for the grace of God go I," because God had an active beheading program for all who crossed Him—and heaven knows there were days when it didn't seem to take much to do that.

"Beheaded?" Jacopo's concern was becoming more pronounced.

"Beheaded."

"Seriously?"

"There are no unserious beheadings, Jacopo."

"How? Beheadings are usually public affairs. I heard nothing of this."

"Do you remember also telling us that two lone travelers would carry considerable sums and a precious treasure?"

"Yes. That's correct. I did tell you that, come to think of it."

"So, how did you know this?"

"The monk told me."

"The monk, who gave you a valuable horse to sell, saying you could keep half the proceeds, also tells you about—in my line of business, Jacopo—high-value targets?"

"Yes."

"Didn't that strike you as strange, Jacopo?"

In an attempt to mimic Alfonso, Jacopo replied sarcastically, "In my line of business, Alfonso, 'strange' is never part of the equation. I am a businessman. What matters is profit. You, of all people, should understand that."

There is nothing more binding, at least temporarily, than camaraderie in crime.

"Does this monk have a name?"

"Oh yes. He is one of the most senior monks in the Monastery. He is the subprior."

Patronizingly, Alfonso said, "I did not ask his rank. I asked his name."

"Paola."

"Paola?"

"Yes, Paola."

Alfonso turned to his underlings, smiled, and repeated, "Paola." The three broke into laughter.

Turning back to Jacopo, Alfonso asked, "When tomorrow are you scheduled to pay Paola?"

"Just before dawn."

"Where?"

"Here."

"We'll join you. You don't mind that, do you?"

"No, of course not! I only hope it doesn't make Subprior Paola nervous."

Smiling, Alfonso replied, "I do." He was still smiling, but his voice took on a hint of threat as he added, "Do you mind returning the money my beheaded friend and colleague paid for the stolen horse?"

Jacopo dove his hand into his pocket and handed a pile of coins to Alfonso, who slowly and carefully counted them. Finished, he looked Jacopo in the eye and said, "Jacopo. You really need to reduce your tavern expenses."

Nervously, Jacopo smiled, replying, "You're right, Alfonso; the cost of doing business is getting out of hand. It's becoming harder and harder to conduct business while maintaining fair pricing I provide to valued customers such as you."

Alfonso stared at Jacopo and replied, "I can't ask the tavern owner to repay us the difference."

The tavern owner nodded, smiled, and interjected, "Thank you for your understanding, kind sir."

Alfonso nodded to the tavern owner, then turned his attention back to Jacopo, saying, "Tomorrow morning you are to provide the proceeds of this transaction to … What was his name?"

"Paola."

"Paola. How could I forget? I think my friends and I could convince Paola to make up the difference of our losses happily, wouldn't you say, fellas?"

Niccolò and Alessandro laughed, and Alfonso said, "I'm sure he would be happy to."

Alfonso laughed with them and then turned back to Jacopo with neither a laugh nor a smile, asking again, "When and where?"

"I told you. Here. First thing in the morning. He has to be back at the Monastery in time for morning prayers and breakfast."

"Oh, we'll certainly give him something to pray about, won't we, fellas?"

More laughter.

"Tavern keeper, where would you suggest three tired souls lay their heads for the night?"

The tavern owner, looking quite relieved his "guests" might move on, replied, "The River Inn, just a few steps to the left when you exit."

"Jacopo, we look forward to seeing you early tomorrow and meeting your 'friend' Paola."

As they left, Jacopo let out a breath of relief, sunk into a chair, and turned to the tavern owner, saying, "A tankard, if you please. On my bill, of course."

En Guard with the Guard

Brisighella, Italy

February 25, 1461

Having lost time with thieves and been saddled with an extra horse, Between Thieves, it was apparent Antonio and Gabriele would most likely not make it to the Monastery of San Giorgio in Ferrara unless they pushed themselves into the evening.

According to Gabriele's chart, there were a few villages that might have food and accommodations for them before they reached Ferrara.

Most villages were atop some hill, providing beautiful vistas and, more importantly, a view that gave ample warning of any approaching armies.

"One of the guards from our monastery has family from Brisighella, probably an hour's ride from here, and he has spoken of travelers staying at a couple of the village's inns. That might be a suitable option for us."

"I am in your hands, Gabriele," Antonio replied.

Gabriele thought, "If only he knew." But instead, the guard said, "If we make good time, perhaps there will be time for your first lesson in swordsmanship."

"Yes. I look forward to that."

Gabriele laughed and replied, "You won't for long."

In response, Antonio, too, laughed.

But nervously.

The trail winding up the hill to the village provided, as promised, a stunning view of the Tuscany landscape below. But now, with not one but two horses in tow, it was a slower climb, and they were both thankful to reach the lanes leading in and through the village.

The streets were lined with two- and three-story stone houses, with shops lining the village's center streets. Two inns were separated by a bakery, a butcher shop, and a tavern.

Antonio said, "I wonder if the bakery serves coffee." That is not all he was wondering.

Gabriele stopped at the first inn, dismounted, and said, "Manage the horses while I inquire inside." The guard vanished, leaving Antonio with four horses. Passersby looked curious and a couple offered a polite, "Welcome, traveler." One man passing by looked and said, "One man and four horses. That's a sight."

Antonio laughed and, for the first time, was conscious of the headless thief's sword now strapped to his waist—not that he would know how to use it, but appearances do carry some value.

Gabriele returned, said, "Wait here," walked down to the second inn, and disappeared inside. The guard came back to Antonio after a short while and said, while pointing to the nearest inn, "We have two options. This inn has two rooms available—overpriced, I think—but no courtyard. The other has only one room with two beds available; however, it has a courtyard."

Antonio glanced between the two inns, then turned to Gabriele, who was waiting for an answer, and said, "Why does a courtyard matter?"

Gabriele sighed, yanking on the sword hanging from Antonio's waist, and said, "Training, Antonio. Training."

Antonio sat in the saddle, thinking, "I didn't sign up for this." Then, staring at Gabriele, who was standing waiting for an answer, he said, "Gabriele, I am a manuscript illustrator."

Gabriele stared at Antonio, then replied, "Antonio. Do you remember this morning?"

"I would rather not, but yes, I do."

"Antonio, this is not Florence. Out here, the sword is mightier than the paintbrush."

"The courtyard, then."

"Good choice. Let's tend to the horses, take our belongings to our room, then begin."

Their room was on the second floor, with two wooden beds and folded woolen blankets at the foot of each bed. The walls were bare stone, with only a crucifix hanging on the wall between the two beds. There was a small table between the beds, and on it was a clay pitcher for water, two clay mugs, and a candle.

At the foot of one bed was a chest for storing belongings, and there was a small window overlooking the inner courtyard below. Although not expansive, it was walled, and in its center was a small fountain trickling water.

Gabriele studied the courtyard below, nodded, and then said, "Perfect. I'll take the bed with the chest, and we'll keep the book in there. Obviously, based on what happened today, it has some value. I sleep with my sword at my bedside, so do us both a favor: if you need to rise through the night for the potty, please don't jump suddenly out of bed." Then, with a smirk, Gabriele added, "It would be a shame for me to cut that off, overreacting, don't you think?"

"I don't think I will ever forget the image of Heinrich."

"Who's Heinrich?"

"Wasn't that the name of the man whose head you lobbed off?"

"Oh, yes. Him. Come, Antonio, buckle on your weapon. We'll take to the courtyard." With a smirk, Gabriele added, "And I'll teach you how to dance."

Antonio strapped on Heinrich's sword, mumbling, "I think I'd rather be teaching you how to paint."

"You said something?"

"No. Nothing."

Gabriele led the way down the narrow stone stairway to the ground floor and then out to the inner courtyard. The door to the courtyard was a thick, arched wooden door, and although it was open when they entered the courtyard, Gabriele turned and closed it.

Antonio was not the least bit comfortable with the schooling he was about to be given. Still wishing to convey an open mind and a positive attitude (which can be a challenge for the well-read), he unsheathed the headless Heinrich's sword and said, "Okay. What's first?"

Gabriele sighed and said, "Put that away."

Totally confused, Antonio re-sheathed the sword and stood facing Gabriele, realizing how little he knew about what his guard knew very well.

"What do you know about swords?" Gabriele asked.

"Only what I illustrate and that I have never been on the receiving end of one. And that yours looks quite different from mine."

There was a trace of pride in Gabriele's answer: "Almost everyone's looks different from mine. Don't forget, my father was a master sword maker. His clients included the monied and the bloodied. The nobility you'd be privileged to meet and those you would not want to meet on the battlefield.

"When people see my sword's hilt above the sheath, they think I am of nobility. Look at the design compared to yours."

Antonio looked at his weapon in detail. Its handle was plain, its cross guard was straight and undecorative, and its grip felt easy to lose.

Gabriele's sword had ornate cross guards with curved ends and intricate designs.

"Nobility's sword designs are primarily for show, to let someone know you are a person from a wealthy family. When I unsheathe my sword, I have seen men gasp. There is nothing but battle about my blade. It's double-edged. Do you see these fullers along the blade? Mine make my sword lighter and provide more agility in combat. Here, take my sword."

Antonio reached with his left hand, not his dominant hand, and his look of surprise was instant.

"I swear this isn't much heavier than some of my brushes."

"Like I said, my sword is mightier than your brushes. But think of it like your brushes: does your art not come partly from delicate wristwork? The art of sword warfare is in the footwork. Come. Stand beside me and match my foot movement."

Antonio joined Gabriele, standing side by side facing the outer courtyard wall.

"I am going to approach my opponent as if making an attack move. But watch my feet and move the way I do." As Gabriele stepped forward, the right foot quickly swung to the left of the left foot.

As Antonio tried to mimic the move, he tripped over his left foot.

"Again." Gabriele demonstrated, moving slower so Antonio could study and replicate the move.

"Again."

"Again."

With each demonstration, Gabriele quickened the pace until Antonio could keep up.

"Okay. Now we're going to do the same move, but left foot over right foot."

Learning this maneuver went quicker and smoother than the first.

Satisfied, Gabriele said, "Well done, Antonio. You know why we do this move?"

Antonio just stared and said nothing.

"It's called a feint. You make your opponent think you're making one approach, but you swing and come from another. Every swordsman knows this maneuver. So now we're going to add another move to the move."

"Another move?"

"Pivot."

"Pivot?"

"You pivot on your leading foot, whether it's right or left, and attack from the side."

So began the practice of this move.

Three buildings down, on the other side of the courtyard, a villager was standing at her second-floor bedroom window, watching. She called to her husband, "Giovanni, come here. Look at this." Her husband came to the window, and they watched together as Antonio and Gabriele practiced their moves.

She asked her husband, "Have you ever seen people dance like that?"

"No. I've heard of it. But I have never been to Éire."

In the courtyard, Antonio and Gabriele took a break and sat on the fountain's stone wall. Gabriele looked at Antonio, wondering if he was up to it, then asked, "Do you feel like trying some of those moves with a sword in your hand?"

Antonio swung a look at Gabriele and answered, "You have been doing this since you were three years old. I have been doing this since just past midday today."

Sensing Antonio's frustration and anxiety, Gabriele patted his knee and said, "Let's do a couple of basics then see if that tavern has edible food."

Gabriele stepped back from Antonio, sword unsheathed, and said, "Unsheathe your sword."

Antonio nervously drew out his sword, not knowing what was going to come next. Whatever it was, he was not looking forward to it.

"There are some basic attack moves. The overhand cut is when you're striking right from above, aiming for the head or shoulders. Then Gabriele demonstrated a swift blow through the air from straight above.

"Now you try it."

Antonio was self-conscious and certainly feebler in his demonstration but mimicked Gabriele's example as well as could be expected from someone more accustomed to paintbrushes and ink than flesh and blood.

"Well, at least you get the idea. Now, a move if you're looking to catch someone off guard is the uppercut to the lower body. It's a surprise no one enjoys."

Gabriele demonstrated the move with such speed it would be hard to imagine anyone even seeing it coming.

"Now, you show me the move."

Antonio's display of the move was both slow and awkward, and Gabriele sensed his embarrassment.

"Antonio, don't forget I have been doing this since I was three.

"Two more basics. The middle slash goes for the torso or arms and is done with hip and foot movements we were just practicing."

Watching Gabriele show the move, Antonio thought, "It looks more like dance than warfare. Until you're on the receiving end of the sword, that is."

Antonio's demonstration of the move was perfectly clumsy, and Gabriele smiled, adding patiently, "That one is going to need some work."

"Okay. Lastly, we have the most basic attack maneuver. It's a straight thrust right at your opponent. It's simple. But you must keep the attack going while your opponent tries to defend themselves. This move can have a lot of subtle and swift twists and turns."

Still at her bedroom window watching the spectacle, the villager called out again to her husband. "Giovanni, come here! Now they're fighting!" Her husband came back to the window, and together they watched Antonio and Gabriele practice sword moves.

"Yes. Definitely from Éire."

Back in the courtyard, after demonstrating the thrust, Gabriele said, "In reality, Antonio, I think the most important thing I can teach you is the defensive moves. Parries block against strikes from above, below, and the side—and, most importantly, the thrust coming straight at you."

Stepping back, Gabriele said, "I'll show you. I want you to come at me with the thrust movement I just showed you."

"But Gabriele! These are actual swords!"

Gabriele smiled, replying, "Yes, so we will have to be real careful. So come on. Do a thrust. And put your heart into it."

Antonio lunged forward in a thrust, sword directed right toward Gabriele.

But Gabriele moved into the thrust, used an upper parry to block Antonio's blow, and kept moving forward using the sword's handle to pin Antonio's sword above his head. Antonio's sword was locked down to his shoulder, and Gabriele kept moving in until their noses almost touched. Face-to-face, eyeball-to-eyeball, they stood, Gabriele not relieving the block. The guard said, "This is my preferred countermove to a thrust. I like to get in real close, look them in the eye, and see what's going on. And let them look in my eye and see what's going on."

Antonio and Gabriele remained locked in this position for only a few seconds. But they were long, silent seconds, with each looking to see what was going on. And it was unsettling to both. For different reasons.

At her bedroom window, still watching, the villager called out again to her husband. "Giovanni, come here! You're not going to believe this!" Her husband shuffled back to the window, looked to the courtyard, shrugged, and said, "That's the Irish: dance, fight, kiss and make up."

In the courtyard, Gabriele stepped back from Antonio, saying, "Let's put the swords away and see what fare the tavern has to offer for our dinner." As they sheathed their swords, Gabriele, smirking, said, "You did not do badly for a manuscript illustrator."

More seriously, Antonio replied, "What happened out there earlier today, what do you think that was all about? You said that the horse Between Thieves belonged to the Monastery. How did it come to be with highway thieves? And what made them think the book was worth robbing?"

Gabriele did not reply and simply led the way from the inn's courtyard through the reception out to the street and turned toward the tavern.

They walked down the cobblestone street, saying nothing. Each was trying to absorb what was "going on" from their eyeball-to-eyeball swordplay lesson.

The tavern had a hanging wooden sign over its door for anyone who might not know this was the tavern, and the only people who wouldn't know would be travelers.

Inside, a brick-oven fire burned in the back kitchen, and a fireplace at the end of the dining area had a roaring fire. Four tables were set up in a semicircle around the fireplace hearth to provide diners with as much warmth as possible on a Brisighella February night. The four tables at the other end of the dining area were for those who, due to timing, missed being seated at fireside tables.

Antonio and Gabriele were relatively early arrivals, and a table by the fire was available. Gabriele quickly secured a seat facing the room, back to the wall.

Once they were seated, the host quickly attended to them, pouring a glass of what the tavern owner assured them was the region's finest wine and fawningly listing the tavern's menu choices, which were—although very appetizing-sounding—limited.

Once he stepped away, Gabriele looked Antonio in the eye and said, "I don't like it."

Antonio glanced at the wine cups and said, "But you haven't even tasted it."

Gabriele looked at Antonio, then cast a glance at the fireplace, then looked back to Antonio, responding, "Why did those thieves have one of the Monastery's horses?"

"Because they're thieves?"

"Antonio, those thieves were from Bologna, at least that is my guess. How did Between Thieves get from Florence to Bologna? And please don't tell me they were just thieves. Those thieves were on a mission."

"As are we."

Gabriele raised a cup of wine, prompting Antonio to raise the other, and they tapped cups and sipped. And then, as if thinking out loud, Gabriele said, "They failed in their mission."

"Especially the one with no head."

Gabriele stared Antonio in the eye and said, "Think. What would you do?"

"If I were headless?"

Gabriele stared at Antonio, wondering how someone this smart could sometimes not be.

"Think, Antonio. Somehow, they have one of our monastery's horses far from home and are out to rob us. Of what? Our money? No. It's the book."

After three days of poring over every page in the book, Antonio thought, "And they could have it."

"So, what do you suggest?"

As he posed this question, the tavern keeper appeared at the table and, having heard the question, suggested, "Our house specialty."

"And what is that?" Gabriele asked.

"It is capon stuffed with roasted chestnuts and served with tenderized turnips and carrots, smothered in olive oil infused with our secret house blend of rosemary, sage, thyme, and parsley, topped with a dash of carefully aged fresh saffron."

Antonio and Gabriele looked at each other with blank stares, and Antonio responded, "That sounds unique. A memorable house specialty, I am sure." Looking at Gabriele, he said, "For two?"

Gabriele nodded, and the tavern keeper turned to his kitchen.

Both deep in their thoughts, Antonio and Gabriele remained eyeball-to-eyeball.

Gabriele asked, "Who knows about our mission?"

Antonio shrugged and began, "The only person I told about Gutenberg's—"

Gabriele interrupted him, leaning into the table closer to Antonio, and whispered, "Best we don't use the word 'Bible' when we are talking in public. Just call it 'the book.'"

Antonio started again. "The only person I spoke to about 'the book' was Abbot Fransisco. When I went to my studio manager to borrow an original copy of 'the book' for reference, he already knew what I was coming for and had it in hand for me. I don't know if he knew why I needed it, but I don't think so. I could see he sensed something mysterious was going on, but I doubt he knew what."

Still staring Antonio in the eye, Gabriele said, "I am head of security at the Monastery. I know of most things that go on. The night after your unscheduled appointment with the abbot, I know he called an emergency meeting with the Monastery's senior clergy. I was not in the meeting; I only know he called one. Such meetings are rare."

Turning to stare out the tavern window, Gabriele pondered out loud, "So how did Between Thieves end up with thieves north of Bologna?"

"Is it possible the Monastery simply decided to sell the horse?" Antonio asked.

Gabriele turned back to Antonio and asked, quite sarcastically, "To thieves?"

"Well, you have to admit, a horse named Between Thieves might have a certain appeal to thieves who, most likely, would not have a grasp of the context of the horse's name."

"Lame."

"The horse is lame?"

Gabriele sighed and responded, "No, Antonio. Your suggestion is lame."

The tavern owner arrived at their table and proudly presented their meals. While it smelled very appetizing, it appeared to be a mystery medley of whatever might have been in the tavern's pantry that day.

Gabriele scooped up a spoonful of the bowl's mystery meal, blowing across it to cool it. Just before slurping a taste, the guard said, "We go back."

Stunned, Antonio responded, "To Bologna?"

"No. Back to the Monastery. To Florence."

Antonio's absence from his studio was never far from his mind, and his immediate thought of returning to Florence was the worry of lost time. Yes, his position was secure. But what about his work?

"We'll lose a lot of time, Gabriele."

"Having another horse in tow will only slow us down more. I already was thinking bringing Pilate was a mistake. And Antonio, something does not seem right. I think a conversation with the abbot is in order."

Nightly Prayers

Brisighella, Italy

February 25, 1461

It was a short walk from the tavern along the narrow cobblestone street to the inn. Three doors from the inn, Gabriele glanced up at one of the narrow stone houses to see a woman and a man standing side by side. They were looking out the window and watching Antonio and Gabriele walk toward the inn.

"Villagers," Gabriele thought, "always with such a hunger for stories to tell about strangers."

When they arrived at the inn, Antonio and Gabriele nodded to the innkeeper and then climbed the narrow stone stairway to the second floor and their room.

A chamber pot sat between the ends of the two beds.

Gabriele, glancing at it, said, "In case you didn't notice, there is a privy in the upper corner of the courtyard."

"Yes, I saw. And smelled, as well."

"Yes, well, the wind seems to be from the southeast right now. That will be the neighbors' aroma for the night, hopefully."

Unbuckling the sword and placing it at the bedside, Gabriele slipped into the bed, pulled up the woolen blankets, and said, "Good night, Antonio."

Antonio replied, "Do you always sleep in your clothes?"

"In unfamiliar places among unfamiliar people, yes. I suggest you do the same."

Antonio unstrapped his newly acquired sword, copying Gabriele and laying it within easy reach by his bedside. Like Gabriele, he climbed into bed fully clothed and pulled up the woolen blankets, resting his head into the goose-down pillow, letting out an audible sigh. Then, after a short pause, he said, "Gabriele?"

"Yes?"

"Are all your days like this?"

It was a moment before Gabriele responded. "No. But my father trained me in case they would be."

The full moon shone through the window, casting its light on Gabriele, who was staring wide-eyed at the room's ceiling. Then, from nowhere, the guard blurted, "I am so sorry!"

"For what?"

"Forgetting our evening prayers."

Now Antonio also lay wide-eyed, staring at the ceiling, and it was a few moments before he replied.

"Are you in the habit of conducting evening prayers?"

Staring at the moonlit ceiling, Gabriele considered the audience. Antonio was the Monastery's most highly respected manuscript illustrator and one who could get an unscheduled meeting with the abbot on a moment's notice. After answering truthfully, the guard's guard would be down.

"No. Not always."

Antonio remained staring at the ceiling, silent in his response, then admitted, "Me neither."

Gabriele's head swung around. Staring at Antonio, the guard replied, "Really? Why not?"

"Have you ever read the Bible?"

"No, it's in Latin."

"So how do you know what it says?"

"I listen to the monks talk about it."

"Do you attend the Monastery's church services?"

"If I am not on duty protecting the Monastery."

"Do you learn more about the Bible's teachings from the church services you do attend?"

"No, not really."

"Why not?"

"They're in Latin. I told you. I don't understand Latin."

"So what do you get from these services?"

"Oh, they're very spiritual. I like seeing the light pouring through the stained glass windows of Bible scenes, the music, the incense ... Have you ever heard of Dufay? I get a lot from the services."

"Sensual."

"Yes! Very sensual."

It was something Antonio had thought about often: incense, choral music, and colorful light streaming in through the stained glass windows all the while the monks keep everyone in the dark. Latin, the language of the intelligentsia and nobility. He smirked as he thought, "Wouldn't it be interesting if, with this mechanical printing Gutenberg has unleashed, they started printing Bibles in languages people understood?" Then he chuckled.

Gabriele heard. "What's so funny?"

"Do you know what they don't say in Latin?"

"No."

"Jokes."

They both started laughing, with Gabriele letting out an "Oh, God ..."

"Shhhh!" Antonio whispered. "With all the reading I have done, I have never come across one reference to God having a sense of humor. Anger? Oh, yes."

They continued to giggle, almost like children. Then Gabriele asked, somewhat concerned, "Is what we're saying heresy?"

"From my experience, that depends entirely on who can hear what we say."

They both continued to stare at the ceiling, knowing they should be sleeping, but they were not.

Antonio reflected on the events so far, and their journey had only just begun. One thing continued to puzzle him.

"Gabriele, are you still awake?"

"Yes."

"When we encountered those thieves, you flung a dagger out of your left sleeve. How did you do that? And why? Is that a second weapon for close battle?"

"I have a little pouch strap on my left wrist, and when I flick my wrist, it frees the dagger to my left hand. Yes, it is a weapon, but that is not its primary purpose."

"What is?"

"Distraction. When my opponent sees it, that draws his attention away from me, and that is when I make my move."

"Like today?"

"Yes. He just glanced away for a second, and in a second, he had no head."

"Ingenious."

"Works like a charm."

"We're supposed to be wary of charms, aren't we? Do you have it on now?"

"Of course."

"May I see it?"

"Certainly." Gabriele got out of bed and went to Antonio's side, slid the left sleeve up, and there was a leather wrist harness securing the dagger. Gabriele gave a quick flick of the wrist, and the dagger was instantly flung into the guard's hand. One thing that struck Antonio was how slender Gabriele's forearm was. You would think a monastery's head guard would be beefier. But as the abbot had said and as Antonio had witnessed, Gabriele's power was in swordsmanship. "And wit," Antonio thought.

Gabriele returned to bed as Antonio asked, "Did your father invent that?"

"No, I did."

"Ingenious."

"Thank you. So you can sleep well because you are well guarded. Good night."

"Good night, Gabriele."

Not So Dumb and Not So Dumber

Brisighella, Italy

February 26, 1461

With a packhorse and a stolen horse in tow, Antonio and Gabriele made their way along the trail leading back to Bologna, meandering through dormant vineyards, passing stone homesteads whose fireplace smoke made them both crave a little more warmth than what their woolen blankets provided.

Along their journey, they talked about their lives and their childhoods—Antonio's with a mother encouraging learning and Gabriele's motherless, with a father who taught Gabriele the skills of being a man from an early age.

At one point, Gabriele laughed, saying, "Brains and brawn. We're quite the team."

"You don't lack brains, Gabriele. Just education. And don't let someone's education intimidate you. I have met a lot of stupid educated people."

Gabriele laughed and replied, "And I have encountered husky, brawny men who barely knew how to chop wood."

The afternoon sun was setting, slowly casting longer shadows and more golden light.

"What do you think, Gabriele? Return to the Monastery of San Domenico when we reach Bologna?"

Gabriele thought for a few moments, then replied, "Antonio, I think we would be better off at an inn. There was something about that subprior. What was his name?"

"Paola."

"Yes. Paola. As a guard, Antonio, I am always on guard. And there was just something about him that put my guard's instincts on alert."

"And he was absent during morning prayers and breakfast," Antonio added.

"There will be inns in Bologna. I'm sure we will find one."

It was dusk when they reached the Bologna's perimeter. They rode slowly, following the streets leading to the town's center. They passed a tavern and, a few doors down, saw a sign reading, "The River Inn."

"I'll go in and inquire about rooms," Gabriele announced, dismounting and turning to Antonio. "You look after the horses and don't forget what I taught you about swordsmanship." The guard winked then disappeared through the inn's doors.

A moment later, Gabriele was back, saying, "Just like the last inn, one room with two beds. The town's stable is at the end of this street. We can tie up our horses and get them fed and watered, and then we're free to do the same for ourselves at the tavern we passed on the way in."

Gabriele mounted Thrice and led the way to the stable.

While there were stalls for twenty horses, there were just five that were available. Both Antonio and Gabriele were happy to dismount and get out of the saddle for the night.

The stable manager greeted them, asked how long they would stay, quickly told them the nightly price for the stalls, and requested payment.

While they got the horses settled, Gabriele's attention shot around to three horses in the end stalls.

"Antonio!"

"What?"

"Don't you recognize those horses?"

The truth was, Antonio could not recognize one horse's ass from another's.

"Not really."

"Those are the thieves' horses."

"You mean the ones with the one who lost his head?"

"Yes. Let's not lose ours."

Gabriele turned to the stable keeper, spoke briefly, and then turned back to Antonio.

"They're staying at The River Inn."

"So now what do we do?"

Gabriele and Antonio stood looking each other in the eye, both playing out options in their heads.

Gabriele then patted Antonio on the shoulder, saying, "I think I know what's going on."

Antonio was taken aback by his reaction to Gabriele's touch: it comforted and surprised him, and he wished it had lasted longer. The guard's touch stirred him. "Strange," he thought.

"What is that?"

With a mischievous smile, Gabriele asked, "Where do you think these thieves got Between Thieves?" It was a rhetorical question, and without waiting for an answer, Gabriele continued, "They got it here in Bologna, and since no one is giving horses away, they probably bought it from someone."

Gabriele turned to the stable keeper, who had stepped away, and called out, "Kind sir, if I wished to buy or sell a horse here in Bologna, who would I seek?"

Without giving it a second thought, the stable keeper replied, "Jacopo."

"And where might we find him?"

"The tavern." Then, laughing, the stable keeper added, "Most of Bologna's business is conducted in the tavern."

"Would a florin cover the costs of tending to our horses, feeding and watering them?"

Like all people in business, the stable keeper valued generous customers.

"Certainly."

Grabbing Antonio's arm, Gabriele said, "Antonio, why don't we have a tankard at the tavern?"

They stepped out of the stable onto the moonlit Bologna cobblestone sidewalk and made their way toward the tavern. Gabriele kept a guarded eye on The River Inn as they passed it.

The tavern was easy to find. Light from candles, torches, and the fire burning in the fireplace spilled onto the street.

Opening the thick, arched wooden door, they found more than a roaring fire. With the full tavern came a cacophony of bellowing conversations and laughter.

Weaving through the tables and random standing or wobbling patrons, Gabriele approached a barmaid. The woman was scantily dressed and obviously an added feature of the tavern besides the endless flow of wine from the wine casks.

"Excuse me. Is Jacopo here this evening?"

With hands full of wine goblets and tankards, the barmaid just nodded toward the far end of the room, answering, "In the corner at the table," and continued her rounds of delivering rounds.

Threading through the crowd toward the corner table, Gabriele turned to Antonio, smiling, and said, "She's cute, don't you think?"

Grinning, Antonio replied, "I don't know. I haven't heard her speak."

At the corner table was a group of men, with one man sitting at the seat with his back to the wall. He was thin and wiry with thick black hair slicked back over his head. He was in an animated conversation with three other men sitting at the table. It soon became clear that this was the table where men made deals, whether for a night's enjoyment with female company, a property whose owners were desperate for a sale, loans at fluctuating rates, or livestock. Especially horses.

Gabriele leaned into the table and said, "I am sorry to intrude on your affairs, but would one of you happen to be Jacopo? We were advised to seek him out."

Cautious but never wanting to miss a business opportunity, the black-haired man responded, "I am he. Who are you?"

Gabriele smiled, responding, "I am Gabriele, and this is my associate, Antonio. We represent Abbot Fransisco of the San Miniato al Monte Monastery and have been tasked with locating a horse stolen from the Monastery's stable."

The thing about the fear of God is that it rarely surfaces until one's life or livelihood is in peril. For Jacopo, this was one such moment. Turning to the other men at the table, Jacopo said, "Gentlemen, would you please excuse us? As we are all aware, matters of the Church take priority in all our lives."

The men nodded, agreed to meet the following day, and excused them-selves from the table.

Gabriele and Antonio assumed the emptied chairs, and Gabriele asked, "Do you know of any horse trades or sales recently that might have seemed out of the ordinary? Suspicious?"

Squirming in his seat and wishing to stay out of the Church's crosshairs, Jacopo replied, "It is such a relief to talk to you of this." Self-preservation is primal. Playing the victim as much as possible, Jacopo told a version of the story, saying an official of the Church had approached him to sell a horse and told him he could keep half the proceeds. Then, darting glances back and forth between Antonio and Gabriele, he pleaded he was but a merchant trader.

"What Church official?" Gabriele probed. Feigning concern and still playing the victim, Jacopo replied, "I do not wish to cause problems with the Church. I hope you can have sympathy for my position."

Gabriele and Antonio turned and looked each other in the eye, both think-ing, "You're looking for sympathy?"

Gabriele turned back and, feigning sympathy, replied, "We understand your situation. Tell us then, who bought the horse?"

Without blinking an eye, Jacopo replied, "Travelers. There were four of them, but they only had three horses and were in need of a fourth."

"Travelers?"

"Yes, as best I could guess, travelers."

"What kind of travelers? What was the purpose of their traveling?

"I don't know. It's not my business to ask others' business."

Jacopo smiled, thinking the matter was closed.

Neither Gabriele nor Antonio smiled. Then Gabriele asked, "Have you seen these travelers since?"

Jacopo squirmed again and said it was funny they asked because the "travelers" had returned, less one, and they were to meet in the morning to "sort out the confusion."

"And the money," Gabriele added.

"Yes, that too."

Gabriele asked when and where they would meet in the morning, then gracefully thanked Jacopo for his help.

Gabriele and Antonio rose from the table and made their way through the tavern, with the barmaid casting a sour look. They had provided no income for the tavern or, more importantly, for her.

Walking back to the stable, Antonio asked, "What do you think?"

"We stay."

"At the inn?"

"Yes. The thieves will either be drunk or asleep by now. Thieves are not known to be early risers. But you and I do not begrudge a dawn sun, do we?"

Antonio reflected on the morning he sought an unscheduled meeting with the abbot. Gabriele had been on guard duty. No, they were not unaccustomed to early mornings.

How things had changed from Gabriele's chilly reception that morning to now.

Gabriele tasked Antonio with informing the stable keeper of their overnight stay and early departure and went to make arrangements at the inn.

Once they were in their room and setting their saddlebags at the foot of their beds, Gabriele looked at Antonio's bag with the bundle tied to it and said, "Antonio, I am curious."

"About what?"

"Our cargo."

"Gutenberg's blunder?"

"Do you mind showing it to me?"

Antonio reached into the saddlebag's pouch and pulled out the exquisitely bound—but flawed—book wrapped in cloth.

"Gabriele, I present to you the Holy Bible our abbot, rightly so, believes is not quite holy enough. Holy is perfect. This draft is not."

"May I see it?"

Antonio passed the book to Gabriele, who took it as if receiving a treasure and, after opening it to a random page, said, "And you can read this? Understand it?"

Antonio cast a glance into Gabriele's eyes and cracked open the door to his safely guarded secret. "I can read it. I can't say I always understand it."

Gabriele looked back to the pages as if looking into a well of mystery. Then, randomly turning to another page and pointing to text, the guard said, "So what does this say?"

Seeing the text Gabriele had fished from the well, Antonio burst out laughing.

"What's so funny?"

Antonio looked at Gabriele, smiled and said, "This is amusing, given that we are both hungry and about to eat."

"Why?"

Antonio then read, translating, "This is from Kings, Chapter 6, verses 28 and 29. It reads, 'This woman said to me: "Come on, let's eat your son today, then we will eat my son tomorrow." So we cooked my son and ate him.'"

"Seriously?"

"I don't know. I wasn't there. Hungry?"

Gabriele looked at Antonio and for the first time noticed a mischievous twinkle in his eye.

Cracking the Bible's spine every night along their journey became entertainment. First, Antonio would find curiosities, and then Gabriele would find random passages that Antonio would translate and read.

Some nights, they laughed. Other nights, not.

The Three Musketeers

Bologna, Italy

February 27, 1461

A monk, three thieves, and a horse trader walked into a bar. The monk, Subprior Paola, was expecting to receive money; the three thieves were expecting to extract money from the monk; and the horse trader, Jacopo, hoped that through this messy situation, he wouldn't need to flee Bologna the way he had to flee Venice.

It was early, and unlike the night before, the tavern was practically empty. The five of them sat crowded around the corner table where Jacopo traditionally held court and conducted business.

The barmaid from the night before was there, looking like she hadn't slept, which was not uncommon given her second job of turning the tavern's paying customers into paying customers of hers.

Of the three thieves, Alfonso was the closest to being equipped with a brain. Subprior Paola had expected to be meeting only with Jacopo, so finding three other men with him took him by surprise and made him anxious, fidgety, and ill at ease. When the barmaid came to the table to take their orders, Paola was quick to say, "I will have a tankard of the blood of Christ."

Jacopo tried a horse trader's diplomacy, starting the meeting saying, "There seems to be some confusion about our recent horse trade."

Alfonso quickly jumped in, saying, "There's no confusion. We bought a stolen horse and we want *all* our money back, not the money less Jacopo's significant tavern expenses."

Paola tried to act in disbelief. "Are you telling me you think that horse was stolen?" He piously added, "I don't steal horses. I save souls."

"How did you come to have this horse? What was its name?"

"Between Thieves," Paola replied.

"Well, it certainly is now," Alfonso answered, adding, "How did you come into possession of the horse?"

"It was a gift."

"A gift?"

"Yes, a gift."

"Who from? Who gave you this 'gift'?"

"A fellow man of God at the San Miniato al Monte Monastery."

"Funny, because it was a guard from that monastery who told us it was stolen."

Jacopo jumped in, suggesting, "Perhaps that guard was lying and actually stole the horse from you. And in that case, you should be searching for the guard to return the horse he stole." Jacopo was feeling better about this discussion and even thought of ways to convince Alfonso to give the money back that he had given to him the night before—because if the horse was stolen from Alfonso, certainly a monk and an honest businessman such as Jacopo should not be held responsible.

Paola added sympathetically, "It's terrible that someone took advantage of you like that."

Alfonso replied, "So you're telling me the guard was lying and stole the horse from me by telling me someone else had stolen it?"

In unison, Paola and Jacopo replied, "Yes."

"I don't buy it."

Jacopo replied, "Yes, you did buy it. That we know. But I sympathize with your situation, and I'll tell you what I am prepared to do: as a gesture of goodwill, I will split the cost of the stolen horse with you. Just return half the money I returned to you yesterday. To be honest, I think that is very generous of me. Would you not agree, Brother Paola?"

"Yes, I certainly do and I would like to reciprocate the kindness by accepting half of the money Alfonso here will return to you as payment in full. Then we can all put this nasty business behind us."

"Wait a minute. You want me to return the money to you that you returned to me yesterday for a horse I don't have?"

"I think I am being very generous," Jacopo said, then added, "We didn't steal the horse, did we, Brother Paola?"

Sorrowfully, Paola shook his head no.

There was a considerable amount of horse trading going on, considering there was no horse.

Or horses, for that matter.

Just before dawn, Antonio and Gabriele left the inn, went to the stable, and told the stable keeper they were to collect their horses and those of fellow guests at the inn. They saddled and gathered Twice, Thrice, Pilate, Between Thieves, and three horses whose names they didn't know. They tethered the herd together and rode out of town toward Florence.

Once clear of the town and out of sight, they untethered the three thieves' horses and gave them hard slaps on their asses, which sent them running but not toward Bologna.

Antonio and Gabriele stood there, both smiling, just admiring the scene of the three thieves' horses getting smaller and smaller as they galloped farther and farther into the distance. They both said nothing, watching the way artists might study their recently finished paintings, standing and staring, proud of their work.

Without looking away from the scene, Antonio said, "That was a brilliant idea, Gabriele."

Gabriele, too, remained fixed on the scene, responding, "Thank you. Yes, I confess I am a little proud of this one." The guard paused, then added, "I wonder what they will do when they find their horses gone?"

Antonio replied, "I suspect they will be taking the Lord's name in vain."

Home Again, Home Again

Florence, Italy

March 1, 1461

Prior Lorenzo sat writing at his desk, his quill pen feverishly and meticulously conveying his theological argument that sacred texts, especially the Bible, should remain the prepotence of the Church. Imagine, he hypothesized, if a layperson such as Gutenberg began printing Bibles in local languages! "Latin is the language of God," he sermonized, adding that he was but a humble servant of the Church.

The sun was setting, and the warm glow of his candlelight contrasted with the deepening twilight outside his window. Shadows from the frescoes on his wall seemed to move in the flickering light, as if dancing to his theological tune.

The Monastery was settling for the night with the sound of chants and a faint clang of a bell, announcing the time for the monks' Vespers.

Lorenzo put his quill pen down and turned to look out at the golden light but was startled to see two people on horseback, silhouetted by the setting sun, approaching with two horses in tow.

He suddenly recognized the riders as Antonio and Gabriele, and his mind scrambled for explanations, especially when he recognized one horse being led as Between Thieves. What did they know? How did they come to be in possession of Between Thieves? Had Subprior Paola betrayed his trust and told them of Lorenzo's plan to prevent the Gutenberg Bible's correction? What happened to that young homeless man so gullibly eager to please the Church? Please him?

Should he wait to find out what they knew? No. He needed to know before they could inform Abbot Fransisco. He grabbed his cloak and scurried down the stone corridor, past biblical story–themed frescoes, to the Monastery's entrance.

During their journey back to Florence, Gabriele and Antonio could only speculate about how Between Thieves ended up with thieves on the outskirts of Bologna. The only thing they knew for certain was that Between Thieves had not wandered off by himself, getting as far as Bologna and then into the hands of thieves by chance.

"Someone took him there," Antonio had said, and Gabriele had replied, "I know."

"But who?" Antonio asked, more to himself than Gabriele because he knew what the guard's answer would be.

"I don't know."

"Maybe it had nothing to do with us," Antonio suggested, though he knew that was just wishful thinking. Then he asked again, "Do you think the meeting Abbot Fransisco called that night was about our mission?"

"I wish I knew. But I don't."

Now the sun had set, and the sky was a deep cobalt blue. Nightfall would not be far behind, and the moon was waning, offering little light.

The sky would be black, punctuated by stars, like pearls glowing and flickering in the endless black of the heavens.

On reaching the Monastery, they took the horses to the stable, and Gabriele instructed Pietro, the stable keeper, to secure, feed, and water them. Then the guard asked how Between Thieves had gotten away. Pietro nervously answered that he did not know. Gabriele's stern head of security and guard demeanor had returned.

Gabriele said nothing more but continued to glare at Pietro. Nervous, Pietro repeated, "I don't know! I really don't know!"

Without replying, Gabriele turned, looked at Antonio, and gave a nod to the Monastery gates. It was the same nod Antonio received when he was admitted without an appointment.

Gabriele surprised the Monastery guards, but they said nothing and only nodded. The gates creaked open, and standing there, baring an unctuous and ingratiating smile, was Prior Lorenzo.

"I am so surprised to see you back so soon. Why did you abandon your journey?"

The corridor walls' torches flickered a strobing light across Lorenzo's sharp-featured face, hooked nose, and unchanging, fawning smile.

Gabriele knew the ways of monasterial intrigue and subterfuge, and Lorenzo's use of the word "abandon" was far more telling than perhaps Lorenzo recognized. There, in one word, was the strategy. Plant the word "abandon" in the abbot's ear.

Calmly but firmly, Gabriele said, "We wish to speak with Abbot Fransisco."

Wringing his hands and shaking his head, Lorenzo replied, "I'm so sorry, but Abbot Fransisco is resting."

Antonio spoke up, saying, "Prior Lorenzo, I know how devoted you are to the abbot, but I think he would be disappointed if we didn't inform him immediately about why we came back." Antonio was playing the disappointed card again.

Lorenzo shot a glance at Antonio, and for a split second, his facade dropped to reveal a venomous glare. The facade returned, and he said, "Certainly. What is it? I shall tell him immediately." It was another snake-mate moment.

But it was short-lived.

Gabriele shot back, "I think it best we tell him ourselves."

All the monks knew the abbot trusted no one more than Gabriele and, to varying degrees, they were jealous of that—none more so than Lorenzo. Gabriele had saved the abbot's life, although the details were never discussed.

"Wait here." Lorenzo turned, shuffled from the entrance, then went down the corridor leading to the abbot's quarters.

Antonio and Gabriele turned and looked at each other. Antonio could see the Gabriele he had been getting to know during their travels—a warmer Gabriele than the steely, head-nodding guard Gabriele he met when he was here at the Monastery with no appointment. Then they turned their attention back to the corridor, waiting for Lorenzo's return. Without looking at Antonio, Gabriele whispered, "This should prove interesting."

Lorenzo emerged from the shadows, saying, "Follow me." He turned and led the way to the abbot's quarters, opening the thick, arched wooden door and, after Antonio and Gabriele were in the room, closing the door behind them.

Three candles lit the room, and shadows from the books' and manuscripts' spines lining the walls' bookshelves looked like a monochromatic, moving mosaic. Standing in front of the book-lined walls, Abbot Fransisco greeted them warmly, Gabriele first, then Antonio.

Obviously with some concern, the abbot asked, "Is Gutenberg's Bible safe? Do you still have it?"

Gabriele answered, "Yes, Father, we still have it, but something unusual and concerning happened."

"Tell me."

Gabriele's answer began with a question. "Did you know that one of the Monastery's horses was missing?"

"Yes. Between Thieves. Apparently, a young man from Florence was seen riding it. North."

"We came across it north of Bologna when four thieves tried to rob us. One was riding Between Thieves."

Alarmed, the abbot replied, "Four thieves? What did you do? Where is the horse now?"

"It's back in the stable. We—"

Antonio interrupted, "Reverend Father, you spoke to me of Gabriele's swordsmanship. There are only three thieves now."

"I see."

"You should have."

The abbot glanced out his window to the starlit sky and, talking to himself as much as to Antonio and Gabriele, said, "I thought it strange that a young man could steal a horse from our stable. A young man whose home was on the streets, I am told. I wonder where he thought he was going. I wonder where he is now."

Gabriele added, "I wonder how Between Thieves came to be with thieves. And there was one other thing."

Antonio jumped in. "They demanded our money and our 'treasure.'"

"Treasure? They used the word 'treasure'?"

"Treasure," Gabriele confirmed. "And 'Bible.' They mentioned a Bible."

Abbot Fransisco turned and looked out the window again, this time saying nothing.

Finally, the abbot said, "Well, it must be corrected. You can resume your journey tomorrow. Antonio, do you still have the letters of introduction I provided?"

"Yes, I guard them carefully."

"Good. Your position at the studio is secure, as I mentioned. I will inform them that there has been a delay in your return. That won't be a problem. I spoke with utmost confidentiality to Cosimo de' Medici about this situation. He is most sympathetic. You may stay here tonight and resume tomorrow. I will also have a couple of other letters for you tomorrow that should help you on your journey."

Abbot Fransisco stood up, indicating that the meeting had concluded.

Out in the corridor, with all the monks retired for the night, Lorenzo had his ear pressed against the door; but through the thick wood, all he could hear was the murmur of conversation. Then suddenly, he heard the iron door latch clang as someone prepared to open it, and he jumped back and stood in the corridor as if he had been waiting to escort them out.

When they opened the door, Antonio and Gabriele were surprised to see him. He stood there with his obsequious smile and said, "I hope this was a satisfactory meeting. Antonio, I will show you out."

Coldly, Gabriele replied, "He is staying for the night, the abbot's guest, so please show him to the guest room. We are leaving again in the morning."

"Certainly."

Lorenzo led the way, with Antonio and Gabriele trailing. Antonio turned and whispered, "Thank you for that."

Gabriele just smiled.

The abbot said nothing of the guest room. But Antonio would much prefer it to a bed in the monk's dormitory.

For the Love of the Church

Florence, Italy

February 27, 1461

Prior Lorenzo left the corridor and entered his privileged quarters in the Monastery, distressed and feeling he could empathize with martyrs that had gone before him.

He sank into his chair at his desk and lit his candle. His quill and ink were on display along with a small stack of paper on one side of the desk and another smaller stack of his writings on the other.

With a slight breeze from the window, the candle's flame flickered almost as if it were a whirling dervish, the walls becoming a kaleidoscope of colors dimming and brightening as the candlelight lit his frescoes and then washed the colors away.

For the good of the Church, Gutenberg's Bible had to remain flawed. People had to distrust anything not originating from the Church. How could the abbot and many others in the Church be so naïve? Machines printing Bibles unsanctioned by the Church? How could they be so blind, so shortsighted? What's next? Printing them in native languages and dumping them on inns' bedside tables? No sooner had he thought that than he admonished himself. "Stop thinking so cynically of the absurd. Focus on the problem."

Lorenzo turned and gazed out his window to the twinkling, starlit sky. He thought, "What I need is divine inspiration." As soon as that thought entered his mind, as if on cue, a shooting star crossed from horizon to horizon directly in front of him.

A tear rolled down from his eye as he humbly mumbled, "Thank you, Lord." Because, in a split second, the star shot across the sky, and his prayer for divine inspiration was answered.

He needed to get ahead of Antonio and Gabriele. What was it about Antonio, anyway? Something. Lorenzo's keen perception led him to suspect that the guard Gabriele was more devoted to guarding the manuscript illustrator than the Monastery and, as such, the very Church itself.

Given the Church's history of intrigue, Lorenzo knew nothing got immediate attention from the Church more than a conspiracy. With that in mind, he spun around in his chair, grabbed a piece of paper, armed his quill pen with ink, and put pen to paper, being careful to use handwriting unlike his own. He began to write, then paused and looked up at a flickering fresco, deep in thought. Then he turned to his paper and continued to write. Yes, poor Latin grammar would further disguise the identity of the note's author. Lorenzo was forever correcting monks on their Latin grammar.

He scribbled feverishly, and when he was satisfied, he leaned back to reread his stroke of genius and smiled. Blowing to dry the ink, he took one more step to forge the document's authenticity: he wiped the paper across the stone floor not just once but several times so it bore signs of dirt. His story would be that it had been slipped under his door. He would rise early, ready to depart, and would urgently rouse the abbot, show him the paper, and tell the abbot he would leave immediately for Bologna.

Lorenzo was so pleased with his ingenuity, borne from divine inspiration, that he could barely sleep. He spent half the night tossing and turning and rose well before dawn, packing his essentials, which, of course, included Lorenzo's best weapon: a letter of credit written in Latin, open-dated and backed by the Medicis.

Dressed and packed, Lorenzo raced to the abbot's quarters and loudly pounded on the door. A second later, the abbot, in his nightgown, opened the door with a look of both displeasure and concern, instantly recognizing the seriousness of finding Prior Lorenzo standing there.

"Reverent Father, I am so sorry to disturb you, but there is an urgent matter."

"What is it? Come in."

Lorenzo stepped into the abbot's chambers, closed the door behind him, and simply said, "This." He handed Abbot Fransisco his artful document. It read:

> *"Ad Lorenzo,*
> *"Est periculum inter nos. Audivi duos monachos susurrantes in umbris de*
> *consilio in Bologna parato. Locuti sunt de irruptione in monasterium ibi,*
> *intendentes furari rara artificia et manuscripta. Hi monachi participabunt*
> *in fructibus huius perfidiae.*
> *"Timeo pro mea salute et debere manere anonymus. Debes celeriter agere.*
> *Vade ad Bologna statim ut eos moneas et adiuvare in tutelam thesaurorum*
> *eorum.*
> *"Tuus in cautela,*

"Frater Curiosus"

The abbot looked up from the letter, stunned. "How did you receive this?"

"It was slipped under my door. As soon I read it and grasped the seriousness, I packed essentials and am ready to depart. I think I should leave immediately."

"I agree with your assessment, given the seriousness of this matter. Go with my blessings. I will keep the letter. Well hidden, of course. You will travel by horse, I presume. Which one?"

"I think Between Thieves. Given the recent activity, he is accustomed to cross-country journeys. I have also been told he is our fastest."

"Wise decision."

"Thank you. And given that there appear to be untrustworthy Brothers among us, I think we should keep our knowledge of this plot unknown. May I suggest you explain my sudden departure was due to news of a very ill family member I had to attend to?"

"Good advice. That is precisely how I will explain your absence."

Lorenzo turned, and as he opened the chamber door, the abbot called out, "Lorenzo?"

"Yes, Reverend Father?"

"Thank you for taking action on this with such haste."

Lorenzo bowed and scraped, replying, "I am but a servant." Then he briskly disappeared down the corridor, hurrying to the stable.

As he entered the stable doors, daylight was only beginning to break. The stable keeper, Pietro—a man well into his fifties who had been a staple of the stable since his twenties, now with graying hair and less nimble limbs —had been dozing on two bales of hay at the far end of the building when Lorenzo appeared. He jumped to attention, saying, "Prior Lorenzo. Such an honor to see you. And at such an early hour."

Lorenzo knew Pietro had been sleeping. Although sleeping while on duty in the stable was not officially condoned, it was unofficially recognized that not just the horses needed sleep.

"Yes. Please saddle Between Thieves. I must leave immediately."

"Certainly," Pietro replied, sprinting to Between Thieves' stall.

In less than five minutes, Between Thieves was saddled, harnessed, and ready to go.

"Not that your business is my business, but when should I expect Between Thieves to be back for watering and feeding?"

"I don't know," Lorenzo replied, welcoming the opportunity to circulate the story of the ill family member. He theatrically feigned emotional distress and laid out the fictitious saga.

"I am so sorry to hear this," Pietro said while watching Lorenzo mount Between Thieves. "I hope they recover well and soon."

"We all wish him a speedy recovery, and meanwhile, I will race to his side. Thank you for your concerns."

Lorenzo brought Between Thieves to a full gallop as he left the stable. He estimated he might have a four-hour lead on Antonio and Gabriele, maybe more given the speed of the Monastery's before-, during-, and after-breakfast rituals and requirements. They would also, no doubt, be traveling slower. With luck, he could reach the Monastery of San Domenico and Subprior Paola in Bologna six or maybe even eight hours before Antonio and Gabriele.

Even before the clanging of the morning bells, Antonio lay in his bed, his eyes wide open, staring at the ceiling, wishing the bed he had not gotten much sleep in was even just half as comfortable as the bed at The River Inn in Bologna. But it wasn't. He thought, "I wouldn't want to be old sleeping in a bed like this." Yet, he was given luxury with this room regardless of how spartan it was. The room had little in the way of furniture: this simple wooden bed, an anorexic pillow, a basic wooden table, and a stool. The room was lit only by daylight leaking in through a small window opposite the doorway.

But this was better than sleeping in the dormitory with a dozen monks, some who snored, some who occasionally burped, and some who occasionally farted. "Perhaps they get used to it," he thought, although anyone who sleeps with someone who snores would tell you one doesn't.

He knew what to expect now that the morning bells were tunelessly chiming. The monks would begin their day in prayer, thanking God for all the nothing they had, and then everyone would take to the refectory for breakfast while one of the monks did the morning reading.

Monastery breakfasts were not hearty, and it dawned on Antonio that after breakfast, when he and Gabriele began their journey again, they could first stop at Mario's bakery for *frittelle* or *cantucci*. This morning's breakfast at the Monastery would most likely consist of bread, some fruit, and water. It occurred to Antonio that horses ate better than monks. Yes, a stop at Mario's would be in order.

When he heard the shuffling of feet in the corridor, he collected his things, left his luxury room, and made his way to the refectory, which was similar to the refectory at the Monastery of San Domenico: a long, narrow room with one long table and a long bench on each side of the table. He had no idea if the seating was preordained or if it was more of a random affair. He thought about people being creatures of habit and assumed the monks would sit in the same spot every day except the one whose turn it was to do the reading during the meal.

As he walked along the corridor, monks in the hallway smiled and nodded to him but said nothing. When he entered the refectory, Gabriele was already seated and, seeing him, the guard motioned to the next spot, saved for him. He was surprised at his own reaction to seeing Gabriele: he was not just pleased but also relieved. "Funny," he thought.

As he sat down, Gabriele asked, "How did you sleep?"

Antonio turned and whispered, "Seriously?" Gabriele had to stifle a laugh. Guards don't laugh.

As the food—bread, some fruit, and water, as anticipated—was being served, one of the monks stood and went to the end of the table to do the day's reading.

"Good morning, my Brothers. May this be a blessed day for all. This morning, I have chosen Psalm 6, a psalm of David and his plea for healing and deliverance from enemies."

Antonio glanced around the room to see how intently the monks were listening. Were they listening or was it just background noise that occurred at every meal? Most monks were just eating, but a few glanced up at the monk reading. Gabriele just ate, looking at nothing but the food on the plate.

The monk continued, "O Lord, rebuke me not in thine anger, neither chasten me in thy hot displeasure.

"Have mercy upon me, O Lord; for I am weak: O Lord, heal me; for my bones are vexed."

Antonio's mind drifted, and he wondered how many of the monks had read any of the Greek classics.

"Return, O Lord, deliver my soul: oh save me for thy mercies' sake.

For in death there is no remembrance of thee: in the grave who shall give thee thanks?"

Antonio turned and looked at Gabriele, whose mother died during childbirth. Who begged for her life? The guard carried guilt over the death, Antonio thought, but what did Gabriele have to do with it? Being born?

Although he was intelligent and had studied the writings of thinkers, Antonio was also astute enough to know that in the Holy Roman Empire, thoughts like that were best left in the mind and not allowed to reach the vocal cords. Letting them out was not good for your health.

The monk continued, " Depart from me, all ye workers of iniquity; for the Lord hath heard the voice of my weeping..

"The Lord hath heard my supplication; the Lord will receive my prayer."

Begging for his life. Who prayed for Gabriele's mother's life? Whoever did clearly did not pray hard enough.

The reading concluded, and Gabriele turned to Antonio and said, "We should be on our way."

They got up, collected their things, and proceeded to the stable. As they entered, Pietro greeted them, and as they went to fetch their horses, Gabriele suddenly blurted, "I don't believe this."

"What?" Antonio was not familiar enough with the stable to notice immediately what Gabriele had seen right away.

"Between Thieves. He's not here." Then the guard turned to Pietro and asked, "Where is Between Thieves?"

"Prior Lorenzo took him. He left to attend to an ill family member."

Antonio and Gabriele looked at each other, and Gabriele said quietly, "Interesting."

Gabriele glanced at their belongings, including the subject of their mission, Gutenberg's blasphemous Bible, and said, "Let's load everything on our two horses. That third horse just slows us down." After rearranging and tossing a couple of items to the ground alongside Gabriele's comment, "We can do without these," Antonio and his guard saddled, harnessed, and mounted Twice and Thrice and made their way out of the stable to the trail in the direction of Florence.

Less than a hundred feet from the stable, Antonio asked, "Are you hungry?"

"I'm starving."

"I know a bakery in town where we can stop before we set out."

They followed the trail into Florence, and Antonio led the way directly to Mario's. When they entered, Antonio was surprised to see Andrea was working. He turned to Gabriele and whispered, "You're in for a special treat this morning. Her name is Andrea. Take a good look."

"Yes, she's beautiful."

"Beautiful? I think she's the source of wet dreams for half the men in Florence."

"Including you?" Gabriele replied.

"She's crossed my mind more than once in private moments."

They got to the counter, and Andrea looked at Antonio, smiled, then looked at Gabriele and said, "You brought me a new friend this morning." Then Gabriele smiled at Andrea, who applied all her seductive charm as she introduced herself. "Hi! I'm Andrea."

"Gabriele," was all Gabriele replied.

"What can I get for you two gentlemen this morning?"

Antonio responded by saying, "I'm surprised you're working in the morning."

Coy and seductive, Andrea replied, "I know. I much prefer my bed in the morning, don't you? But my father has his annual cold, and he's the one who's in bed. What can I get you?"

Pointing to the shelf below, Gabriele coldly said, "I'll have a panini."

Surprised, Antonio turned to Gabriele. "That's all?"

Sternly, with guard-like authority, Gabriele replied, "We have a long journey. We should get on our way," bringing idle chat to a full stop.

Antonio ordered a few things for the trip.

Andrea always wore something low-cut so that whenever she leaned forward to fill an order, a man's eyes instinctively had but one place to go —as Antonio's did while she worked.

Gabriele just looked forward but could see where Antonio's attention had been drawn.

As she handed the order to Antonio, Andrea smiled provocatively and said, "Nice to see you, Antonio." Then she turned to Gabriele and added, "And nice to meet you, Gabriele. I hope I see you again."

Gabriele forced a smile, answering merely, "Thank you," and turned toward the door, telling Antonio, "Let's go."

Without saying another word, Gabriele was out the door and mounting Thrice with Antonio almost having to sprint to keep up. "Ever the guard," Antonio thought as he mounted Twice and followed Thrice as they headed out of the city.

Gabriele led the way and put Thrice into a good pace. Antonio struggled to keep up as he rode while trying to put his food in his side pouch.

From behind, Antonio could not see the look on Gabriele's face, and Gabriele thought that was a good thing. As they made their way out of the city, the guard thought, "Why did that make me so angry? I don't like that it did."

"To Lorenzo,
"There is danger among us. I have overheard two monks whispering in the shadows about a plan being hatched in Bologna. They spoke of a raid on the monastery there, the thieves intending to steal rare artifacts and manu-scripts. The monastery's monks would share in the proceeds of this treachery.
"I fear for my safety and must remain anonymous. You must act quickly. Go to Bologna at once to warn them and assist in safeguarding their treasures.
"Yours in caution,

"A Concerned Brother"

ALL THAT IS SACRED

THE FOOT SOLDIERS

Sasso Marconi, Italy

March 2, 1461

There was not much to the village of Sasso Marconi or (in the eyes of Lorenzo at least) its inhabitants. The village was small, comprising a few uninspiring one- and two-story houses, a church (of course), and most importantly, an inn where Lorenzo hoped he could rest, have a meal, and have Between Thieves watered and fed before he made the last leg of his journey to Bologna and the Monastery of San Domenico. He was eager to hear from Subprior Paola about what had happened and why his well-thought-out plan had failed.

Having to make a trip to discover what went wrong annoyed him, but more importantly, he was anxious to meet with Paola to plan a different course of action. He was confident Antonio and Gabriele would return through Bologna seeking accommodations at the Monastery of San Domenico since they carried the abbot's letters of introduction requesting they and their horses be fed and provided shelter. Lorenzo had not thought through an alternative plan. Although he was displeased with Subprior Paola, he and Paola shared the same conviction that control of the Bible should be kept within the purview of the Church. With their shared beliefs, Lorenzo begrudgingly admitted to himself that two priors were better than one.

March is rarely kind to a landscape's appearance, at least in the northern hemisphere, and this unkindness showed on Sasso Marconi's surrounding agricultural landscape. Barren, raw, and colorless, it was as drab as any day could be although it was not raining. Granted, at this time of year, precipitation would most likely be snow that many would view as nature's beautiful winter blanket. However, Lorenzo saw it more as a disguise for the eyesore of March's desolation.

Lorenzo dismounted from Between Thieves and stretched, stiff from being saddle-bound for so long, then tied Between Thieves to the hitching post.

The inn was a two-story stone building in the village square with nothing but a plain wooden door entrance; inside was equally inornate, but in the small dining area there was at least a fireplace with a fire crackling, providing some heat. Not a lot. But some. There were three tables, two occupied by four people each, couples in their thirties. They turned to see who had just entered and, not recognizing Lorenzo, simply smiled and went back to their meals, wine, and discussions.

A plump woman, likely in her fifties, sat at a reception desk. As Lorenzo entered, she looked up, smiled, and said, "Welcome, traveler, welcome!" She stood up, which did not bring her head much higher than it was when she sat. She was short. "Come in, come in where it's warm! Will you be staying with us this evening?"

"No, I was hoping for a meal for myself and feed and water for my horse, and then I'd like to continue on to Bologna. Is there someone who can tend to my horse while I dine?"

"Of course! I will call my husband." She turned, opened the door behind the reception desk a crack, and called out, "Giovanni! Can you come help attend to a guest's horse, please?"

No sooner had she turned back to attend to Lorenzo than Giovanni, standing six feet, four inches, emerged through the door, ducking his head as he entered the reception area. "Yes, Ginevra, did you call? I didn't hear what you needed."

Straining her neck up to respond, Ginevra replied, "Yes, Signore ..." She turned to look at Lorenzo to have him fill in the blank.

Lorenzo, always welcoming an opportunity to make his stature known, corrected, "Prior Lorenzo."

Suitably impressed, Ginevra replied, "Prior Lorenzo, an honor," then turned back to her husband. "Prior Lorenzo would like his horse fed and watered. Would you be so kind?"

"Of course, my pleasure." Giovanni ducked out the front door.

Ginevra turned back to Lorenzo, paying suitable attention and saying, "It's an honor to have a guest such as yourself, Prior Lorenzo. With which monastery are you, if it is not imprudent to ask?"

People knew the San Miniato al Monte Monastery's stature, and, as Lorenzo expected, Ginevra was suitably impressed.

"Please, Prior Lorenzo, take a seat in our humble dining lounge, and I will be right over to tell you our menu."

Lorenzo took a seat at the only available table, which was too far from the comfort of the fire, but it would suffice. As soon as he sat down, Ginevra came to his table to announce the inn's offerings.

"I am pleased to provide you with a choice of The Pilgrim's Respite, The Medicis' Modest Banquet, The Friar's Fasting Fare, or the daily special."

"What is The Medicis' Modest Banquet?"

Ginevra, with an intimate and almost whispered delivery, replied, "Chicken pie, braised leeks and onions, and erbolata tart. With wine, of course."

"And what about The Friar's Fasting Fare?"

Ginevra, now with an Italian flare that over the centuries would become world-famous, replied, "A carefully selected blend of root vegetables and barley with a side of roasted turnips and cabbage and a hearty rye bread. With wine, of course."

Winter fare in Tuscany was often a creative mix of root vegetables and fowl or fish differing mostly by the names innkeepers created for the meals. Lorenzo stared at Ginevra briefly, then finally replied, "You can't go wrong with a Medici meal, can you? I'll have that."

Moments later, Ginevra was serving a piping hot portion of The Medicis' Modest Banquet, which lived up to its name of "modest." While bowing away, she said, "I hope this is to your liking, Prior Lorenzo."

As Lorenzo ate, Giovanni returned from caring for Between Thieves, and seeing the couple together piqued Lorenzo's curiosity. "I wonder if they have children," he thought.

Lorenzo's bowl emptied quickly, and he was eager to continue his journey. He thanked his host and hostess, paid for his and Between Thieves' meals, and was soon on his way.

As he left the village, he thought again, "I wonder if they have children."

After riding for an hour on the road to Bologna, Prior Lorenzo saw three men walking toward him.

The three men, Alfonso, Alessandro, and Niccolò, had spent two days scouring the countryside, looking for their horses. They saw a lone man approaching on horseback.

As they neared each other, Alfonso looked, squinting, then yelled, "Wait a minute! You!"

Lorenzo looked at them, none clearly of any consequence, and replied scornfully, "What? What is it you want?"

"That's our horse!"

"What do you mean, this is your horse? This is not your horse."

"It sure as hell is! We paid good money for that horse!"

Lorenzo felt uneasy, realizing he was venturing into unknown territory. His first defense was to try a sympathetic, "you must be confused" tactic.

Feigning compassion and sympathy, Lorenzo said, "I am sorry to disappoint you, but I believe you are confusing my horse with another. It's happened before."

"With those markings? *With those markings*? You're telling me there are other horses with markings like that? I've seen hundreds of horses in my day, and none have markings like this. That's our horse!"

Not realizing he was about to dig himself in even deeper, Lorenzo tried a sterner, authoritarian approach. "Sir, I can assure you, you are mistaken. In fact, this horse belongs to one of the most revered monasteries in the Holy Roman Empire."

"Monastery? *Monastery*?" Alfonso turned to Alessandro and Niccolò. "You see? I told you! I told you it was him!"

Nearing hysterics, Alfonso turned back to Lorenzo and belted out, "That's right! That's right! A monastery! We bought the horse from a horse trader in Bologna; he'd gotten it from a monk in a monastery to sell to raise money. However, a guard from another monastery stole it from us, saying it was stolen from his monastery, and he stole our other horses, too! That's why we are on foot!"

Acting as though they could reason with him, Lorenzo made an effort to defuse the situation and said, "Do you mind explaining that again?"

Unfortunately, that only worsened matters; Alfonso's hysterical state also caused him to become somewhat incoherent.

"The monk! I mean the monastery ..."

"Which monastery? You mentioned two."

"The one that had the horse!"

"When? You said they both had the horse."

"When we bought it!"

"But I thought you said you bought it from a horse trader."

Alfonso was now beginning to hyperventilate. Alessandro and Niccolò both looked on, stupefied, unable to follow the train wreck of thought.

Alfonso now spoke slower, taking breaths between each phrase as he lapsed into full hyperventilation.

"We bought ... the fucking horse ... from a fucking horse trader ... who said he got ... the fucking horse ... from a fucking monk ... selling it ... to raise fucking money ... for his fucking monastery ... but a fucking guard ... from another fucking monastery ... stole our fucking horse ... and cut the head off our fucking friend, by the fucking way ..."

Lorenzo interrupted, "Wait a minute. Wait a minute. Now you're telling me someone lost their head over this whole affair?"

Lowering his head to the ground, hyperventilating, Alfonso muttered, "That's it. That's it!" Then he swiftly drew his sword.

Lorenzo had but two weapons: A letter in Latin they could not read. And Between Thieves.

He yanked on Between Thieves' reins, bringing the horse's front legs into the air and startling the three thieves because being trampled by a horse can be extremely painful, if not fatal. This depiction of equestrian power and might would go on to appear in paintings, television shows, and spaghetti western movies.

Startled, the three thieves jumped back as Lorenzo took Between Thieves into a full gallop down the road toward Bologna.

For a moment, the three thieves ran after Lorenzo. They quickly gave up running but did not give up walking in the same direction. Toward Bologna.

Full in Bologna

Sasso Marconi, Italy

March 2, 1461

For miles, Gabriele and Antonio rode in tandem with Gabriele taking the lead through the winding, narrow cobblestone streets of Florence. The March morning air was icy, and people scurried about, beginning their day of work or chores bundled in woolen coats and hats. They clung to themselves, trying to prevent what body heat they had from being sacrificed to March's frigidity.

Antonio and Gabriele, too, were bundled, and their horses' breaths punched into the wintry morning air, leaving a trail of tiny storm clouds as they made their way from the streets of Florence into the great white north of Tuscany's winter landscape.

Gabriele's mind recoiled from a struggle to understand why they were attacked and what made their cargo so special to an irrational and recurring rage resulting from the stop at Mario's bakery. Why?

After riding silently for miles, Gabriele heard Antonio in the rear say something. Turning around, the guard said, "Did you say something?"

"Do you see the stone walls ahead? Do you know what that is? Have you ever been here before?"

"Yes, sort of, and no."

"You might enjoy seeing this. I'll explain it as we pass."

They maneuvered their horses into a side-by-side trot. And they were talking again.

They were passing the village of Fiesole, which had stunning views overlooking Florence; its ancient ruins were still lodged in the Tuscany soil that once was claimed as Etruscan soil.

Gabriele gazed at the ancient stones and remnants of what no longer was.

"Such a beautiful view of Florence, but I always wonder about the ruins in midst of these villas only Florence's wealthy occupy."

Antonio replied, "Like many things, its beauty was a source of envy—not to mention its location. Very strategic. Being a pagan center didn't help it either. We all know the true path to God is worth fighting for.

"We call it Fiesole. But it was originally called Vipsul in Etruscan and in Latin, Faesulae. It was an Etruscan city and once more important than Florence. Saint Romulus is the Christian town's patron saint. The Cathedral of San Romolo houses his relics and remains. Have you never visited?"

"No. My duties tie me to our monastery. As we can see, temples and places of worship are always at risk of being brought to ruin."

Antonio wondered how some things remained and wondered what had vanished; what was vanquished from the collective soul of all? It was also the first time he heard Gabriele speak of anything more than their mission and directions.

As they passed by the city's walls, Antonio pointed to a collection of rubble and ruins and, with his hand pointing like the arms of a clock, said, "See that? Those temple ruins are rumored to have been dedicated to the Roman goddess Minerva."

"Who was she?"

Antonio turned to Gabriele, smiling, and replied, "She was the goddess of wisdom, strategic warfare, handicrafts, and the arts—a versatile goddess as far as goddesses go. A bit like the Greek goddess Athena."

As they rode, to the left were ruins of large tombs, and Antonio explained what they were. Smirking, Gabriele asked, "Is that where they bury goddesses when they get new ones?"

The guard looked away before seeing Antonio's reaction. He was smiling, just staring at Gabriele, wondering, "Why do I like this man so much given how intimidating he can be?"

As they rode across the rolling Tuscany hills, the bright March sun only marginally warmed the day. The vineyards, olive groves, and fields—once lush, beautiful, and tended by focused farmers—were now winter barren, but time melted as Antonio gave a running narrative on much of what they passed and what had passed in what they passed.

At one point, Gabriele turned to Antonio and asked, "How do you know all this?"

"I don't just illustrate manuscripts, Gabriele; I read what I illustrate. I may spend considerable time on one letter in a word. In that time, I vanish into other worlds, worlds where that letter or word may have been born. I read. I fall into the books I illustrate. I vanish from our world into theirs."

Gabriele just stared at Antonio, thinking, "This man ..."

When they reached the foot of the Apennine Mountains, they stopped. Gabriele looked up the trail leading up the mountain and said, "We're lucky."

Antonio looked up the mountain and, seeing its incline and narrow trail, failed to see any good luck at all. "How's that?"

"It's not snowing."

Gabriele began the climb, and Antonio followed. Gabriele, in the lead, called back to Antonio, advising, "Don't forget, Antonio, animals can sense fear. And through the mountains, you don't want to be riding a frightened horse. Keep your nerves."

For the next few hours, there was no conversation. All focus was on over-coming the mountain. Occasionally, a rock became unearthed by the horses' hooves and tumbled down the mountainside. Both Antonio and Gabriele knew not to look. Conquering the mountain meant conquering fear.

Once they crested the mountain, Gabriele let out a sigh and said, "Good. Going down will be easier." With a wry smile, the guard added, "But not by much."

As they eased their way down the mountainside, Antonio found himself wondering, once again, how a manuscript illustrator had found himself riding a horse down a mountain, being pursued by armed thieves, going to Mainz to confront a German he had never met and tell him he made a mistake and demand he fix it. As any rational person would, Antonio wondered why he didn't just keep his mouth shut.

When they and their horses reached the bottom of the mountain, all still alive, Gabriele pulled out the crumpled map of questionable accuracy and said, "There should be a village up ahead. We can rest, get the horses and ourselves fed, and then push on to Bologna. Sound good?"

"Sounds better than going back over the mountain."

With each passing hour, they delved inch by inch into each other's lives— crevasse after crevasse, life incident after life incident, the comedies and tragedies that made up the mosaics of who they were.

To a degree.

As they approached Sasso Marconi, Gabriele glanced at the map and then proudly informed Antonio, "It's almost where it says it is." Both were looking forward to getting out of the saddle for a rest, and the horses would appreciate having them off their backs.

It was a small village, but whether large or small, a small village or a larger city such as Florence, the first thing to find in any place was the town square. That was not a challenge in Sasso Marconi, nor was it a challenge to decide where to find a meal because they had a selection of one.

They both dismounted, stretched, then tied Twice and Thrice to the hitching post and made their way through the unadorned wooden door. Ginevra's appearance from behind the reception desk surprised Gabriele; the hostess was already standing.

"Welcome, travelers, welcome!" Although she was somewhat height-challenged, there was nothing diminutive about Ginevra's warmth.

"Will you be staying with us tonight?"

Gabriele, glancing into the dining room, replied, "No, but we would appreciate a meal and the warmth from the fireplace."

"Of course! Please. Take a seat in the dining room, and I'll fetch my husband to tend to the horses. Then I'll be right back to share our menu offerings with you."

Although two of the three dining room tables were occupied, the table closest to the fire was free. As they sat down, the other guests smiled and nodded hello. Gabriele took the usual seat, facing the room.

Ginevra stepped behind the reception desk, opened the door behind it a crack, and called to her husband, Giovanni, to tend to the horses. When he ducked through the doorframe, Gabriele, watching, commented, "Well, that makes you wonder."

Antonio, with his back to the desk, turned just in time to watch Giovanni duck through the inn's front entrance. Then he turned back to Gabriele, asking, "What?"

"Whether they have children."

Before Antonio had time to respond, Ginevra was at the table.

"Today, we are pleased to offer a choice of Sasso Marconi Medley, Reno River Rage, Farmer's Caring Cooking, or the daily special."

Glancing at Gabriele, Antonio replied, "What is the Sasso Marconi Medley?"

With famed Italian gusto, Ginevra replied, "It is capon stuffed with roasted chestnuts and served with tenderized turnips and carrots, smothered in olive oil infused with our secret house blend of rosemary, sage, thyme, and parsley, topped with a dash of carefully aged fresh saffron."

Antonio replied, "That sounds delicious. I'll have that."

Gabriele followed suit, sort of. "I'll have the ... What was the second one again?"

"Reno River Rage."

"I'll have that."

"Don't you want me to describe it to you?"

"No, I trust it's fine."

When Ginevra returned and served their meals, Antonio received a beef dish.

Gabriele received what appeared to be a fish stew.

Antonio looked at it and said, "Maybe you should have asked."

Gabriele shrugged and replied, "Let's just eat and get on our way."

They ate in silence, as it is when people are hungry, and as soon as they finished they went to the reception desk, where Ginevra was standing or sitting. As they were paying, Ginevra inquired, "So where are you traveling from?"

Gabriele answered, "Florence."

Ginevra replied, "Well, isn't that funny! We just had an important guest from Florence." Feeling she had some bragging rights for the stature of their inn, she added, "A prior from the San Miniato al Monte Monastery."

Gabriele and Antonio looked at each other, and Gabriele replied quietly to Antonio, "Funny, indeed."

They thanked Ginevra, and as they walked out and mounted Twice and Thrice, Gabriele said, "Well, that settles that."

"What?"

Stating the obvious, Gabriele said, "I think we should find other accommodations in Bologna rather than the Monastery of San Domenico."

They rode in silence across what in summer was lush but was now quiet and dormant in winter's rest. While the landscape was tranquil, their thoughts, each private and internalized, were not.

As they approached the city's outskirts, Antonio said, "Gabriele, I feel somewhat uneasy."

"I understand."

"I am not sure you do."

"What do you mean?"

"You see yourself as the head of security for the San Miniato al Monte Monastery."

"Yes. So?"

"I see you as the head of security for a well-paying client. I keep my thoughts about the Monastery and anything related to it to myself. Doing otherwise might not be good for business."

At first, Gabriele said nothing, and they rode in silence.

After several long, awkward minutes, Gabriele said, "Antonio, as head of security for the San Miniato al Monte Monastery, my assignment is to protect you. As I understand the assignment, that protection is unconditional."

Antonio said nothing as they entered the city and made their way along the winding cobblestone streets toward the town's center in search of an inn. Night was falling, and candles and lamps burned in the windows of the stone houses lining the streets. Then Antonio expressed what he had never expressed about anything to do with the Monastery: an opinion.

"I don't trust Prior Lorenzo. I don't like Prior Lorenzo. And I think the feelings are mutual."

They were just entering the town's square, and ahead was a four-story inn, taller than most of the others, with candles and lamps burning in the windows. Gabriele had not replied but, as if changing the topic, said plainly, "Let's try that inn."

After dismounting their horses and collecting their saddlebags, Gabriele said, "I don't like or trust him, either, if that makes you feel any better. Why don't you take the horses around to the inn's courtyard, and I will arrange for a room. It's March. I doubt there will be a problem getting one."

Antonio watched as Gabriele, saddled with the saddlebags—one of them carrying the book—turned and entered the inn through the arched doorway.

As the inn's door closed, Antonio suddenly felt very empty, alone, and exposed.

He walked the horses along the narrow walkway next to the inn to the inn's courtyard and stable. A stable boy got up from a bale of hay, asking if he was a guest of the inn, and Antonio said flatly, "Yes. Feed and water." Antonio began to turn back to the inn's entrance but then realized how the boy might interpret how he had spoken. The boy might think he meant, "You are a nobody. You don't matter."

He turned back to the stable boy and added, "Please." And then he reached into his saddlebag's pouch, took out a half-florin coin, and handed it to him.

Stunned, the boy said, "Really?"

Turning to make his way to the inn's entrance, Antonio shrugged, tossed a hand in the air, and said, "It's on the Church."

Gabriele was standing in the lobby waiting for Antonio with a big grin. The guard said, "Third floor. And guess what? Feather mattresses!"

A small smile made its way out of Antonio's sudden emotional pit, and he replied, "Maybe they needed the straw to feed the horses."

The inn was surprisingly well occupied, and the only availability was a setup they were quite familiar with: one room with two beds.

Their evening routine had been random Bible readings. Gabriele would open Gutenberg's Bible, sometimes commenting on the illustrations, often asking Antonio how long it would take him to create a similar illustration. The guard was always astounded to learn how quickly Gutenberg's press could produce dozens, even hundreds, in so little time.

Gabriele would also randomly open to text for Antonio to translate and read.

This night Gabriele opened to Corinthians, Chapter 14, verses 34-35, and Antonio translated from Latin and read, "Let your women keep silence in the churches: for it is not permitted unto them to speak; but they are commanded to be under obedience, as also saith the law. And if they will learn any thing, let them ask their husbands at home: for it is a shame for women to speak in the church."

Gabriele chuckled, then said, "It sounds like being a guard. We don't speak in church, either."

Gabriele then stared out the window at the street below and said, "Yes, women should know their place."

Then, turning to Antonio, the guard said, "Wouldn't you hate to be a woman? We're lucky we're not, aren't we?"

Antonio replied, "I have often wondered where my mother got the courage to let her intelligence show."

"How did your father treat her?"

"In public? Like every man treats his wife, as someone to be obedient. But in private, at home behind closed doors, I remember there being more. He listened to her. It was she who suggested I should learn the languages. But could she have made that possible? No. That was my father. He was a bookbinder. And what did he have access to? Manuscripts of many languages."

Gabriele turned back to the window. "I remember asking my father why he had not remarried, and his answer was, 'Because I am still with your mother.'"

Gabriele turned back, pulled the blankets back on the bed, and said, "As I said, Antonio, we're lucky."

Paola Doesn't Pay Off

Monastery of San Giorgio

March 2, 1461

Prior Lorenzo rode through the narrow cobblestone streets of Bologna, which were busy with merchants and townsfolk scurrying around, bundled for the cold March air.

Although it was not as prestigious as Florence, Lorenzo liked Bologna. It was quaint. But what was most remarkable was Lorenzo's destination: the Monastery of San Domenico. Following Bologna's main winding street led him to the monastery, whose façade, with its Gothic origins, was now tastefully adorned with current Renaissance features, providing a sense of the institution's history while conveying a modern-day influence suggesting continued relevance.

Here—unlike at his monastery, San Miniato al Monte—a resident, or sometimes the abbot himself, greeted all visitors, expected and unexpected, unless local unrest necessitated guards.

Lorenzo approached the entrance and dismounted from Between Thieves. A monk approached, bowed, and greeted Lorenzo, welcoming him to the Monastery, asking about Lorenzo's needs and wants, and inviting him inside for food and beverage.

Lorenzo thanked the monk and took little time to introduce himself as the prior of the San Miniato al Monte Monastery in Florence.

The monk bowed again, saying, "Such an honor, Prior. Do you wish to speak with the abbot? I am confident that the abbot would gladly receive you."

"No, Brother, thank you, but I wish to speak with Subprior Paola. He and I met and talked at the conference a year ago, and I wish to confer with him again to discuss further readings I have had on topics of our discourse."

"Certainly, certainly. Please, come in and make yourself at home in our humble monastery. I'll show you to the vestibule and will advise Subprior Paola of your visit."

The monk opened the large, thick wooden door entrance, which was framed in stone. Six scenes, almost like a stone précis, depicted the origins of man and the story of God: the creation of Adam; Adam and Eve and the original sin; Abraham preparing to sacrifice his son Isaac at God's command; the birth of Christ; the Crucifixion of Christ; and, of course, the Resurrection.

Passing through the doorway, Lorenzo thought of how succinctly the stone storytellers had summed up God's story and God's promise.

"Follow me and you will live forever." That's a hard benefit to beat.

As the monk led Lorenzo to the vestibule to wait while he sought Paola, Lorenzo thought more about that archway. Yes, stories. The history of humanity was a never-ending string of personal stories, some bound through a common theme. Such was the Church's story. And stories are all in the telling. Dwelling on that only strengthened his conviction that the flawed, mechanically produced Bible must remain that: flawed. It was the Church that needed to control the weaving of the stories. The archway, like the stone itself, had only strengthened Lorenzo's resolve.

Lost in his own story, the voice of Subprior Paola snapped Lorenzo back to reality.

"Prior Lorenzo! What a surprise! What a delight it is to see you!"

As it had been when Antonio arrived at the Monastery with no appointment seeking an audience with the abbot, Lorenzo's smile slithered like a snake from ear to ear.

"Subprior Paola, likewise, a delight to see you as well." Lorenzo extended his hand for a handshake, but his handshake was limp. It was almost as if, instead, Paola should kiss his ring.

"Subprior, where might we discuss church matters without disruption?"

By "disruption," Lorenzo, looking Paola in the eye, was really saying, "Without being overheard."

Paola looked at Lorenzo, then offered, "Allow me to escort you to a guest room where you may stay during your visit." Paola led Lorenzo from the vestibule through a stone corridor adorned with frescoes and tapestries, more of the Bible's narrative laid out pictorially. After all, learning is most effectively accomplished through visuals, and the Church was a master at visual storytelling and spent considerable sums on its creation.

An arched wooden door opened to one of the Monastery's guest rooms, offered to visiting dignitaries—or sometimes lucky travelers seeking accommodations when the rooms were unoccupied by more important guests.

The room, furnished with a simple wood-frame bed and a small table and chair, had only a small window looking out over the garden and courtyard, now donned solely in February's gray rather than the vibrant and lush colors of a Bologna summer.

Entering the room, Lorenzo sat on the side of the bed as Paola closed the door behind them. Then, gesturing to the chair, the prior said, "Please, sit so we may talk."

Paola pulled the chair from the table and turned it around to face Lorenzo.

As Paola was sitting, Lorenzo let out a deep, slow sigh, then looked up from staring at the floor. He looked Paola in the eye and said, "I was surprised to see our guard return the horse I sent you via the messenger. It confused me, and given our joint mission, it concerned me.

"I contrived a conspiracy that will occupy my abbot and have him looking within our monastery for a ghost that doesn't exist—a ghost that informed me via an unsigned letter that there was a threat to our monastery that emanated from here in Bologna, hence my need to depart immediately. And here I am, having traveled on a horse that is getting to know the countryside well."

Letting it sink in which horse he was referring to, Lorenzo followed that with a question that set the tone: "Can you explain why our plan failed?"

In the question was the subtle, unspoken insinuation that somehow the blame for the plan's failure would rest on Paola's shoulders, a subtlety not lost on Paola.

Paola squirmed in his seat and tried to shift the blame from himself to fate, an all-powerful force whose origins no human has ever explained, at least rationally.

But Paola was about to do that very thing: explain fate. "Let me explain—"

"That would be very helpful of you, Subprior Paola." Lorenzo's use of Paola's title was an overt reminder of who held the seniority.

Paola explained what he knew of the situation and went into great detail about the meeting with the three thieves and the horse trader, Jacopo.

"And what became of the messenger I sent? Did he sleep well, as I wished he would?"

"I don't know."

"You don't know? How can that be?"

"He disappeared."

"Disappeared? He disappeared? From all my reading of our texts, I have never read of anyone disappearing. Exactly how did he disappear?" Sarcastically, Lorenzo asked, "Did he disappear before your very eyes?"

"Of course not." Paola then explained that he and his fellow Brothers had been taken with a sudden virus necessitating an immediate trip to the necessarium. When they returned, the messenger was gone, and they had looked everywhere for him. With no luck.

Lorenzo looked away and stared out the window, wondering how the messenger could have just disappeared without a trace and without a horse.

"Did you look down the well?"

Wishing to confirm they had thought of everything and happy there was finally a question to which he could answer "yes," Paola said he personally had indeed looked down the well, concerned because that was their drinking water supply.

With the inquisition concluded, Lorenzo returned to the topic of their original mission.

"Do you think our guard and that loathsome illustrator would suspect you had anything to do with this … this calamity?"

The inquisition may have been over, but the sting was not.

Paola responded, "I can't see how they would!"

"Good. Tell me, Paola, what did the thieves you met with—and handled adeptly, I must say—look like?"

Finally. A compliment. Paola described the thieves and Lorenzo responded by asking almost rhetorically, "They would have been traveling on horseback, correct?"

"I assume so, yes, based on the story they told me and the horse trader, Jacopo."

Lorenzo told Paola of his encounter with three men on foot who were claiming Between Thieves was their horse. Puzzled, he stared out the window again, and most likely thinking out loud, said, "That must have been them. But why were they on foot?"

Although the question wasn't for Paola, he answered anyway. "I have no idea about that. However, when I met with them, they seemed quite fixated on their finances. Perhaps they sold their horses to the horse trader, Jacopo."

"I doubt it, Paola. The business of highway banditry is difficult to conduct on foot."

Lorenzo stood up and walked over to the window, looking out at the void of March's landscape while he tried to put the pieces together and concoct another strategy.

He turned back to Paola and said, "It's favorable they are not suspicious of you. They would have left Florence after I left on my journey here, so they will most likely come here for food and accommodations for themselves and their horses. Perhaps it would be wise to keep Between Thieves from plain view at the stable. Can you see to that?"

"Certainly, Prior Lorenzo. And do you have a plan for when they arrive?"

"As much as I dislike and distrust that illustrator—there is just something about him that doesn't sit well with me—we must remain disciplined and focused. Antonio is of little consequence. He has no voice or authority within the Church. He is just a hired tradesman. And the guard? Of little consequence, either. The abbot tasked him with protecting the illustrator."

Smiling at his own cunning and strategic acumen, Lorenzo pointed out, "If the abbot had thought this through, he would have assigned the guard the priority of protecting the Bible."

Not understanding and unable to read Lorenzo's scheming mind, Paola asked, "What are you thinking?"

Lorenzo turned away from the window. Smiling and looking Paola in the eye, he said, "They know nothing of your involvement, so they will undoubtedly seek accommodations here. And what will they do while they are here?"

"Eat?"

"Sleep, Paola, sleep. They will be exhausted from their journey, but they will feel safe here. That means they will sleep soundly."

Turning and pointing to the latch on the guest room's door, Lorenzo pointed out, "You have no locks on these doors. Remember, what are we after? Not them. It's that Gutenberg monstrosity. And we get it through a means as old as civilization itself."

"You mean ..."

"Of course. We steal it while they're sleeping. It would make an excellent fire starter for a morning fire in one of the Monastery's fireplaces." Then, as though standing on a pulpit, Lorenzo proclaimed, "Then let the world know of this flawed Bible. Let the world doubt and distrust any biblical work spouted out from some machine. Let the Church be the harbinger of truth and ecclesiastical authenticity. Ours is a divine mission, Paola. The Church will recognize that once it regains its clarity." Then he smiled at Paola, adding, "The Medicis, too, will see us as guardians of the Church's authority."

Inspired, Paola's mind drifted to a fantasy of an audience with the Medici family, an unimaginable dream in which a Medici might actually listen to anything he had to say.

"What do we do now?" Paola asked.

"We wait, Paola. We wait. When they arrive, I will remain out of sight. Instruct your Brothers to say nothing of my presence. Tell them mine is a confidential mission."

And wait they did, indeed.

Nightfall was ascending, and Lorenzo had no idea what time Antonio and Gabriele would have left Florence, nor could he even guess.

Paola had one of the Monastery's lay staff take Between Thieves to the far end of the stalls and cover him with a horse's blanket, thus providing some warmth for the cold winter night and also hiding the steed's distinctive markings. The worker was also to fetch Lorenzo's belongings.

In some ways, Paola's instructions to the layperson foreshadowed George Boldt's revolutionary hotel concept, which he would introduce late in the nineteenth century at New York City's iconic Waldorf Hotel. It was called "room service."

Yet, there they were in 1461, and Lorenzo had just been provided precisely that service.

As night enveloped the Monastery, it was soon apparent Antonio and Gabriele would not be arriving that day. "Just as well," Lorenzo thought. He, too, was tired after his journey from Florence and welcomed the promise of a good night's sleep without having to attend to any middle-of-the-night subterfuge liberating Gutenberg's Bible from Antonio and Gabriele's quarters.

At the conclusion of the evening's prayers and rituals, Lorenzo retired to his guest room, a luxury by monastic standards. Pleased to see his belongings, he undressed for a night's sleep, slipped under the bed's woolen blankets, and was soon asleep, drifting into another world over which he had no control—the world of dreams, often forgotten, sometimes frightening, and never predictable.

When the morning sun's rays broke through the horizon, ousting night's darkness, light crept into Lorenzo's room and woke him from a deep night's sleep with not a dream or nightmare to recall.

He rose, dressed, and left his room to join the Monastery's morning rituals, prayers, and breakfast. In the refectory, as breakfast was being served, the abbot stood and announced, "Today, we are blessed to have as our guest the prior from the San Miniato al Monte Monastery, Prior Lorenzo. I thought I would ask Prior Lorenzo to provide our breakfast reading."

Although surprised, Lorenzo rose from the table and to the occasion, reviewing Psalms stored in his memory's catalog.

He walked to the head of the table, turned to face the monks, smiled, and said, "Given the responsibilities we all bear within these walls, I would quote several passages, starting with Matthew, Chapter 16, verse 18.

Proud of his memory and proud to display it, he spoke without reading: "'And I say also unto thee, That thou art Peter, and upon this rock I will build my church; and the gates of hell shall not prevail against it.'"

He glanced around the table to see who might have understood his reference to the Church.

He continued on. "From Acts, Chapter 20, verse 28, we are told, 'Take heed therefore unto yourselves, and to all the flock, over the which the Holy Ghost hath made you overseers, to feed the church of God, which he hath purchased with his own blood.'"

He recited several passages, all from memory, each referencing from one context to another the importance of the Church, or so they could be interpreted.

After concluding his from-memory reading, the abbot stood and complimented Prior Lorenzo. The monks nodded in agreement.

As he glanced around the table, he saw Paola smiling, obviously proud of having Lorenzo as his guest given how Lorenzo had so impressed not just his fellow monks but the abbot himself with his reading from memory.

After breakfast, Lorenzo joined the other monks in their rituals and prayers and helped with their duties throughout the day while always monitoring the Monastery's door, anticipating Antonio and Gabriele.

They never arrived.

As the day's sun set, Lorenzo's concerns grew. After the evening's meal and prayers, he asked Paola to join him in his guest room. Once they were there, out of earshot with the door closed, Lorenzo confided, "I don't like this."

With his annoying habit of trying to look on the bright side, Paola suggested, "Perhaps something in Florence delayed them. Perhaps as head of security, the guard had issues or duties to attend to. Perhaps the illustrator had work that set them back."

Lorenzo just waved him off, saying, "Having this Bible corrected is our abbot's priority. To him, the mistake is a significant embarrassment. Having it corrected is of utmost importance." Then, looking Paola straight in the eye, Lorenzo said, "Imagine embarrassing yourself in the eyes of the Medicis. Especially as an abbot."

Paola could not even imagine having an audience with the Medicis, let alone embarrassing himself in front of them.

"I understand your point."

"If they are not here by midday tomorrow, let us confer here in my quarters so we can determine another course of action to pursue."

Lorenzo then opened his door, thus ushering Paola out. Paola bid good night, thinking it a positive note, adding, "Prior Lorenzo, sleep well knowing that the Lord is with us."

Lorenzo smiled and nodded, closing the door as Paola departed. Once it was closed and Lorenzo was alone with his thoughts, he immediately processed Paola's parting words of encouragement, thinking, "'Sleep well'?"

He didn't.

By midday the following day, Lorenzo accepted that his prey would not be walking into the web he had spun as he had hoped. As planned, he met with Paola in his guest room immediately after the midday meal.

Lorenzo again sat on his bed, facing his table; and again he motioned for Paola to sit so they could strategize, although Lorenzo knew that task rested with himself.

Devising a strategy was often a simple matter of addressing questions. The first question was a straightforward one, and he posed it to Paola.

"What do we know?"

Paola answered, "I don't know what we know."

With a sigh, Lorenzo responded, "What do we not know?"

Paola looked at Lorenzo and replied, "Anything, it would seem."

Lorenzo was no longer listening to Paola; he began thinking out loud.

"I think it's safe to assume Antonio and his guard will not be coming here."

"I think you're right."

Lorenzo continued, barely aware Paola was sitting there facing him.

"We know where they are going, and we would be wise to assume they are now past here."

Lorenzo then smiled, shrugged, and said, "We also know they have to come back. All we need to do is prevent the corrected Bible from making it back to the Monastery."

"What about your prolonged absence from your monastery? It is surely felt."

"Almost certainly, Paola. So you are right; I need to extend my absence. I will have you send a courier with a communiqué to my abbot. Have you trusted couriers you could summon now?"

"Yes, through our chain of couriers, there is no sleep. I assure you I can get your communiqué to Abbot Fransisco in good time and I will ensure the couriers understand the urgency of the brewing conspiracy."

"Excellent. Do you know the beauty of a conspiracy, Paola?"

"No, I have not considered that."

The teacher replied to his student, "Conspiracies have no bottom."

"No doubt, Abbot Fransisco will cast a suspicious glance in every corner of the Monastery, trying to identify the author of the note slipped under my door.

"Yes, I will be absent longer than planned. So clearly, the conspiracy has spread farther than here at the Monastery of San Domenico. But Abbot Fransisco is not to worry because I have reliable information on the conspiracy's origins and am in full pursuit. I will not rest until I root out and quash the conspirators."

Leaving no lie languishing, Lorenzo added, "As for the sick-family-member cover story, I will suggest that there are signs of recovery—clearly proving the power of prayer—and that I will continue in prayer at my family member's side until full recovery."

"I see," replied Paola, now operating on blind faith. Sort of.

"But if that Bible is corrected, won't that make Gutenberg aware of the mistake and thus lead to the other Bibles being corrected and defeat our purpose? We want people to distrust Scriptures other than those originating from within the Church."

For once, Paola made a good point.

Lorenzo thought for a minute and then asked, "How many inns are there in Bologna?"

"Five."

"Tomorrow, first thing, I need to find out where they stayed in Bologna and when. I will continue after them. I can travel faster than them. After all, I will be on our fastest horse, and I have a greater sense of urgency than they do. As for Gutenberg being made aware and correcting all the other flawed Bibles scattered across the Holy Roman Empire, rumor has it Gutenberg is facing legal difficulties." Then Lorenzo leaned forward, smiling, and rhetorically asked, "Who's going to pay for that correction? No one."

Lorenzo had a shrewd understanding of not just biblical verse but the human psyche itself.

He knew full well no one likes to pay for their mistakes.

Stage Fright

Verona, Italy

March 5, 1461

After several days of travel in relative peace and ease, Antonio and Gabriele were confident that they had slipped through Lorenzo's intended noose. During the hours riding side by side, they shared stories—sometimes laughing, sometimes solemn—but slowly, story by story, their familiarity with the complexity of each other's lives grew.

Sometimes, they would ride for hours silently, comfortable with the voiceless stillness, listening only to the sounds of their surroundings—an occasional bird, sometimes cattle in the distance if they were close to a village, periodic church bells when passing through small villages. Often the only sound was the wind, sometimes gentle, sometimes not.

Antonio would catch himself staring at Gabriele, observing every nuance of the guard's body language and facial expressions. Then, when he realized what he had been doing, he would look away and force his focus elsewhere, sometimes reflecting on his work and often wondering how the studio was managing without him.

He had been promised his position would be secure, as if he could just walk back into a life that seemed more and more distant the longer he was away—the more he rode, side by side with Gabriele, farther and deeper into a fate-driven unknown. However, the studio would have adjusted to his absence; at first, other manuscript illustrators would have commented that the studio just wasn't the same without him, but as each day and week went by, that would fade. Someone would have taken over his tasks and most likely his art board, and when he walked back in after weeks away, yes, there would be a job waiting for him. But would there be a place for him in the realigned social order of the working studio?

Gabriele did not have that worry. Having saved the abbot's life, there was no threat anyone could replace Gabriele in the abbot's heart and mind.

Gabriele's worry was the man sitting in the saddle on the horse that rode along beside Thrice.

Gabriele could sense Antonio was being drawn in, could sense his eyes, and didn't have to see him staring; Gabriele could feel it.

The afternoon sun was becoming an early evening sunset as they approached the Verona gates.

Antonio, seeing the gates, asked, "Are you familiar with Verona?"

"I know of it, yes."

"You're aware Venice annexed it?"

"Vaguely. I try to close my ears to politics. In my profession, we only get involved in politics when politics fail."

"I think the threat of Florence's conflict with Venice is real."

"I am aware of tension, yes. I have overheard Abbot Fransisco speak of it."

As they neared the gates, two guards emerged, standing directly in front of them and blocking the gate's entrance.

Antonio initiated their inevitable exchange with as bright and friendly a greeting as he could muster. "Good afternoon, sirs." Then, pointing behind the gate, he added cheerfully, "Verona looks every bit as beautiful as I have been told. We look forward to seeing it."

Coldly, one guard answered, "Not yet. Do you have papers? What is the purpose of your visit?"

"Yes, of course." Antonio rummaged through the abbot's assortment of letters of introduction. As he did, Gabriele, pointing to the guard's sword, said, "That is an exceptionally well-designed sword."

The guard cast a quick glance at his sword, wondering what had caught this traveler's attention. Then, looking back at Gabriele, he answered somewhat suspiciously, "How would you know? You haven't even seen it."

"My father was a master sword maker. I can tell just by looking at the hilt."

The guard's pride in his prized possession showed. "Really?"

"Oh yes." Gabriele listed off well-known noblemen for whom Gabriele's father had produced swords that were as much works of art as they were weapons.

Gabriele knew how closely a man tied his ego to his sword. Now the first guard, no longer scrutinizing Antonio, withdrew his sword and asked, "What do you make of this?"

"You got that in Venice, didn't you?"

Shocked, the guard said, "Yes, but how could you tell?"

"The pommel. They only make them that way in Venice. Beautiful."

Both guards were now beaming with sword pride.

Antonio, now with papers in hand, offered them to the senior guard, who just glanced and said, "Yes, yes. I am sure they are fine. What is the purpose of your visit?"

Before Antonio could say a word, Gabriele jumped in, saying, "We are traveling and just seeking an inn for the night."

The guard went for the bait.

"Where are you headed?"

"Lugano … a Swiss town."

Not only did the guard go for the bait, but he also came back for seconds.

"What's there?"

"We're attending a sword maker's trade show."

The guard turned to the other. "That's something I wish I could attend."

His fellow guard agreed, saying, "Me as well."

They waved Antonio and Gabriele through the gates into the Verona streets. Once out of earshot, Antonio said, "Who taught you to lie like that?"

Without missing a beat and straight-faced, Gabriele replied, "Prior Lorenzo."

"What prompted you to come up with that story?"

"You didn't want them searching our bags and discovering 'the book,' did you? And having to explain that?"

"No, that would not have been favorable. But how did you come up with that sword story so quickly?"

"Antonio, men view their swords as an expression of their manhood."

As they continued along the cobblestone streets, Antonio thought, "What an intimate observation for a man to admit to another man." Then he glanced at Gabriele's sword. It was beautiful. A work of art in metal. "No surprise," Antonio thought, "Gabriele's father was a sword maker."

They wended their way toward Verona's square, following the winding cobblestone streets. Each street was lined with a mix of Gothic and modern Renaissance stone houses, most adorned with frescoes and colorful banners. There was no mistaking Verona's vibrancy. Multiple market stalls also lined the street, and there was no shortage of activity. Though bundled for the winter air, along the streets they trotted, customers haggling with vendors; people seemed to come and go, all in a hurry, most likely in search of warmth as much as the vendors' wares. One stall selling colorful woolen hats was especially busy.

Entering the town square, they saw three inns. In the square's center stood an elevated wooden pavilion, and it seemed preparations were being made for some presentation or event because stools were being arranged in a semicircle facing it.

As Antonio and Gabriele were passing a man walking toward them on the street, Antonio called out to him. "Excuse me, sir. Would you happen to be from Verona?"

The man stopped, smiled, and replied, "Yes. Are you in need of directions?"

"No, I wonder which of the three inns in the square you might recommend."

Pointing across the square to a three-story Gothic building with its name, "The Adige River Inn," painted in gold on a black wooden sign, the local advised, "If you have not been to Verona before, I recommend it. It has spectacular views of our river, especially in the morning. And of the three inns, I have been told they provide the best care for a traveler's horses."

Antonio thanked him, and smiling, the local replied, "My pleasure. Enjoy your visit."

They crossed the square, dismounted, grabbed their saddlebags, and entered through the inn's arched wooden door. Welcoming warmth emanated from both the dining room's crackling fireplace and the innkeeper, a tall, gray-haired man who was well past his prime yet had somehow maintained, against all worldly odds, a youthful enthusiasm and the talent of making every guest who walked through the inn's doors feel like they were the most important person he had ever met.

"Welcome! Welcome! Seeing your bags, I assume you will stay with us tonight. Wonderful! One room or two?"

Without hesitation, Gabriele replied, "One room, two beds. If that's possible."

"It most certainly is, and I am pleased to add, with a river view. Seeing your bags, I also assume you have horses that need attending?"

"Yes," Antonio replied. Then he added with a little smirk, "Is everyone in Verona as friendly as you?"

"Oh no, we have resident politicians."

Antonio chuckled and added, "Best not to let them know you have two Florentine guests."

The innkeeper shrugged, responding, "Politicians squabble. Most people just want to get on with their lives with the least amount of misery possible. People here have no issues with people from Florence. Venice? Well, that's another matter." He added the last comment with just enough spice of mischief to amuse without offending. "Actually, we have other guests from Florence."

Antonio and Gabriele both thought the same thing: Lorenzo. But how could he have gotten here before them?

Calmly, Gabriele asked, "Who might that be?"

"Didn't you see them setting up in the square? It's a theatre group from Florence, the Florentine Performers or something. We must be on their circuit because they pass through every couple of months. People seem to enjoy their performances."

Intrigued, Antonio asked, "What are they performing?"

"Oh, I wouldn't know. I am always working when they're putting on performances. They always perform right around dusk, so the torches lighting their stage area add drama, or so I'm told."

Antonio and Gabriele thanked him, took their saddlebags to their room, and tossed them on the beds. Antonio asked, "Gabriele, do you want to go watch our fellow Florentines perform?"

Almost as if confessing a sin, Gabriele replied quietly, "I have never been to a play."

"You've never been to a play? All the more reason." Leaving no room for protest, Antonio opened the door and did something with Gabriele he had never done before.

He issued an order.

"Come on. Let's go."

People were gathering in the square and finding seats on the stools. The stage was on a two-foot raised platform, and torches burned on the side flats. The blue sky dimmed, soon becoming a deep cobalt blue before darkness fell; then torchlights would illuminate the stage, revealing who and what the audience's eyes would be drawn to.

Antonio and Gabriele took seats beside a couple in their mid-forties. Antonio sat beside the woman, and her husband—who was not looking as enthused to be there as his wife but upstaged her with his enthusiasm for the wine—sat on her other side.

Antonio turned to her and asked, "What are they performing?"

She turned and looked at Antonio, surprised that someone sitting to watch a play would not know what he was about to watch.

In a tone suggesting this was something he should have known, she whispered, "*Everyman!*"

Gabriele leaned into Antonio's ear and even more quietly whispered, "What's that?"

Antonio whispered his answer, "It's a story about us."

Shocked, Gabriele intensely whispered, "Us? How do they know about us?"

Antonio found Gabriele's shock amusing, even bordering on endearing. He whispered his response, "Us ... mankind ..."

Gabriele was silent for a few moments then asked, "How long is this play?"

Before he could reply, two stagehands brought torches to center stage to reveal a character sitting in a chair, happily drinking wine from a soup bowl, surrounded by props of wealth and pleasure: gold coins that didn't quite look like gold, fine robes, and wine goblets.

"That's Everyman," Antonio whispered to Gabriele.

Just as Everyman took a long drink from his goblet, a character dressed in a black hooded robe entered from stage left.

"That's Death," Antonio whispered. The actor playing Death looked young for the role, Antonio thought; but when he spoke, his voice had such thundering, menacing depth that it even startled many in the audience, some jumping out of their stools. It was almost incongruous, as if the audio did not match the visual.

Death had belted out God's command and God's summoning. As the play progressed, Antonio explained—character by character, consequence by consequence—the play's progression in a whispered style that, centuries later, sportscasters would emulate at golf tournaments.

As Antonio watched the play, he found himself studying Death closer and closer until he realized he recognized him as someone he had often seen on the streets of Florence. He whispered this to Gabriele, adding, "I always wondered what he did. Now I know. He was a starving actor."

Good Deeds, Knowledge, and Fellowship played out their roles, the play culminating with Everyman stepping into his grave accompanied only by Good Deeds. Stagehands whisked the torches from the stage, leaving it in complete darkness. At that precise moment, a resonating voice—the voice of God—delivered the parting words, "Blessed is the soul who finds salvation in love and virtue. Everyman's story is yours to heed. Live wisely, for all must reckon."

A rumbling, spontaneous applause erupted as the stagehands returned torches to the stage and the cast re-emerged, concluding the performance with gracious and humble bows.

Antonio turned to Gabriele and said, "So now you've seen a play. This troupe is from Florence. Why don't we go tell them how much we enjoyed their performance? Especially the actor playing Death. What a voice!"

"Why not? I confess, his performance startled me off my stool."

At the stage, the performers, all still in costume, were packing up props and stage gear. Still in a black robe, Death was easy to find.

He was packing items in a trunk when Antonio and Gabriele approached him.

"Excuse me," Antonio said, "we just wanted to tell you that your performance was impressive and memorable."

It was as memorable as his response because when he replied, "Thank you," his voice was soft, quiet, and self-conscious. Antonio told him they, too, were from Florence, then said he believed he had seen him in Florence and asked his name.

"Guglielmo." You could barely hear him say his name. It was as if it were an embarrassment.

Both Antonio and Gabriele sensed his awkwardness, and in an attempt to set him at ease and warm the conversation, Antonio replied, "A pleasure to meet you, Guglielmo. My name is Antonio, and this is Gabriele. I am a manuscript illustrator, and Gabriele is the head of security at our San Miniato al Monte Monastery."

The second Guglielmo heard that, his eyes widened. He jumped back and let out a screech of terror. "Franco! Franco! Franco!"

Within a second, a stocky man in his thirties ran to his side and said, "What is it, Guglielmo? What's the matter?"

"They're from the Monastery!"

Franco's's head swung instantly, and he glared at them both, looking them both in the eyes, back and forth. Then he bluntly and abruptly said, "What do you want? Why are you here?"

Antonio, confused, replied, "We just wished to tell Guglielmo how much we enjoyed his performance."

Franco barked, "Are you in the habit of seeking out dead men?"

Antonio and Gabriele looked at each other as if the other could provide a clue to what Franco was talking about. But neither could.

Franco kept grilling Antonio and Gabriele until he was certain they knew nothing of Guglielmo's story.

Then he told them.

Antonio and Gabriele stood, speechless, listening to Franco and casting glances at Guglielmo. The young man stood like a statue, motionless, staring at the ground.

When Franco finished, Gabriele said, "Guglielmo ..."

Guglielmo looked up from the bottom of his lonely world to Gabriele, who said, "In a few weeks' time, we will be back in Florence. When we are, and when you and your troupe are in Florence, I would like you to come to see me. There is someone I would like to introduce you to."

"Who?"

"Our abbot."

"Me? Why would an abbot meet me? I'm a nobody."

Franco shot him a glance and said firmly but kindly, "Guglielmo, I thought we agreed you would never say that again."

"Sorry."

The four stood there silently until Gabriele said, "Until Florence, Guglielmo."

Antonio and Gabriele then turned and began the short walk back to their inn.

Neither spoke.

In their room, Gabriele turned away from Antonio, but not before Antonio caught a glance of a tear running down the guard's cheek.

He heard Gabriele whisper, "Good God."

Even more quietly, Antonio responded, "If only."

A Band of Thieves

Bologna, Italy

March 5, 1461

It took visits to only two inns in Bologna to learn where Antonio and Gabriele had stayed—and when they had left. They had a few days' lead, which both frustrated and angered him. "But then," he thought, "they won't have the same sense of urgency as I do."

And they were not riding Between Thieves.

Prior Lorenzo had now been pushing Between Thieves hard and he knew the horse was tired. So was he.

Traveling along the Roman-era road, he saw the gates to the village Soave in the distance and thought that would be a good and even appropriate place to stop for a meal and have Between Thieves watered and fed. From there he would head to Mantua or even Cremona—if he could push Between Thieves there—with its violin-making shops seemingly on every second corner, or so he had heard.

He liked Soave's significance. It was an ecclesiastical center and home to the Church of San Lorenzo, the only church in the area. Lorenzo always felt more comfortable knowing he was among kindred spirits. And, of course, its namesake did not escape him; he felt perhaps his mission was worthy of a sainthood, too.

The gates to the village were open, giving entrance to narrow cobblestone streets lined by two- and three-story stone houses. Typical of many Italian towns and villages, the roads did not lead directly to the village center but turned away from it, leading to another village gate and exit. Lorenzo always thought how simple and ingenious this urban planning was: any advancing army would march into town, following the street that would only lead them to another gate, and march right back out again.

Nowhere is the power of confusion more potent than in warfare.

Lorenzo stopped when he saw an elderly couple walking toward him on the street and asked them for directions to the village center, where he might find an inn or tavern for a meal and care for his horse.

The man replied, "It's simple, just follow this for two more blocks, turn left at the house with the yellow-painted door, follow that for about three blocks until you see a tiny one-story house, turn there, and then head straight in. That will lead you to the square, where there are two inns. Both provide meals, but I prefer Antonio's. His is the one with the green-painted arch over the doorway. You can't miss it."

Just to be clear, Lorenzo repeated the instructions, a practice in communication that would continue to evolve for centuries, even into aviation to prevent pilots from landing on wrong runways even though they sometimes did. Even, occasionally, at wrong airports.

"Okay."

Pointing down the street, Lorenzo said, "Two blocks this way until the house with the yellow door, turn left and go about three blocks until the one-story house, and turn ... which way?"

The elderly man thought for a moment, and you could tell he was trying to visualize the route in his mind's eye. After a second, he pointed with his left arm and said, "That way."

"Okay, left there, and that will take me to the town square?"

"You can't miss it."

Lorenzo missed it and soon found himself at a gate leading out of the city.

After seeking directions from locals twice more, Lorenzo finally entered the town square, and sure enough, there was the inn with the arched green-painted doorway.

Lorenzo decided to try the other inn across the square.

He dismounted Between Thieves, tied him to the hitching post, and opened the arched door to the three-story stone inn. He saw a reception desk in front of him and a dining area to the right with five tables—three of them occupied by what appeared to be couples, two of them empty—

and at the far end a large stone fireplace with a warm, welcoming fire crackling.

To the left was a common seating area with two couches and two chairs, all unoccupied, and a small wooden table with an unlit candle.

As he entered, a man exiting middle age looked up from the reception desk and broadly smiled, saying, "Welcome, pilgrim, to Antonio's Inn. How may we be of service to you? Are you seeking accommodations or perhaps a meal on this cold winter day?"

Confused, Lorenzo replied, "I thought Antonio's Inn was across the square, the building with the green-painted arch over the doorway."

"No, that is Marco's. We have a friendly competition to see which one of us can provide the most congenial accommodations and the most satisfying, memorable meals. No matter where a traveler stays here in our village —everyone calls it 'Little Bologna'—we want them to remember us all fondly. And tell others. So now that you are here, I can assure you that you won't find anything better here in Soave. How may I help you?"

"I would like a meal before I continue on my journey to Bolzano, and I would like my horse watered and fed. Is that possible?"

"Certainly. We can care for your horse in our courtyard. Would you like directions to the courtyard entrance?"

"Directions? No, thank you. Would it be possible to have someone take my horse there for me?"

"Of course. I will have someone look after that for you. In the meantime, please have a seat in our dining room, and I will be right back to explain our menu."

The innkeeper turned and disappeared through a doorway directly behind the reception desk. Lorenzo entered the dining room, returned polite nods and smiles to those who looked up as he walked in, and took a seat at one of the open tables; he thought it was not close enough to the fire for his liking but would suffice.

A few moments later, the innkeeper reappeared to attend to Lorenzo at his table.

"Your horse is being cared for."

"Thank you."

"What takes you to Soave, if I may ask?"

With only a slight hint of arrogance, Lorenzo replied, "I am Prior Lorenzo from the San Miniato al Monte Monastery, and I am traveling to the Monastery of San Giorgio in Ferrara on monastery matters."

Bowing and scraping, the innkeeper replied, "Such an honor to have such an esteemed guest. Prior, today, I am pleased we can offer you Soave Farmer's Special, Tuscany Hills Winged Delight, and the daily special."

"What is the Tuscany Hills Winged Delight?"

The innkeeper, with an Italian flare that over the centuries would become world-famous, replied, "Stuffed pigeon."

Lorenzo, always the critical thinker, asked, "With what is the pigeon stuffed?"

"I don't know. I'll go ask the chef." But as the innkeeper turned to leave, Lorenzo, who had a schedule to keep, stopped him and said, "No, no, no, that's fine. I'll have that."

When the innkeeper returned shortly with Lorenzo's meal, he also brought a goblet of wine. Presenting it with a humble smile and a slight bow of reverence, he said, "Please. The inn's pleasure."

Lorenzo offered a tiny hint of a smile and nodded his thanks.

As the innkeeper walked away, Lorenzo lifted his goblet, took a sip of his wine, and then looked at it somewhat bewilderedly, thinking, "This doesn't taste like Chianti." He just shrugged, took another sip, and began his meal, which he found surprisingly delicious for such a little village.

Finished, he went to the innkeeper, now sitting at the reception desk, and said, "If you could please have my horse brought from the courtyard, I will settle my account and continue on my way." Then, almost reluctantly, Lorenzo added, "The stuffed pigeon was stuffed well."

"Thank you, sir. Give me one moment, and I will have your horse brought out for you." He disappeared through the door behind the desk for only a moment before returning, settling into his chair to present the tally.

"Okay. That will be half a florin for the horse care …"

Lorenzo immediately thought, "The horse must have had the organic hay,"

The innkeeper continued, concluding, "And that will be two and a half florins for the meal."

"Two and a half florins?" Lorenzo protested. "That seems quite expensive for a village meal."

"Sir, we are a completely self-sustaining community. We receive no papal subsidies whatsoever."

Lorenzo thought, "Always looking for handouts from the Church, aren't they?"

The innkeeper's words, "Plus, we import our wines," only increased Lorenzo's displeasure.

Outraged, Lorenzo protested, "But you said the wine was compliments of the inn!"

"Oh, sir, it is! But in order to do that, we have to charge more for the meals!"

Lorenzo begrudgingly slammed three gold florins on the desk, turned, and left.

Outside, he unhitched Between Thieves and put his left foot in the stirrup; then, as he spread his legs to mount, he unintentionally released an audible and prolonged burst of gas, the spirit of a stuffed pigeon winging its way back to the winds.

Looking around and seeing there was no one to witness his graceless exit, he sat tall in the saddle and made his way out of Soave with greater ease than he had making his way into it.

There was only one problem. Actually, there were three. Their names were Alfonso, Alessandro, and Niccolò.

Lorenzo had just left the inn and rounded a corner, and only the heavens knew who was more surprised: he or they.

While he had the advantage of horsepower, they had the advantage of weapons; Lorenzo's only weapon was less effective in situations like this, a letter in Latin they could not read. Their swords came out, and even Between Thieves felt nervous surrounded by thieves.

Alfonso, the leader of the three and the one best equipped with a brain, was the first to speak.

"Well, well, well, Prior, isn't fate a mysterious thing indeed." Alfonso's sword, while not quite at Between Thieves' jugular, was in easy striking range. He wanted neither to startle the horse nor give him room to escape.

"I see you still have what belongs to us. A horse."

Lorenzo, practiced in the art of on-the-spot scheming, replied, "Is that all you're after? A horse?"

Alfonso looked him straight in the eye and replied, "With a dash of revenge as interest."

Lorenzo's scheming was already two steps ahead of Alfonso's.

"So what would you have then? The brief satisfaction of short-lived revenge and one horse between the three of you. What then?"

Alfonso didn't answer because he sensed Lorenzo was going somewhere with this. His thief's instinct told him the pot was about to be sweetened.

"Why settle for a horse when instead you could have significant sums of money?"

"We're listening."

"I am after the very thing you were after when you tried, unsuccessfully, to rob that tradesman and his guard. That failure lost you this horse and … What was your colleague's name?"

Alfonso turned to Alessandro and said, "What was his name?"

Alessandro turned to Niccolò. "What was his name?"

Niccolò replied, "Heinrich."

Alessandro turned to Alfonso, saying, "Heinrich."

Alfonso turned to Lorenzo and said, "Heinrich."

"Heinrich," Lorenzo confirmed.

Niccolò then added, "I think."

Lorenzo looked at Niccolò, replying, "I'm sure you do."

Although the three had not sheathed their swords, Lorenzo had captured Alfonso's full attention.

"That item you were after was, for most purposes, quite worthless."

The three thieves looked at each other, and each—with varying degrees of capacity—was trying to figure out how they had lost three horses, a sum of money, and a colleague for something worthless.

Lorenzo provided the answer: "But it is worth considerable money to me. Money I can get, given my credentials, from almost any financier in the Holy Roman Empire."

This was a subtle way of communicating that he was not carrying this money and therefore would be pointless to rob right there and then. He was, after all, between thieves.

Lorenzo told the group about Antonio and Gabriele, explained their destination, and concluded with the unfortunate point that they had a lead and that the four of them would have to make good time.

Alfonso stated the obvious, or what he thought was the obvious. With a what-do-we-do-now shrug, he said, "We'd have to buy horses."

Lorenzo began to reply, "My dear … I'm sorry, what's your name?"

"Alfonso. This is Alessandro and Niccolò." They all nodded polite hellos.

"My dear Alfonso. Why buy a horse when you can rent one, ride it into the ground, and then return it?"

It was that quality of thinking that would spawn the birth of the insurance industry.

"And I can help with that."

In a mere two hours, they were all mounted and about to leave Soave when Alfonso turned to Lorenzo and said, "In our business, you'll also need a sword."

"Good point."

"Yes. Let's hope it has one."

The Understanding

North of Verona, Italy

March 6, 1461

It had not rained in over a fortnight, so the banks of the Adige River were dry, and crossing at a shallow ford would be easy for the horses even when bearing passengers.

As they reached the stream, Antonio and Gabriele dismounted and led their horses, and themselves, to water.

The forest's edge was just a few hundred yards past the stream's northern shore. Here, the river was narrow and shallow, and Antonio and Gabriele knew to take advantage of a stream or river's passing favorable conditions rather than waiting and risking the difficulties of rising water, should it rain.

Gabriele looked skyward and, seeing a thin band of cirrus clouds advancing from the east, said, "Best we cross today."

"How far to Trento, do you guess?"

Gabriele referred to the crumpled chart and shrugged. "Three to five hours. I only know this forest trail from what others have told me. It's a winding and hilly path, but its other side borders Trento's southern edge."

Then, with a small, subtle smirk, Gabriele added, "And I understand travelers are well-fed by clergy at the Trento Cathedral."

"I'm sure Twice and Thrice will appreciate our effort to reach there today. As I am sure we will, too." Antonio mirrored Gabriele's smirk as they mounted and took their reins. They rode their horses across the stream and made their way to the forest's edge.

The forest trail was hard to see. A few hundred feet from the forest's edge, they stopped as Gabriele scanned the landscape while referring to the chart.

THE TYPO

The sun was beginning its late afternoon decline, promising the golden hour, prompting Antonio to ask, "Are there meadows in this forest should we need to bed for the night?"

"Antonio, horses are not comfortable being tied down in a forest at night."

Scouring the forest edge, Gabriele added, "Nor am I, for that matter."

Then, scanning, the guard spotted it. "There's the trail."

Gabriele and Antonio left the open, well-lit field for the forest shadows. Not only was the setting light creating a different world but so also was the emerging sound. Twice and Thrice's breaths became more pronounced, more audible over a bed of early-spring insect mating calls, nocturnal bird screams, and a world coming alive when it felt the world should settle for rest and peace. Shadows from the retiring late afternoon sun were becoming longer.

And darker.

Were it not for a rising full Moon, the forest's narrow trail would have melted into the ever-darkness of what moments before had been evergreen.

Suddenly, all the forest's nocturnal sounds, owls' cries, and even their horses' breaths seemed to fall silent.

What followed was the soft sound of footsteps breaking the forest's fallen leaves and twigs. A sound not from one direction but from all.

Then the first growl.

Instinctively, Antonio began to gently stroke Twice's neck.

Antonio softly but urgently instructed Gabriele, "Calm your horse. Calm your horse."

Wolves.

They seeped out from the trail's edges from all directions, moving slowly, circling them.

Facing them was the pack's leader.

Calmly, Antonio twice repeated, "Calm Thrice." Then he added, "And yourself."

The pack's leader had now moved from the forest shadows to the moonlit path, teeth bared, growling, saliva dripping from its lips. It was clearly guiding the pack in for the kill.

While continuing to stroke and calm his horse, Antonio slowly and carefully dismounted while maintaining eye contact with the wolf pack's leader.

As his feet grounded, Antonio lifted his arms perpendicular, hands outstretched, and faced the circling pack—never breaking eye contact with the pack's leader, whose growling and aggression had become increasingly pronounced.

Antonio squatted little by little, bending at the knees, bringing himself eyeball-to-eyeball with the wolf. Creature to creature. Spirit to spirit.

While stroking Thrice's neck, calming the horse, Gabriele muttered, "Jesus Christ."

Without breaking eye contact with the wolf, Antonio softly responded, "He's not here right now."

Antonio and the wolf remained locked in eye contact. Then, millimeter by millimeter, millisecond by millisecond, Antonio eased one outstretched hand to face the pack's leader and then extended the back of his hand toward the wolf's face. And teeth.

Neither broke eye contact with the other, but the wolf inched forward, then slowly and cautiously sniffed at Antonio's outstretched hand. For a moment, the pack's leader just stared at Antonio; then it glanced at the horses and Gabriele before looking back again at Antonio.

Then, slowly, the wolf backed away, turned, and slipped back into the forest, vanishing into the cloak of darkness.

Its pack followed.

For several moments, Antonio remained crouched, listening to the forest.

As the nocturnal sounds came back to life, Antonio got up and climbed back into his saddle.

He turned to Gabriele, smiled, and said, "They must feed well in Trento. It seems the wolves weren't that hungry."

Gabriele watched as Antonio settled into his saddle. Then the guard asked, "Who taught you that skill?"

"It's not a skill, Gabriele. It's simply an understanding."

As they made their way along the narrow moonlit trail, Gabriele was in the rear, studying Antonio, thinking, "And trust."

"Yes. Trust. Can I trust him?" the guard wondered.

WILLIAM LOWER

Sick and Tired

Monastery of St. Augustine

March 7, 1461

The journey from Trento to Bolzano was an ambitious trek. While the valley provided inspiring views of the towering mountains, the road became rugged at times, and their focus was on balance and control of Twice and Thrice.

Antonio and Gabriele talked little through this leg of their journey; both focused on the obstacles speed eating into their finite supply of daylight.

Though occasionally rugged, the road was the primary route for travelers and merchants; and where travelers and merchants existed, so did bandits.

They passed travelers both on foot and horse, and Gabriele paid close attention to men approaching on horseback, always issuing the same command to Antonio as they approached: "Be alert." As men on horseback approached, Gabriele would take the reins in one hand with the other hand on the sword's hilt. Bandits would always approach in a friendly manner, trying to engage their target with idle, harmless greetings intended to make the target believe they could let their guard down. The bandits would pass their targets casually, feigning friendliness, but the moment they passed, they would swiftly make an about-turn and attack from behind.

Gabriele had drilled the ways of bandits into the artisan traveling companion's head. "Antonio, on roads such as this, I trust no one on horseback, not even old women."

Antonio chuckled and said as if perhaps Gabriele was being overly suspicious, "Old women?"

Gabriele returned his gaze and, without a trace of a smile, replied, "How do you know they're women?"

People on foot, although not completely immune from suspicion, were not as great a concern to Gabriele. In that situation, besides swordplay skills,

Gabriele also had the advantage of a horse. But even people on foot were scrutinized for any sign of a crossbow under their cloak.

On the road, Gabriele was always on guard, relaxing only when there was no sign of other people and no place along the trail where bandits could stage an ambush, such as from behind the boulders ahead or from the shadows of a tree grove.

Gabriele was mindful of daylight, trying to formulate a plan in the event darkness appeared before the sight of Bolzano. The trail was narrow in places, making encounters with people traveling in the opposite direction an intimate affair, especially if the approaching travelers were traveling by wagon—precisely as the ones approaching them were at a particularly narrow stretch of the trail. Gabriele, always watchful, took a hand from the sword's hilt at the sight of two children sitting beside their father; they were either fighting or playing, so often hard to tell with children, but they were animated. Unlike with horses, it has always been a challenge to harness a child's energy.

Gabriele knew from other travelers they had passed that the village Egna was on the route to Bolzano, but the guard was unsure of its distance, what accommodations they might find, and what meals the village might have for both them and their horses. Gabriele decided to ask the man with his bouncing children as they maneuvered around each other on the narrow trail.

With a smile, Gabriele began what would be a limited conversation with a lighthearted remark of their situation: "Tight through here! I understand there's a village called Egna ahead. Would you know how far and where we might stay and get something to eat there?"

The man smiled and replied, "*Es tut mir leid, aber ich spreche kein Italienisch. Ich habe das Wort 'Egna' erkannt, weil wir gerade von dort kommen, aber darüber hinaus fürchte ich, dass ich Ihre Frage nicht verstanden habe. Könnten Sie mir bitte helfen?*"

Knowing Antonio's language skills, Gabriele replied to the German, "*Un moment, s'il vous plaît,*" and, with only a tinge of desperation, called Antonio following directly behind.

With no room to ride Twice between the wagon, Antonio had to dismount but didn't mind since a stretch of the legs was always welcome after hours in a saddle. Gabriele explained the language barrier and told Antonio what had been asked. Antonio turned to the German, thinking to himself he would welcome the opportunity to practice his German language skills— but hearing his mother tongue, the man spoke so quickly Antonio struggled to understand half of what he said. But the two muddled through and, at the conversation's end, bid each other a fond *"Verabschiedung"* as the wagon squeezed by. The German family continued their journey, leaving Antonio and Gabriele to do the same.

"What did he say?"

"He said Egna is about an hour from here, and there is an inn called Gasthof zur Sonne he preferred over the other inn, Osteria del Vino, because he preferred the food at the Gasthof zur Sonne, particularly the *speckknöde*. He also suggested we not leave Egna before sampling a glass of Gewürztraminer and said that he doesn't speak French."

"What does French have to do with it?"

"I have no idea."

Gabriele looked at the sun to the west. One hour to Egna. Eat and have the horses fed and watered and try to make it to Bolzano that day? There would be a full moon, which would make some night travel possible.

Gabriele moderated an internal debate: "Why the hurry? Because we lost time. Whose time? Everyone's. But whose time matters?" Gabriele thought for a moment. "Antonio's time. I know he worries about what will await him after a lengthy absence. Is that your problem? It shouldn't be. But why do I feel it is? Because you're letting your emotions get in the way. Just do your job," the guard thought.

The trail had widened, and Antonio was able to ride beside Gabriele. The sun shone low over the western sky, casting a golden light on the mountains to the east, adding to their majesty. It also cast a golden light on Gabriele, riding to Antonio's right.

After riding silently for a mile, Antonio, staring at the mountain backdrop behind Gabriele, said, "Beautiful."

Gabriele turned and looked at the vista, marveling at its beauty and majesty but also conscious of what this beautiful golden light meant. The view would dim from sight as the sun sank lower and lower over the horizon.

Gabriele turned to Antonio and said, "How do you feel about riding with only moonlight to light the way?"

"For how long?"

"Maybe three hours."

"The horses need to be fed."

"So do we. Maybe we can try whatever it was that the German pilgrim suggested, get the horses fed and rested, and then push on. The terrain should be easy following the valley."

As they approached Egna, little of the sun's golden light was left, but the full moon was just breaking over the horizon. They would not be riding in the dark.

The narrow, twisting cobblestone street was lined with mostly two-story Gothic-era stone houses painted in a random array of primary colors, with a smattering of the modern Renaissance influences on the occasional building.

The village was small, as was the town square. The restaurant was easy to find. The stable for the horses' care and feeding was directly across the square, and the stable's keeper assured Antonio and Gabriele they would be attended to immediately. Gabriele had a talent for making requests understood as instructions.

The Gasthof zur Sonne was a welcome break from hours in the saddle. The dining area had a welcoming roaring fire, and though it was small and clearly popular with the locals, two tables were vacant. About twenty people sat at tables, all in animated conversations. Two tables were occupied by four men each, and judging by their girth, they were most likely farmers. But regardless of their vocations, it was clear they were fond of German cuisine. These were not small men. Couples occupied the other tables, and Antonio and Gabriele found seats at a table by the window. Tapestries hung on the inn's stone walls, and Antonio pointed out to Gabriele the difference between Egna's artistic style and Florence's.

As a rotund waiter approached the table, Antonio posed a dinner-related question to Gabriele.

"Should we ask about the specials?"

"Antonio, that has not served us well in the past. In the interest of time, perhaps we should ask for the special and dispense with its description."

When the waiter arrived at the table, Gabriele said, "We'll have two of your daily specials."

The waiter, somewhat surprised, asked, "Don't you want to hear what it is?"

Antonio glanced at Gabriele, then turned to the waiter and replied, "Certainly. Tell us about your daily special."

"Speck."

"Speck?"

"Speck."

"Okay, we'll have two orders of speck."

"Anything to drink?"

"Two glasses of your house wine." Turning to Gabriele, Antonio added, "It might help us stay warm for the ride."

As the waiter turned to the kitchen, Gabriele said, "You didn't even ask what that was."

"Would it matter?"

"You're right. Most likely not."

They ate quietly and quickly, and as they ate, several times Gabriele glanced out the window to the rising moon. The mountains lining their trail would block the light sooner than if they were trailing over open farmland.

Antonio looked out the window and made a remark about the moon's beauty, then turned back to Gabriele, asking, "Are you not worried about bandits, traveling at night?"

Gabriele smiled and replied, "Antonio, generally people don't travel at night. With no one to rob, why would bandits be out there? Besides, at night you'll find most bandits in taverns being served and serviced by barmaids."

"I never thought of that."

With a smirk followed quickly by a glance back at the meal, Gabriele quipped, "You never thought of being serviced by a barmaid?"

It was more than a humorous line. For Gabriele, it was a probe. Over the days, the guard had felt Antonio's gaze without even seeing it, sensing his attention. And although Gabriele made every effort to keep a distance (with varying degrees of success), the guard was beginning to have a recurring thought: "He prefers men." Then self-discipline immediately kicked in. "Not my concern. Not my business."

Gabriele stood up abruptly, assuming command again and walking to pay the bill, again taking the lead. "Come on. Let's go."

It wasn't long before the little village of Egna had faded from view and they rode alone through a moonlit mountain valley pass. The valley comprised only meadows and fields ending at the base of the surrounding mountains. There were no forest groves, no threats—at least, none that could be seen.

However, more than the sun had gone down. So had the temperature.

"Are you cold, Antonio?"

"Yes, a little."

Self-admonishing, Gabriele said, "I wish I had thought to take a moment to haggle with one of those street merchants we saw in Egna selling blankets. Another might have helped."

Through the icy-cold night air, following a moonlit mountain trail, they rode, often covering a couple of miles before speaking. Riding side by side, Antonio could hear Gabriele's teeth chatter as the cold settled in, slowly making its way to the guard's bones.

Antonio was not immune to the cold either; after a couple of hours of riding, it was difficult to focus on anything but the desire for warmth. At one point, Antonio asked Gabriele if they should stop and try to get the horses to lie down and curl up against them for their body heat.

"Not a good idea," was all Gabriele said in response. Even speaking depleted energy, and all their energy was needed to keep the body's fire burning.

By the time they reached the Monastery of St. Augustine, the monks had retired for the night. A solitary guard was stationed at the Monastery's entrance, although he, too, had to be woken.

Through chattering teeth, Gabriele informed the guard of their mission from the San Miniato al Monte Monastery while Antonio leafed through his letters of introduction and found the one addressed to the Monastery's abbot.

The guard went inside the dormitory and woke two monks, advising them of the monasterial guests who had arrived. While all guests were welcome, those from another monastery were always treated like dignitaries.

Reading the letter of introduction, written in Latin and signed by Abbot Fransisco himself, got the monks' full attention.

One of the monks turned to the other and said, "Brother Jonathon, please light the fire in the calefactory so our guests can warm themselves from this cold air. And wake another Brother to prepare the guest rooms."

Rooms. Plural. They were indeed being treated like royalty, each being provided a private room. The monk in charge instructed the guard to take Twice and Thrice to the stable and have the stable boy fetch feed and water and cover the horses with blankets. "I am certain they must be cold, as well," he added.

Moments later, both Gabriele and Antonio were standing in front of the calefactory's fire, rubbing their hands together as their bodies began to absorb the fire's heat. Antonio could feel his body loosening and only realized then how his body had instinctively tightened while riding through the cold night air.

Turning to Gabriele, Antonio asked, "Feeling better?"

"Much. Thank you."

They stood facing the fire until a monk arrived to inform them that their rooms were prepared and that their belongings had been brought in from the horses. The thawing duo followed the monk through the biblically illustrated stone corridors to their guest rooms. Though the walls were lined with frescoes and tapestries, none were lit well enough to see the actual designs. The hanging torches had been extinguished for the night, and the only light came from the flickering flame of the torch the monk, who was leading the way, was carrying.

Their rooms were side-by-side and the monk had already lit each room's candle. He informed them he had added an extra blanket for each of them, advised them when to expect morning prayers and breakfast, then bid them blessings and a good night's sleep.

Looking into the room, Gabriele said, "This bed is a welcome sight. I will see you at breakfast. Good night, Antonio." The guard entered the room, smiled at Antonio, and closed the door.

When he was in his room and had closed his door, Antonio realized he had not had a room to himself since Florence, a life that now felt like a distant memory.

He blew out the candle, removed his shoes, and slipped into the bed, grateful for the extra-heavy woolen blanket. Being under heavy wool blankets felt like being in a warm cocoon.

Light from the full moon cast a cold blue light on the room's stone walls.

Nothing hung on these walls except for a small iron crucifix above the small table and chair.

He stared at it for a moment, but his eyes grew heavy, and soon he slipped into another world over which he had no control. A world with a series of incongruous events unfolding in his mind in dreams he sometimes remembered and sometimes did not, dreams that brought guests—some welcome, some not—ushering him through often schizophrenic nocturnal journeys. Though those journeys evaporate into the dawn's breaking light, the emotions dreams stir often remain, sometimes so strongly they dominate a mood for the full following day. Emotions triggered by events, real or surreal, that lie in wait in the subconscious, waiting for their victim to let down their psychological defenses, their guard, as they slip into a restful state of sleep—but not always that restful—as the ringleader-less circus begins its cerebral performance.

So it was that night, with a man luring Antonio from one threatening circus act to another, each with unexpected dangers, each evoking fear. Meanwhile, the man just smiled and laughed, dragging Antonio from one disjointed event to another. That man was Gabriele.

As the morning sun swept the circus back under Antonio's cerebral rug, he stretched his arms, his situational awareness coming back to life as he recognized where he was and why he was there. Clearing his mind, he rose, preparing to join the drone of the morning prayers, have breakfast, and get on their way.

He opened the door to the corridor just as two monks were passing, and he asked for directions to the refectory. Pointing down the hall, one monk said, "This way. Your timing is good, breakfast is about to be served. Please. Come with us. I am Brother Jonathon, and this is Brother Franco." Antonio nodded a hello to them both, told them his name, and walked with them to the refectory, now almost full. This refectory differed from the ones in the San Miniato al Monte Monastery in Florence and the Monastery of San Domenico in Bologna. Rather than being long and narrow, this refectory was shorter but wider. There were two long tables with benches on either side, but the tables' lengths were not the twenty-foot length of the tables at other monasteries.

Scanning the room, he was surprised not to see Gabriele, but he immediately thought, "Still sleeping, no doubt. Yesterday's was a longer, harder ride than most days' have been." He turned to Brothers Jonathon and Franco, excusing himself and advising them he was going to wake his companion.

When he reached the room, he gave a light rap on the door and then opened it. He saw Gabriele still in bed with wet-looking hair, as if the guard had just stepped out of a bath.

"Gabriele, are you awake? Are you okay?"

Answering, Gabriele's voice was weak and soft. "Antonio, Antonio, I don't feel well, and I am so very cold." Antonio stepped to Gabriele's bedside and saw perspiration running from the guard's forehead. Gabriele was clutching the blankets as if clinging to them for life. But that was precisely what Gabriele was doing. Antonio put his hand on the guard's forehead; it was burning with fever. And no one should be cold under two thick woolen blankets.

"I'm sorry, Antonio. I just need to rest for a few more minutes, and then we can go."

"I don't think we're going anywhere. I will be right back."

Antonio darted into his room, grabbed the blankets off his bed, rushed back to Gabriele, and laid his blankets on top of the others.

Weak and almost inaudible, Gabriele said, "Thank you, Antonio."

Antonio felt Gabriele's forehead again. It felt hotter than just a few minutes prior.

"I'll be right back."

Antonio left the room and ran to the refectory, running up to Brother Jonathon and Brother Franco. Turning and seeing Antonio running toward them, Brother Jonathon rose; and as Antonio reached him, he saw the anxiety on his guest's face and asked, "What is wrong?"

"Gabriele … my partner … burning up with fever. Is there someone here who tends to the ill?"

"Brother Jakob, at the next table. Come."

Brother Jonathon rushed to the adjoining table to a tall, dark-haired, thin man in his mid-thirties. Seeing them approach, Brother Jakob stood, obviously accustomed to being approached by someone with urgency.

"Brother Jakob, this is Antonio Strozzi. He and his traveling companion come to us by introduction from Abbot Fransisco of the San Miniato al Monte Monastery in Florence, and his companion, Gabriele, appears to have taken ill. Could you please come to help attend to him?"

By mentioning Abbot Fransisco, Brother Jonathon was communicating these were not just any guests. These were guests that should be granted every courtesy.

"Take me to him." Brother Jakob's voice was soft and low. In response, something was triggered in Antonio, and he thought perhaps it was hope. To Antonio, Jakob's sounded like not only a voice of compassion and care but, more importantly, a voice of confidence.

The three monks, followed anxiously by Antonio, scurried to Gabriele's room. Once there, Brother Jakob took the stool by the room's table, placed it by Gabriele's head, then sat and put his hand on the guard's forehead, saying, "Good morning, Gabriele. My name is Brother Jakob, and I tend to those who become ill in our monastery."

Gabriele replied with a weak, "Good morning."

"Clearly, you have a fever. What other symptoms are you experiencing?"

Gabriele's eyes darted around the room, seeing who would listen, then weakly replied, "I have made several trips to the necessarium, and I generally ache all over. I am weak. Making it to the necessarium was difficult. I'm sorry."

"Sorry? Sorry for what?" Brother Jakob replied. "More than a person's soul is provided sanctuary here in our monastery. The vessel carrying that soul, the body, is as well." Turning to Brother Jonathon, he said, "Have someone fetch two buckets of water, one at room temperature and the other cold from deep in the well, as well as some cloths and a cup for drinking."

Brother Jonathon hurried out the door and as he did, he turned to Brother Franco and said, "Have someone go into town and fetch Hans Müller. Ask that he come immediately. Inform him we suspect a case of pestilential fever in a very important guest."

Within a second, Brother Franco was out the door. Then Brother Jakob stood, announcing he was going to fetch some items from their infirmary. As he walked out the door, Antonio followed him and closed Gabriele's door behind him.

"Brother Jakob, before you go, please, a couple of questions. First, what is 'pestilential fever'?"

"It is a disorder that attacks a person's intestines first, often followed by other bodily ailments and, sometimes, failure."

"Failure. What does that mean, 'failure'?"

Brother Jakob paused for a moment, looking Antonio in the eyes, then replied, "It means they are delivered to God."

"Tell me, Brother Jakob, of the people who develop this fever, do any manage to postpone their meeting with God to a future date?"

"Oh, yes. Some do."

"Are you able to tell who is likely to survive and who is not?"

"Antonio, if you could tell that, your name would spread across the land as quickly as this fever itself. I have not heard of an elderly person surviving pestilential fever." Then, with a reassuring smile, Brother Jakob added, "But Gabriele is not elderly, is he?"

What Gabriele had was not pestilential fever, as Brother Jakob said it was, but rather typhoid fever, which was not identified until the nineteenth century.

Brother Jakob was about to walk away, but Antonio stopped him with one more question. "This Hans ... who is he?"

"Hans Müller. He is Bolzano's apothecary. He is the only one I know of, next to God, who can perform miracles."

"Is that what this will take? A miracle?"

Smiling, Brother Jakob replied, "We all believe and trust in the power of God. But it doesn't hurt to have a miracle tucked up your sleeve from time to time, does it?"

Antonio watched Brother Jakob walk away down the stone-wall corridor —a corridor lined with frescoes and tapestries, each depicting important biblical stories that, in their totality, were supposed to answer one simple question.

Why?

Antonio had read and illustrated the Bible's stories many times over, and in his mind they failed to do that.

He shared that belief with no one.

Antonio stepped back into the room to see Gabriele showing no signs of life. His heart pounded for a split second until he saw the guard's chest slowly rising and falling with each labored breath.

Antonio sat on the stool by the bed and took his partner's hand, hot to the touch. Feeling him, Gabriele turned, eyes only halfway opening and a small smile fighting to reach out to the world from behind the fever's delirium, and said, "You're still here? Don't you have more important things to do?"

"At the moment, no."

Lorenzo Catching Up

Verona, Italy

March 7, 1461

Lorenzo, riding Between Thieves with his new band of thieves, was eager to learn if anyone had seen Antonio and Gabriele in their travels. He asked everyone he encountered about them. He found the response from the guards at the gates to Verona peculiar.

"Oh, you're referring to the one with the sword! Yes, they went through here the day before yesterday." The guard then glanced at Lorenzo's sword and chuckled. "Odd," Lorenzo thought.

Two days. Lorenzo was trying to keep up the pace, but the thieves' horses were not as swift as Between Thieves; yet, there was nothing he could do about that other than push for a longer day of riding, which he was doing.

Alfonso rode beside Lorenzo, with Niccolò and Alessandro trailing behind.

Their abruptly formed partnership, borne when the thieves were looking to retake the horse they believed belonged to them and get a taste of revenge, began with understandable awkwardness; a monastery prior and a band of thieves on a mission together.

Passing through Verona, Lorenzo stopped to inquire at each of the three inns, and his stop at the last of the three bore fruit. Gabriele and Antonio had stayed at The Adige River Inn. Alfonso, hoping to call it a day and inspect the local taverns and their barmaids, said presumptuously, "So then, we're settling here today?"

"No. We push on."

Crestfallen, with dreams of wine and barmaids vanishing, Alfonso let out a heavy sigh. He followed Lorenzo to their horses, and they began their foray to Trento.

Spring was displaying its annual signs of hope: green clusters of grass sprouting between the patches of receding, melting snow. Hope springs eternal annually, only to be vanquished later by the crushing blow of arctic air. Hope, like life itself, is cyclical.

Alfonso and Lorenzo's initial conversations were stiff; what does a thief say to a monastery prior, and what is the content of a prior's small talk with a thief?

"So when did you begin ... you know ... banditry?"

"What many people, and I suspect you as well, fail to understand is that this is simply a business. Some people are shoemakers. Some people are bandits. It's just business. Do you think a shoemaker gets up in the morning and says, 'I can't wait to make another pair of shoes today?' No. It's just a business. As is mine. I suspect, in your shoes the shoemaker made for you, you'd say I have fallen out of favor with God."

Lorenzo turned and looked at Alfonso, replying, "It doesn't matter if you think you have fallen out of favor with God. How would you know? But you don't want to fall out of favor with the Church."

Alfonso returned Lorenzo's stare and then, smiling, replied, "All the more to prove my relationship with you is a sound business decision."

Lorenzo returned the smile, commenting, "I must admit, for a bandit, you seem quite shrewd."

"It's not shrewd. It's strategic. Every business venture I undertake is strategic. Is this person I am considering robbing worth the risk?"

Alfonso continued to expound his theories and views on strategic banditry, sounding every bit like how you might expect a Harvard MBA to speak today.

"Those two behind us?" He gave a nod to the pair trailing behind. "They're no brain trust, but I can trust them to do what I tell them to do. Doing this on my own would not be very profitable. I need them, and they need me. Much like you need us, and we need you." Staring philosophically to the sky, deep in thought, he added, "Prior Lorenzo, when viewed strategically, most decisions in life are business decisions, right down to timing when to go to the necessarium—with the exception of in emergencies. Decisions in emergencies are rarely strategic. Those are usually a matter of survival."

Niccolò and Alessandro followed behind, just as they followed orders.

Both were shorter, scrawny men and both came from Bologna. At five foot five, Niccolò was the taller of the two by one inch. They had known each other since childhood and had played childhood games of stealing food from street venders' stalls. While it was a game, it was a game borne from need. They each came from large families of small means. Meals at their homes were free-for-alls with the horde of brothers and sisters fighting over what little food made it to the table.

Their childhood vendor-robbing game evolved into a vocation, and they fed and clothed themselves through their honed skill of robbery. Their technique was standard fare: one would distract the vendor through a variety of methods while the other scored the hit.

 It was during one vendor-robbing episode that Alfonso discovered them. He had watched them in operation and followed them after they made their escape. While they could sprint to make their escape, they didn't have the stamina of long-distance runners. Alfonso caught up with them after a couple of blocks, invited them to a tavern for a wine, and recruited them. As a one-man operation, Alfonso knew he had to expand his capabilities if he was going to expand his business. Niccolò and Alessandro were an investment: they needed both horses and swords, and those were substantial expenses. But they brought loyalty. And Niccolò and Alessandro were eager apprentices; they followed Alfonso's instructions and orders without question. For them, this was career advancement. They were no longer petty thieves; they were now bona fide highway bandits.

Riding behind Alfonso and Lorenzo, mile after mile, hour after hour, all they could see was Alfonso's one free arm—sometimes waving in the air during his animated monologues—and their horses' asses with their periodic dumps.

Niccolò turned to Alessandro and asked, "What do you think?"

"What do you mean, what do I think?"

"About this?"

"What about this? What this is that?"

"About what we're doing?"

"We're not doing anything."

"I know. That's what I mean. What do you think?"

"About doing nothing? I hadn't given nothing much thought."

"We're not doing anything."

"Yes, but we're being paid."

"Not much. And at least when we rob someone and get just a little, we don't have to spend hour after hour with them, day after day with the person we robbed like we have to with this Lorenzo guy."

"Alfonso says the real money comes when we catch those other two, that guard and the other guy. Alfonso knows what he's doing."

"Tell that to … What was his name?"

"Heinrich."

"Yeah, tell that to Heinrich."

"Poor Heinrich. He was just trying to impress Alfonso."

"Yeah, and that guard was such a skinny, nothing-looking guy. Have you ever seen anyone handle a sword like that before?"

"Never."

"I think that might be why Alfonso didn't engage. And I think Alfonso wants more than money from this."

"What do you mean?"

"I think he also wants revenge. Alfonso can get real pissy if he thinks someone's got the better of him. Remember that horse trader guy?"

And so their journey went. One of the many unsolved mysteries of the human experience is how someone who knows almost nothing can talk about nothing endlessly, all day long.

In front of them, although it was a long day's travel on horseback, Lorenzo was enjoying the fresh spring air and the scents erupting from nature, which were bouncing back to life after a dreary, dormant winter.

Listening to Alfonso, Lorenzo found himself surprised learning about the strategic thinking that went into banditry. Always strategic, he was equally surprised at the respect he was gaining for Alfonso. "How odd," he thought.

As they rounded a corner in the trail, the Monastery of St. Augustine came into view on the horizon.

Almost as if the question were strategically crafted and timed, Alfonso asked, "Where do we intend to bed for the night?"

It was a good question. Traveling by himself, Lorenzo would arrive at any monastery's door, introduce himself (by title, of course), and receive comfortable quarters and food for himself and Between Thieves. However, seeking such courtesies would prove awkward when arriving truly between thieves.

"Trento. I will need to attend to some business there, and we'll stay at an inn. I'll get a room and find one for you and …" His voice turned to a whisper. "What were their names again?"

"Niccolò and Alessandro."

"Right. Your colleagues. And a stable for our horses, of course."

The business Lorenzo needed to attend to was quite simple. He needed money. This was where his weapon revealed its power: an open-ended line-of-credit letter, backed by the Medicis, would end his shortage of funds in short order with but a quick visit with anyone servicing the financial needs of merchants or nobility in Trento. While he was not nobility per se, with a letter showing Medici backing, he practically was. With the needed funds, he could continue his journey, stay at monasteries en route while parking his colleagues at inns, and perhaps, while visiting monastries, he could recruit others to support his mission to have the Church maintain control of ecclesiastical matters.

As they rode past the Monastery, Lorenzo glanced at it. He wondered if stopping to inquire about Antonio and Gabriele would be a good idea but quickly dismissed the thought. How would he explain his company of thieves? Besides, it seemed Antonio and Gabriele were avoiding monasteries. They had bypassed the Monastery of San Domenico in Bologna. Better to inquire at the inns in Trento.

The ride into Trento's center provided a spectacular mosaic composed of Romanesque and modern Renaissance architecture propped against a backdrop of the towering Alps. Lorenzo cast a longing glance as they passed the Trento Cathedral with its Romanesque façade and its prominent bell tower, wishing he could indulge in a visit. But he couldn't while with thieves and with a schedule to keep. How far had Antonio and Gabriele gotten? Lorenzo, riding Between Thieves between thieves, crossed the Ponte del Duomo, leading them into the town's center. Lorenzo turned to Alfonso and instructed, "Let's find an inn and get settled. Make sure the horses are cared for while I attend to some business. If we're lucky, the innkeeper might have seen those two."

They weren't lucky. At least not in that way. They were all tired of riding, so they stopped at the first inn they found in the town center. It was a rather plain and somewhat tired three-story Gothic structure, unembellished and uninspiring, but it would suffice. Lorenzo asked for two rooms: one for three thieves and one for a monastery prior, although that is not how he explained it to the innkeeper. The innkeeper had no recollection of two men fitting Antonio's and Gabriele's descriptions, but he did know of two people working in the local market area who provided financial services to merchants and nobility. And how to find them.

And find them Lorenzo did. Of the two, the one most receptive to his Medici-backed letter was a short, skinny, beady-eyed man approaching his forties. He was happy to meet Lorenzo's needs at an almost reasonable exchange rate, not that the interest charges interested Lorenzo. His, at least in his eyes, was a monastery mission; and for those matters, money was no object, especially since it was someone else's.

"Ultimately, the Church will thank me," Lorenzo thought as he made his way back to the inn, comfortable now that he had a way to pay for it. "I'm certain of that. I'd bet money on it." He had. Only it wasn't his money.

When he reached the inn and stepped into the lobby, he looked to the right into the dining area, expecting to see his colleagues. After all, they had all mentioned several times during the last few hours of their journey how hungry they were.

The dining area was empty. Lorenzo turned to the innkeeper, who had hardly noticed Lorenzo's presence, and asked if he knew his colleagues' whereabouts.

"Oh, they went across the square to the tavern. To get something to eat."

Lorenzo was conflicted over where to park his suspicions about his colleagues' motives. The fact that the inn's dining area was empty? The inn was rather drab. It was possible the food could be,too—or even inedible.

He went across the square to the tavern, and opening the door was entering another world. While the town square was serene, inside the tavern was the opposite, as if the door were not only soundproof but also a portal to another dimension. With a beam-strutted, low ceiling and a roaring fire, the room had maybe fifteen tables, all overcrowded with an incongruous assortment of characters who seemed to have only one thing in common: they had all consumed a lot of wine. Consequently, whatever was being discussed was funnier, judging by the enthusiastic laughter; and in order to be heard, everyone was trying to talk over the laughter, which somehow seemed to make things funnier by the minute. Except to Lorenzo. He scanned the room and spotted his three business partners at a corner table, laughing like everyone else. Alfonso had his arm around the waist of a barmaid, who was also laughing, although whether that was to increase the customer's gratuity or propose after-hours services was unclear.

Everyone was laughing. Except Lorenzo.

He squeezed his way through the crowd (who would have no chance of escape if the fire were to spread beyond the fireplace, he noted), arrived at his partners' table, and caught Alfonso's eye. Alfonso greeted him cheerfully with, "Lorenzo! Lorenzo! Pull up a chair and join us!" Turning his attention to the catch in his arm, he added, "This is Maria. Maria, this is my friend and business partner, Lorenzo."

"*Mucho gusto!*" Maria greeted.

Lorenzo, skilled at concealing seething rage behind spurious smiles, produced one as he nodded to Maria, thinking, "Great. And now a Spaniard in the works. How strategic."

Looking around the room and then back to his trio of thieves, Lorenzo said, "Alfonso, I am glad you and your colleagues have been able to get some well-earned relaxation, but I think we should return to the inn, perhaps get something to eat there. It's so busy here it might take a long time to get food, and we need to rise early tomorrow and push on. We have a long trip ahead of us."

Alfonso sighed, turned to Maria, and said, "My darling, perhaps later we can meet." Then he stood up, with Niccolò and Alessandro following suit like baby ducks following their mother, and the quartet pried themselves out of the rollicking tavern's grasp and returned to the glum and lifeless inn.

The dining area was still unoccupied, so they took the table closest to the fire, and Lorenzo waved to the innkeeper for attention. The innkeeper left the reception desk and as he reached the table, he said somewhat apologetically, "We only have our daily special today, I'm afraid."

Foolishly, Alfonso asked what it was, but since it was all they had, what did it matter? Shrugging and again sounding apologetic, the innkeeper replied, "Stuffed pigeon."

Quickly, Lorenzo replied, "Four, please." Stuffed with what was of little consequence. The innkeeper then retreated through a door behind his reception desk leading to the kitchen.

As the four shuffled in their seats, Lorenzo, not accustomed to wearing one, was trying to adjust his sword to make himself more comfortable. Alfonso, seeing Lorenzo's inexperience, asked, "Has anyone ever taught you anything about how to use that?"

"Not really, but I have been to a few swordplay tournaments and watched quite attentively."

"Tomorrow, before we leave, we'll spend half an hour in the courtyard so I can teach you at least the basics. Nothing is more dangerous than drawing your sword and not knowing how to use it."

"I look forward to it," Lorenzo lied.

When the innkeeper arrived, balancing four bowls, he asked as he served them to the guests, "Would you care for wine with your meal?"

Lorenzo and Alfonso both replied, Alfonso saying, "Yes," while Lorenzo replied, "No." There was a brief stalemate as Lorenzo and Alfonso stared at each other, but it was Lorenzo who held the trump card.

"It's not in the budget."

Alfonso just sighed and turned to his meal.

The four ate in silence for several minutes until Lorenzo said, "It tastes like no pigeon I have ever tasted before."

Relieved it was not just his lack of experience eating a meal comprising more than one ingredient bringing him to the same suspicion, Alfonso enthusiastically agreed, "That's what I thought, too!"

Once their meals were finished, they got up and walked up the narrow, dimly lit wooden stairway to the second floor and their rooms, the three thieves to one and Lorenzo to another.

"You are probably not accustomed to the discipline of rousing as early as we do in the Monastery, so I will wake you at dawn." As if he could read Alfonso's mind, which, in fact, he was, he added, "And leave Maria for another time. Get some sleep. You will need it."

The three disappeared into their room, and watching to ensure their door remained closed, Lorenzo stood for a minute until the room fell quiet. Lorenzo then adjourned to his quarters.

Lorenzo Learns Swordsmanship

Verona, Italy

March 7, 1461

Alfonso felt as if he had just fallen asleep when there was a rap on the door followed by Lorenzo sticking his head in the room, announcing, "It's dawn; time for us to get going. I will meet you downstairs in the dining area and I will order breakfast for us."

The only thing that could have gotten the trio to rise more quickly than the promise of food would have been the promise that Maria was waiting downstairs to service them.

As he made his way down to the main floor, Lorenzo pondered the discussion he had the day before with Alfonso, wondering to himself if the promise of food was shrewd. Or strategic?

That was academic. All that mattered was that it worked.

The four quickly and silently ate their breakfasts, which consisted of an egg, what appeared to be a slice of ham, and a small assortment of pickled root vegetables.

Once he was finished, Alfonso took charge. He turned to Lorenzo, pointing to his sword hanging from his belt, and said, "I will have Niccolò and Alessandro fetch and saddle our horses while I teach you a little about how to use that thing."

Alfonso led the way out of the inn's rear doorway leading to the courtyard. The door to the courtyard was a flimsy, arched wooden door; and although it was open when they entered the courtyard, Alfonso, smiling to himself, turned and closed it.

"I'm going to enjoy this," Alfonso chuckled to himself.

"Must I?" was Lorenzo's thought.

Lorenzo was not the least bit comfortable with the schooling he was about to receive, and wishing to avoid the experience altogether, he said to Alfonso, "Isn't this what I have you and ... What are their names?"

"Niccolò and Alessandro."

"Yes, your colleagues. Isn't that what you three are for?"

"Tell me, besides being a monastery prior, are you also a predictor of the future? You don't know what we might encounter on our journey, and neither do I. Do you really want to be completely unprepared?"

If there was one thing Lorenzo found distasteful, it was enduring the experience of having to admit someone else was right. Like right now.

Reluctantly, Lorenzo unsheathed his sword and said, "Okay. What's first?"

Alfonso sighed and said, "Put that away."

Frustrated and confused, Lorenzo re-sheathed the sword and stood facing Alfonso, feeling very much like a scolded school child. And not liking it in the least.

"Lorenzo, the first thing you need to learn is how to use your feet. Come. Stand beside me and match my footwork."

Lorenzo joined Alfonso, standing side by side with him, facing the outer courtyard wall.

"I am going to attack my target, but watch my feet and move the way I do."

As Alfonso stepped forward, he hopped from one foot to the other, standing on his right, then left, then right again, and then left again.

As Lorenzo tried to mimic the move, at first he lost his balance and fell over.

"Get up, and let's do that again." Alfonso demonstrated, moving slower so Lorenzo could study and mimic the move.

"Again."

"Again."

With each demonstration, Alfonso quickened the pace until Lorenzo could keep up.

As Lorenzo's ability to keep up with Alfonso improved, he felt proud of himself, thinking, "Yes! I can do this!"

Satisfied, Alfonso said, "Not bad, Lorenzo. You know why we do this move?"

Lorenzo just stared and said nothing, thinking only that it reminded him of exercises the monks occasionally did in the Monastery courtyard.

"To cause confusion. Your target doesn't know how you're coming at them. You know it's working when you see fear in your target's eyes. Then you make your next move."

"Next move? What move?"

"The kill."

"The kill?"

Lorenzo lamented to himself that he thought his life in the Monastery had spared him the messy and distasteful work of combat and warfare.

"You leap forward and go right at them. Like this." Alfonso showed his hopping maneuver, then suddenly leaped forward.

So began that practice.

Three buildings down on the other side of the courtyard, a villager was standing at her second-floor bedroom window, watching. She called to her husband. "Heinrich, come here. Look at this." Her husband came to the window, and together they watched as Alfonso and Lorenzo practiced their moves.

She then asked her husband, "Have you ever seen people dance like that before?"

"No. I've heard of it. But I've never been to Hungary."

In the courtyard, Alfonso and Lorenzo took a break, leaning up against the courtyard's stone wall. Alfonso, sensing Lorenzo might think the lesson was over, said, "Now we're going to try those moves with a sword in our hands."

Lorenzo swung a look at Alfonso and asked, "Do you do this every day?"

"Of course not. Only when I'm robbing people, and even then, only when a person doesn't voluntarily surrender their money."

Alfonso, sensing Lorenzo's reluctance, said, "A little practice and we'll be on our way."

Alfonso stepped back from Lorenzo, sword unsheathed, and said, "Unsheathe your sword."

Nervously, Lorenzo drew out his sword, not knowing what was going to come next. Whatever it was, he was not looking forward to it.

"There are some basic attack moves. The overhand cut is when you're striking right from above, aiming for the head or shoulders." Then Alfonso demonstrated a swift blow through the air from straight above.

"Now you try it."

Lorenzo was self-conscious and feebler in his demonstration but mimicked Alfonso's example as well as could be expected from someone more accustomed to quill pens and ink than flesh and blood.

"Well, at least you get the idea. Now, a move if you're looking to catch someone off guard is the undercut to the lower body. It's a surprise no one enjoys."

Alfonso's demonstration only further raised Lorenzo's frustration and anxiety.

"Now, you show me the move."

Lorenzo's display of the move was both slow and awkward, only furthering Lorenzo's sense of inadequacy: a feeling he deeply resented.

Alfonso could sense this and didn't want to push Lorenzo too far. He was, after all, the one who held the purse.

"Two more basics. The middle slash goes for the torso or arms."

Watching Alfonso show the move, Lorenzo thought, "This is so distasteful. There are much better ways to get money than through ways like this."

Lorenzo's demonstration of the move was clumsy, and Alfonso tried not to laugh, merely commenting, "That one is going to need some work. Okay. Last, we have the most basic attack maneuver. It's a straight thrust right at your opponent. It's simple. But you have to keep the attack going no matter how your opponent tries to defend themselves. This move can be tricky."

Still at her bedroom window watching the spectacle, the villager called out again to her husband. "Heinrich, come here! Now they're fighting!" Her husband came back to the window, and together they watched Lorenzo and Alfonso practice sword moves.

"Yep. Definitely from Hungary."

Back in the courtyard, after demonstrating the thrust, Alfonso said, "In reality, Lorenzo, the most important thing you need to know for survival is defensive moves, the parries. Blocking against strikes from above, below, and the side—and, most importantly, the thrust coming straight at you."

Stepping back, Alfonso said, "I'll show you. I want you to come at me with the thrust movement I just showed you."

"Alfonso! These are real swords! I do not wish to become injured because of training that is most likely unnecessary!"

Alfonso replied, raising his voice, "I'm just trying to teach you skills to stay alive!"

Lorenzo put his foot down. "That's what I'm paying you for! It's your job to keep me alive!"

"And what if I'm dead? Then what are you going to do? Perhaps you have the power to raise me from the dead. Will that be your salvation?"

And so a heated argument began over life and death, roles and responsibilities. An argument that grew louder second by second.

At her bedroom window, still watching, the villager called out again to her husband. "Heinrich, come here! You're not going to believe this!"

Her husband shuffled back to the window and looked to the courtyard. Hearing the argument even from three houses away, he shrugged and said, "That's the Hungarians: dance, fight, and end up just arguing."

After several bouts of going-nowhere arguments, Lorenzo said, "Let's just call it a day and get on with our day. Agreed?"

"Agreed."

They were soon saddled and went from inn to inn to find out if anyone had seen two men matching Antonio's and Gabriele's descriptions.

No one had.

The Apothecary

Verona, Italy

March 9, 1461

The covered horse-drawn carriage pulled up to the Monastery of St. Augustine entrance. Brother Jakob rushed to open the carriage door, and out stepped a tall, thin man with a full head of thick gray hair, a leather satchel slung over his shoulder. He was well into his sixties and bore a sage look—patient, but with purpose. Brother Jakob reached out to shake his hand, saying, "Herr Müller, so good of you to come on such short notice."

Müller's voice was low and deep, and he spoke slowly. His gaze made it appear that no matter what he was doing, he was always deep in thought.

"My duty. Please. Take me to your patient."

There was an urgency to Brother Jakob's pace, and Herr Müller, with his long, spindly legs, had no problem keeping up; in fact, it appeared this was his normal walking pace.

As Brother Jakob opened the door to Gabriele's room, Antonio jumped and introduced himself to Apothecary Müller.

Gabriele lay sleeping, a cold, damp cloth covering the guard's burning forehead. Two buckets of water were at the bedside, with a drinking cup in one.

The apothecary looked at Antonio and asked, "What is our patient's name?"

"Gabriele."

"Would you mind if I took your seat at our patient's side?"

Antonio leaped off the stool. "Of course not!"

The apothecary's voice was low, lilting, and calming.

On every visit he made, Müller knew he had two types of patients. The first was the person afflicted, and the other was the group of family or friends at the bedside tending to the patient, themselves suffering from heightened anxiety whether they recognized it or not. His calming voice was his treatment for them, and in his satchel were herbal remedies for a variety of afflictions he encountered in his practice. While others believed in bloodletting for treatment, he did not.

"God has given us cures for all that affects us. They are there in nature. It is our job to find them," was his message to all a patient's friends and family.

Müller turned to Antonio and asked, "What have been Gabriele's symptoms?"

As Antonio spoke, Müller stared intently, nodding, conveying his understanding. When Antonio finished his briefing, Müller turned to Brother Jakob and instructed him, "Please bring me two cups of heated water. Bring the water to a boil first, then bring them directly to me along with two spoons. And bring a little honey. The herbal treatments I have are healing, but they are not that pleasant tasting."

Brother Jakob responded, "Right away," and rushed out the door.

Alone with the apothecary, Antonio asked, "Herr Müller, what do you think?"

Müller looked at Antonio and then turned his gaze to Gabriele. Reaching for the cloth on Gabriele's forehead, he dipped it into the bucket of the colder water, then placed it back and replied with questions, not answers.

"Has Gabriele been drinking fluids?"

"Yes. Water mostly, but he was able to take tea a little while ago. Then he fell back asleep."

"Tea. That's good. When Brother Jakob returns with the hot water, I'll prepare some of my … tea," he said with a smile.

"What is it?"

"These are herb blends I have brought from Bologna. A gifted herbalist in the area develops recipes known for miraculous results."

Concerned, Antonio asked, "Is that what Gabriele needs? A miracle?"

"That is a question I am not qualified to answer. I don't know the workings of miracles. Only herbs. Don't forget who gave us nature, Antonio. He who gave us everything."

Antonio turned his gaze to Gabriele and thought, "Did He give us illness, as well?" But that was not a question to ask in a monastery.

The door opened and Brother Jakob came in carrying a tray with two cups of steaming water, a small bowl of honey, and two spoons, all as requested. Brother Jonathon followed.

"Good! Set them here beside me." Müller opened his satchel and retrieved two pouches, each with a unique blend of herbs. Curing herbs, he mentioned to Antonio. He poured two spoonfuls from one pouch into one of the steaming cups, added honey, stirred his blend together, and glanced over to his patient. He leaned closer to Gabriele and gave a little shake of the guard's shoulder, calling softly, "Gabriele ... Gabriele ... I have something for you to drink. Can you sit up?"

Slowly, Gabriele's eyes opened, and there was a look of surprise at seeing a room full of people when it seemed only a minute ago Antonio was the only one there.

Gabriele looked at Antonio and asked, clearly confused, "How long have I been sleeping?"

"A couple of hours. This is Apothecary Müller, and he has some tea that should help you feel better."

Gabriele began to sit up but struggled, and Müller reached to help.

Once the guard was sitting up, Müller handed over his steaming tea, instructing, "Drink this. This is what your body needs."

Gabriele took a slow sip, and a face of complete bewilderment with a dash of displeasure followed. "What in the name of God is this?"

Even Müller let out a little laugh, remarking to Antonio, "In my experience, seeing the return of a sense of humor has often been an early sign of recovery."

Then Müller turned to Gabriele, adding, "It may taste like it came from the necessarium, but it's what your body needs. Drink up."

Gabriele followed the apothecary's advice, finishing the drink and then handing the cup back to Müller while wearing the look of just having taken a large bite of a very sour apple.

"Good. Now I am going to prepare another drink for you to take in an hour."

"Better or worse?"

"Better. Or so I have been told."

"You mean you've never tasted it?"

"Gabriele, for some reason that's a mystery to me, I never get sick. I've taken a sip and have not minded it, but I've never had to drink an entire cup of it. But you do."

Müller took the second cup of hot water, mixed in herbs from the other pouch, and stirred in some honey. When everything dissolved, he stood up, turned to Brother Jakob, and said, "Repeat this two-drink regimen this evening before Gabriele settles for the night. Then again in the morning."

Müller said he would return the following day to check in on his patient, and as Brother Jakob was about to escort the apothecary out, Antonio said, "Brother Jakob, could you have my bed brought in? I'll stay with our 'patient.'"

"Certainly."

Once they were in the corridor, Brother Jakob quietly asked, "So, what do you think?"

Hans Müller gave a little shrug. "I always try to determine if there are signs indicating whether one will make it. So far, I cannot identify those signs. He's young. That's in his favor. And he is alive well enough to know my teas are not the best-tasting beverages." Smiling, he turned to Brother Jakob and said, "Come to think of it, that might be one of the evidence-determining factors I'm looking for. Unfavorable responses to my teas' taste."

Brother Jakob smiled.

Müller, at the door now, parted, saying, "I think we will know in the next day or two which direction he's heading. Keep him in your prayers."

Brother Jakob brought Antonio's bed into Gabriele's room, and Gabriele downed the second cup of less bad but still bad-tasting tea and was soon in slumber again. Antonio had fresh, cold deep-well water brought in and continued to keep a cold cloth on Gabriele's forehead.

Antonio would sleep for an hour, wake up, and change the cold compress. This continued through the night. At dawn's breaking light, Brother Jakob arrived, entering the room after a light knock on the door.

"Antonio, join the Brothers in the refectory for breakfast. You need to eat. I will watch over Gabriele until your return."

Antonio stood, cast a glance at his sleeping partner, then asked Jakob to fetch him if there were any signs, good or bad. Assured after Jakob said he would, Antonio left the room and walked down the stone corridor, studying the frescoes and tapestries as he walked. He knew the stories depicted and knew what those stories were supposed to teach. Supposed to. How many times had he labored over pages, telling those stories one letter at a time, spending days, sometimes weeks, on just one story?

He knew the stories and saw them for what they were: stories.

In the refectory, he ate in silence, looking only at the food on his plate. The morning's reading was simply background noise to the thoughts that screamed in his head.

And the more he thought, the more confused he became. The image he could not avoid or erase from his mind's eye was Gabriele lying motionless on the bed. How many times did he suddenly flinch, thinking Gabriele was no longer breathing?

Slowly eating his modest monastery breakfast of fruit, a little cheese, and bread, he took one grape at a time from his plate and chewed on them slowly, forcing himself to consider the possibility that for the remainder of his journey, he may be alone. He struggled to take his emotions, lock them behind a door, and think rationally. What would he do? Go back? Or continue on? As he deliberated over his options as a lone traveler, he accepted his reality.

There was no going back.

Go back, having lost the abbot's most trusted guard and having failed to have "the book" corrected? No, there was no going back. How would he continue alone?

He would just have to find a way. It was as simple as that.

Antonio forced himself to keep his emotions in check. With breakfast finished, he returned to Gabriele's room to see Brother Jakob on his knees in prayer at Gabriele's bedside. Seeing that, the air was suddenly sucked out of Antonio's lungs.

Gabriele was dead. That was all he could see, watching Brother Jakob kneeling in prayer at Gabriele's side.

Seeing Antonio, Brother Jakob stood and said, "How was your breakfast?"

Antonio couldn't even speak.

"I took the time for prayer while you were gone. We never know if our prayers are heard, but we do know they can't hurt."

Antonio glanced over and saw Gabriele's chest slowly rising and falling.

"Jesus Christ," he thought.

For the next two days, Antonio sat by Gabriele's side, refreshing the cold cloth compress and preparing Hans Müller's teas, taking it as a good sign that Gabriele complained more about the taste.

At times, when Gabriele was sleeping, Antonio would just stare at his patient, his feelings becoming more and more complicated. "But he's a man," Antonio would think, and another voice in him would answer, "So what?"

Hans Müller would make a couple of visits during the day, caring for the patient while also trying to ease Antonio's worry.

Brother Jakob would frequently stop in, now with the routine of bringing not just Gabriele's cups of hot water for the medicinal herb concoctions but also food for Antonio. Antonio had politely asked to stay by Gabriele's side. Secretly, he did not want to leave and walk back in to find someone kneeling at Gabriele's side in prayer, as if he were praying to God to accept the soul of their departed servant.

That instant—that split second when he found Brother Jakob kneeling in prayer at Gabriele's side and Antonio had believed that Gabriele had died —made Antonio realize that if Gabriele were to die, he wanted to be there holding his partner's hand. Antonio hoped that by holding Gabriele's hand, even in unconsciousness Gabriele would know, would be able to sense that he died loved.

Late in the afternoon of their third day there, that possibility seemed more probable: Gabriele's fever was causing delirium. No longer in this world, Gabriele was calling out from another world, the past world and the pain points in the guard's life, particularly in childhood. "Why can't I have a mother?" "Do you miss her?" "Tell me again! Tell me again! Tell me again what she was like!"

Antonio remembered hearing about Gabriele's father from the talks of their childhoods; when Gabriele asked why he had not remarried, he had answered, "How could I do that? I am still with your mother."

Antonio thought, "Delirium purges all of life's pain points. That purge, is that so you can go free?"

Gabriele became quiet again. The disjointed soundtrack of a life lived stopped playing. But Gabriele's chest continued to slowly rise and fall.

Late in the afternoon of the third day, it happened as if water doused a fire.

Gabriele's fever broke.

Climbing out of the stupor of delirium, Gabriele sat up, turned, looked at Antonio, and said, "Are you still here?"

Antonio smiled, looking at Gabriele—who looked every bit like a wreck —and replied, "Yes. And I'm glad you are, too."

CAT AND MOUSE

LORENZO'S HUNT

Innsbruck, Austria

March 9, 1461

The ride toward Innsbruck, Austria, from the south provided one of the most spectacular vistas in the known world. Nestled in the Tyrolean Alps, the town provided a different approach to color than Lorenzo's hometown, Florence. While colorful with a myriad of hues—unlike Florence, where primary colors were the norm—Innsbruck's traditional use of more pastel colors created a more sublime beauty, most striking during the day's end, when post-sunset unveiled a cobalt-blue sky backdrop to Innsbruck's multicolored pastel enclave. Lorenzo admired the beautiful town from afar.

However, as their trek brought them gradually closer to this stunning vista, it was not what Lorenzo could see that he focused on but what he could not: Antonio and Gabriele.

The journey from Trento to Innsbruck was slower paced than the previous leg. Lorenzo wanted to stop at each of the monasteries en route to inquire about Antonio and Gabriele. He would have his thieves wait out of sight of the monasteries, giving them and their rented, overworked horses time to rest while he made inquiries.

The town of Bolzano created the greatest delay. There were several monasteries in the area, each requiring a visit, and in Bolzano was a fork in the road. Which route would they have to take to reach Innsbruck? That town was all but guaranteed to be a stop on their journey to Mainz.

He sought the prior at each monastery, wishing to be on equal footing with whom he spoke. As peers, conversations would be more relaxed and most likely less formal than when he spoke with monks beneath his station.

During conversations with his peers, he steered discussions toward Gutenberg to gauge their sentiment and subtly planted seeds of potential doubt.

The more he left monasteries empty-handed, the more active his scheming mind became. His first stop was the Franciscan Monastery in Bolzano, now over two hundred years old; while Gothic in its origins, it was being modernized with fresh coatings of frescoes. The monks and, indeed, its prior were congenial and inviting. They took pride in their aid and commitment to the community's poor. "Book of Luke, Chapter 4, verse 18: how ironic," Lorenzo thought.

Although Lorenzo was casting bait for the prior's thoughts on Gutenberg, the prior did not bite. Asked about Antonio and Gabriele, the prior said that he had not seen nor heard anyone mention two men fitting Lorenzo's description.

With a sigh and a practiced expression of gratitude, Lorenzo thanked his fellow prior for his time and courtesies. After they gave each other blessings, Lorenzo left, mounted Between Thieves, and rejoined the thieves, saying only, "Nothing. Let's continue."

The next stop was the Dominican Monastery on the Piazza Dominican, conveniently close to the Cathedral of Bolzano, which meant Lorenzo had two stops in one.

The Dominican Monastery was an architectural marvel with but a single nave in its original design and octagonal pillars supporting its vaulted ceilings. A monk welcomed Lorenzo, then escorted him to meet with the monastery's prior. As they walked through the corridor, artists were at work creating modern frescoes along the stone walls. Lorenzo always applauded the Church's modernizing to remain relevant to the populace it served. To a degree. Taking too much liberty could undermine the Church, Lorenzo believed. Following this line of discussion with this monastery's prior bore a little more fruit than Lorenzo's conversation with the prior at the Franciscan Monastery. This prior responded, "Yes, we must always be conscious of potential consequences from hastily made decisions." The conversational door to a discussion on Gutenberg did not open. And his host had not seen or heard of two travelers fitting Antonio's and Gabriele's descriptions.

With two stops in Bolzano proper, Lorenzo granted his thieves a temporary reprieve of visitation rights (and funding) to the tavern in the town square.

While he very much needed them, he also welcomed a respite from his loquacious new comrade, Alfonso. "If banditry was not his vocation, he certainly could have found a home within the Church," Lorenzo mused.

It was on his walk from the Dominican Monastery to the nearby Cathedral of Bolzano that Lorenzo's musing took him to fresh thinking.

It struck him that perhaps he was overlooking the obvious. Man's nature to be self-serving was a building block for the Church. Applying guilt to man's nature was profitable.

Made to recognize reality and reality's threat to his instinctive self-serving interests, perhaps Lorenzo could turn Antonio from an adversary into an ally. Why had he not thought of this before? He dismissed this oversight, blaming it on his pious servant's role within the Church. "It's just not my nature to be self-serving," he thought.

By the time he reached the steps of the Cathedral of Bolzano, he had also reached the conclusion of taking another tack.

The visit to the Cathedral of Bolzano bore no more fruit than any of his other monasterial visits.

Through the power of his deductive reasoning, he realized he had no way of knowing if he was behind or ahead of his prey.

How would he know for certain? After all, anything is possible in the universe of the unknown.

From that insight, he bore a plan. Actually, it was merely an addendum to an existing plan but could still prove useful. He would put this plan into action at the next monastery stop and at every monastery stop.

The next monastery stop would be the Muri-Gries Monastery, but before he continued his trek he would have to extricate his faithful (faithful as long as they were being paid) comrades from the town square tavern, just steps away from the Cathedral of Bolzano. Funny, he thought, how easy it was to find a tavern in such proximity to so many churches and cathedrals.

Finding the tavern was easy. It was the only building in the town square with a sign that included the word "tavern"; it was a single-story stone building with a simple, small wooden door entrance. Anyone six feet or taller would have to duck to enter.

Although it was the middle of the day, the tavern's minuscule leaded-glass windows provided little light for its interior; so when Lorenzo opened the wooden munchkin door, it was, once again, as if he were opening the portal to another dimension.

Flickering candlelight supplemented the limited daylight, and although it was midday, one could easily conclude that no men in Bolzano worked. Men and a few select women packed the tavern, everyone laughing, with some yelling to be heard over the wine-induced merriment.

Lorenzo, however, was not amused.

Now, as was becoming his instinct, he looked in the tavern's corners to locate his travel companions. Sure enough, there at a corner table laughing like everyone else was the trio. As to be expected, Alfonso had his arm around the waist of a barmaid or some such service provider.

Lorenzo squeezed his way through the crowd, arriving at his partners' table, now appearing like a predictable apparition whose sole purpose was always to ruin the party. He caught Alfonso's eye, and the thief greeted him cheerfully, "Lorenzo! Lorenzo! Pull up a chair and join us." Turning his attention to the catch in his arm, he added, "This is Catalina. Catalina, this is my friend and business partner, Lorenzo."

"*Mucho gusto*!" Catalina greeted.

Lorenzo sighed, thinking, "Now another Spaniard in the works."

"Alfonso, I am glad you and your colleagues have been able to get some well-earned relaxation, but we must be on our way."

Alfonso sighed, turned to Catalina, and said, "My darling, perhaps another time." Lorenzo led them out of the tavern to the harsh reality of midday sunlight, Alfonso, Niccolò, and Alessandro following suit, as always, like baby ducks following their mother.

The trip to the Muri-Gries Monastery was short, but the stay there was not. Lorenzo could have left his comrades at the tavern and returned to retrieve them later, but by that time, they would most likely not have been able to sit in a saddle without falling off. The ride was less than thirty minutes, but just before reaching the Monastery, Lorenzo dropped off his band of thieves in a clearing and instructed them to wait until he returned. He knew they would lie in the grass and sleep off the tavern's entertainment.

Dismounting, Alfonso, comforting Lorenzo, said, "Take your time. Don't worry about us." Lorenzo was not the least bit worried: he held the purse. And without the purse, they had no way to finance a return trip to the tavern unless they were to rob someone, which Lorenzo had forbidden while under his employ.

The approach to the Monastery was a striking sight of the old blending with the new. The church itself and its bell tower were less than fifty years old, but they were built on a much older structure dating back over two hundred years—a nobleman's fortification now donated to the church, the nobles no longer needing to fortify themselves from pesky armed neighbors near and far.

Vineyards, just beginning to show signs of spring growth, occupied the land surrounding the Monastery.

Several monks were tending to the fields, and one turned to greet Lorenzo, offering a warm welcome. Lorenzo never wasted much time; he introduced himself by title and asked if he might speak with their prior.

Monks were never slow to bow to seniority. They welcomed Lorenzo, then advised their prior of his visit.

Lorenzo did not wait long before the welcoming monk returned with his prior in tow.

After introductions and blessings, Lorenzo got straight to the point.

It was no surprise to learn the Monastery's prior had not seen or heard of two men matching Antonio's and Gabriele's descriptions. Lorenzo then asked if they might have paper, ink, and sealing wax so he could leave a letter for his friend in the event he showed up on his journey. He actually needed several pieces of paper in order to leave messages at each monastery.

The prior showed Lorenzo to a guest room with a table and chair, provided Lorenzo with his writing materials, and left him to compose his correspondence.

With the guest room door closed, a stack of paper in front of him, a lit candle for the sealing wax, and a jar of ink, Lorenzo settled in his chair, thinking of how best to word his letter.

His first instinct was to compose it in Latin as he did all his writing, but just as he was about to put quill to paper, he stopped.

No. Too formal. Antonio would expect that from Lorenzo. Perhaps plain Italian would be better. More friendly. More conversational. More personal. More intimate. And reading something in plain Italian would surprise Antonio and possibly disarm him.

What salutation? "My Dear Antonio"? No, that might do more harm than good. "Greetings, Antonio"? No. That might sound like he's coming from another planet. After considering many salutations, each with its own sense of perversity, he elected to keep it simple.

"My Esteemed Antonio,

"I trust this letter finds you well, though I imagine your days are stressful, being absent from your vocation, which has made you so revered. It is precisely your brilliance that compels me to write—not as an adversary but as someone who admires your dedication and shares your concerns about the future.

"Antonio, think about the so-called marvel of Gutenberg's press. A marvel, they say—but at what cost? When I learned of your discovering Gutenberg's blasphemous flaw, I could not help but wonder what thoughts passed through your mind. Did you not see how that dreadful contraption could one day render your sacred craft obsolete?

"I write to you not to alarm but to enlighten. We are not so different, you and I. Both of us serve higher purposes—yours is your devotion to your craft, and mine is my duty to safeguard the Church's authority over the sacred Scriptures we both value so much.

"Antonio, we face a common threat. If this printing press is allowed to proliferate unchecked, what will become of us? Of you? Will there be any need for master illustrators if books are churned out by machines?

"Antonio, I believe we are on the same side in this matter. You may not see it yet, but our fates intertwine. Together, we can ensure this mechanical menace does not undermine the divine order we both hold dear. I admire your loyalty to the abbot—it is a quality I respect deeply—but consider this: loyalty does not mean blind submission. Sometimes, true loyalty requires us to act in ways that protect those we serve from threats they cannot yet perceive.

"I propose an alliance—not one bound by formalities or declarations but by mutual understanding. Let us work together quietly, subtly, to expose the flaws in Gutenberg's creation. Let us remind the world why the human hand—the artist's hand—cannot be replaced by cold machinery. You have already uncovered its imperfections; let us use that discovery as a foundation for something greater.

"I know this may seem bold, even presumptuous. But think about it, Antonio. Think about what is at stake—not just for you or me but for all who cherish beauty and divinity in their purest forms.

"I eagerly await your thoughts.

"Yours in shared purpose,

"Lorenzo"

Though it was long, Lorenzo thought the letter struck the right balance and might strike a chord with Antonio.

Pleased with himself, he began to write multiple copies of the letter he could leave at each monastery he visited. The irony that Gutenberg's press would have made his task much easier escaped him.

He thanked his host, regrouped with his comrades-in-arms, and pushed on.

Each stop at monasteries en route to Innsbruck bore the same results.

Brixen Cathedral, Säben Monastery, Novacella Abbey, and finally, the Stams Monastery were all stops on the way to Innsbruck. The Cistercians, Augustinians, Franciscans, Dominicans—no channel to the divine was overlooked in the search for Antonio and Gabriele.

While the search bore no results, Lorenzo was now leaving breadcrumbs at every monastery he visited. And he would continue to do so at every monastery stop en route to Mainz.

Due to the many stops, the quartet was late arriving to Innsbruck but not so late that the three thieves' heads didn't turn as they rode past a tavern, making note of its appearance for navigational purposes. Lorenzo had informed them he would find an inn for them while he sought accommodations at the Franciscan Monastery, which was only blocks away from Innsbruck's town center.

Neither the three thieves nor Lorenzo was sorry to bid each other a good night.

Bible Studies

Augsburg, Germany

March 11, 1461

The journey was tiring, and they still had hundreds of miles ahead of them. Sitting in the saddle hour after hour, day after day, took its toll on them physically. Instinctively, usually in an inn's courtyard or a monastery's cloister, Gabriele would do back stretches and yoga-like exercises to preserve and restore the spine's integrity. Antonio copied the movements one day and instantly recognized the relief they provided, which prompted him to ask who taught Gabriele these techniques. Somewhat bewildered by the question, the guard replied, "Taught? No one taught me this. If you pay attention to what your body is telling you, it will just come to you." After thinking about Antonio's question for a few more moves, something occurred to Gabriele, prompting the question, "Do you think there are people who pay to be taught this?"

"There are," Antonio replied.

Gabriele's thinking was centuries ahead of its time. Beyond anyone's imagination in Gabriele's epoch was that a communication channel would be created that would allow people to view these exercises in their own homes—after agreeing to monthly payments for guidance on how to do these simple, instinctive-if-you-listen-to-your-body exercises. Fees that would renew automatically and almost require a court order to cease, thus paying for a person's exercise routine for eternity (or until they no longer have a bank account). This concept was beyond anyone's wildest imagination in that era. Theirs was not an advanced civilization like the one we are fortunate to live in today.

What Antonio and Gabriele were tasked with remedying was but an incidental flaw in what would ultimately change the course of history. Knowledge and information would no longer be controlled and held beyond the walls of money only nobility and the Church possessed.

Whether Lorenzo knew of the larger implications of his desire to keep control of the Scriptures within the Church, only Lorenzo's ghost knows.

Control information and communication, and you control society.

After a long day's ride and a welcome dinner, Antonio and Gabriele retreated to their room at Augsburg's Finest Inn. They put their saddlebags at the foot of their beds as they did every night, then Gabriele turned to Antonio and said, "All the evenings we have occupied ourselves reading from Gutenberg's creation, I have never seen its actual mistake. Show me this flaw."

Antonio always enjoyed poring over the tome's pages, studying how letters were crafted, planning the spacing of type, visualizing colors to be used, determining where decorative type was appropriate and pleasing to the reader and where not. He enjoyed poring over Gutenberg's Bible.

Carefully untying the cloth's binding and unwrapping the book, he picked it up, gently turning the pages until he reached page 149. Then he pointed to the Book of Luke, Chapter 4, verse 18.

"There."

Looking at the page somewhat in awe, Gabriele asked, "I am still amazed you can read all this. You understand all of it?"

"Every word."

"I can't imagine how these pages came off a contraption of some kind. Can you describe it? How does it work?"

Antonio described all he had heard and learned of Gutenberg's invention to the best of his knowledge, never having actually seen one.

"How long would it take for that machine to print this page?"

"After the type is placed on the plate for printing, maybe the time it takes to light that candle."

"Really?" Even though Gabriele knew little of the publishing industry, it was easy to imagine the time difference between a machine and a professional illustrator producing the same outcome.

"How long would it take you to create a page like this?"

Antonio studied the page, looking at the details and the use of illuminated initials, gauging time, and replied, "Two or possibly three days."

"What do you think about all day while doing this?"

"I think about what the words mean, what they say."

Staring at the page, which could have been written in Greek instead of Latin and Gabriele wouldn't have known the difference and the guard commented, "That's right. You can read Latin."

Gabriele stared at the page in silence, then asked, "You understand every-thing written in this book?"

"I know what it says. I would not say I understand."

"In church, when priests read from the Bible, it often sounds like music but without an instrument, just the human voice. You never understand what they're saying, but it always sounds like the voice of authority."

Staring again at the page, Gabriele took the book and randomly opened to another page more to the front of the book. Then, pointing to the text, the guard said, "Okay. What does this say?"

Looking at the text Gabriele pointed to, Antonio burst out laughing.

"What's so funny?"

"Gabriele, you may have skills in games of chance."

With Antonio still chuckling, Gabriele asked again, "What's so funny?"

"What you have turned to is one of the pillars of the Bible's story. Randomly, Gabriele, you turned to Genesis 1, verses 26 to 27, which reads: 'And God said, Let us make man in our image, after our likeness … So God created man in his own image, in the image of God created he him; male and female created he them.'"

"Yes, that is what the priests mention in some sermons."

"Yes, that is what they mention," Antonio repeated. Looking at him, Gabriele sensed there was something Antonio was not saying.

"Why? What is it about that?"

Just as he had wondered before he embarked on this journey if he should just have kept his mouth shut, Antonio now wondered if he should have just kept the book shut. Because now, he found himself at the gates to the sacred grounds, the sacred, well-guarded grounds of what he believed. It would take centuries of Gutenberg's influence to have some people (not all) realize you can't believe everything you read.

"Oh, nothing. I just found it amusing that simply by chance, you opened to that passage."

Guard-like and focused, Gabriele stared at Antonio, then finally said, "Antonio, do you know what skill I have developed as a guard?"

"No, what is that?"

"The skill to recognize when someone is not telling me the truth." There was a small smile on Gabriele's face.

So there he was; the gates flung open to his sacred grounds, with no one there to guard it. Antonio looked out the window at the town square below. Lamps and candles were lit in windows in the buildings surrounding the square. A few merchants, dressed for the colder weather, still had their stalls open for business, hoping to entice some of the day's last stragglers before closing up shop.

Antonio turned back to Gabriele and said, "Remember when you asked what I did, what I thought about when I worked on manuscripts? I told you I think about the words I am creating. I disappear into the stories I am telling. You remember that, correct?"

"Yes."

"Let me ask a question: do you believe in God?"

"Yes, of course! Everyone believes in God ... except for maybe witches and people like that."

Antonio stared at Gabriele, recognizing he was about to grant entry into his sacred grounds, realizing that to do so exposed him to very real risks.

They sat there just staring at each other, each trying to read the other's mind. Then Antonio just spat it out: "Do you think God is that stupid?"

"*What?*"

"Think about it. That statement tells us one of two things: If God created man in his image, then God is flawed because we certainly know man is. Or that statement is in reality just a reflection of man's arrogance, claiming we are like gods."

Gabriele, pointing to the Bible, said, "Go back to where you found the mistake here."

Antonio turned to the page he knew too well, page 149.

Pointing to the error, Gabriele said, "If they consider this blasphemy, what do you think they'd think about what you're saying?"

"Oh, I'd be burned at the stake along with the witches."

Gabriele laughed and replied, "Well, if they try, I'll bring a bucket of water to save your wretched soul."

"Make it holy water. Just to be safe."

Gabriele closed the book and suggested Antonio provide "interesting" reading each night on their journey, suggesting it could just be the entertainment they needed.

After blowing out the candles and settling for a night's sleep, Gabriele spoke through the darkness.

"Antonio?"

"Yes?"

"I think I'm going to go to hell."

"Why do you say that?"

Chuckling, Gabriele replied, "Because I had never thought of it, but I found what you said somewhat amusing."

"Then we're both going to go to hell. But first, we have to get to Mainz."

Unshared Secrets

Lugano, Switzerland

March 13, 1461

Antonio lay with his eyes open, staring at the ceiling in the darkness of their inn's room, which looked out to the town square below and Mount Brè in the background.

But that view was now shrouded in the evening's darkness. If he looked out the window, he might have seen some lamps burning in the buildings' windows below in the square. But the heavy drapery was closed, which helped keep the cold out.

Somewhat.

Tapestries depicting various biblical scenes covered their inn room's walls; these tapestries offered warmth against the Swiss-mountain winter night rather than any spiritual merit.

Gabriele was asleep in the bed across the room. They were lucky. Although not a luxurious inn by any standards, it had feather rather than straw mattresses. A luxury.

Still, he couldn't sleep. He couldn't understand what was happening to him. Was he falling in love with a man? Now, every time he looked into Gabriele's eyes, he had to look away out of fear that Gabriele, looking him in his eye, would see his attraction, his feelings.

Antonio used to tell himself he was in love with Andrea at the bakery, but now he recognized it for what it was: sexual want. Now he found himself sexually attracted to his guard, not because Gabriele was a man but because of how he was feeling. He had an ache for Gabriele, an ache new to him.

He found himself watching Gabriele's every movement, every gesture, being drawn in by every move until Gabriele would turn to say something to him; then he would quickly turn away, not wanting Gabriele to see that he had been watching every move, savoring every gesture, hungering to reach out and hold him.

For a moment, toying with the idea of honesty, he wondered what would happen if he just told Gabriele how he felt. No sooner did the thought enter his head than there, in the darkness, in the stillness, in the quiet of this Lugano night, he soundlessly laughed to himself, wondering if doing that would cause him to have the same fate as the thief who tried to rob them. With the self-deprecating humor only a dark, forlorn, rejected lover can have, he thought to himself, "Oh well, at least it would be quick."

Light was clawing its way around the edges of the window's coverings, indicating that soon they would collect their things, wash up as best they could, have a quick breakfast in the small dining area on the inn's ground floor, do the usual morning's half-hour fencing lesson in the courtyard, and be on their way.

Gabriele stirred, stretched, then sat up.

"Antonio, are you awake?"

"Yes."

"How did you sleep?"

"Oh well, you know."

"Yes, I know. Even though my bed at the Monastery is but a wooden-frame bed with a straw mattress, it is my wooden-frame bed with a straw mattress."

Antonio sat up and turned to sit sideways on the bed facing Gabriele. For a moment, he just stared at the guard, a small smile on his face. It was strange how just looking at Gabriele made him feel at peace. Then he said, "So what's first: fencing lessons or breakfast?"

"Half an hour in the courtyard, then we eat, and we go."

The route via Lugano was a longer way to Mainz, but they chose it believing Lorenzo would not. This route would lessen the likelihood of an encounter with him.

Antonio had become more accustomed to wearing a sword on his side. After the incident with the thieves, Gabriele had stopped in a shop in Bologna to purchase two sharpening kits that each included a small whetstone, an oilstone, and a leather strop. Each night, they would use mostly the whetstones to sharpen their blades while they chatted. It became an idle routine.

They collected their things and made their way down the narrow wooden stairs to the door at the rear of the inn's main floor. The door led to the small courtyard and stable where Twice and Thrice were hitched.

The courtyard was enclosed by a small stone wall with iron gates opening to the back lane, which led out to the town's square. It was cold, and each breath they took produced tiny clouds that, within seconds, vanished into the heavens.

As they stepped into the courtyard, Gabriele pulled a sudden surprise attack on Antonio so swiftly that it seemed Gabriele's sword just magically appeared in the guard's grasp. Antonio was totally unprepared and jumped back, startled. Had this been an actual attack, it would have been no contest. He would have been finished.

Gabriele then said, "That can happen anywhere, around anyone carrying a weapon, whether or not you see the weapon."

The guard smiled and added, "I know that was a little unfair, but I wanted you to have a true sense of what a surprise attack feels like."

"You mean like a heart attack?"

Gabriele stepped farther into the courtyard, turned, and said, "Come on, show me what you've got."

Antonio drew his sword almost naturally and began practicing attack moves.

Gabriele easily blocked them but kept repeating, "Again! Again! Again!" On one move, Gabriele commanded, "Pivot! Pivot!"

After twenty minutes, Gabriele said, "Okay, let's go eat."

As they made their way back to the lobby and dining area, Gabriele thought, "He's getting better. Now it might take someone several moments to kill him instead of one."

The inn's dining area was almost full, but Antonio and Gabriele were able to take two seats at a long table where eight other people were already eating. A few looked up and nodded a hello, while others engaged in conversation paid no notice.

The dark-haired, middle-aged woman wearing an apron came to take their order but began by giving them their choices, which were limited. Beer (or herbal tea if they insisted), fresh bread with cheese, ham or salami, or oat porridge, but they had run out of eggs.

An elderly man sitting two seats down and across from Gabriele advised, "The bread is warm, the porridge sticks to your ribs, and the cheese is well aged."

Gabriele thanked him and turned to the waitress. "If it's warm and fast, that sounds perfect."

The idea of fast food was a foreign concept, as it would remain for several centuries, and the waitress, somewhat surprised, replied, "Coming right up!" Then, turning to Antonio, she added, "The same for you?"

Antonio nodded his thanks, and the waitress turned and headed for the kitchen, no doubt to tell the staff about the peculiar request for a speedy meal.

Always on guard, Gabriele had over the years developed a fine-tuned perception of people.

And Gabriele could read Antonio. He was becoming attached. Gabriele caught his glances, observed his nuanced behaviors he may not even have noticed, sensed he was becoming attracted, and it was discomforting. Gabriele kept affection locked in a box.

It never occurred to Gabriele what to do if a man made any romantic advances. It was not something people thought about, but if they did, they never talked about it. Yes, some people whispered about some men being effeminate, and as in any social dynamic, there was always gossip and guessing—but it was not something visible in society. It was, after all, the Holy Roman Empire. No one knew whether God was peering through their bedroom windows. But no one could prove He wasn't.

What would Gabriele do if Antonio did make any romantic advances? The thought of it was causing considerable anxiety and concern. Gabriele stared into the bowl of porridge, eating silently, lost in thought, lost in loneliness. Love was not something Gabriele ever entertained. And with Antonio? The voice in Gabriele's mind raged: "Stop! Get on with your job."

Their bowls and plates now emptied, Gabriele looked up to Antonio and said somewhat abruptly, "Are you ready to go? If we keep up a good pace, we can make it to Kufstein today. Between here and there are mostly mining villages. And you know what miners are like."

"No, actually, I don't."

"You've led a privileged life. Let's go."

Gabriele got up and paid for the meal with Antonio, who was following behind, wondering to himself, "Did I say something to annoy Gabriele?" If there was one thing Antonio had learned through their journey, it was that an annoyed Gabriele was someone to be reckoned with. Take headless Heinrich, for example.

The Letter

Monastery of Tegernsee

March 20, 1461

Antonio and Gabriele were within five days of reaching Mainz. Throughout their journey, they had sought accommodations at both inns and monasteries, a decision based on logistics: if a monastery was too far off their route, they would find an inn. Their route was the primary trade route that stretched from China into the heart of Europe. With a steady flow of merchants and pilgrims and a smattering of bandits, there were inns for travelers in almost all the towns and villages they passed. Even bandits need to sleep.

Antonio was looking forward to their stay that night at the Monastery of Tegernsee south of Munich.

A robust publishing center, the Monastery was a Mecca for manuscript illustrators and biblical scholars, and Antonio knew his stature as one of Florence's premiere manuscript illustrators would be recognized and likely result in courtesies extended beyond the courtesies offered to most travelers seeking accommodations.

He looked forward to viewing the Monastery's collection of manuscripts. Seeing the works of other manuscript publishers often provided inspiration for his own work.

The grounds leading up to the historic monastery were lush, bursting with spring's fresh growth, and fragrances carried by gentle breezes enveloped Antonio and Gabriele as they made their way to the Monastery gates. The Monastery itself was an aesthetic blend of the old and the new. Its Gothic roots were tastefully complemented by the trending Renaissance influence.

Monks were tending the grounds, and one stood at the doors, preparing to greet arriving guests. As they dismounted, the monk approached to help with their saddle gear and to welcome them.

Gabriele made the introductions. The guard's impressive status as the head of security for the San Miniato al Monte Monastery was quickly upstaged when the monk learned who the traveling companion was.

"Antonio Strozzi?" Known artisans of the era commanded celebrity status among the knowing and the enlightened.

"Our abbot will be delighted, I'm sure, to know of your visit. Please. Follow me."

The monk led them through the vestibule and the freshly painted, fresco-lined stone corridors leading to the hall of guest rooms. Neither Antonio nor Gabriele had seen such expansive guest accommodations. But given this was a center of scholarship and artistry, it was not surprising.

As the monk led them to rooms for their accommodations, he introduced them, particularly Antonio, as they passed or encountered Brother monks.

Once introduced, one monk said, "Antonio, if it would be convenient, I would like you to come to the library once you get your guest rooms. There is something I would like to show you."

Nothing piqued Antonio's interest more than an invitation to a library. Manuscripts were the building blocks of Antonio's life.

Just as in the Monastery of St. Augustine, Gabriele and Antonio were treated to private rooms located side by side. As they opened their doors to unload their saddlebags, Antonio turned to Gabriele and, with a benign smirk, said, "Let's hope that leaving you in private will not cause a replay of your stay at the Monastery of St. Augustine."

Gabriele gave a demure smile, responding, "Let's do more than hope. Let's pray."

Antonio just smiled, ignoring the suggestion, and asked, "Do you want to join me in the library?"

"Certainly."

The monk tour guide waited by their doors, and when they re-emerged, he led them through corridors decorated with tapestries and frescoes. No one would have been able to fathom the value of the art they waltzed through as if it were just everyday decor. And to them, at that time, it was.

The library they entered was the biggest both Antonio, despite his training and education, and Gabriele had ever seen. It took both their breaths away. Three of the room's four walls were lined with shelves holding possibly several hundred manuscripts, each with ornate, often gold-leaf–accented spines, row upon row, knee-high to almost the ceiling.

You could tell the inviting monk enjoyed and took pride in seeing their reactions to viewing such treasures. After the impact, the monk turned to Antonio and said, "Antonio, allow me to show you something." He walked over to a shelf and began to remove one of the manuscripts. As it came into view, Antonio was more stunned than he was by the immensity of the library in which he stood. This library and the Monastery's reputation were iconic.

Amazed, Antonio watched as the monk presented a manuscript Antonio recognized immediately. It was a manuscript he had created. It was almost a year's work.

"This was gifted by your Abbot Fransisco to our library."

Antonio was speechless.

Gabriele was in awe and wore a smile of immense pride, thinking, "Yes, this is our Antonio. And for the moment, my Antonio."

The attending library monk carefully returned the manuscript to its place on the shelves of the revered Monastery of Tegernsee's library walls. Antonio stood silent, staring at the spine of his manuscript, realizing that he would leave behind more from his life's journey than a tombstone. It struck him as odd. He had never thought of that.

It was easy to see that the library monk had enjoyed giving Antonio a life memory. From the look on Antonio's face, it was easy to see he had not considered his impact.

Smiling, the librarian caretaker monk said, "I am sure our abbot would be delighted to welcome you to our home here. Please, follow me."

As they wound through the art-lined stone corridors of one of the Holy Roman Empire's most esteemed monasteries, Gabriele turned and whispered to Antonio, "I was well aware of how respected you are at our monastery, but I did not know you are respected to this extent."

Antonio shrugged and whispered in response, "Neither did I."

Around a corridor, a stone wall led to an arched wooden doorway with its ornate door shut. The librarian gave the door a gentle knock. A second later, the door opened, and there stood the Monastery's abbot. Tall, slender, and silver-haired, his face wore the marks of time, but the warmth of his smile was timeless.

The librarian began, "Abbot Fabian, may I—"

"Yes, I know."

Although communication across Europe was slow at that time, communication within the monastery walls was not.

The abbot smiled, extended his hand and ring, and said, "Welcome, Antonio." Then, turning to Gabriele, he said, "I trust you are the trusted guard?"

Gabriele bowed and replied simply, "Father."

Stepping away from the door and gesturing to his study, Abbot Fabian said, "Please. Join me."

The abbot's study was much like Abbot Fransisco's study in their home monastery, San Miniato al Monte, although this abbot's study had not three walls lined with manuscripts but five. Its sixth wall housed an arched window overlooking the Monastery's cloister and grounds.

Gesturing to two chairs facing his desk and the monastic throne, Abbot Fabian said, "Please. Sit and be comfortable. You must be tired from your journey."

They all settled in their chairs, and the abbot turned to Antonio and said, "Antonio, your work rivals the finest of even what we produce here in our modest monastery."

Antonio smiled, replying, "Your kind words mean much to me," but what ran through both his and Gabriele's minds was: "Modest?"

Reaching across his desk to a small stack of papers, Abbot Fabian said, "We have recently been fortunate to have another visitor from your monastery. Your Prior Lorenzo visited and left a letter for you, Antonio, if you happened to pass through."

Handing the letter to Antonio, the abbot said, "If there is anything we can do to make your visit with us more restful, please do not hesitate to ask."

Standing, indicating the meeting's conclusion, he added, "My door is always open to you, as are the doors to our monastery. We welcome you to our evening meal and prayers."

Antonio and Gabriele left the abbot's study, and it wasn't until his door was closed and they were out of earshot and alone, making their way back to their guest rooms, that either spoke of the letter in Antonio's hand. Neither looked at the other as they spoke; they just continued toward their rooms.

Antonio said merely, "Lorenzo."

"Perhaps a love letter?"

Antonio gave a slight laugh at the humor, but he was not much amused knowing that Lorenzo remained, although elusive, a threat.

Gabriele said, "I am very curious what he would put in writing to you. Read it to me, will you?"

"Of course."

In the privacy of Antonio's room, Gabriele anxiously watched as he broke the letter's seal and unfolded the paper. Antonio, before even reading it, said, "You won't believe this."

"Believe what? What does it say?"

"Here, look for yourself."

He handed the letter to Gabriele, who, without looking at it, said, "You know I can't read Latin."

"Look at the letter."

Gabriele only then looked at what was written.

Stunned, Gabriele blurted out in disbelief, "It's in plain Italian!"

Antonio took the letter back, read it, and then remarked, "Yes, and there is nothing plain about it at all." He handed it back to Gabriele, saying only, "Read."

Gabriele slowly read the letter, not once but twice, and then said, "Do you know what is most disturbing about this letter?"

"What?"

"It means he's ahead of us."

They both stood silently, each trying to plan for what is most difficult to plan for: the unknown.

Antonio then asked, "Gabriele, this is more your world than mine. My world sits back there on the bookshelf in the library. How do you think he could make this journey alone?"

"Not easily. But there is something even more troubling."

"What's that?"

"Do you think this is the only monastery where he has left this letter? How would he know we were going to stop here?"

"Well, this monastery is renowned for publishing. He would certainly guess I would be interested in stopping here."

"So he would bypass all the other monasteries and just leave a letter here, this far into the journey, and nowhere else? I don't think so. But that's not all I am worrying about him distributing to monasteries."

"Why? What else?"

"Rumors. Didn't you find the meeting we just had with the abbot a bit unusual?"

"No. Why?"

"Antonio, think how the monk in the library fawned over you. And the abbot? Almost dismissive."

"You are far more skilled in interpreting monastery mysteries than I. What do you think?"

"We don't know if Lorenzo has left a trail of untruths for us to follow. I think after tonight, we stay away from monasteries."

Antonio let out a sigh and said, mostly to himself, "What have I gotten myself into?"

Reaching for the door, Gabriele smiled and replied, "I don't know, but it's my job to get you out of it." Then, giving him a friendly slap on his back end, the guard said, "Good night, Antonio. Sleep well."

As Gabriele closed the door, Antonio sat on his bed's edge, wondering who he could trust. Gabriele. Who else? "God only knows," he thought. And God doesn't write letters.

Exchanging Breadcrumbs

Burgbernheim, Germany

March 22, 1461

Antonio and Gabriele did not make long goodbyes at the Monastery of Tegernsee.

After reading Lorenzo's letter, they were both uneasy with even small, inconsequential exchanges with a monk. They were alert, warmly greeting everyone but trusting absolutely no one.

The letter, so casually and conversationally written, not in Latin like everything else Lorenzo wrote, had succeeded in planting doubt and distrust.

For the first half day of travel, the letter consumed both Antonio's and Gabriele's minds, and the conversation consisted simply of a string of statements and questions and out-loud thoughts.

"What did he expect me to do? Warmly greet him and say, 'Lorenzo! So good to see you again! After careful consideration, I think you're right'? Is that what he expected?"

"Does he really think you could so easily be swayed to be disloyal to the abbot? My sense is the abbot quite likes you even though you're not with the clergy."

"My sense is that the abbot really trusts you. He as much as told me."

Gabriele turned to Antonio and asked, "If you have the letter in easy reach, may I look at it again?"

Antonio reached into his saddle's side pouch and handed the letter to Gabriele.

Gabriele reread the letter and then said, "Listen to this: 'I admire your loyalty to the abbot—it is a quality I respect deeply—but consider this: loyalty does not mean blind submission. Sometimes, true loyalty requires us to act in ways that protect those we serve from threats they cannot yet perceive.' Does that sound arrogant to you? Or am I just a lowly guard?"

"A lowly guard? Gabriele, you fail to recognize the value of trust. There are a few things that strike me about that letter. First, his feeble attempt to feign friendship would be laughable were it not for what's at stake. But two other things are more striking."

"What are they?"

"One you've identified: arrogance. The other is that he would know you, too, could read the letter."

"Unless he thinks I don't know how to read and write."

Antonio smiled, turned to Gabriele, and asked, "Do you know what arrogance is?"

"What?"

"A vulnerability."

They rode in silence through the rolling Bavarian landscape on trails that passed crops rising as they do every spring, as if rising from the dead. They weaved through forest patches and tiny villages where people smiled and waved.

They both glanced at the Monastery of Oberndorf as they passed it, and Gabriele said, "I wonder if there's a letter there waiting for you?"

Antonio thought for a moment and then said, "Why don't we find out?"

And why not? Breadcrumbs.

They were greeted warmly, and Antonio introduced himself and asked if a colleague had left a note for him. And indeed, he had.

It was the same letter.

As they stood in the monastery's vestibule, Gabriele asked the monk when their colleague had left the letter. "You just missed him. He stayed the previous night and left this morning."

Gabriele looked at Antonio and said, "He is not far. Our paths could easily cross."

Antonio stared out the vestibule window overlooking the monastery's cloister. Then, smiling, he said to Gabriele, "Perhaps we should respond to Lorenzo's letter." Then Antonio laughed.

"What's so funny?"

"The answer to his letter."

"Why? What will it say?"

Laughing, Antonio replied, "'Me subtiliter aestimas. Teque nimium extollis.' " Which means, 'You underestimate me. And overestimate yourself.'" Antonio continued to chuckle.

"That's strong, and I agree, but I am not clear about the humor. Is there some humor in the Latin I'm missing?"

"No, the humor will be in how the letter will be signed."

"How will it be signed?"

Antonio smiled, looked into Gabriele's eyes, and replied, "Gabriele."

Gabriele laughed.

The monk was obliging. Equipped with paper, ink, and a quill, Antonio took considerably less time handwriting multiple copies of this letter than Lorenzo took rewriting his tome, letter after letter.

As they rode away from the Monastery, Gabriele pointed out the obvious. By leaving their letter at each monastery and church of any consequence, they might also get a good indication of whether they were ahead of or behind Lorenzo.

While the stops slowed their progress, they did provide Lorenzo's road map. A letter awaited them at the Monastery of Wessobrunn, the Monastery of Reichenbach, and the Monastery of Heilsbronn, each farther and farther from Oberndorf as they progressed to Nuremberg—a logical stop before they set their sights on Mainz. But at each stop, they also left a copy of their letter.

The Battle of Breadcrumbs had begun.

As the sun began its journey to the center of the Earth, Antonio and Gabriele made inquiries about suitable towns for a night's stay and decided on the village of Uffenheim. Several travelers had mentioned The Rose and Crown, run by a couple, Johann and Anna Bauer.

Uffenheim was a small older village of half-timbered houses, many with overhanging upper floors. The town square almost made up the entire town itself; it had a more visually muted presence, with buildings mostly the color of the natural material used in their construction, many accented with ochre, terra-cotta, or muted greens.

However, The Rose and Crown Inn, a three-story building, was painted in a deep red, and many travelers said you couldn't miss it—one of the few times the use of that directional guide proved accurate. Antonio and Gabriele tied Twice and Thrice to the hitching post and opened the door to the inn. The deep red color of the inn suggested that it was more upscale, and if there was any doubt, the ornate iron hardware on the door should have put those doubts to rest. The wrought-iron strap hinges had a curved floral decorative flare extending out across the door.

The door opened to a vestibule and reception area furnished with stuffed, fabric-covered chairs; to the right was the dining area and a fire burning in a large stone fireplace, and to the left was a common area, also furnished with atypically comfortable seating choices, from chairs to benches.

As soon as they entered, the blond woman in her late twenties seated at the reception desk stood to greet them. Standing almost six feet tall, she towered over both Gabriele and Antonio. Extending her hand in greeting, she smiled and said, "Welcome to The Rose and Crown. Will you be staying with us tonight?"

Antonio was taken aback by more than her height; she had greeted them in Italian.

Antonio, somewhat confused, asked, "*Sprichst du Deutsch?*"

She replied, "*Ja, natürlich, ich bin Deutscher, aber ich nahm an, dass du Italiener wärest. Liege ich falsch?*"

Antonio replied, "No, we are Italian. I apologize. I was simply surprised to hear you speak Italian. Your Italian is perfect."

With a little bow that almost brought them eye to eye, she replied, "Thank you. My name is Anna Bauer. My husband, Johann, and I wanted a quieter life, so we bought this quaint little house and moved here from Frankfurt. Life in Frankfurt was getting too fast and too busy for us."

Gabriele thought, "If this is quaint, I wonder what they consider luxurious?"

"How long will you two gentlemen be staying with us?"

"Just one night," Gabriele replied.

"Well, I hope your stay is comfortable for you. Your room will be the one at the end of the hall on the second floor. I see you have saddlebags. I assume you would like your horses fed and watered, so I will have Johann tend to them."

Antonio nodded and replied, "Thank you."

Then Anna continued with an invitation to dinner. "We have a tradition in The Rose and Crown. We invite our guests to sit together for the evening's meal, chat, hear stories, laugh, and sometimes make new friends. You are not obliged to join us, but most people find the evening enjoyable. That may be why you heard of us in your travels. A day's journey can get monotonous. Stories of each other's travels can be entertaining, and Johann and I especially enjoy hearing of people's tales and lives. It provides us with the vitality we experienced in Frankfurt without having to put up with living in Frankfurt."

Antonio and Gabriele looked at each other, both shrugging a "why not" shrug, and Gabriele turned to Anna and said, "That does indeed sound like it could be an entertaining meal. What time?"

"We gather after Vespers when the church bells ring."

Antonio and Gabriele thanked Anna and took their saddlebags to their room.

Once they set their saddlebags at the foot of their beds, Gabriele was the first to sit on the bed and immediately commented, "A feather mattress!" Then, stretching out on the bed, the guard said, "I love you, Thrice, but this is so much more preferable to your saddle."

Antonio laughed and replied, "Don't get too comfortable. We're joining them for dinner, not breakfast."

Gabriele sat bolt upright, spun on the bed to sit in its middle, and asked, "Don't you wonder where Lorenzo is right now? And what he's up to?"

So Close, Yet So Far

Burgbernheim, Germany

March 22, 1461

Lorenzo sat at a table in The Knaves Inn's dining room, too far from the room's fireplace for his comfort.

His travel partners, much happier to be in a land that served more beer than wine, were laughing, recounting past victorious encounters.

Lorenzo offered a feeble smile, feigning amusement, as if he had been listening.

He hadn't.

His only preoccupation was thinking, "Where are Antonio and Gabriele?"

Had he known, what would he have done? Sat them down and talked reason to them? Explain reason to a manuscript technician and a guard?

Alfonso motioned to the waitress, calling her over for the third time to order more rounds. Lorenzo turned his gaze out the window.

"Lorenzo! Lorenzo!" Alfonso's enthusiasm only grew with each passing round. "Isn't she a wonder? Beatriz, this is our comrade, Lorenzo. Lorenzo, this is Beatriz."

"*Mucho gusto!*"

Lorenzo manufactured a smile, nodded, and then turned his attention back to the cosmos that was out beyond the inn's window, just beyond his reach.

What he would have done had he known that there in Burgbernheim, they were but six miles apart, only the God he worshipped knows.

Story Time

Uffenheim, Germany

March 22, 1461

Uffenheim's church bells tolled as the sun dipped below the horizon, their sound piercing the evening chill while a fire crackled in The Rose and Crown's dining room.

The circus performers, the inn's guests, seemed to appear from all corners: through the inn's front door, from a back stairway Antonio and Gabriele did not know existed, from behind them, from the floor above theirs, and some—they could have sworn—from the fireplace itself.

Long table candles flickered, casting light against the stone walls as the room filled with the aroma of roasting meats and baking bread. Unlike monastery meals, this held all the promise of a pending feast.

People settled into chairs around the dining room table, each nodding a foreigner's hello to each other.

Like a circus ringleader, Anna appeared from behind swinging tavern doors, waving her arms in the air and shouting, "Welcome! Welcome! Johann and I welcome you! Tonight, our home is your home. First, please introduce yourselves and tell us what you do. Johann will be out shortly to tell you about our fare this evening. But first, let me begin: My name is Anna, and I am the hostess of The Rose and Crown. Your turn."

A local farmer, his elbows resting on the table, nervously wrung his thick farmer's hands and said, "My name is Otto, and I farm lands close by."

From around the table came an assortment of greetings. "Hello, Otto."

Next to Otto, a slender young man greeted with, "Hello. My name is Lukas, and I am studying theology and will be attending a conference in Nuremberg."

The table responded, "Hello, Lukas."

Following Lukas was a flamboyant, mid-thirties, colorfully dressed woman who proudly announced, "Hello. My name is Margarete, and I supply textiles."

That implied she was a merchant.

"Hello, Margarete," the table responded.

So it went.

Frederick, the blacksmith. Isabella, the herbalist. Jakob, the traveling musician, who produced a flute to substantiate his claim. Hannah, the baker—everyone loves bakers. You could tell by the enthusiastic hellos she received.

Sophie, who merely said she was from Nuremberg but, judging by her wardrobe of silk and fine cotton, appeared to be no ordinary resident. She was nobility.

Benedikt, another merchant, though an aging one.

"Hello, Benedikt."

Then came Antonio, who said, "My name is Antonio, and I am a manuscript illustrator."

The hellos that followed were like recognition of a celebrity's attendance.

Following and last was Gabriele, who said, "My name is Gabriele, and I am a swordsman."

Even Antonio's head swung to look, and there was a notable pause before the obligatory "Hello, Gabriele" followed.

Had it been the twentieth or twenty-first century, the dinner would have felt very much like an AA meeting.

At the conclusion of the introductions, like a well-managed stage play, Johann entered from the kitchen bearing a platter laden with a crispy crusted roast pork, a scent of herbs and spices trailing from it; bratwurst; bowls of a barley-based vegetable stew of carrots, turnips, and peas; and freshly baked rye bread.

While Anna's height seemed to dwarf her guests, she was dwarfed by her husband, Johann, who stood six foot two.

As he put the platter in the table's center, he introduced himself, said hello to everyone, then disappeared back into the kitchen. While the bread was being passed around, Johann re-emerged with a second platter laden with an assortment of cheeses, butter, pickled vegetables, fruit tarts, and honey cakes.

It was little wonder why so many travelers had recommended The Rose and Crown Inn: it would be impossible to leave hungry.

With guests asking each other about their journeys and their lives, Sophie turned to Gabriele and asked, "Gabriele, what does a swordsman do?"

Gabriele looked into the depths of the fireplace, thinking before responding, then said, "A good swordsman simply makes people nervous."

After a brief pause, the table erupted in nervous laughter.

A Memorable Meal

Burgbernheim, Germany

March 22, 1461

Lorenzo sat at the table with his partners in pending crime, waiting for their meals to be served between the rounds. The beer came in good time —the food, not so much.

Beatriz finally arrived with what appeared to be overcooked, lukewarm pottage that had a film of grease floating on top; stale, rock-hard bread; and a mystery meat almost as hard to cut as the bread.

WILLIAM LOWER

A Stone's Throw

Burgbernheim, Germany

March 23, 1461

Lorenzo had to bang on Alfonso and his team's door several times to bring them out of their stupor, with visions of Beatriz dancing through their heads, and back into the real world of pursuing greater riches than the meager per diem he was paying them that barely covered the daily cost of beer or wine.

Lorenzo's pounding finally got a "What? What?" from what sounded like Alfonso. Lorenzo, the taskmaster, replied, "Breakfast will be on the table momentarily but only for a few minutes, and then we depart."

Their travel pace had been considerably compromised by the brief stops at monasteries to inquire about Antonio and Gabriele and leave the letter Lorenzo hoped might make Antonio think twice about what he was doing.

The breakfast differed little from dinner the night before. The bread was stale; the porridge resembled cruel gruel.

The inn clearly served leftover meats from the previous night (which themselves appeared to be leftovers from the day before), and the cheese smelled like it aged under a goat's armpit.

More importantly to Alfonso, Niccolò, and Alessandro, someone watered down the ale.

It was not a meal to linger over, and for that, Lorenzo was thankful.

Lorenzo and his posse made their way out of Burgbernheim onto the trails meandering through the agricultural lands, rolling hills, and occasional forest patches not yet cleared for growing crops.

Lorenzo's focus, however, was not on the bucolic vistas along his journey but on monasteries where he would stop, trying to get an idea of where he was time- and distance-wise in relation to Antonio and Gabriele.

And the more he thought about his journey's mission, the more righteous he felt about his purpose. Don't give sacred texts haphazardly to machine operators and mechanics; give them to scholars. That so many in his world failed to recognize that view only strengthened his resolve. Occasionally, he permitted his mind to drift into fantasies of adoration: recognition for saving the Church and its authority and domain over all things spiritual.

The first monasterial stop on his thrust to Mainz was the Burgbernheim Monastery, the reason he had chosen the village of Burgbernheim for a layover.

From there were a series of stops that included the Marienberg Monastery —an influential Benedictine abbey—and its nearby St. Burkhard Abbey, then the Neustadt am Main Abbey—a Benedictine monastery—and the Monastery of Langenzenn. The objective was to make it to Würzburg, where he would stay for the night after finding an inn with Spanish wait-resses for his comrades.

Each monasterial stop added to the journey's travel time. First, he had to arrange a spot for his comrades to wait, out of sight of the monastery and without the means to spend their time (and his monasterial money) waiting in a nearby tavern.

The St. Burkhard Abbey was the first monastery he could confirm Antonio and Gabriele had been to; a welcoming monk happily produced a letter they had left behind, saying, "You just missed them."

Lorenzo smiled and thanked the monk before opening and reading the brief correspondence.

His instant reaction was anger at the imprudence and audacity of the message itself, but that reaction was usurped by astonishment.

The letter's author was the guard, of all people.

Could Gabriele write and read in Latin? What did he know about this guard, other than the abbot's trust in him and his own jealousy over that trust? Nothing. But Lorenzo always felt that there was something secretive about that guard, Gabriele. Lorenzo prided himself on his keen sense of awareness of buried secrets.

Thanking the monk, Lorenzo mounted Between Thieves and galloped to rejoin his squad.

Seeing his arriving at the pace he was traveling, Alfonso knew there was some pending urgency. Turning to Niccolò and Alessandro, he said, "Get your wits about you. Get mounted and get ready to move. It looks like he's in a hurry."

And he was.

Lorenzo rode up to Alfonso and said, "We just missed them, and they are not far ahead. Let's get moving and let's make good time."

They traveled at a quicker pace than they had previously, resting only when they knew their horses needed rest, food, and water.

Traveling through towns and villages, including Erlangen and Bamberg, they stopped at any significant monasterial or religious center, such as the Bamberg Cathedral.

At each stop, people greeted him warmly and told him that his colleagues, Antonio and Gabriele, had visited and left a letter for him.

Each time someone gave Lorenzo the letter, it forced him to feign pleasure, a charade that became increasingly difficult.

Having traveled at an intense pace for two days, he stopped for the day, choosing The Bishop's Solace Inn from the dozens of Würzburg inns for the simple reason he took comfort from the word "solace." He felt he very much needed and deserved solace.

The inn, which was in the town's square, provided an impressive view of the hilltop fortress and residence of the Würzburg prince-bishops.

What he would have thought, what he would have done, what events would have unfolded had he known that across the square at another Würzberg inn, Antonio and Gabriele were also resting for the night is anyone's guess and something only the Muses might know.

The Eyes Have It.

Würzburg, Germany

March 25, 1461

Ever since Gabriele had asked to see the flaw in Gutenberg's Bible, they had developed an evening pre-bed entertainment routine: Antonio would find amusing, poignant, or outrageous biblical quotes, read them, and they would either laugh, discuss, or become solemn at uncomfortable truths of mankind's narrative.

After his selection, he would hand the book to Gabriele, who would open pages randomly and point to verses by chance.

This, too, often created comedic results.

Through their biblical studies, they learned if a slave owner struck either a male or female slave and the slave died, the slave owner would be punished (although the punishment was not defined); if the slave survived a day or two, there was no punishment. Antonio had quoted Exodus 21:20–21.

There was the questiinable and certainly not lawyer-approved promise that prayers would be answered found in John 14:13–14 q

The selections from the Bible on their journey were a mirror of life itself, bending to the will of randomness.

These evenings' entertainments had created a slow-growing and invisible bond between the two lone soldiers marching to the defense of Gutenberg, no doubt unaware of the impact Gutenberg's genius would have on their world and the world to follow.

They estimated they were now two days from Mainz, two days from whatever would unfold when they confronted Gutenberg with a flaw in the product borne from his genius.

Now, in the Germanic territories of the Holy Roman Empire, their meals were heartier and heavier, and their bodies commanded more sleep in order to divert their energy to digesting.

Tired and ready for sleep, they retreated to their room overlooking Mainstraße in Würzburg and they sank, sitting on bedsides, facing each other.

Gabriele looked at Antonio and, though weary, said, "Night's reading. You start. But maybe tonight, let's make it brief. I'm tired, so you must be, too."

Antonio sighed, grabbed the Bible, and gazed into the infinity for a moment, thinking of where he might find the shortest passage requiring the least amount of discussion. After a few moments, he turned to Corinthians, Chapter 13, verses 4 to 7, and read, "Love is patient, love is kind. It does not envy, it does not boast, it is not proud. It does not dishonor others, it is not self-seeking, it is not easily angered, it keeps no record of wrongs. Love does not delight in evil but rejoices with the truth. It always protects, always trusts, always hopes, always perseveres."

Handing the book to Gabriele, he said, "Good thoughts to sleep by. Find your biblical surprise, and then we can sleep."

Gabriele took the book, randomly opened to a page, pointed to a verse, and handed it back to Antonio, saying, as was their standing joke, "It's Greek to me."

Antonio took the book, read the passage Gabriele had selected by chance, by fate, then slammed the book shut. He turned his gaze once again to the infinity outside, infinity just on the other side of the window, his nostrils flaring and eyes watering.

"What's the matter? What's the matter?"

Reopening the book to the passage Gabriele had by chance revealed, Antonio read, as monotone as he could manage, "This is Leviticus, Chapter 20, verse 13, and it reads, 'If a man also lie with mankind, as he lieth with a woman, both of them have committed an abomination: they shall surely be put to death; their blood shall be upon them.' " The air in their room ceased to move. No sounds penetrated the walls or windows. They each stared straight ahead, neither looking the other in the eye.

This was the moment Gabriele feared. Inside, Gabriele was shattering in pain and boiling over in rage, yet nothing of either showed. Gabriele, the guard, was on duty and on full alert.

Staring out the window in search of the source in infinity, Antonio began to speak. And Gabriele knew what was coming.

"Gabriele ..."

What followed knows no qualifiers. What followed has no disclaimers. What followed is, at times, tossed around so cavalierly and insincerely, it is an obscenity to the infinity that was out the window, just beyond Antonio's reach.

"I love you."

The two sat there, frozen in time—time that never freezes. It's experience that freezes. Not time. After those three simple words, neither knew what to say next.

Though Gabriele's exterior was expressionless, inside, the guard's pain and rage collided.

The pit in Antonio's stomach was in search of new bottoms not to be found.

There sat two souls, each lost in their private universes of loneliness.

Gabriele was the first to speak. "Antonio, I'm sorry—"

But before Gabriele could continue, Antonio interrupted, "No, I'm sorry."

Gabriele got up and went over to Antonio's side, sitting on his bed and taking his hand, and said, "I am touched more than you can imagine by your words."

No matter how well cushioned, rejection's blow is never softened, no matter how soft the words.

Antonio continued to stare out the window to infinity, then said, "I'm sorry. I should have said nothing."

"Antonio, I know men love. It is not for me to judge if a man loves a man. What matters is love, wouldn't you say?"

Antonio gave a feeble nod. "Yes, that's what matters."

"Antonio, I can only imagine how difficult it must have been for you to say those simple words to me. And I am sure that love is a private matter to you."

"Yes. Yes, it is. Very private. And unsettling."

"You placed trust in me to tell me that. Antonio, I will not betray that trust."

Antonio broke his stare from the empty infinity just outside the window and turned to look in Gabriele's eyes to sense if there was truth in the promise of no betrayal. There is so much you can see in the eyes that can't be explained, as there was with the wolf, who was intent on attack but did not. The eyes talk. And Gabriele's eyes were not lying.

Softly, Antonio said, "Thank you."

"Antonio, we all have secrets. Some big, some small. You have trusted me with a very intimate secret, Antonio. So I will share mine with you, a secret no one knows and a secret I would like to remain secret."

Looking up from the floor, Antonio said, "And what's that?"

"Antonio, I am not a man."

Antonio's head shot around to look Gabriele straight in the eyes, and at that moment, all that moved in that room were the pupils of their eyes.

They exploded in bloom.

The eyes have it. They always do.

THE ENCOUNTER

A GENIUS IN TATTERS

Mainz, Germany

March 31, 1461

Gutenberg's diminished workshop was on the ground floor of a narrow stone building on Krämergasse Strausse; it was a humiliating decline from the heady days when his brilliant invention of a moveable-type printing apparatus broke new ground and in the process left him, by bank measures, broke.

In the center of his dimly lit production center that was often in disarray was the altar of his artfulness, ingenuity, and creative mind: a printing press. Metal-forged type pieces lay scattered throughout his shop despite the fact that they had a storage spot in the stacks of type trays; but in the frenzy of the printing press production, returning them to their storage was of secondary importance to the turmoil and urgency of mass print production.

At sixty-three, with an unkempt salt-and-pepper beard, a full head of hair, an empty pocket, a mercurial disposition, and a passion for the impossible, Johannes Gutenberg stood staring at his contraption as it pressed, page after page after page, a local bakery's help wanted poster.

Behind him, at the far wall, was an oven for forging metal for type. The smell of ink, melting tin, and aging wood permeated the room. Hans, his twelve-year-old apprentice, approached from behind, nervously gave a tug on Johannes' threadbare sleeve, and said, "Herr Gutenberg, today is month's end."

Irritated by the interruption to his watching what was once a dream performing its magic, Gutenberg swung around, bursting from the bubble of magic taking place before his eyes, and said, "What?"

Hans, too young not to be intimidated, turned and looked for reassurance from Harald, an older, grown employee. Harald nodded, and Hans turned back to the inventor of the about-to-be-burgeoning world of mechanics and repeated, "Today is month's end."

Gutenberg stared at the imp Hans and replied, "So, Hans, you are a keeper of calendars?"

Hans glanced back to Harald, who nodded again in reassurance; Hans turned back to Gutenberg and said, "No, Herr Gutenberg, it is just the day I believe we are to be paid."

For a moment, Gutenberg just stared at Hans, expressionless, then turned and sat on a worktable bench.

All the while, Bartholomew Bakery's help wanted posters, with the help of Harald, continued to be pressed from the plate of Gutenberg's brilliance.

"Yes. It is." He then glanced over to Harald, who nodded as he had to Hans.

Gutenberg nodded and shuffled to a tiny office at the back of the production floor, stepped in, and closed its door while Hans and Harald stood on the production floor, casting glances to each other. Moments later, Gutenberg re-emerged from his office, first making his way to Hans, and held out his hand. Hans opened the palm of his hand, and Gutenberg handed over a few coins.

Hans smiled and said, "Thank you, Herr Gutenberg. It is a privilege to be learning from the master." Still smiling, he added, "And being paid."

Gutenberg turned and walked over to Harald, handing over a few scant coins, saying, "Thank you, Harald, for all you do under difficult circumstances."

Harald smiled, looked Gutenberg in the eye, and said, "Fust has taken the fruits of your genius, but there are two things he can't take."

Gutenberg looked Harald in the eye, then looked around their meager production center and responded, "And what might those be?"

Harald took the aging Gutenberg by the hand and said, "He can take the fruits of your genius, but he can't take your genius. And the other thing he can't take?"

Gutenberg looked him in the eye and fell for the bait. "What?"

Harald smirked and winked, saying only, "Your name."

Gutenberg laughed and said, "That and a half a gulden will get you a bun at Bartholomew Bakery."

The March sun had long set. Hans and Harald had lit the candles and oil lamps.

Gutenberg smiled, looked at them, and told them he was looking forward to seeing them the following day as he stood and unwound the screw to the press.

Hans and Harald set what they were doing aside, took their coats, bid Gutenberg a pleasant evening, and scurried out the door to Krämergasse Strausse.

With candles and oil lamps burning and his masterpiece now motionless, having produced multiple Bartholomew Bakery help wanted posters, Gutenberg sat staring at his genius mechanism. How this would speed and broaden information.

But it was not Gutenberg who would reap financial or creature comforts.

It was Fust.

Gutenberg sat on the bench, staring at his marvel. Under the candle and oil lamp light, as he smiled at its ingenuity, a tear leaked from his eye. He quickly wiped it away with his ink-stained hand, leaving a blackened stain across his face, almost as if he were preparing for nocturnal war.

It's a Mainz, Mainz World

Mainz, Germany

March 29, 1461

After hours of riding through rolling hills of agricultural land and winding through the narrow streets of the tiny villages sprinkled across the land-scape, they crested one hill, and there in the distance were the gates.

They both stopped as if on cue, trying to process what would follow.

No one had sent Gutenberg advance notice of their coming or, more importantly, of their purpose.

The trip had taken weeks, and Florence now was a distant memory, as were their former lives.

Gabriele turned to Antonio, asking, "Can you believe it?"

Staring at the Mainz gates in the distance, Antonio replied, "I am trying to."

They stood, staring at the gates to Mainz for a few more moments, collecting their thoughts, adjusting their focus from the challenge of getting to Mainz to the challenge of being in Mainz, the challenge of finding Gutenberg and compelling him to admit to his mistake and correct it, whatever that required. How difficult would that be? What did one of his machines look like? How much work was involved in setting up one page for printing?

Putting Twice into a trot, Antonio led the charge with a simple, "Here we go."

And off they went.

Gabriele had used her sword ploy at many city gates they had to enter on their journey, but this was different.

These were the German territories, and the Holy Roman Empire was not all one happy family. At Mainz, they would check papers. But Mainz, like

Florence, had a thriving publishing trade, and business was business—and business is always welcome.

As they approached the walled city, Gothic towers, tall and imposing, underscored the strength and history of the community. The Medici-driven and -funded Renaissance elegance was less pronounced.

As they approached the gates, two guards greeted them and asked for papers and purpose, but they were not as imposing as Antonio and Gabriele feared they would be. One guard walked around their horses, looking at their saddlebags, then asked, "Are you bringing items to sell in Mainz?"

Gabriele twisted the truth, replying, "No, we are here to seek Gutenberg and do business."

One guard replied, "I'm sure he would welcome that." The guards then gave each other a look with the smirks of an insider's joke.

Stepping aside, the inspecting guard said, "Enjoy your stay. There are several inns along the river that travelers tell us are quite agreeable."

They proceeded past the gates, then Twice and Thrice carried them through Mainz's winding, narrow dirt streets teeming with merchants peddling their wares and products. Some did so enthusiastically, some aggressively, but all were eager to make a sale, a deal, or a trade.

The city was alive and vibrant.

Children ran up and down Mainz's muddy streets, laughing and shrieking, and as Antonio and Gabriele passed a rambunctious group, Antonio wondered if he could remember life without the burden of living and the almost impossible challenge of being free of a constant worry about life itself. But life's mayhem did occasionally bear fruit. One such fruit was riding on the horse beside him. "Fate," he thought. Or was God, in the heavens, charting out each person's events and rendezvous as they journeyed through life? Was He busy planning … what? A hundred million journeys in a constant state of flux, colliding within the impossible-to-imagine maze of other moving parts in the confined sphere of life here on Earth?

He realized what he was doing and stopped. Antonio was aware of his unfruitful tendency to allow his mind to wander. Through the course of spending three days crafting one page, his mind would drift. To where? Most often, nowhere. "The problem with thinking," Antonio thought, "is thinking itself." Where did that get you? Most often, confused.

A woman shooed the cluster of screaming and laughing children away from the front of her stall of fruits and vegetables. They were blocking the way of potential customers.

From a tavern, still several blocks away, Antonio and Gabriele could hear a tuba-dominated brass ensemble playing.

"Have you ever tasted beer?" Antonio asked.

"No. What does it taste like?"

"That depends on where it comes from. Just like wine. Depends on the soil where the plants grew its ingredients. But from what I know of beer, it all has a similar effect on people."

"It gets them drunk."

"And gives them gas."

"Gas?"

"Yes. Sometimes, being around someone who has consumed a lot of beer smells like walking past the necessarium."

Gabriele was silent for a moment, then asked, "And people drink this voluntarily?"

Antonio laughed and replied, "You'll see. Let's find an inn, then a tavern for a meal."

Several inns were on the street that followed the shoreline of the Main river. One inn, the Gasthaus zur Krone, looked welcoming. How many inns on their journey had names that referenced a crown, they couldn't remember. The name's purpose was to suggest their inn was fit for royalty, although it was doubtful royalty had ever graced the doorsteps. But implying an inn was suitable for royalty meant it was at least passable.

This was true of the Gasthaus zur Krone. It was fine. It would do. Neither Antonio nor Gabriele were strangers to straw mattresses.

Finding a tavern was easy. All they had to do was follow the sound of the tuba, a sound so pronounced that they were able to find its source from several blocks away.

With candles and wall torches lit and a fire burning in the corner fireplace, the tavern was warm and welcoming. The throng of patrons yelling to be heard over the quartet's trumpet, sackbut, flügelhorn, and tuba made it also very noisy.

A jolly, ruby-cheeked aging German wearing an apron around his round belly arrived at their table and plunked down two mugs of beer, saying, "Beer, I assume. Would you like to know our daily special?"

Antonio and Gabriele gave each other a quick glance, and Antonio nodded to the waiter.

As though he had said it a hundred times before, the German rattled off, "An abundance of bratwurst accompanied by savory schnitzel, caramelized carrots, our house sauerkraut, two cheeses, and bread."

Antonio and Gabriele looked at each other, both surprised, and Antonio replied to the waiter, "You don't have fresh, grain-fed beef slowly cooked in a broth of thyme, carrots, cubes of potato, chopped onion, minced garlic, a generous cup of wine, and salt and pepper to taste?"

"No, that was yesterday's special. We ran out."

"The special sounds special. Two, please."

Leaning into the table closer to Antonio and speaking just loud enough to be heard over the din, Gabriele asked, "Are you certain it's the beer that gives people gas?"

Antonio looked around the tavern at the crowd enjoying their beer, the house special, and loud conversations with their friends and answered, "No, not really."

Gabriele took a sip from her mug and made a face as if she had just taken a large bite from a sour apple, not unlike the look on her face when tasting Hans Müller's herbal remedies.

"It's an acquired taste, apparently," Antonio advised.

They ate their meals in silence, save for the sound of the enthusiastic quartet and dozens of people battling to be heard over it.

Most evening meals they ate in silence, both hungry from a long day's journey.

Once finished, they paid for their meals and the partly consumed mugs of beer and wandered back to the inn, the quartet's music fading away the closer they got to their night's accommodations.

"How do you think tomorrow will go?" Gabriele asked.

Leadership on their trip to Mainz had been Gabriele's domain, given her role as protector and guide for the journey. But now, they were about to enter Antonio's world: the world of the printed page.

"I don't know. I have heard he is temperamental."

Gabriele said nothing but thought, "Best he is not with me." Gabriele had the skill of taking the temperament out of people in short order.

"But he won't want it known that his work is flawed or imperfect. He may not enjoy having to correct it, but he'll do it. That is my guess. Don't forget, this work bears his name. Few people want shame associated with their name."

They reached the Gasthaus zur Krone and stepped inside. Unlike the tavern they had just left, it was, thankfully, quiet. After a long day's journey, they always welcomed sleep, but never more so than now.

Antonio watched Gabriele undress. Naked, she reached into her saddlebag for a nightgown Antonio had purchased at a stall in Würzburg and slipped it over her head. Reaching down, she stretched it out like a dress, then twirled like a ballerina, beaming with a childlike smile, and said, "I love this."

Antonio smiled and said, "It's just a nightgown, Gabriele."

She stopped, turned, and faced him, no longer smiling as she corrected him. "No, Antonio. It is not just a nightgown. It is a woman's nightgown, and I never buy women's clothes, nor will I. I do nothing that could reveal I am a woman. My father raised me to be a man, and so I shall remain. He taught me how to be independent. My mother must have been an amazing person. She was the one who taught him to think like that, or so he told me. Throughout my childhood, whenever he witnessed a woman living a subservient life, treated little better than livestock, he would highlight her plight, asking me, 'Is that how you want to live?' All my life. Pointing that out, then asking over and over again, 'Do you want to live like that?' You must have had a remarkable mother, Antonio, pushing you, encouraging you to learn the languages you have learned."

"She was an amazing mother. I wish you could have met her."

"I wish I could have met mine."

They stood, locked eye to eye like they were diving into a deep, subterranean, and secret pool together.

"I am not big and muscular, Antonio. But you put a sword in my hand, and there isn't a man I fear."

"I don't doubt that."

Gabriele took a step toward Antonio, took his hand, and said, "These beds are small, Antonio. But I think the two of us can fit in one. Don't you?"

Meeting the Master

Mainz, Germany

March 29, 1461

Gutenberg's shop was close to Antonio and Gabriele's inn, so they walked —although the walking was not as easy as it might have been in Florence, with its cobblestone streets. Here in Mainz, many of the narrow streets were dirt and mud.

Antonio held Gutenberg's Bible wrapped in cloth as they walked. Finding Gutenberg's shop was easy: he (and his troubles) were well-known in Mainz among merchants and tradesmen, and when asked about his shop's location, almost all concluded their directions with a dubious "Good luck!"

Gutenberg's shop was in the Dietmarkt district, where most commerce was conducted. They passed a shop selling handblown glass products, several shops selling wine, and one shop with a window displaying an assortment of brass musical instruments, some recognizable. They passed an apothecary, and just before the end of a block was Gutenberg's unmistakable place of business: it was the only shop with multiple printed papers displayed in the street windows.

Antonio and Gabriele looked at each other, both taking a deep breath as Antonio reached for the wrought-iron door latch and mumbled, "Here we go."

The door opened to a scene of mechanical chaos. There in the center of the room was a machine that looked like a wine press or blunt-bladed guillotine.

In the back of the shop, molten metal was being forged for the type characters. A young apprentice ran between the workers, one hammering at a letter and the other arranging type on a plate for the press. The apprentice obeyed orders from all sides—the plate setter, the type hammerer, and Gutenberg himself.

When Gutenberg looked up and saw Antonio and Gabriele standing at his door, he smiled, stopped whatever he was doing, and came to greet them. Could this be? Customers?

As they introduced themselves, unwrapping the Gutenberg Bible to reveal it, Gutenberg's smile evaporated. Staring at it, he said, "Oh. That. What is it you want?"

Antonio spoke, using skills he had learned from his most important client, Abbot Fransisco. Flattery is an effective precursor to asking for the impossible or the laborious.

"Herr Gutenberg, I am a manuscript illustrator from Florence."

Gutenberg continued to frown, saying nothing and waiting for this impetuous tradesman to get to the point.

"Herr Gutenberg, it is such a privilege to meet the genius behind this Bible's creation."

Gutenberg continued to frown, saying nothing and waiting for this impetuous tradesman to get to the point.

"The typography is masterful, and the illustrations a marvel to the eye."

Gutenberg continued to frown, saying nothing and waiting for this impetuous tradesman to get to the point.

"However, there is one thing that needs your attention."

Gutenberg continued to frown, saying nothing and waiting for this impetuous tradesman to get to the point.

"There is a minor mistake, but a mistake Abbot Fransisco believes needs to be corrected."

Gutenberg came to life. "Mistake? *Mistake*? I don't make mistakes in my work! I only make mistakes when choosing business partners! Show me this mistake!"

Antonio opened the Bible, turning to page 149, Luke, Chapter 4, verses 18 to 19, and there, before Gutenberg's eyes, was the word "*Deus*" with a lowercase "d."

Gutenberg stared at it for a moment and then muttered, "Jesus Christ."

Softly, Gabriele replied, "He's not here right now."

Gutenberg looked at Antonio and his armed guard and said, "Yes. This came off my press. But not while I was in control of it. My former business partner and, regrettably, financier sued me, won in our questionable court system, took possession of my press and the work I had in progress, continued with them under my name, and has made a handsome living for himself. And what am I doing? Working off a lesser press making help wanted flyers for a bakery."

Gabriele glanced over to a table, where there was a stack of papers for Bartholomew Bakery announcing it was looking for a young woman to work the afternoon shift. Looking at it, Gabriele wondered, "What is it with bakeries and their buns-in-the-oven approach to business?"

With his eyes fixed on Antonio's and his index finger pointing to the "d" in "*Deus*," Gutenberg declared, "This is not my mistake. It is Fust's. And it would give me great pleasure to assist you in your efforts to have him correct his sloppiness."

Antonio closed and rewrapped the Bible, and they agreed to meet the following morning and, together, meet with the Bible's maker. As they opened the door to leave, Antonio turned to Gutenberg and thanked him for his time and help. Gutenberg grumbled, and the shop sprung back to chaos.

Confrontation with Fust

Mainz, Germany

March 31, 1461

Johann Fust, stroking his long scraggly beard, stood admiring a page fresh off his printing press. While his employees wore work clothes covered in ink and oils, Fust dressed as the nobleman he was, in the latest fashions made of the finest materials: silk, wool, and cotton. The nobility were not ones to get their clothes—or hands, for that matter—dirty.

His production floor, while not elaborate or huge, was not as small and dingy as Gutenberg's. The windows on Fust's production floor had lead-glass panes and were high in the room, just below the ceiling, but they were not deep. Opening and closing them required a small ladder.

Two typesetters were placing type from the type drawers onto a plate, preparing it for printing. Two other employees were preparing the press for printing, and three others scampered to fetch supplies and materials as the senior employees barked out commands.

Fust enjoyed watching the preparation for printing and always wanted to see, hear, and smell the press once it began to operate. "Those sights and sounds," Fust would silently muse, "are the sights and sounds of money."

When he heard the door to his production floor open, he looked up, surprised to see Gutenberg and two young men. Both his curiosity and suspicion were aroused.

Startled, Fust exclaimed, "Gutenberg! What are you doing here? What would bring you here? We finished our business. You know that."

Gutenberg marched over to a production table and slammed the Gutenberg Bible on it, saying, "Your sloppy work. That's what brings me here!"

Fust was incensed. "This is not my work. It is yours!"

"It is my name, but this did not come off my press while I was in control of it. It came off my press once you took control of it."

Getting indignant, Fust scoffed, saying, "Gutenberg, I have made you the laughingstock of Mainz, and this clumsy accusation is only going to give me more ammunition in Mainz's society. Who are you to call my work sloppy?"

Then, turning his attention to Antonio and Gabriele, he added, "And who have you brought with you? A new pair of naïve apprentices fawning over the great Gutenberg?"

Turning to them, he asked, "Tell me, has Gutenberg paid you anything yet? Or will he pay you on a future date?" Fust took pleasure in humiliating Gutenberg over his lack of finances.

Antonio replied very matter-of-factly, "No, I am a manuscript illustrator from Florence."

Fust burst out laughing. "A manuscript illustrator? Well, well, well. Enjoy your career. While it lasts."

Fust most enjoyed humor when it was at someone else's expense, and his laughter only diminished somewhat when Gabriele added, "And I am the head of security at the San Miniato al Monte Monastery in Florence and am here at our abbot's request to have your oversight corrected."

Fust took Gabriele a little more seriously than Antonio but shrugged it off, saying, "It's Gutenberg's Bible. It's Gutenberg's mistake."

Fust's employees had all either completely stopped what they were doing or were only pretending they were still doing their jobs. The truth was, unsurprisingly, they were captivated by the drama unfolding in front of them.

Then Fust asked, "What is the alleged mistake, anyway?"

Gutenberg tore open the Bible, quickly flipped to page 149, and, pointing to the typo, shouted, "Right here, Fust, right here! This is such an amateurish mistake! I could barely believe my eyes!" Looking around the room at Fust's employees, Gutenberg snarled, "I wonder which one of you is squirming right now? One of you certainly set this page."

Indignant, Gutenberg returned his stare to Fust, proclaiming, "I may make mistakes in choosing business partners, but I do not make mistakes in my work!"

Begrudgingly, Fust went over to a table with the open Bible, saying, "Show me this supposed error."

Growing more outraged with every passing minute, Gutenberg, pointing to the page, yelled, "Luke. Chapter 4, verse 18. Fust, for your enlightenment, the word '*Deus*' commands a capital 'D'! Even heathens know that!"

Fust, wanting to end this confrontation and get on with his day (and a pending lunch engagement), turned to Gabriele and said, "In deference to your monastery and as a sign of goodwill, I will send you back with a full refund for this book's purchase." He added, "With the understanding that this generosity is not an admission of any guilt on my part whatsoever."

"Law school," Antonio thought. "This man had to have attended a law school somewhere. Only lawyers talk like that."

Antonio responded immediately to the offer. "Herr Fust, I made that very suggestion to our abbot, that he ask for a refund. But he rejected that suggestion, saying that what he wants is for the Bible to be corrected."

Agitated, Fust responded, "Do you have any idea what is involved? Look at that plate!" Fust pointed to a plate a typesetter was setting, preparing it for the press. Getting more agitated the more he thought about it, Fust blasted, "Do you have any idea how much work goes into printing one page, Herr Manuscript Illustrator? But then, how could you? You're just a manuscript illustrator, a florin a dozen!"

Calmly, Antonio replied, "That's not true."

"How dare he speak back to me," Fust thought. He asked, "What's not true?"

"Your pricing."

"What pricing? I never said what this costs me."

"No. The price of manuscript illustrators. It's not a florin a dozen; it's a florin and a half a dozen. Prices have gone up. Inflation."

"Why you impetuous—" But before Fust could unleash to the world whatever gem of an insult he had in store for Antonio, the production door burst open, and in barged four men, all brandishing swords.

In the lead was Alfonso; beside him, Niccolò and Alessandro. Behind them, Lorenzo locked eyes with Antonio, breaking into a smile that looked like a snake slithering from one ear to the next.

Alfonso, also relishing this moment, stared at Gabriele, his smile so much like Lorenzo's you would not be faulted for believing the two were related. "I told you we'd meet again."

"I'll take the Bible. Thank you very much," Lorenzo commanded.

Gabriele turned to Antonio and calmly asked, "Do you know what I hate the most?"

Gabriele's demeanor was so unflustered and nonplussed, for a moment, it took the foursome off guard.

"What?" Antonio replied.

It was just a split second interlude, but in Gabriele's world, a split second was often the second that mattered.

"A surprise attack." Those words had not completely passed her lips before her sword was in hand, in the air; and as she faced Alfonso, you could detect a small, subtle, and disarmingly gentle smile on Gabriele's face. Alfonso's smile vaporized, and all you could see on his face was wrath. Whether that anger was at Gabriele or himself for falling for her deception is anyone's guess.

For a moment, the room was a tableau. No one moved. The foursome didn't move. Antonio and Gabriele, both of their swords now unsheathed, didn't move. None of the employees moved, although you could see the one closest to the door glancing back and forth between the armed men and the door itself, perhaps trying to perform basic physics in his mind: once everyone in the room became a moving part, would he be able to get to the door before any of the moving parts could get to him?

The remaining employees didn't move, and each had a look of garden-variety terror on their face. Fust didn't move, and he, too, studied the mechanics of reaching the door and escaping before any moving parts could get to him, but you didn't need a degree in physics to know that would not be possible.

Gutenberg did not move nor did he take his eyes off Fust.

Everyone remained frozen. As in chess, the game and its dynamics can depend very much on the first move. All stood for several moments staring at each other, each making game plans and trying to read their opponents.

Like a commander well behind the front lines, it was Lorenzo who shattered the standoff as he issued the order, "Get the book!"

All the pieces on the chessboard began their moves. The employees, mere pawns, ducked behind and beneath tables and work desks—except for the one who had been evaluating the physics involved in getting out the door, which he did.

Fust, trying to defy all odds, attempted a dash for the door, completely overlooking the fact that Gutenberg was directly behind him. While he was much older than Fust, Gutenberg easily grabbed Fust by his collar, stopping him in his tracks, simply saying, "Oh, no you don't!"

It is wise to never underestimate temperamental old men.

The real battle was between the armed opponents. The three thieves, each wanting a slice of revenge over the fate of their now headless colleague, Heinrich—whose name they often forgot—simultaneously attacked Gabriele. Flicking the dagger from up her sleeve did not provide the same distraction as it had with headless Heinrich, but it did serve as a little protection from her left side. To a degree.

While three pieces on the chessboard made a coordinated attack on the queen, Gabriele, they opened the board for the bishop to attack the king in the only way the bishop could attack: head-on. With the sword positioned for a frontal thrust, Lorenzo lunged forward very peculiarly, hopping from one foot to the other, still wearing his snake-like smile. But Antonio paid little attention to Lorenzo's facial expression. It was his feet he watched. As soon as Lorenzo was within inches of striking range, Antonio waited until Lorenzo hopped to his left foot. Then Antonio quickly crossed his left foot over his right and, with a simple parry, threw Lorenzo off his attack and off-balance, wiping the smile off his face. Now Lorenzo's face showed the side he always tried to mask: seething rage and hatred.

He lunged again. And again. And again. Each time he was out-feigned by Antonio's footwork; and each thrusting attempt was easily parried, first a side parry, then a thrust parry, then a side parry again, followed by yet another thrust parry. With each successful parry, Lorenzo became increasingly frustrated and enraged—and the more his feelings intensified, the clumsier his attacks became, to the point where Antonio was almost amused.

The room was a battle of two swords against four, but the reality was it was one sword against one sword and three swords against one.

Gabriele's battle was not as easy as Antonio's. Not only were there three swords against one, but Gabriele's opponents were far more experienced with swords than Lorenzo.

While she managed to keep two assailants at bay, parrying a two-pronged frontal thrust from Alessandro and Alfonso, Niccolò swept in from the side. Although her dagger did provide a little defense, Niccolò managed to get a swipe across Gabriele's hand clutching the dagger. There was a sharp sting. And blood.

At seeing first blood, all three of the thieves, while continuing their assaults, broke into smiles. Niccolò, emboldened by drawing first blood, stepped up his aggressive attacks. With each attack, he slipped closer and closer to Gabriele's side, where she would be most vulnerable.

The violent clanking of swords became more intense, and the time between engagements was shortening.

While repelling every attempt Lorenzo made to break through with a thrust, Antonio caught from the corner of his eye a move that was a mere second from happening: Niccolò was past ninety degrees to Gabriele's left and was quickly inching into position for an attack from the rear. Within a second, he was, and Antonio watched as Niccolò set up for an uppercut from behind. That would be a simple yet fatal blow.

Just as Niccolò began to raise his sword, Lorenzo attempted another thrust, only this time, his rage had overcome what limited skills he had. In a fit of pure, burning anger, he attempted an uppercut, charging with a low poised sword, and Antonio did to Lorenzo what Gabriele had done to him: a parry turned into a counter-attack. With a swift swipe, Antonio targeted Lorenzo's grip, knocking the sword from his hand and throwing Lorenzo off balance.

From the corner of his eye, Antonio saw Niccolò with his sword positioned to deliver a fatal blow.

In that split second, what instantly sprang to Antonio's mind was what Gabriele had drilled into him over and over again. Pivot! Pivot! Pivot! And pivot Antonio did. As Niccolò was about to deliver his blow, no doubt proud of his maneuver, he suddenly felt excruciating pain from his back and looked down to see the tip of Antonio's sword protruding from his intestines—Niccolò's last vision in life.

Niccolò's split-second demise directly behind Gabriele happened as Alfonso was in the middle of a thrust attack. He was taken off guard seeing Niccolò collapse, which gave Gabriele that split-second advantage of a parrying counter-attack. As she had done with Antonio in the courtyard, she pushed forward, turning her defensive move into an attack, closing the distance until she was nose-to-nose with Alfonso. She sought his gaze, as she always did, wanting to see the look in her opponent's eyes and let him see the look in hers. Seeing the fear and surprise in Alfonso's eyes, she smiled. Then, in a move never seen before in sword battle, she kissed him and leaped back, saying, "You know what that was?" As she pivoted and began a thrust to plunge her sword through his heart, the last thing Alfonso heard on this Earth was Gabriele saying, "That was the kiss of death."

Alessandro, the last remaining of the thieves, dropped his sword and fled through the door and into obscurity.

Lorenzo, in the process of getting back on his feet, made a feeble attempt to reach for his sword but quickly felt the tip of Antonio's sword pushing against his jugular and stopped.

"Please do, Lorenzo, and spare us the burden of having to care for and feed you on our return trip." It was now Antonio who wore a smile. Not Lorenzo.

Lorenzo tried pleading. "Antonio! Don't you see that keeping the flawed Bible is in your best interests, too?" Then, glancing over at Fust's press that was the genius of Gutenberg, he said, "Can't you see how that contraption is going to put you out of work? No one will need manuscript illustrators, Antonio!"

"I don't know, Lorenzo. I am confident I will be able to carve out some kind of future. Tell me: what will you do outside the monastery walls?"

Gabriele, stepping over Alfonso, turned back to Fust, saying, "Now, where were we?"

Fust, hysterical, replied, "Where were we? Where were we? Look! There is blood everywhere! All over our floors! There is blood all over the pages I have just printed! And look! Look! I have blood all over my clothes!

Calmly, as if speaking to a child in the midst of hysteria, Gabriele replied, "Fust, look on the bright side: at least it's not your blood."

Antonio turned to Gutenberg and asked, "Herr Gutenberg, how long should it take to have this page reprinted?"

Thinking out loud, Gutenberg replied, "Well, they don't have to redesign the page, merely copy what has been done." Looking at Fust's employees, he continued, "Depending on the skill of his employees, they should be able to prepare the page for printing in one day, print the second day, and let the ink dry overnight ... Two days, perhaps."

Antonio turned to Fust and said, "Herr Fust, as you must certainly know, Florence—as here in Mainz—is a thriving publishing center. Certainly, a businessman of your stature would know that industries are communities. In these communities, people talk and share experiences and information, wouldn't you agree? And a significant difference between Mainz and Florence is the Medici family."

Snidely, Fust replied, "What is your point, Herr Manuscript Illustrator?"

"A sad reality, Herr Fust, is that rumors travel faster and farther than truth. And rumors have destroyed businesses. The Medici family, I am told, makes a point of keeping their ears to the ground."

Fust said nothing.

After a few minutes of silence, Antonio asked, "Herr Fust, when can we expect to have a corrected manuscript to take back to our monastery and the abbot?

Gutenberg, without any attempt to hide his pleasure at a small morsel of revenge, then added, "And remember, Herr Fust, there were 180 of these Bibles scheduled for production. You no doubt finished them, earning considerable money. And sold them where? All across Europe?" Smiling, Gutenberg added, "You certainly face challenges."

Fust, forever the businessman, turned to Antonio, then to Gabriele, and asked, "How much would you two gentlemen charge to distribute the corrected texts?"

Without hesitation, Gabriele replied, "You can't afford us."

Although Fust tried to mask his indignation, he was unsuccessful as he replied, "How would you know what I can and cannot afford?"

Gabriele turned to Gutenberg and asked, "Herr Gutenberg, how much interest was Herr Fust charging you for the loan to turn your genius into reality?"

Gutenberg practically spat the words out. "Sixteen percent."

Gabriele looked back to Fust and said, "We will deliver your correction. Our fee is everything you own."

Fust threw his arms in the air in disgust.

"Plus sixteen percent."

Although monetarily bankrupt, for a moment, Gutenberg felt like the richest man in the world. Such is the incalculable value of retribution, no matter how short-lived.

Resigning himself to his profit-eating task, Fust blurted, "You'll have your correction in three days." Then, waving at the bloodied production floor, the bloodied printed pages, and the recently departed Alfonso and Niccolò, he asked, "What am I to do with this?"

Lorenzo, though still with the tip of Antonio's sword at his jugular, smugly spoke up. He hoped he could leverage Fust's position and forge an impromptu partnership borne from Lorenzo's on-the-spot scheming agility.

"Yes, Gabriele, what are you going to do about this? The way I see it, while I was here with guards of my own to fulfill our abbot's wishes, you and this tradesman here, under the employ of Gutenberg, came here seeking revenge for Gutenberg—and thus, you two are guilty of murder. Isn't that right, Herr Fust?"

Pulling on his straggly beard, clearly giving this idea careful considera-tion, Fust replied, "I like it, I like it." Gabriele's sword swooshed through the air, and Fust suddenly found himself in the same situation as Lorenzo: with a sword's tip at his jugular. Gabriele said, "If I or we are guilty of murder, what difference does it make if it is two or three?"

Ever the calm businessman, Fust turned to Lorenzo and replied, "While I admire your initiative, I think I will stick with the reprinting. After all, it's only one page."

All Lorenzo managed to do was bring Gabriele's attention to him. With the commanding stature of the head of security, Gabriele walked over to Lorenzo, stared at him and, seeing his pouch slung around his neck, asked, "What do you have in the pouch? Money, I hope. Our funds are running low, and now we have you to feed as well on our return journey."

"These are my personal belongings."

Pandering, Gabriele replied, "Now, Prior Lorenzo, you know as well as I that in the monastery, there is no such thing as 'personal belongings.' Toss the pouch over, but be slow and careful as you move. Antonio is a manuscript illustrator and not as skilled with a sword as I am. A foolish or sudden move could result in your throat accidentally being cut."

Lorenzo glared at Gabriele as he slowly removed his pouch and tossed it to her feet. Picking it up and opening it, Gabriele said, "Good. I see we have a little more money and the monastery seal, of course." Then she pulled out the letter Lorenzo carried and opened it. Seeing it was written in Latin, she handed it to Antonio, saying, "Latin. Do you mind?"

With little risk of Lorenzo attempting anything stupid, given the monastery's head of security's skills, Antonio sheathed his sword and took the letter. As he read, he slowly smiled and said, "This letter, backed by the Medicis, authorizes a line of credit be extended to"—Antonio paused and looked at Lorenzo, then to Gabriele—"the bearer of this letter. If his dead thief-partners understood what this letter said, Lorenzo would not be alive today. This is a bottomless well of money."

As Gabriele, Gutenberg, Fust, and Antonio were sparing and arguing, over the mechanics and responsibilities of correcting the Bible, Lorenzo slowly slid backward and slyly grasped his pouch, empty but for one thing: his monastery's seal. Once close to the door, he made his move: he jumped up and sprinted out the door and onto the streets.

Fust laughed, saying, "It seems your fish has gotten off the hook."

Antonio turned and stared Fust straight in the eye, replying, "Who said he was our fish, Fust? You said you could have this Bible corrected in three days? Make it two. Seems you'll have your work cut out for you." Then, looking Fust and his wardrobe up and down, Antonio added, "You do know how to work, don't you?"

Worth the Wait

Mainz, Germany

March 31, 1461

On their walk back to the Gasthaus zur Krone, Antonio said, "Let me see your hand." Blood trickled from the swipe that the now deceased Niccolò had taken across Gabriele's dagger hand.

"It's nothing."

"Nothing is nothing. Let me see."

Antonio took Gabriele's hand and saw that while the cut ran across her hand, it was not deep. But a cut is a cut, and an infection is an infection.

Looking straight ahead as they walked, Gabriele said quietly, "Remember. You're holding a man's hand."

Just as quietly, Antonio replied, "And heart. We'll have the inn send for someone to treat this wound."

And they did. The attending city physician wrapped the wound in cloth and concluded the appointment saying, "It's nothing, really."

Gabriele turned to Antonio and smirked, communicating the timeless, universal, wordless message that reads, "I told you so."

The next two days Antonio and Gabriele spent with Gutenberg in his workshop. The method of type creation and the font design fascinated Antonio.

Gutenberg took pride in showing Antonio his printing process, but he was occasionally interrupted by questions from his nervous apprentice. Gutenberg would bark his responses, and the apprentice would scurry back to his tasks and duties.

At one point, while Gutenberg was expounding on the process of forging each letter needed for the press to Gabriele, Antonio walked over to the apprentice and said, "You know, I was once an apprentice, just like you."

"You were, Herr Strozzi?"

"Of course, we all start somewhere. And like you, I had a famed teacher. His name was Fra Angelico. When people learned he had trained me, it opened doors that otherwise might have remained closed. But being trained by him was not easy. He did not suffer mistakes kindly."

The apprentice glanced over at Gutenberg, now in excited, animated discussion with Gabriele, explaining all the mechanics behind the genius of what he had created.

Antonio asked, "What's your name?"

"Hans, Herr Strozzi."

"Well, Hans, I believe that once you learn and gain experience working with Gutenberg's press and are grown and making your own way, saying Gutenberg trained you will give you credentials others only dream of. So let him bark. After all, barking dogs don't bite, do they?"

"Thank you, Herr Strozzi."

"Don't thank me. Thank him."

THE JOURNEY HOME

ON THE ROAD AGAIN

Mainz, Germany

April 3, 1461

At dawn's break on the morning of the fourth day in Mainz, Antonio and Gabriele loaded their saddlebags to prepare for the long trip back to Florence. The last thing to do in Mainz was to stop at Fust's foundry and printing facility and collect the redeemed Bible.

When they opened the door, Fust turned and, with a sour look on his face, said, "There on the table. There's your book. Take it and leave."

Antonio walked over to the table, opened the Bible, and turned to page 149. There was *"Deus"* with a capital "D." At the end of the table was a large stack of printed pages, and you could still smell the ink. There sat 179 corrected pages.

Antonio smiled, looked at Fust, and said, "Well done, Fust. I am impressed. I wish you luck with the distribution of the corrections. I am sure, if I know our Abbot Fransisco, he'll be following up with communiqués to fellow monastery abbots throughout our Holy Roman Empire. If I were in your tailored shoes, I would not want to overlook any Bible in need of correction."

Antonio took the Bible and left. Gabriele, stone-faced, had not taken her eyes off Fust, and she waited until Antonio was safely out the door before backing out and closing the door behind her.

As Antonio was securing the Bible in Thrice's saddlebag, Gabriele commented, "We have a long journey. Hopefully, our return to Florence will not take as long as our journey to get here."

Gabriele had ensured Antonio understood anytime she was in public view she was Gabriele, the man. Gabriele, the swordsman, not to cross.

Antonio, as he was mounting Twice, smiled and said, "I think our return trip to Florence will be much more enjoyable than the journey to get here."

"How so?"

Antonio reached into his saddlebag and pulled out the letter he had liberated from Lorenzo. He held it in the air and said, "Think of it as a paid vacation."

Antonio knew full well there would be no public display of affection from Gabriele, but he could read her well and was probably the only one who would recognize her small, almost imperceptible smile.

To Florence on a Wing and a Prayer

Worms, Germany

April 5, 1461

Lorenzo had a two-day lead on the race back to Florence. He hoped his correspondence to Abbot Fransisco while en route to Mainz would have entrenched the abbot's concern of a deep-rooted conspiracy spreading among a traitorous cadre within the monasterial community.

It was solely the San Miniato al Monte Monastery's seal (his only possession), his agile imagination, and his oratory skills that would see him through his long trek back to the sanctuary of his monasterial position.

His mission in Mainz had failed, but that did not mean the lowly tradesman and his treasonous guard partner had succeeded. They, too, had to return to Florence. And knowing he would have a two-day lead, Lorenzo had time to plan and plot to prevent their safe return.

For his hasty departure, he was thankful for Between Thieves. He set an aim for the first monastery of significance en route, where his monastery's seal would surely afford him a warm welcome, food, and accommodations. More importantly, it would also give him access to financiers who, seeing the seal, would secure him funds for his return journey. After all, it was common knowledge within the nobility and the monasterial circles that his San Miniato al Monte Monastery in Florence had trusting relations with the Medici family. With that came convenient access to Medici money. The San Miniato al Monte Monastery seal was as good as the gold from which it was forged.

Knowing Antonio and Gabriele would wait two days for Fust to correct the Bible, Lorenzo was confident he could take his time at the Monastery of St. Peter in Worms, even though Worms was close to Mainz. The Monastery of St. Peter was also one of the most renowned religious centers in the Holy Roman Empire, and was now over three hundred years old.

The monastery, with its pier-basilica design, eastern and western choirs, and four flanking towers, was the burial site for several Holy Roman emperors. Like Lorenzo himself, this setting had stature. Its significance inspired Lorenzo. Such a fitting place to design plans to ensure the Holy Scriptures remain in their rightful place, within the walls of institutions such as this.

Fust may be busy working on correcting his blasphemous, careless blunder, but that did not mean the corrected Bible needed to make it back to his monastery.

Here in St. Peter's Cathedral in Worms, Lorenzo would have the time for inspiration and planning.

His welcome had been warm, and once he made his position known, further evidenced by his revered golden seal, the monks gave him a guest room suitable for a person of his station. The attending cleric was only too happy to provide the paper, quill, and ink he requested.

At the conclusion of the meal service and evening prayers, Lorenzo retired to his guest quarters overlooking the grounds and, beyond that, the town of Worms.

Glancing out the window before sitting at his table and taking quill and ink to paper, he hoped he would see another shooting star, a sign from the heavens. But he did not. However, that did not deter him from his mission, his role as guardian of the holy Church's domain. Now, equally important as his mission was his responsibility to prevent the story of the incident at Fust's from reaching Abbot Fransisco's ears. More than the corrected Bible needed to be disappeared. Now, so did Antonio and Gabriele.

But how could he stop Antonio and the Monastery's mutinous guard?

He reflected on the power of the Church; it was the power of the Church he needed to harness. Where was its actual power? Adoration? Worship? Faith? No. Those were not the actual powers that kept its flock faithful to the Church and its commands. No.

That power was fear.

Did we not preach to fear the wrath of God?

Deep in reflection of the dynamics of the Church, Lorenzo kept circling around and around and around. How could he instill fear in Antonio and his feckless guard?

Then, as if the shooting star had indeed shot across the sky, Lorenzo's brilliance shone again. He smiled. It was so simple. Yet so powerful.

Trying to instill fear in them was a fool's errand. But what if he turned it around? What if he could weave and spread a story that made them the ones to be feared, instilling suspicion of them in the clergy he encountered on his journey back to the sacred sanctuary of his monastery? What if he could do that?

And what is man's instinct when it senses something or someone menacing threatening it?

Man's instinct is to kill it.

From flies to bears: kill it.

Like many great ideas, it was all in the execution. A fly, you can see. A bear, you can see. But what is most fearsome is that which you cannot see.

Antonio's and Gabriele's appearances were nothing to be fearful of. Quite the opposite. They were attractive young men, almost innocent looking. Could he use their look of innocence against them? Like Medea and Circe of Greek mythology: Both beautiful. Both deadly.

What would be their story?

Lorenzo's keen strategic focus always remained on the core objective. What did he want? Distrust of any sacred texts not emanating from the confines of the Church, his Church. Additionally: to silence Antonio and Gabriele.

If there could be holy water, it only stood to reason there could be unholy water. And being transported through the appearance of innocence made it all the more terrifying.

What if the Bible they were transporting had been sprinkled with unholy water by the Devil himself, turning anyone who touched it or even looked at its pages against God and all who tried to spread His word?

Armed with a quill, ink, paper, and the revered San Miniato al Monte Monastery's seal, Lorenzo put his talents to work.

"*Socii mei Pugnatores Ecclesiae Nostrae,*

"*Scripsi ad te cum corde onere urgenti et metu. Ad me pervenit quod duo apparent innocentes,* Antonio Strozzi *et* Gabriele, *terram nostram sacram inter Worms et Florentiam percurrunt sub specie quae veram naturam eorum celat. Hi enim sunt agentes Diaboli ipsius, missi ad fundamenta fidei nostrae subvertere.*

"*Hi viri Bibliam portant, contaminatam aqua inhonesta, quae ab Principe Tenebrarum superpositum est. Haec non est liber ordinarius; est vas corruptionis. Te oro, ne fallaris aspectu eorum. Paginae huius libri maledicti potentiam habent capere animas eorum qui audent tangere vel etiam spectare, transformantes innocentes in instrumenta mali—agentes quorum solum munus est compromittere et minari voluntatem divinam Dei in Terra.*

"*Celeriter et decisively agere debemus. Te rogo ut sociorum tuorum championum Ecclesiae coniungas et paratus sis ad hanc insidiosam minacem congredi. Liber quem portant non debet aperiri; ad cineres reducendus est ne malignitas eius inter nos disseminetur. Ne deficiamus in officio nostro ad fidem nostram et populum nostrum ab hoc vilem deceptione tuendum.*

"*Deus nobis vires in hoc tempore necessitatis tribuat.*

"*In ministerio Christi,*

"Prior Lorenzo

"*Monasterium San Miniato al Monte*

"*Data die Mercurii, v. Aprilis, A.D. MDLXI.*

"My Fellow Champion of Our Church,

"I write to you with a heart burdened by urgency and dread. It has come to my attention that two seemingly innocent figures, Antonio Strozzi and Gabriele, are traversing our sacred lands from Worms to Florence under a guise that conceals their true nature. They are, in fact, agents of the Devil himself, sent to undermine the very foundations of our faith.

"These men carry a Bible tainted by unholy water, sprinkled upon it by the Prince of Darkness. This is no ordinary tome; it is a vessel of corruption. I implore you, do not be deceived by their outward appearance. The pages of this accursed book possess the power to ensnare the souls of those who dare to touch or even gaze upon them, transforming the innocent into instruments of evil—agents whose sole mission is to compromise and threaten God's divine will on Earth.

"We must act swiftly and decisively. I urge you to rally your fellow champions of the Church and prepare to confront this insidious threat. The book they carry must not be opened; it must be reduced to ashes lest it spread its malevolence among us. Let us not falter in our duty to protect our faith and our people from this vile deception.

"May God grant us strength in this hour of need.

"In Christ's service,

"Prior Lorenzo,

"San Miniato al Monte Monastery

Wednersday, April 5, 1461"

Once the letter was crafted, Lorenzo took to making copies to be distributed by couriers throughout the route back to Florence, a task that occupied him for half the night.

Though he had little sleep, Lorenzo rose at dawn for morning prayers and breakfast, but first he requested the services of and a meeting with the Monastery's most trusted courier. His name was Frederico, a young man who had chosen to be a messenger of God—not as an ordained monk but as a swift, horse-powered deliverer of urgent inter-monasterial communiqués. Frederico's reputation had spread as quickly as the messages he carried. "This is from Frederico," implied urgency and action. Frederico and his messages traveled day and night to the monasteries and major churches littering the trade route between Mainz and Florence, easily surpassing the hapless duo oblivious to the traps that lay before them.

The only other issue Lorenzo faced was money. Or more to the point, lack of it.

Today, it's hard for us to imagine a world void of Bitcoins, intercontinental-linked cash dispensers, and multiple branch banks that trust each other to give cash to a person they have never met before but is vouched for by another of their bank's branches.

In medieval times, being trusted with cash was a "who you know" arrangement.

And Lorenzo knew Bertold, who knew Günther, who knew Gerbrecht, who knew Hartmann, who kept a considerable amount of various currencies secured in secret sanctuaries in his sprawling Worms domiciles. So Lorenzo conned Bertold, who conned Günther, who conned Gerbrecht, who conned Hartmann to part with funds using a non-lawyer-approved promise that the Medicis would back this loan—a promise made credible only by Lorenzo's possession of his monastery's seal and his oratory skills. And his smiles.

In today's world, the word "conned" is often replaced with the word, "fucked." So Lorenzo fucked Bertold, who fucked Günther, who fucked Gerbrecht, who fucked Hartmann, who was the one who was truly fucked because trying to begot the Church in the age of the Inquisition was a sign of wisdom deprivation. There was little chance Hartmann would see his money again.

At midday, with his pouch fattened by Hartmann, Lorenzo mounted Between Thieves and made off for Florence.

Pleased with himself and his success in Worms, he rode through the pastoral, agricultural lands, confident that his weeks of diligence and refusal to allow the blasphemous forces outside the fortresses of holy Church walls would prevail. Beyond swatting at spring's flies hatching from the ground under Between Thieves' hooves, the spring ride was idyllic. He rode under the warmth of God's sun, at peace with himself, his mission, and all things divine, knowing his story would be spread as fast as any story could spread. With a network of monastery couriers, it would spread even through the darkness of night.

Meanwhile, in the privacy of the wide-open spaces, Antonio and Gabriele were free to talk, laugh, and enjoy the fresh air as lovers, as friends, and as sharers of secrets neither shared with anyone but each other.

They planned their return journey with every intention to make each moment they had together out of sight and sound of other eyes and ears the most precious moment they were granted while here in this world.

Gabriele valued the freedom to laugh almost as much as she valued life itself. It was a freedom she had never dared to indulge in before now. As they rode across the fields and over streams, she would occasionally look around to her sides, front, then behind. Confident there was not another human soul in sight or sound, she would tilt her head back, looking to the heavens, and yell at the top of her liberated lungs, "Yes! Yes, yes, yes!" so loud Antonio quipped, "Aren't you worried God will hear you?"

"Worried? *Worried*? No! Thankful!"

At the sight of any human dwelling or presence, from a shepherd to a distant stone house, Gabriele would fall silent again, fall back into her protected shell. Gabriele the guard was always on guard.

As they passed through the narrow cobblestone streets of Worms, Antonio told the history of the now three-hundred-year-old St. Peter's Cathedral, explaining its role in the 1122 signing of the Concordat of Worms, the 1235 wedding of Emperor Frederick II and Isabella of England, and the burial of Holy Roman emperors on its grounds.

"How do you know all this?"

"Remember, Gabriele, I not only read the manuscripts I illustrate, but I also remember some of what I commit to paper."

Gabriele stared at the cathedral as they rode by, wondering what secrets it must hold—as well as what is told in manuscripts. "The universe holds many secrets," she thought.

While tempted to stop, they decided to push on. Paid vacation or not, they both had lives to return to in Florence.

The rolling hills they traveled through were lined by miles of rows of grapevines, which were coming to life after a dormant winter's rest.

Monks and farmers were tending to the vineyards, casting passing glances and waves as Antonio and Gabriele rode by.

They had given preference to inns over monasteries for their return journey, and although not on the direct route back to Florence, Antonio wanted to visit the Carthusian Charterhouse in Kiedrich. Although it was a modest town with mostly Gothic structures, it did have contemporary additions such as Saint Michael's Chapel—which was only twenty years old—and there were construction plans for a church dedicated to Saint Valentine. Eltville am Rhein was just a short distance farther and would have better inns than Kiedrich, but Antonio wanted to see choirs at the Charterhouse. It was developing a reputation for distinctive harmonies in Latin-language liturgical music, which was something Antonio would enjoy hearing if they were fortunate enough to visit while a choir was practicing.

They rode to the entrance, and a monk working on the grounds, seeing them approach, came to greet them. Antonio and Gabriele introduced themselves, and Antonio expressed an interest in seeing where the choir might perform or rehearse.

The attending monk smiled meekly, saying, "Please wait here, and I shall return momentarily."

"Momentarily" wasn't quite momentarily, and Antonio and Gabriele were just discussing whether to forego this stop and continue on their way when the church doors flung open and four guards appeared, two bearing swords and two armed with spears. Even Gabriele, a seasoned guard, was taken by surprise and knew it would be foolhardy to attempt to engage.

One guard said, "Come with us and bring your saddlebags, but *do not* even attempt to open them." Flanked by the two guards with swords and followed closely by the two guards with spears, they were led inside. They only got a passing glimpse of the chapel before the guards led them down a narrow stone stairway lit only with two torches. The stairway steered them to a tight stone corridor lined with closed wooden doors, and only two more torches lit the way. It seemed as if this corridor ran the length of the church down its middle, explaining the absence of windows.

One guard opened the first door and, motioning to it, barked at Antonio, "Toss your bag in the room, then turn around and place your hands behind you." As soon as Antonio had done as instructed, he felt two strong hands bind his wrists with rope. Then the hands shoved him in the room and slammed the door, and he heard the clank of an iron bolt. The room was small but tall, possibly three meters, and at the top of the wall opposite the door was a small window that only admitted enough light to keep the room from complete darkness. There was not one piece of furniture in the room. It was simply cold gray stone.

A few moments later, he heard, faintly, what sounded like another iron bolt slamming into place. After that, he could hear nothing.

"Gabriele?" he called out.

He heard no answer.

The Savior

Nuremberg, Germany

April 9, 1461

With a bustling population of twenty thousand people, second only to Cologne in western Germany, Nuremberg had diverse economic activities of toy manufacturing, textiles, and metalwork production. But what most appealed to Lorenzo was its respectable showing of religious centers, including St. Lorenz Church, a namesake he bore with pride. Indeed, Lorenzo sat tall on Between Thieves as he paraded along the winding cobblestone streets. He passed the St. Sebaldus Church, which was just a few streets away from the Franciscan Monastery, riding like arriving royalty. In the few stops he had made, the clergy welcomed him as a church hero. The copies of his message, traveling via courier day and night to churches and monasteries dotting the trade routes, stood like beacons guiding him on his journey home and into Church legacy, the defender of Church authority.

The fear of unholy water had gripped the community of Christ; and churches, cathedrals, and monasteries welcomed Lorenzo almost as a second savior. His choice of where to rest his head that Nuremberg night was the Frauenkirche, the Church of Our Lady. It had passed its centennial less than ten years prior and was a suitable resting spot for a monastic celebrity such as him—even though he always presented himself in a veil of humility, like a shrinking violet. The Church of Our Lady was significant, having been founded by the Holy Roman emperor Charles IV. It was, to Lorenzo, a relatable significance.

As he dismounted Between Thieves, a minister opened the door to greet the guest, who quickly introduced himself.

The minister's eyebrows shot to the heavens, and he replied, "Prior Lorenzo? What an honor to have you grace our humble home! We all know of you here! Please, I will have someone tend to your horse. Will you be staying with us tonight?"

"If you can accommodate me, yes, it would be a welcome reprieve from a long day saddle-bound."

"Of course, please, let me show you to a guest room. I hope it will be to your liking."

While the church's exterior was simple, the only highlight its coat of arms, stepping through the doors was a different story. The interior housed many works of art with an impressive display of statuary. The minister led Lorenzo to a small but comfortable room at the rear behind the altar.

"Please. Relax, and I will fetch our priest, who will be most pleased to greet you, I am sure.

Lorenzo settled his bags and sat at the room's table. He glanced out the window to the views of the rear church grounds, where gardens just beginning to blossom sent sweet scents for Lorenzo's pleasure.

A few moments later, a tall, thin gracefully aging priest wearing a black robe and a cross around his neck gave a light knock on the door and stepped in the room. He extended his welcoming hand for a greeting rather than offering a ring to be kissed and introduced himself, saying, "Welcome, Prior Lorenzo. My name is Father Martin, and I am pleased to meet you."

Lorenzo took Father Martin's hand in both his hands, gave a slight bow befitting for attending royalty, and replied, "My pleasure, I am sure."

"Come. Join me in our dining room and tell me about your travels. I am most eager to hear your stories, especially how you learned of this satanic threat to our faith and the faithful."

Father Martin led the way along the corridor, which was lined with statuary and artwork. Lorenzo followed, crafting his backstory to the communiqué now whisking its way, courier by courier, throughout the Holy Roman Empire.

They reached the dining room and sat at a table. A minister served tea while Lorenzo elaborated on his story with a focus on the phrase he was careful to apply to his letter, "It has come to my attention …" Those six words relieved Lorenzo of any firsthand responsibility, laying that burden on a humble worshipper whom he knew only as Hans—who was outside the room where this dark ritual with the unholy water had taken place. Hans had overheard the entire exchange, and while he had not seen the Devil himself, he described his voice as the deepest, most gravelly voice he had ever heard—a voice that made his spine tremble. Once he heard the instructions this demon issued, he had raced to relay the story to Lorenzo, believing the prior would know best what to do.

Father Martin replied, "A fascinating story, and we can only be thankful this young man, Hans, had the foresight to advise you."

"Thankful, indeed," Lorenzo replied.

Father Martin stood, saying, "Well, thank you, Prior Lorenzo, for your speedy response and action. We will indeed watch out for these two agents of the Devil. Please join us for dinner and prayers. If you need anything to make your stay more comfortable, please tell my ministers, and I will ensure they take care of you."

Lorenzo stood and offered an ingratiating bow as the priest left the room and Lorenzo to his own devices.

Sitting back in his chair and staring back out the window, Lorenzo was thankful for his meeting with Father Martin. It made him realize there would be more tightening to his narrative required since this communiqué was indeed traveling quickly and would reach Florence long before him.

Yes, his narrative would require refinement.

The Double-Edged Sword

Kiedrich, Germany

April 9, 1461

Father Peter, a tall, thin elderly priest with silver hair and a black robe, sat at the table in the small dining room at the rear of the church. With him were two of his younger clergymen and two of the guards who had locked Antonio and Gabriele in their cells.

Father Peter read aloud the urgent letter that had arrived by courier.

At its conclusion, he remained staring at the letter while the others waited for his thoughts and conclusions. What were they to do with these two?

The younger priests waited to hear what Father Peter would say, and the guards—frightened at the thought of putting themselves in the hands of the Devil's agents—waited for instructions.

Father Peter put the letter on the table and smiled. The younger priests looked at each other, astonished. What could be so amusing about the matter that was before them?

"So this is the handiwork of the great and powerful Lucifer? This is the best he can come up with? Lucifer himself?"

The younger priests stared in disbelief. How could Father Peter treat this matter so lightly?

"No one actually saw this event, did they? It was overheard by a young man we only know of as 'Hans,' who reported it to this Prior Lorenzo."

Father Peter turned to the guards and asked, "Who did these two say they were?"

A guard answered, "One said his name was Antonio and that he was a manuscript illustrator. The other claimed to be Gabriele, the head of security for the San Miniato al Monte Monastery in Florence."

Suddenly, Father Peter looked surprised. "Where?"

"The San Miniato al Monte Monastery in Florence."

"Was he armed?"

The second guard held up Gabriele's sword and answered, "Yes. With this."

Father Peter looked at it and said, "It looks like a nobleman's sword."

The second guard replied, "That's what's so unusual." He unsheathed the sword, adding, "This is a warrior's blade. I have never seen anything like this."

Father Peter got up from the table when he saw the sword, Lorenzo's letter in hand, and said to the guards, "Come with me."

When he heard the bolt to his barren cell clank, it startled him. Since his arrival, bound and thrown into the cell, Antonio had heard nothing except an occasional bird's faint chirp, which reached him through the tiny window high in the dungeon's wall.

When the door opened, Father Peter entered carrying two wooden stools, and two guards followed. He set the stools on the floor as the guards untied Antonio's bound hands. The priest gestured for Antonio to sit on a stool, taking the other himself. The guards exited, leaving the door open.

When Father Peter spoke, his voice was low and soft, and he stared Antonio in the eye as he asked, rhetorically, "You are Antonio?"

"Yes. Antonio Strozzi."

"My name is Father Peter." Spreading his arms into the air, he continued, "This is my church. Actually, it's not really mine, is it? It's God's church. This is where people come to worship. This is where people come for spiritual advice. People baptize children here. We lay souls to rest, we join couples in holy matrimony, and every week, we celebrate and worship God together."

Then, looking up at the tiny window, he added, "Evil has no home here."

He looked back at Antonio and said, "I understand you are a manuscript illustrator."

"Yes. In Florence."

"So you read Latin?"

"Yes."

Father Peter, saying nothing, handed Antonio the sheet of paper Antonio had not even noticed Father Peter was carrying.

It was Lorenzo's letter. Antonio, grasping the seriousness of its accusations, began to protest, almost stammering, "This … this … this is …"

But Father Peter cut him off, concluding Antonio's sentence: "… unforgivable." He continued, "Antonio, people come to seek God's forgiveness through me for a variety of indiscretions, lapses in judgement, and other personal matters we call 'sins.' I came to sit with you in this cell to ask for yours."

Antonio glanced back at the letter and replied, "Father, I am but a manuscript illustrator. However, it strikes me you are not the one who should ask for forgiveness. But how did you …"

"How did I know? Abbot Fransisco and I go back many years. As young students of the Scriptures, we studied together and have remained friends. Close friends. A few years ago, he informed me about a guard who had saved his life, a guard by the name of Gabriele. While returning from a visit to the Medici residence and carrying significant sums, he and his sole guard were attacked by three armed bandits who made it clear they knew Abbot Fransisco carried money. As one bandit lunged toward the abbot, his sole guard's swordsmanship put an end to him with a strike through his throat. With agility the abbot had never seen, the guard engaged the other two—one did not live to tell the story while the third turned and ran. All of this happened, according to Abbot Fransisco, in little more than a blink of an eye.

"Right now, that guard is doing what you should be doing: eating. You must be hungry. Come. Let's join him."

Antonio and Father Peter stood, and as Antonio began to pick up his stool, Father Peter said, "No, I will carry that. Just grab your bags, and perhaps you can show me this book of Gutenberg's. I have yet to see one."

Up on the main floor, they walked through the body of the church, past the pews and colorful stained glass windows lining the cathedral walls. Antonio followed Father Peter around the altar to a rear door that led to a small hallway. At the end was a discreet dining room.

Gabriele was at the table with one of the priests, eating. Seeing Antonio and Father Peter, she said, Gabriele-businesslike, "Antonio. Good to see you. I'm glad you seem in good health."

"You, too, Gabriele."

Pulling a chair out for Antonio, Father Peter said, "First, we'll get you fed, and then perhaps you could show me this book."

After he and Gabriele had eaten, Antonio placed Gutenberg's Bible on the table in front of Father Peter, who, thrilled, carefully turned the pages and lightly ran his fingers over the engravings, remarking on its magnificence.

"And you saw the presses that made this?"

"Yes."

"Marvelous. Just think how this will spread the good word."

His was precisely the opposite point of view of Lorenzo's.

Closing the Bible, Father Peter said, "We must ensure your receptions at your various stops as you journey back to Florence are not repeats of this one."

Then, holding up Lorenzo's letter, he said, "This arrived by courier. And the chain of couriers travel day and night. Lorenzo was through here two days ago, so he does have a lead on you. You can expect no matter where you stop, this letter will have preceded you.

"I will send couriers out immediately that will also travel day and night. This story and the truth will be dispensed with the utmost urgency.

"Lorenzo needs to sleep. A chain of couriers does not. It will take a few days, but eventually, the truth will overpass him. And my instructions, in the name of the Church, will be to ignore his communiqué and let him continue on his journey back to his San Miniato al Monte Monastery.

"By separate couriers, I will also send an urgent message to my friend Abbot Fransisco, along with a copy of Lorenzo's letter. I am confident the abbot will address Prior Lorenzo appropriately."

Riding High in April

Bologna, Italy

April 12, 1461

During his travels through the Holy Roman Empire's German territories, Lorenzo embellished his unholy water chronicle. His monasterial seal ensured he and Between Thieves were well provided for as his story and fame spread from village to village, town to town, church to church, and monastery to monastery.

Lorenzo had the comfort of a two-day lead and the confidence that day and night couriers would be laying the unholy water trap.

So Lorenzo rode in peace, taking his time to ensure his message preceded him. He had lingered in Heidelberg and taken his time in Worms, visiting all the town's holy homes.

That wasn't his first mistake. But it was a mistake. In Bruchsal, Karlsruhe, Pforzheim, Basel, and especially Zurich, people treated him as the second savior.

But as he got closer to Florence—particularly in Asti—his reception, while courteous and accommodating, did not result in discussions of any consequence.

With day after day of polite dinner conversation, worry dined on Lorenzo's ego.

When he reached the Monastery of San Domenico in Bologna, he conferred with his co-conspirator, Subprior Paola, telling him of his unholy water plan. But he confessed he was unsure if his strategy had borne fruit.

He had Paola reassure him of his loyalty, a conversation punctuated by only subtle reminders of his Medici connections. He suggested Paola recruit the eyes and ears of Bologna's finest—such as the horse trader Jacopo and his network of the less than orthodox—to watch for signs of

Antonio and Gabriele. With Lorenzo, suggestions were politely worded instructions.

Lorenzo reminded Paola of the mission: keep that book out of circulation. And given the encounter in Mainz, it would be preferable if Antonio and Gabriele were to disappear and never be heard from or seen again.

What Lorenzo did not know was history would repeat itself right across town, right there in Bologna.

The following morning, Prior Lorenzo mounted Between Thieves and, now firmly in the hands of fate, began his ride into destiny.

Parting and Sorrow

Florence, Italy

April 12, 1461

As they crested the hill and saw the town of Bologna in the distance, Antonio and Gabriele became quiet. So much had happened since they first bypassed Bologna's Monastery of San Domenico weeks ago, when they evaded Lorenzo—at least temporarily. Then, they were the manuscript illustrator and guard, and now they were lovers. Neither spoke as they rode past the Monastery, heading into the town to find an inn for the night. They both were wondering, after this night, when they would have another night together. Each contemplated how they could go back to the life they had before the world had experienced its first typo. And they had experienced each other.

Antonio was the first to speak.

"What do you think? The River Inn again?"

Gabriele looked at Antonio, smiling, and said, "You mean an inn that caters to horse traders and highway bandits? That sounds romantic. Why not?"

As they got closer to the town's edge, Antonio turned and just stared at Gabriele. Sensing his look, Gabriele turned to him and said, "What are you thinking?"

Antonio looked away, turning his gaze straight ahead in the direction they were riding. "Nothing."

Gabriele continued to stare at Antonio as they rode and, after a few silent moments, said, "Yes, me too. Nothing."

The sun was setting as Twice and Thrice took their first steps from the dirt trail onto the winding cobblestone streets. Lamps were being lit in the houses' and shops' windows, and street vendors were closing their stalls for the night.

Now, in public view, Gabriele the guard was back on duty. Antonio was accustomed to this routine. He would not see Gabriele his lover again until they were behind closed doors.

When they arrived at the inn, Gabriele said, "I'll go in and make sure they have a room for us. Wait here." She dismounted and disappeared through the inn doors while Antonio waited with the horses. A few moments later, Gabriele came back and said, "We're in luck. Same room. Let's drop our things in the room and get something to eat. I've asked them to care for the horses."

When they reached their room to drop their saddlebags, they closed the door behind them. They stood and stared at each other, neither saying a word. Antonio took Gabriele's hand, and Gabriele, looking him in the eye, said only, "I know."

She turned and opened the door, and they made their way out. Looking and acting more like a him than a her, Gabriele led the way down the stairs, and they headed to the tavern to eat. Stepping through the tavern was like stepping back in time. It seemed as if nothing in the world had changed. Except them. The tavern was moderately full, but there was a table for them. Jacopo was in the corner conducting business and the barmaid was busy conducting hers.

Once they were seated, the waiter arrived at their table to announce the day's menu and to take their order.

"Welcome! Allow me to tell you about today's specials. I am pleased to offer The Pilgrim's Respite, The Medicis' Modest Banquet, The Friar's Fasting Fare, and a new addition to our offering, The Nobleman's Winter Fowl." Antonio looked at Gabriele, then turned to the waiter and asked, "What is The Nobleman's Winter Fowl?"

The waiter replied, "Stuffed pigeon."

Antonio replied, "Pigeon is fowl?"

Proudly, the waiter replied, "Here, yes."

In unison, Antonio and Gabriele replied, "I'll have that."

WILLIAM LOWER

"And a tankard of wine?"

"For two," Antonio replied.

When the waiter returned with their wine, Antonio raised his glass to Gabriele and said, "To a successful trip."

Gabriele raised her glass to his and said, sounding very businesslike, on guard, and guard-like, "A very successful trip."

Over dinner, in a crowded tavern, they spoke in code. The small talk disguised the big conversations they had not had.

"Are you looking forward to returning to your routine in the studio?"

The coded answer was a shrug and "It's almost hard to imagine. It feels like I have been gone a lifetime."

The coded acknowledgment was "I understand."

The waiter brought their dinners, and they ate in relative silence—a silence you have when your vocal cords are paralyzed, but your mind is screaming.

When dinner and the imported wine were finished, Antonio paid the waiter, and they walked back to the inn in silence.

When they were safely behind their room's closed door, they fell silently into each other's arms and stood as one. One statue. Two parts, but one entity.

Gabriele then looked around their room and said, "I think I'm going to miss this place."

They slowly and wordlessly undressed each other, then slid into the narrow straw-mattress bed, leaving the other one untouched.

Neither slept well, slipping in and out of consciousness, reluctant to let sleep rob them of what they each feared would be their last night together.

After a quiet breakfast at the tavern, they were once again road-bound on Twice and Thrice.

They rode silently through the winding streets and only spoke once they were free and alone together, making their way across Tuscany's rolling hills of fields and vineyards, crossing streams and heading to the inevitable: the final destination of Florence and the end of enchantment.

"I'm sure Abbot Fransisco will be pleased to have you back."

"The studio's star will be back to shine again."

Unasked by either was the question, "How do you drift back into the status quo after this, after what we've been through?"

It was dusk when Florence came into view. The late afternoon sun cast a golden glow across the city's walls and houses, and on the hill stood the San Miniato al Monte Monastery. Monks would be deep in the evening's prayers. As though announcing their return, the monastery's bells began to ring.

The Meeting of the Minds

Florence, Italy

April 13, 1461

Between Thieves' pace quickened with no urging from Lorenzo. It was like Between Thieves could smell home and his friends, could sense comfort after having been so road-weary for so long. Maybe Between Thieves could sense or smell Pietro, who tended to him and the other horses in the monastery stalls. Maybe he missed when Pietro would stroke his neck for no reason other than to say a passing hello as he was being fed or groomed. Whatever his reason, Between Thieves quickened his pace as he approached Florence's San Miniato al Monte Monastery.

Over the miles, as he neared his monastery, Prior Lorenzo had fine-tuned his story of routing out a deep-rooted conspiracy. He was, praise be to God, happy to be home in the Monastery after a successful journey. His only concern was the unknown whereabouts of Antonio and Gabriele. It was possible his unholy water scheme had worked. He did not know if it had or if it had not. But he was the prior, and his word at the Monastery was obeyed.

As he approached the Monastery, two guards attended the Monastery's doors. They said nothing after his greeting, but they were laypeople: guards. As he dismounted, he instructed one to return Between Thieves to the stalls. The other guard said, "Welcome back, Prior Lorenzo. Yours has been a long absence. Abbot Fransisco informed us of his pleasure at receiving you immediately upon your return."

Lorenzo smiled and replied, "Of course."

He studied the guards' faces closely to see if he could detect any sign of pending trouble. But that was the trouble with the guards. The good ones projected nothing. And Gabriele had trained the guards well.

As one guard led Between Thieves away, the other opened the door for Lorenzo and closed it behind him after he entered.

The Monastery was as quiet as a tomb. He heard no prayers, no chants, no bells. Had he been as perceptive as Antonio, he might have heard a spider walking across its cobweb.

Needing no escort, he walked through the fresco-painted, tapestry-lined stone corridor leading to Abbot Fransisco's study and quarters. When he reached the door, he gave a light knock and waited.

And waited.

When he finally heard the latch to the door, he took a deep breath, which was immediately taken away when the door opened. Standing there, stone-faced but with purpose, was Gabriele. The abbot, sitting at his desk, did not look up. Across from the abbot sat Antonio.

Stepping aside, Gabriele motioned for Lorenzo to join them.

Quick-witted as always, Lorenzo exclaimed, "Reverend Father! I hope these conspirators have not deceived you!" The abbot did not look up and continued to stare at the book on his desk in front of him. There sat Gutenberg's Bible.

Calmly but with authority, Gabriele, gesturing to the empty chair across from the abbot and beside Antonio, said, "Prior Lorenzo. Please be seated."

As Lorenzo sat, he stared at Antonio, but Antonio had not even acknowledged that Lorenzo was in the room. Abbot Fransisco opened Gutenberg's Bible and began slowly leafing through the pages, not yet having looked at Lorenzo.

The only sound you could hear in the abbot's study was the rustling of Gutenberg's pages turning. And a spider walking across its cobweb.

One page. Then another. Then another. And yet another.

Abbot Fransisco then reached for a piece of paper on his desk to the right of the Bible. With that in hand, he began to speak.

"Prior Lorenzo, I studied this letter you gave me that was 'slipped under your door' and I compared its paper to the paper that sits on your desk. The same weight. The same texture. The same finish. The same paper."

Lorenzo began to protest, "Abbot Fransisco, I am a passionate servant of the Church, I—"

But Abbot Fransisco cut him off. "Spare me the sermon, Prior Lorenzo. As abbot of this monastery, I do not consider myself a servant of the Church. I consider myself a servant of God."

The abbot then reached for another piece of paper on his desk and held it up. "Then there's this." It was Lorenzo's cleverly crafted unholy water opus. "Unholy water?" The abbot said nothing more but would not release Lorenzo from his stare. There was nothing more to say to Lorenzo. Nor was there anything more worth listening to from Lorenzo.

Releasing Lorenzo from his visual grip and turning back to his desk, Abbot Fransisco said, "I will organize a meeting with fellow abbots to determine a suitable penance. Prior Lorenzo, from this moment onward, you shall be known as the prior prior, Lorenzo. In the meantime, Gabriele, will you please escort Lorenzo to our cell? Lorenzo, this will afford you time to reflect. When you are not fasting, bread and water will be served."

Gabriele opened the abbot's door and gestured for Lorenzo to leave the abbot's study. As he shuffled out to the corridor, Gabriele walked behind, closing the door. No one but Antonio would have noticed the almost undetectable smile on Gabriele's face.

The abbot then reached to his desk and handed Antonio a sealed letter, saying, "I know your love of manuscripts and the written word, Antonio. As promised, this letter requests a viewing of the Vatican library for you. I understand it is something to behold."

"Abbot Fransisco, I am most grateful for your kindness. A visit to the Vatican library would be a life treasure for me. On our journey, as you foresaw, Gabriele saved me from what would have certainly been a fatal encounter. Might I beg your indulgence and ask to have Gabriele's protection for the journey to the Vatican?"

The abbot smiled, looked out his window to the courtyard, and replied, "So it seems we have something in common. Gabriele has saved both of our lives. He has also trained his guards well. We are in excellent hands. Yes, Gabriele can provide security for your Vatican visit."

Antonio stood, bowed, thanked the abbot again, and excused himself.

With Antonio gone, Abbot Fransisco sat at his desk, alone with his thoughts, the Gutenberg Bible in front of him. He opened to page 149, Book of Luke, Chapter 4, verse 8, and stared at it for a moment. Then smiled.

Thus was born not just the age of the printing press but the age of the proofreader, as well.

The Voice

Monastery of San Domenico

April 14, 1461

Bologna was just coming to life as she reached the town's southern edge. Transitioning from the dirt trail to the cobblestone streets, her ride's quiet tranquility ended as her arrival was announced, step by step, by the clopping sound of the hooves echoing off the stone walls of houses and shops lining these cobblestone streets.

She passed merchants and vendors setting up stalls offering various textiles of wool and silk, but the stalls with the fresh spring produce most attracted her; she was always interested in which herbs foragers had gathered, particularly favoring spring's fresh asparagus.

As she gazed at the offerings while she passed, many of the vendors tried to entice her to stop. "I picked these this morning. Any fresher and you'd have to eat it whence it grew," one called out, and they both laughed.

"I can't tell you how tempting that is. Perhaps, after concluding my business, I'll find you on my way home," she replied.

"It won't be as fresh then," the vendor replied. They both laughed again.

Spring brought out a freshness in people, too, she thought. Passing by one vendor's stall, she could smell the rosemary even from a few feet away. Even more tempting was the smell from the bakeries' morning ovens: fresh pastries and warm breads.

It was a beautiful sunny morning, and you could smell life. The land had woken and had shaken off winter's hibernation.

Animals, too, were announcing and trumpeting both morning and spring. Besides the clopping of the hooves, roosters called out the morning's arrival, and in the distance, she could hear cattle. It wasn't just the city waking; it was the world, the heavens. And after winter's dormant, dreary days, there was now the promise of better, warmer days to come.

A young couple walked past, laughing, holding hands, and getting caught up in each other as if there were no one else in the world.

And for them, there wasn't.

As she made her way along the winding, narrow streets lined with stalls and red brick houses, she could see Bologna's distinctive twin towers, the Le Due Torri, in the distance. And popping out of neighborhoods spread across the town were church steeples, their bells calling out to the faithful.

Weaving her way through the town, she thought of him. "This one's for you," she said, not through spoken words but silently through the soul, adding, "You deserve this. You paid for this, almost with your life."

Silently to the heavens, to the energy that spins the world in circles, she said it again, "This one's for you."

Two monks were outside the Monastery of San Domenico, tending to the spring gardens. One looked up, glanced down toward the town, and saw her approaching; although, from a distance, he could not tell if the form approaching was male or female.

All he could see was a person wearing a heather-green hooded cloak riding a donkey toward them. He watched as she approached with the donkey's slow pace, soon hearing the donkey's hooves on the cobblestone walkway leading up to the Monastery's entrance. It wasn't until she was closer that he recognized it was a woman riding the donkey. By now, the second monk had also looked up.

They watched as she advanced until she was just a few feet away. It was then that they both gave a little bow and one said, "Welcome, traveler. How may we assist you in your journey?"

Calmly, Seraphina said, "I wish to speak with the abbot."

The two monks looked at each other, then back at her, and the one who had greeted her replied, "Most certainly. The abbot is always pleased to give blessings to faithful travelers. What shall I say you wish to speak of with the Reverend Father?"

"Treachery."

Then, raising her arm and pointing to the wooden door lined by its stone archway, with the intricate carvings depicting man's origins and destiny with God, she added, "From within."

Death had a voice.

EPILOGUE

IT ALL ADDS UP

The Vatican

December 21, 1461

The sun had just cracked the horizon, and the first rays of the day's sunshine burst into Antonio and Gabriele's room at the Host Seraphina della Seta overlooking the central square, Piazza del Campo, in Siena. They had spent the previous day in the city, adding a day to their journey; but Siena, rivaling even Florence in its beauty and significance, was well worth a day's visit.

Gabriele rolled over and opened her eyes to see Antonio still deep asleep. She lay there just staring at him, watching his chest slowly rise and settle from sleep's slow and deep breathing. She would have to wake him soon if they were to make it to the Vatican City that day in time to visit the Vatican library. But for the moment, she lay still, watching him, savoring the calm beauty of this instant's serenity and peace. They had chosen an inn that had feather—not straw—mattresses, and that combined with thick feather pillows made getting out of bed much less inviting than getting out of a hard, straw-mattress monastery bed. For people like Antonio and Gabriele, this was a rare and cherished luxury. She tried to imagine what living like this daily would be like. Would they just take it for granted? Would they just think there was nothing special about this when there was everything special about it?

As more of the rising sun's light lit the room, she reached over and ran her hand through Antonio's thick ink-black hair, then leaned over and gently kissed his cheek. Antonio smiled as he opened his eyes and turned to look at her. She put her hand behind his neck and pulled his lips to hers. He was pressed against her leg, and she could feel him coming to life; so she slid her leg over him, then slid down over him, locking his eyes in hers as she heaved. She took his wrists and held them over his head, and he smiled and whispered, "My guard."

"Your guardian angel," she corrected.

"Laughter in lovemaking," she thought. She wondered how they got this lucky. Orgasmic.

A deep sigh of competition has its own sound, its own feel. It was a sigh they both let out.

She slipped out from under the covers and went naked to the window to view the square and some landmarks they had visited the day before. From the window, she could see Palazzo Pubblico, the Torre del Mangia towering above it, and the Siena Cathedral in the distance.

Unnerved, Antonio quickly blurted out, "Gabriele! The windows are open! People can see in!"

Without moving or even turning around, continuing to view the city below, she answered, "We're on the third floor. People never look up. Going about what they have to do, people just look down. Seems that's just what people do to get by. They just look down. They're taught not to look up." Then she turned, facing Antonio, and added with a seductive smile, "They might see something they can't have."

"Come here, you."

"No, Antonio." She began to dress, and as was her way, she instructed, "If we are to get to the Vatican City today, we need to get moving."

As the sigh of competition is unique, so is the sigh of disappointment. Antonio threw back the covers and got up to dress, as well.

As Antonio was about to open the door, Gabriele said, "Antonio, do you know what I hate about going out into the world?"

"What?"

With a demeaning yet playful tone, she answered, "Having to go out as a man."

Antonio laughed and opened the door, and they both stepped back into the world, each as something they were not.

A man.

And a believer.

They walked down the narrow stairway to the inn's lobby, and the chubby, cheerful innkeeper—a woman in her late forties—gave them an exuberant and bright good morning greeting, asking if they enjoyed their stay.

Gabriele, ever the reserved guard, replied, "It was quite comfortable. More than we are afforded at our monastery. Thank you for your hospitality."

They left through the inn's rear door to the courtyard where they had tied Twice and Thrice. The inn had fed and watered the horses and covered them with woolen blankets for the cold winter night. Even the horses enjoyed a luxury not provided at the Monastery.

As they left the courtyard to make their way through the Piazza del Campo, a few market vendors were setting up stalls for the day. In the background, the Palazzo Pubblico was a dominant view.

It was a chilly morning, and they could smell smoke from wood-burning fires emanating from the stone and brick homes lining the cobblestone streets.

They had not eaten, and Antonio said, "I can smell a bakery. Why don't we ask someone where it is and get something to eat while we ride?"

Gabriele turned and, with a wink and a smirk, said, "You have a nose for bakeries, don't you?"

Antonio just rolled his eyes and then turned to a man setting up a stall and asked for directions.

Just a few buildings away, they stopped, and as Antonio was about to dismount, Gabriele said, "No, I'll handle this. I know how you are with bakeries."

Antonio just smiled, shook his head, and sat waiting patiently while Gabriele dismounted and attended to the bakery business.

A few moments later, Gabriele re-emerged bearing four cream *frittelle*, half a dozen *cantucci*, two pieces of *torta della nonna*, and two panini.

Antonio stared wide-eyed and asked, "Do we have any money left?"

Gabriele, always careful to maintain her guard's demeanor and persona in public, answered very matter-of-factly, "It's a long journey. We need food." Handing him a panini, Gabriele instructed, "Here, take this as we get going."

With Siena's city gates behind them and the Tuscany trail in front, they settled in for the day's journey through the frost-covered, rolling hills. They unwrapped their panini, happy to relieve the morning hunger. Gabriele was always careful not to let her guard down as the guard in public. Intimate conversations only took place when there was no risk of being seen or heard by anyone. The trail between the dormant winter vineyards was such a place.

Now that their mission's reward was actually happening, Gabriele asked, "So how do you feel about actually, finally, being able to get into the Vatican library?"

"Excited. Curious. Nervous."

"Nervous? Why nervous?"

"There will not be a book in there in any language I cannot read. Besides everyday Latin, there will be manuscripts in Greek that I can read, although I have never actually carried on a live conversation in Greek. But when people say, 'It's Greek to me,' I always respond, 'So what?' But who knows what I'll find."

"Even so, aren't you excited?"

"Oh, yes. On the shelves of the Vatican library are the works of some of mankind's most profound thinkers. But critical thinking and dogma don't always make good bedfellows."

By midmorning, the ground frost had burned off, and, although it was not warm, the bite of a cold winter morning had also worn off.

The day was the winter solstice, providing the picturesque Tuscany land-scape with the least amount of daylight of the year. Most living things were resting except for the few species of bird that had not flown south for the winter.

Occasionally, they passed a bundled shepherd tending a flock of sheep. Along one stretch of the trail, a lone chapel bell rang out, cutting through the dense, cold winter air.

After several hours of riding and with but two *cantucci* remaining, they approached the walls of Viterbo. It was once a papal residence, resulting in an impressive array of Renaissance architecture. They entered the town, making their way along the narrow cobblestone streets, and stopped at the first inn they saw. They tied their horses and went in to eat before the last leg to the Vatican.

The stone inn had a low ceiling lined with wooden beams, and their good fortune held: a roaring fireplace with an empty table in front of it welcomed them.

Gabriele, with her trained and practiced no-nonsense and assertive approach to people, greeted the innkeeper's welcome with an emotionless "Good afternoon." She followed that with, "May I assume my colleague and I may take that open table?"

The innkeeper gestured to the table and said, "Please, sit and warm your-selves by the fire; I will be right over to tell you about our menu for the day."

They settled at the table, Gabriele, as usual, with her back to the fire and wall, facing the room and anyone who might approach the table.

The innkeeper, ever the seasoned host, brought two tankards of wine to the table, saying, "If you please, be certain to tell fellow travelers of our hospitality. Let me tell you about our choices today. Our kitchen has prepared Papal Perfected Peasant Fare, Viterbo Vineyards *Vellutata di Volpe*, Tuscany Trusted Treasure, and the daily special."

Antonio asked, "What is the Papal Perfected Peasant Fare?"

The innkeeper, with an Italian intimacy that would become world-famous over the centuries, replied, "A modest stuffed pigeon."

Antonio and Gabriele turned and looked at each other, then Gabriele quickly turned to the innkeeper and said, "A modest pigeon. Sounds perfect for our journey. We'll both have that."

The innkeeper walked away, and Antonio and Gabriele stared into each other's eyes, faces blank, speechless.

Finally, Antonio said, "I don't know what to say."

Gabriele responded, "I don't know what to think."

"I think it's best not to think," Antonio replied, and lifting their tankards, they clinked and sipped. Antonio then slowly set his tankard back on the table and calmly whispered, "Imported."

The innkeeper returned and, with a great flourish, presented their meals. He said, "*Buon appetito*" and bowed away from the table.

They each took a taste, both expressing pleasure at what was to be their meal. As Antonio said, "It's delicious!" Gabriele agreed, adding, "And it tastes nothing like pigeon we had before."

After the meal was finished and paid for, they left, got back on Twice and Thrice, and turned to make the final leg to the Vatican library.

As they rode out of the village with less than an hour's ride ahead of them, Gabriele looked at Antonio and asked, "How do you feel?"

"I have absolutely no idea." With a little chuckle, he threw in, "I wonder if this is how Adam felt just before he took a bite of the forbidden fruit."

As they neared the Vatican City, they both became quiet and focused. But they were not without anxiety.

Antonio had picked this day for the visit because it was the shortest day of the year, and early darkness might help with an undetected departure. It was also four days before Christmas, and much of the staff would be engaged in preparing for the holiest day in Christianity.

Preparations would be underway for Vigil Mass on the twenty-fourth and the Mass celebration on the twenty-fifth. Many of the Vatican's staff would need to prepare and hang decorations, boughs, and wreaths, a very labor-intensive task that would take them away from their regular duties, including those in the Vatican library.

There were also the preparations for the ceremonial processions for Christmas Day, which required coordinated and intricate logistical and security planning. This was the Vatican's most important annual undertaking. It had to be flawless.

As they made their way through the narrow streets leading up to the Vatican Hill, they rounded a corner and saw St. Peter's Basilica under construction and renovation—renovations that further disrupted the balance at the Vatican. The Constantinian Basilica was also visible; legend held that it was built over Saint Peter's tomb.

The Apostolic Palace stood to the right, and the Vatican library occupied the ground floor.

After dismounting, Gabriele and Antonio secured Twice and Thrice where other horses were tied.

They reached the library entrance, where a guard greeted them. With authority, Gabriele said, "Good afternoon. We wish to see the library prefect. A letter from Abbot Fransisco of the San Miniato al Monte Monastery in Florence requests our entrance to the library for manuscript research. I am head of security at the Monastery, and Antonio Strozzi is our most valued manuscript scholar. If you could please direct us to the prefect, that would be appreciated."

Gabriele was not asking; she was issuing an order.

The guard looked down at the letter in Antonio's hand, then looked back at Gabriele, simply saying, "Follow me."

They were in. The guard led them down a corridor lined from floor to high ceiling with exquisite paintings of a quality even Antonio had never seen. To the right was an office. The guard knocked on the door, then opened it.

Seated at an ornate desk in a room lined with tapestries and frescoes was a balding man in his mid-thirties. He neither smiled nor frowned. Ignoring Antonio and Gabriele, he simply stared at the guard, waiting to hear why he'd been interrupted.

The guard explained the request, and only at that point did the prefect stand and come from behind his desk. Seeing the letter in Antonio's hand, he gave an icy smile and asked to read it.

Breaking the Monastery's seal, he opened the letter and read. The letter introduced Antonio and Gabriele, explaining who they were, that Antonio was a highly respected artist—proficient in five languages: Latin, Italian, Greek, German, and French—and was well versed in the Greek classics. The letter explained how important Antonio's work was to the Monastery and expressed gratitude for allowing him access to the library so that he might continue his important work.

What the letter said precisely was, "*Spero hanc epistolam te in bona valetudine et summis spiritibus invenire. Scribo tibi in mea qualitate Abbatis monasterii Sancti Miniati ad Montem, instituti venerandi dedicati studio scientiae et conservationi textuum sacrorum.*

"*Hanc humiliter peto tuam eminentiam ut permittas illustratorem nostrum magistrum, Antonium Strozzi, et caput securitatis nostri, Gabrielum, ad accessum in pretiosos thesauros qui in Bibliotheca Vaticana servantur. Antonius est artifex summus, peritus in quinque linguis—Latina, Italica, Graeca, Germanica et Gallica—et bene versatus in classicis Graecis. Eius peritia necess est pro nostris inceptis quae manuscripta antiqua illustranda et transcribenda intendunt pro futuris generationibus.*

"Dum opus nostrum momenti est, credimus accessum ad amplam collectionem tuae bibliothecae nostras conatus valde augere posse. Promittimus nos summos gradus reverentiae et curae erga omnia materia quae forte occurramus servare.

"Gratissimi erimus si hanc opportunitatem nobis concedere digneris. Si fieri potest, etiam quaesumus de protocolis quae sequi debemus durante nostra visitatione.

"Gratias tibi ago pro tua consideratione huius petitionis. Exspectamus responsum tuum favorabile cum magno studio."

The prefect looked up from the letter, glanced at Antonio and Gabriele, and then said, "As you must certainly be aware, this is a very busy time for us. I am short-staffed, but I am also aware of and have great respect for the San Miniato al Monte Monastery. I have one guard available who can escort you during your visit. Please wait here."

He left the office and walked briskly farther down the corridor to where the manuscripts were housed. A few moments later, he returned with a lanky man in his mid-twenties. The prefect said, "This is Giulio. He will escort you during your visit, and I hope the resources are helpful to you." He then returned to his desk, sat down, and reached for the papers there. The meeting was over.

Giulio said, "Please follow me." They left the prefect's office, closing the door, and the entranceway guard turned and went in one direction. Giulio, Antonio, and Gabriele turned and went the other. They rounded a corner, and there in front of them was row after row of shelves lined floor to ceiling with ornately bound manuscripts. Many had gold leaf decorations, and there was an extraordinary array of style and color. The collective was like an expansive, detailed, and elaborate painting.

As they walked, Gabriele looked up to the ceiling and exclaimed, "Oh my God!"

"What?" Giulio looked in the direction Gabriele was looking and repeated, "What?"

Gabriele shot him a look and said, astonished, "You don't see that?" She quickly returned her gaze to the ceiling.

"See what?"

"You're in charge of security, and you don't see that?"

Giulio kept straining his eyes to the ceiling, saying, "See what? I don't see anything unusual."

The longer Giulio looked, the more animated Gabriele became.

"The Vatican library! The Vatican library of all places!"

Gabriele's performance was stellar. There was not a hint of hysterical woman. It was a pure, incensed male security professional.

As Gabriele gave her award-winning performance to an audience of one, Antonio slipped around a corner. He had a rough idea of where to go since he knew approximately where he would find the Codex Vaticanus, one of the oldest extant Bibles in Greek. It was such a manuscript treasure that those who had seen it had talked about it.

And where it was.

He scanned the manuscripts' spines as quickly as he could, gliding up and down the aisles. He could tell when he was getting closer by the increasing age of the works he saw.

He knew he had limited time. Gabriele could only maintain the charade of a security risk lurking in the Vatican library ceiling for so long. And the library would soon close for the day. It was already late afternoon.

But then, there it was. It was breathtaking to see it. It is one of civilization's greatest written treasures.

But that was not what he was looking for. There were rumors of a couple of other sacred texts older and rarer. As he scanned the Codex Vaticanus' neighboring manuscripts, his eyes suddenly landed on one—not because it stood out but because it didn't. It was unadorned and looked older. There was no artistry in the markings on the spine. He carefully eased it from the shelf, his hands trembling. Handling works of this antiquity and fragility required such caution.

He carefully opened the book to a random page in the middle to not crack the binding. How many people had ever seen this? How many people alive today have ever seen this?

Antonio handled the book delicately, afraid it would crumble in his hands. Revealing the pages was a painfully slow process.

The book's pages finally unveiled themselves in front of him, and even with his proficiency in languages and experience with so many varied manuscripts, he had seen nothing like this.

The pages merely contained different symbols and numbers.

He struggled to make sense of it. Astrological calculations? Didn't the Babylonians interpret celestial movements as signs and messages of divinity? The ancient Greeks used numerical symbolism, but this wasn't the case. Minoan maybe? Something completely unknown. There have long been rumors of lost knowledge in human history. Had he found evidence of that?

He studied the pages carefully, racking his brain.

Then suddenly, he recognized one symbol, no longer in use, but he knew what it was.

He stared in disbelief.

It was the symbol of a currency.

What Antonio held in his hands was a ledger sheet dating back to the birth of the Church.

His heart pounded. Trembling, he gently closed the manuscript, slid it back to its grave on the bookshelf, and scurried to get back to Gabriele to leave. She was still masterfully engaging Giulio in the Emperor's New Security Breach as he rounded the corner where he had left them.

He grabbed her arm as calmly as he could and said, "I'm done. We can go now."

Gabriele turned to Giulio as she was being ushered out and said, "Don't worry. I will say nothing of this to anyone. I will leave it for you to manage."

They rounded the corner to the corridor leading to the library's entrance or, more important now, its exit.

As soon as they did, they saw the library's door was open. The sun had set, leaving a morphing blue sky in its trace. December's full moon had just risen.

Standing in the open doorway, silhouetted by this cold moon rising in a deepening cobalt-blue sky, stood Pope Pius II.

ACKNOWLEGEMENTS

A brilliant editor is integral to creating industry-standard, professional fiction. I would like to thank Claire Hernandez for her dedication, sharp eye and literary acumen.

Claire is a professional editor who specializes in fiction manuscripts. She graduated at the top of her class from UC Berkeley's Professional Sequence in Editing program, and has edited everything from novels to advertisements for major brands. Storytelling is her passion, and she is committed to helping authors produce manuscripts that are polished, clear, and error-free.

You can reach her by email at clairehernandez.edit ing@gmail.com . Her services include copyediting, developmental editing, line editing, proofreading, and beta reading.

Cover Image: 12th century illustration of St. John the Evangelist / Lebrecht Authors / Bridgeman Images

www.ingramcontent.com/pod-product-compliance
Lightning Source LLC
Chambersburg PA
CBHW030237120726
47903CB00005B/1520